MONUMENT EDITION

KATE

BEAUMONT

J. W. De FOREST

With An Introduction By JOSEPH JAY RUBIN

INTRODUCTION

After two days of passage from New York slowed by fog and heavy swells, De Forest's steamer reached the low shores of Charleston's harbor early in the morning, 6 November 1855. The coast with its "long beautiful sweep" of foliage stirred him more than the sight of the city. The houses, he told his brother,

> were three storied, very high between floors and half surrounded by enormous verandas. The material was a dark ugly brick, sometimes disguised, but not improved, by stucco. For the stucco is affected badly by the warm humid atmosphere, and grows, in a few years, miserably dark, spotted and ugly. Few of the houses are well proportioned, and only one has met my eye which compares in point of architecture with our pretty residences of New Haven. In short, both from far and near, the city has an old, mouldy appearance, resembling some of the brick-built towns of foggy old England.

De Forest had promised to send home his "*first* impressions" of this first visit to a slave state. An account of Irish and German menials, "elevated by finding someone beneath them," filled his letters. The ragged Negroes seemed inferior to those of the North; the laughter of the young and strong could not cancel the "woe-begone air" of the old.

Service and food at the hotel were capital but expensive — fifteen dollars a week.

Because he came not as a lonely stranger from Connecticut, but as one of the entourage of his future father-in-law, Dr. Charles Upham Shepard, in his third decade as Professor of Chemistry and Mineralology at the South Carolina Medical College and long-time member of the local New England Society, the thirty-year-old traveller gained more than sight of the polished brass of closed doors, high walls, and back streets "brim-full of pickaninnies." The obvious enjoyment written into his letters together with a tone hostile to the Abolitionists brought warning by return mail not to succumb to the "seduction of slavery."

A city that "thought the strongest kind of beer of itself," Charleston offered evidence to support the boast that in "intellects, morals, and manners it stood head and shoulders above any other American municipality." Professional men and planters — some of whom as De Forest noted proudly were also of Huguenot ancestry — had met every fortnight since the 1820's to hear papers by members and guests: Legaré spoke on the Greek Republics, Maury on hydrography, Lyell on geology, Everett on Washington, Agassiz on fossils. Open discussion afterwards excluded only politics and religion — wise restrictions for one who believed in "Free Soil, Kansas squatters, Sharps' rifles, and Mr. Seward," and satirized fashionable theologies and denominational apologetics. Then, supper around a table worthy of Brillat-Savarin.

An invitation to the New England Society inspired a poem, though he had "only the fag-end of two evenings to write it." He argued the doctrine of the resurrection of the body with a member who was a "mighty stickler for literal interpretations of the Scriptures." Other Charleston institutions also offered enough excitement to keep the visitor with his love of science there until 1856 and encourage his return. Possessor of a tradition of inquiry from the time of Lining and Garden, up to Holbrook and his work on American herpetology, the city and its environs contained an illustrious group linked by training and research with Pennsylvania, Yale, Edinburgh, and the Sorbonne. Men like Gibbes, the three Ravenels, Holmes, and others had been host to the American Society for the Advancement of Science. Agassiz ranked the fossils, minerals, and shells in the Museum — the oldest in America — above any other with the exception of Philadelphia's

Academy. The Elliot Society of Natural History, named after the botanist, published original work and displayed a cabinet with worldwide contributions.

The library had extensive holdings. The theater on Meeting Street kept some of the tone brought to it from 1837 to 1847 by managers like Abbott and Forbes. De Forest, whose ready allusions to Sheridan, Boker, Home, and others show his love of drama, could see a favorite, Boucicault's *London Assurance*. Local memory would lead Major Lawson of *Kate Beaumont* to place a Shakespearean tag on the feud between the two Hartland families, for the most popular actress to play in Charleston was Julia Dean; her Juliet to Edwin Booth's Romeo became legend.

The author of a first novel, *Witching Times*, soon to be serialized in *Putnam's*, walked along the bazaar-like King Street to the bookstore with the large plate glass windows and John Russell printed in gilt. Simms, Timrod, and Hayne came to buy domestic and foreign titles and plan a periodical to "give utterance . . . to the opinions, doctrines and arguments of the educated mind of the South." A greater boon was the chance to hear the creator of *The Newcomes*, whose concept of the novelist as judge, parson, as well as painter of social tableaux he admired. "We are to have some fine things soon in the literary way," De Forest exulted. "Thackeray lectures this week." Thackeray gave *The Four Georges* in February 1856 (there was a first visit in 1853) and "stayed a fortnight having a pretty merry time." The city was European, the Englishman concluded, "with an aristocracy and a very pleasant society, ruling patriarchally over its kind black vassals, hospitable, tolerably lettered, keeping aloof from politics as almost all the gentlemen of the States are forced to do."

De Forest had anticipated amenities like the dancing assemblies. ("The town is alive with balls," Thackeray noted.) He also found wisdom. "I never yet saw a South Carolinian who was not a gentleman, and a most intelligent and well-informed one," the Northerner concluded. It was his good fortune to learn in time that the state bred a variety of citizenry. From the first study of the *History of the Indians of Connecticut* (1851) in his early twenties until the last years of his long life, the concept of social survival absorbed him; a later source book was *Primitive Culture* (1871) by the Oxford anthropologist, Edward B. Tylor. Here in the South he found not only the "most powerful single individual in the world," the planter, but the "semi-chivalrous" farmer-mountaineer, the low-down or poor white, and the Negro. Through Lillie Ravenel he would summarize this ante-bellum society:

> There are low people everywhere. But I do say that the better classes of Louisiana and Mississippi and Georgia and South Carolina and Virginia, yes, and of Tennessee and Kentucky, are right nice. If they don't know all about chemistry and mineralogy, they can talk delightfully to ladies. They are perfectly charming at receptions and dinner parties. They are so hospitable, too, and generous and courteous! Now I call that civilization. I say such people are civilized.

Meanwhile he crossed the threshold of homes and churches, absorbed anecdotes, gossip, and fact with the plan of issuing observations like Olmsted's *A Journey in the Seaboard Slave States.* "The only serious drawback on my general happiness is that there is no gymnasium in Charleston. If there was, I suppose they would only set their negroes to work in it." Not even the climate perturbed him. When he caught cold in the winter rain he cured it by taking fifteen drops of camphor in half a tumbler of hot water!

On 19 January 1861, the steamer *Columbia* landed De Forest, by now the author of two travel memoirs and two novels, for another stay in Charleston. As South Carolina no longer considered itself one of the United States — the partisans of the Honorable Peyton Beaumont triumphant over Judge McAlister's — he found all conversation dominated by "those two eternal subjects, Secession and Fort Sumter." There were fewer signs of business in streets shabbier than four years ago and half-rotted wharves empty of ships and freight. Not even the approach of Race Week brought traditional crowds; the New Orleans and Metropolitan Burlesque failed to draw expenses. Legislators at his hotel belonged as before to the aristocracy: "South Carolina is an oligarchy in spirit, and allows no plebeians in high places." But their dress was less ornate than customary, for "dandified suits and superb silks seem to have departed during the present crisis." Portents of the desperate adventure were everywhere. A sword-clanking officer reminded De Forest of the Austrians who stalked the cafés of Florence. Wrapped in a gray Inverness cloak, he stood in Citadel Square and watched the drilling of the elderly cavalry of the Home Guard; at the Battery, once so tranquil, he counted four new iron field-pieces.

Though old friends remained courteous — "You feel as if you were in Paradise, hearing Dante address Beatrice as 'gracious lady'" — they no longer talked of literature or science but of the inevitable future Northern electors shaped with their choice of Lincoln. Edmund Ruffin had come from Virginia in 1842 to begin the *Report of the Commencement and Progress of the Agricultural Survey of South Carolina* (1843). With Dr. Shepard and the paleontologist Francis S. Holmes he pioneered the mining of phosphates vital to Southern soil. Now Ruffin marched as a volunteer with the Palmetto Guards. The literary club had adjourned forever. The Elliot Society appended a note to the last number of its *Journal*: "The publication of this paper is interrupted by the political crisis in America but will be resumed as soon as practicable." After issuing six volumes of *Russell's Magazine* (one with a debate on duelling), the King Street coterie suspended publication and dispersed, quoting their laureate,

> *Could we climb*
> *Some mighty Alp, and view the coming time,*
> *The rapturous sight would fill*
> *Our eyes with happy tears!*

Traditionally this was the pre-Lenten gay season. Instead the Northerner's days became "full of surprising reports and painful expectations. If a door slammed, we stopped talking, and looked at each other; and if the sound was repeated, we went to the window and listened for Fort Sumter. Every strange noise was metamorphosed by the watchful ear into the roar of cannon or the rush of soldiery." Yielding to the war frenzy, De Forest searched the *Mercury* and *Courier* for news of troops and installations. When his return ship grounded near Sullivan's Island he seized the chance to tour nearby Fort Moultrie; some of its eight-inch guns now pointed at Sumter. White volunteers worked through the night side by side with Negro men and women to strengthen the batteries.

The second try to clear the harbor succeeded. On the *James Adger*, De Forest moved away from the coast and the pines, Sumter's five-sided brick wall and its stone embrasures. When next he saw Charleston, weeds sprouted through the interstices of neglected pavements. General Gillmore's shells had exploded among warehouses and mansions, and with non-sectarian impartiality ruined the Huguenot Church and the Catholic Cathedral.

The datelines from many bivouacs show how the volunteer Captain of I Company, Twelfth Connecticut, extended his knowledge of the South. Assigned to the Louisiana theater of operations, he experienced the sand of Ship Island, cypress and tangled cane beyond Carrollton, the heat, mud, mosquitoes, and red ants of Parapet. At Thibodeaux leaking levies turned roads into quagmires; Algiers was a "dirty, rascally suburb" of New Orleans. Beleaguered Port Hudson and two command posts forced Biblical comparisons, for the alligators of Brashear City bellowed all night like the bulls of Bashan, and at Vermilion Bayou he and his men foraged like the locusts of Revelation.

Unlike the "grim abolitionist" who first commanded the brigade, De Forest never succumbed to indiscriminate hatred though he met overt provocation or silent hostility everywhere. At Carrolltown he heard the mutter of "Damn Yankees"; the newsboys of New Orleans would not sell papers to Union soldiers and restaurants refused service. The Cajuns near Thibodeaux, unlike Longfellow's exiled Acadians, were "ignorant, stupid and unpoetic." But the camp-weary infantry-man had one of his memorable evenings in the elegant home of Creoles like the brothers Meurice of *Miss Ravenel*. The cultivated men and women of this new race, as he proclaimed them in a letter home and in the novel, took him back to the time spent as a young sightseer in Paris.

De Forest always praised the verve and courage of the Confederate soldier and itemized the skills that lessened the casualty lists of the "famed veterans" of the Army of Virginia. He eulogized Colonel Mc-Pheeters of the Crescent Regiment and other dead heroes of Mouton's command; he pitied the prisoners so cold in their coarse wet cotton that they stripped the ragged blankets from their dead comrades.

The economic plight of the Confederacy made him compassionate early. "If the war does not end soon, the South will starve," he told his wife in July 1862. In addition to the food taken by foragers like his adept servant, George, indiscriminate looting and plundering by Negroes and runaway soldiers — "mere wantonness" — lay waste an entire region. Detailed on court martial duty, De Forest heard ample testimony of the "multifarious anarchy which we and the rebellion have brought."

Transfer to the Shenandoah in 1864 as part of Emory's Nineteenth Corps brought him to a valley whose loveliness surpassed his native

Connecticut. But "hot marches, heavy guard duty" and a diet of green corn and green apples "made a rough campaign of it." Though weakened by malaria and the miserable rations — a Sanitary Commission lunch of coffee, bread and "butter too!" earned special mention home — De Forest's itinerary now included Opequon, Fisher's Hill, and Cedar Creek, where the enemy order of battle listed old friends in the Second South Carolina. "I never on any other battlefield saw so much blood as on this. . . . The firm limestone soil would not receive it, and there was no pitying grass to hide it." By the end of the year he was too weak to remain on active duty.

II

"When he comes home I shall insist upon his writing a history of this war," Dr. Ravenel tells Lillie after reading Captain Colburne's authoritative combat report of Sheridan's victory. The real Colburne — De Forest — helped by a desk assignment in Washington, needed less than a year to shape his marches from Ship Island to the Shenandoah into *Miss Ravenel's Conversion from Secession to Loyalty.* An inspired fictional strategy added the monumental Virginian, Colonel Carter, and his "well built" nemesis, Mrs. Larue.

Despite the implications of the title, the irony of the novel, like that of its predecessors and two tales of a visit to a spectral "Isle of the Puritans," is in the exposure of De Forest's hostility to the New England milieu. Current slurs are hurled at Southerners: "Saint Paul, Pascal, Wilberforce couldn't have remained respectable if they had been slaveholding planters." But those pointed Northward appear often: "What Yankee ever was known to remain an Abolitionist after having once tasted the pleasure of living by the labor of others." Colburne's New Boston is as feckless as the Salem of *Witching Times* whose "bloodthirsty old Christians" drove Rachel More to Virginia; it is a place "absolutely noxious to social gayeties, amenities, and graces." De Forest went so far in "A Night at Sea" (*Harper's,* July 1869), in his assault on a humorless mother and son of the Old Dominion for never lightening the "solemnity of events and surroundings," as to conclude they "would certainly have fruited into full Puritans had they been New Englanders . . . instead of Virginians."

Though quick to reject the generalizations in Dr. Samuel Cartwright's "Slavery in the Light of Ethnology." De Forest indulged his own bias and typed Northern neighbors. The old men are "long and lean and brown as the Ancient Mariner"; their utterance is "untuned, monotonous, and slightly nasal"; they view praise as a "snare of Satan." The old maids are "grave, sad, sickly" with "narrow-shouldered, hollow-chested" souls. He is also cruel to New England youth. At Professor Whitewood's dinner party, Colonel Carter first stirs Lillie because he is a robust male. The home-town faculty scion is a "pale bit of human celery."

Partial redemption for New Boston comes through the exemplary Colburne and the faculty members of Winslow University who hail Darwin. But De Forest reveals in "The Oversoul of Manse Roseburgh" (*Galaxy,* February 1870), the cause of his scorn for New York. He asks of the idler

> Why did he not turn his hand to art, or science, or literature? Why is it that the wealthy and leisurely New Yorker never thunders and flames in these directions? The Earl of Derby translates Homer for us, and the Duke of Argyll gives us an essay on Primitive Man, and the Prime Minister of England discusses the Greek Mythologies. But the *bourgeois* patrician, half Carthaginian and half Sybarite, who inhabits the island of Manhattan, has no other idea of life than to pass it either earning or spending money.

Other Northerners in *Miss Ravenel* bear the novelist's animus: Ben Butler, demagogue in uniform; Van Zandt, Knickerbocker lush with his thirty bottles a day; Gazaway and the Governor of Barataria, interminglers of war, politics, cowardice and promotions. He dramatized their derelictions but for the present avoided a series of scenes with the Southerners Dr. Ravenel called "whiskey-soaked, negro whipping, man-slaughtering ruffians."

Howells in *The Atlantic* review of July 1867 that initiated almost forty years of friendship named De Forest "the first to treat the war really and artistically." But the critic who would always soften the older man's edges thought it wise to find "rich and wholesome juices" in the pale celery: "It is the goodness of New Boston, and of New England, which, however unbeautiful, has elevated and saved our national character; and in his book there is sufficient evidence of our author's appreciation of this fact, as well as of sympathy only and always with what is brave and true in life."

The fiction after *Miss Ravenel* exploited continued experience in the South. But when the time came for De Forest to cast his *Honest John Vane* and *Playing The Mischief* he returned home for the Congressman who sells his vote to the Credit Mobilier lobby and the young widow who lifts $100,000 from the Treasury with a fraudulent claim. Vane's roots are as shallow as his credo, but Josie Murray traces her lineage to Goody Umberfield "attainted of witchcraft as far back as the boyhood of Cotton Mather."

In uniform at the end of the war, De Forest accepted an assignment to Greenville, South Carolina, as acting Assistant Commissioner in the Bureau of Freedmen and Refugees. (Dr. Shepard had returned to the Medical College "at the urgent invitation of his former colleagues.") In October 1866 he rode like Kate Beaumont and her sister Nellie in "creaking, rolling, staggering cars" out of the silent desert that was Charleston some two hundred miles northwest to the upland headquarters of his area of responsibility: Greenville, Pickens, and, later, Anderson counties — 3,000 square miles of wooded hills and mountains, small farms that grew corn and fed livestock. Though spared the devastation that followed Sherman, many of its 80,000 natives could cry out, like the impoverished Simms, "Alas! Alas! We are mere cherry stones in the hands of fate who delights in flinging!"

By the time De Forest reached the "lonely, rusty station-house" he knew the differences between prewar Charleston and Greenville could not be measured by mileage or terrain. He had come to a region whose history since the Revolution was shaped by its hostility to minority rule enforced by low country planters through a restrictive system of parish representation. The thirty years before the Civil War saw further fracture of loyalties. Here at Glassy Mountain, farmers in their Dark Corner stronghold rejected nullification. Sam Hicks, who dares fight Armitage for Sally Huggs, is a Dark Corner man whose courage comes from heritage rather than tumblers of Pickens District nectar, "fresh from the mill, clar as water, an' strong as pizen." Hicks is no "ordinary low-downer, educated in the depressing vicinity of great estates, and subservient to the planting chivalry." He is a mountaineer, "as independent and fierce and lithe as a wild-cat, and disposed to fight any man who trespassed upon his rights or person."

The low country Beaumonts are Huguenot Episcopalians; the original McAlisters are upland Scotch-Irish Presbyterians. But it was a novelist's generalization rather than historian's fact that based the feud on a rigid pattern of ethnic, religious differences. A reader of *Kate Beaumont* would remind De Forest that the leaders of the Nullifiers, Calhoun and McDuffie, came from the same stock as their antagonists. Charlestonians like James L. Petigru and Judge Daniel Huger were Unionists who, like their Greenville friend, Benjamin F. Perry, sought suffrage and education reforms. Throughout the 1850's Perry and his many supporters resisted editors, politicians, and educators like James C. Furman, head of the local university, who waved the blue cockade of secession. But when Perry could not prevail upon them to keep from "playing before high Heaven a ridiculous farce or a bloody tragedy," he sent his son to fight against the North. Out from Greenville rode at least six volunteer companies though many men of the district remained loyal to the Union. Now a common ruin encompassed all survivors. As De Forest noted, history had refused to follow the logic of a sequence desired by *De Bow's Review* and Rhett's *Mercury*.

The Bureau Major spent fifteen months in "raising the blacks and restoring the whites . . . to a confidence in civil law." In his office on the ground floor of the old courthouse, he heard complaints of freedmen and farmers and wrote reports of outrages. He learned of petty thievery, assaults, bushwhackings. The erstwhile "high-tone" and the chronic "low-down" came to him for charity: corn, shoes, coats. He became the confidant and recorder of case studies in misery. He visited — officially — an establishment like Nancy Gile's and talked with Sally Huggs: "I never saw so many Cypriots as in this village." (The classical learning of this self-taught scholar often reveals itself in these allusions. Of bristly Peyton Beaumont he wrote, "Paches, the Athenian admiral who massacred the garrison of Notium, might well have had such a countenance.") His encounters ranged from Perry, recently the Provisional Governor, owner of one of the finest law libraries in the South, or Charles Hopkins, Negro philanthropist, to illiterate "lone women" called widows by courtesy, or Uncle Peter born in the Congo. De Forest's accurate ear remembered the tone and accent of his supplicants, as well as the cause of their misery.

Because his wife and young son remained in New Haven, he

searched for ways to fill time after official hours. The Piedmont climate a thousand feet above sea level invigorated him more than the Mediterranean during earlier convalescence and helped restore his health. He walked the countryside within view of the Blue Ridge, past "slatternly farm houses" and eighteen by twenty-five "log cabins chinked with mud and destitute of window-glass" like the one in *Kate Beaumont* where aided by a pound of tallow candles, three gallons of raw whiskey, and Sam Toney's fiddle he staged the cracker ball — the single assemblage in all nineteenth century American literature Baudelaire would have memoralized in *Les Fleurs Du Mal,* for here were "the perfect perfumes of the Flesh."

He surveyed oldfields and used one to mount the duel between Frank McAlister and Tom Beaumont. He met farmers like the original Fate Ferguston (*Galaxy,* January 1867), "possessor of sixty acres of rough upland, who had never owned a negro, and never wore other clothing than blue cotton jean or gray woolen homespun." Greenville's eight to ten streets always had low-down women smoking their clay pipes and remarkably tall, handsome girls of the "respectable class." On "sale-day" he watched "little oxen or the sorriest of horses and mules" haul last assets in canvas roofed wagons or buggies shaded by white umbrellas to be bartered for bacon and hominy.

Not all the town was homespun. The First Baptist Church with its fluted Ionic columns had been designed by two Philadelphia disciples of Greek revival architecture, Sloan and Stewart. The beauty of its spire, we learn in *Kate Beaumont,* forced the envious Presbyterians to replace their "bob of a belfry." (Actually it was the Methodists who were spireless.) De Forest discovered other reasons for Greenville's reputation as the Athens of the up country. He lived at the three-story brick Mansion House with its parlor large enough for fireplaces at each end. Years ago professional men and planters fled coastal summer heat and fever and vacationed in Greenville. Names like Poinsett and Hayne appeared on the Mansion House register. In its great ballroom, mused De Forest, "there had been gayeties of proud ladies." Now there were only "sad meditations." He marvelled at his host's ability to provide bountiful meals with five permanent boarders and no more than ten transients.

With the exception of lawyers who offered advice — and found themselves written into the scene in the back room of Duffy's grocery

— the young men of Greenville did not seek the company of the Northern officer. But other "elder and solider citizens" invited him to share the intellectual wealth added to the area by Furman University, a Baptist seminary, and a college for women (which De Forest ribbed gently in "Annie Howard" (*Hearth and Home*, March-May 1870), as the Adiron Female Academy led by President L. Manlius Brown). Founders of a literary society brought him into weekly meetings and invited the use of thirty American and European periodicals; in some he could read his own essays, fiction, and poetry. Among the members were men like John A. Broadus, linguist and theologian, and Perry, biographer and editor. The talk varied from the development of the phosphate mines, South Carolina's base for economic recovery, to the higher criticism of the Bible brought to the state as early as 1829 by Thomas Cooper, the chemist who questioned the authenticity of the Pentateuch. (*Harper's* in April 1867, ran De Forest's "Mrs. Pullet's Perversion," with a wife who attempts after a nightcap of bourbon to convert her husband to a grander religion. But he refuses to read a key text, *The Ninety-Nine Reasons why a Bethelite Sexton became a Pontifical Warden.* Snubbed by the formal Pontificalians, Mrs. Pullet returns to the Bethelite fold. "'Verily,' Mr. Pullet used to say, 'wrath is a converting ordinance.'")

His hosts — old friends of Simms' — found De Forest's judgment of Southern literature as provocative as his latitudinarianism. Since Jefferson and Legaré — first in Mrs. Chester's list of authors — there had been, he insisted, "a vast declension." With the exception of two or three novels by John Pendleton Kennedy and *Sunnybank* (1866) by Marion Harland, the "elder romances of Dixie, produced under a mixed inspiration of namby-pambyism and provincial vanity, strong in polysyllables and feeble in perception of character, deserve better than any other results of human labor that I am aware of, the native epithet of 'powerful weak.' The novelist evidently had but two objects in view: first, to present the Southron as the flower of gentility; second, to do some fine writing for his own glory."

De Forest never surrendered, like hundreds of thousands, to *The Planter's Northern Bride* (Caroline Lee Hentz, 1854), or to the other purveyors of plantation myth. These did not suffice to win the praise of the reader of Taine who knew race, period, and environment. One ponders the ranking of *Sunnybank* — also highly rated by Thomas

Nelson Page — with the *Swallow Barn* sketches. The novel mentions the pre-war struggle between Secessionist and Submissionist, and shifts its setting from a James River plantation to besieged Richmond. Technically, chapters told from alternating points of view seemed impressive and the matching of a Southern girl with a Northerner is the formula of *Miss Ravenel*. That lusty prankster, Sut Lovingood, would soon amuse De Forest. But he continued to ignore all of Simms including *The Forayers* (1855), with the epical Captain Porgy and Marion's Colonel Horry mentioned in *Kate Beaumont*. Nor did he praise John Esten Cooke's *The Virginia Comedians* (1854), T. B. Thorpe's *The Master's House* (1854), Lanier's *Tiger-Lilies* (1867), or the poetry of Timrod.

There were evenings of music — Beethoven, Gounod, Mendelssohn — which the guest enjoyed, and Negro minstrelsy which he endured. The circus came to Greenville and two profane Baltimore "plug-uglies" with a lantern illumination of *Pilgrim's Progress*, holy writ to De Forest. The Howling Gyascutus described in the eighth chapter of *Kate Beaumont*, a chaste variant of Huck's Camelopard, the novelist first saw at a fair sponsored by a local congregation.

III

In his essay "The Great American Novel" (*Nation*, 9 January 1868) — published the month he put away his regimentals — De Forest admitted joining the contest for the prize. Among obstacles immense as the lack of copyright he listed a changing society and a nation of provinces:

When Mr. Anthony Trollope commences a novel, he is perplexed by no such kaleidoscopic transformations and no such conflicting claims of sections. Hundreds of years ago English aristocracy assumed the spiritual nature which it holds with little change to the present day. . . . At this time it is a unit of social expression. . . . There you have something fixed to paint; there you have the novelist's sitter. . . . All successful English romances are written with references to this class; they may attack it, they may defend it, they always paint it.

The material he sent from his Greenville files to *The Atlantic, Galaxy*, and *Harper's* documented the current chaos within the Southern province. A regional critic questioned his source but admired the result: "It would be as difficult to make up a consistent representation of a Southern life from the note-book of a Freedman's Bureau Officer as to get a true idea of American politics from an exclusive study of Mr. Nast's venomous, pungent, and rascally caricatures, but so much the greater credit to Major De Forest for the degree of success he has attained." Indeed, when he refused to traffic in the spurious sentiment of "Rum Creeters Is Women" (*Harper's*, March 1867), he recorded inexorable fact. "I do not feel justified," he ended one tale, "in seeking to punish the slayers of a soldier who was a deserter, and of a loyalist who was a bandit and murderer."

Two memorable Greenville episodes of war enmity kept alive by the lawless reappear as "Brownville" fiction. "Fate Ferguston" and "Parole D'Honneur" (*Harper's*, August 1868), contain semi-chivalrous farmers who live in "rolling landscape, not more than half cleared, the original forest deciduous, the new growth pines, bottoms of rich blackened earth, uplands of pulverous gray, the numerous streaks of oldfield either barren red or brown with weeds." A survivor of years of violence, De Forest did not hesitate to detail the brutality of drunks who club the father of the leader of the local guerillas, then capture Ferguston at a corn-husking and ride him to his death in the woods — as years later others would kill Joe Christmas.

For definition of the low-downer, De Forest moved north of Greenville to the town of Saxonburg where "since the war everybody . . . had gone more or less bankrupt." Selnarten Bowen ("An Independent KuKlux," *Galaxy*, April 1872), tries to "jine" the Klan because the "niggers is gone in for stealin' worse'n ever." A witless dupe in the struggle between "carpet bag adventurers" and "reactionist desperadoes," Bowen commits murder with a rusty Enfield. De Forest interpolated a genealogy of this "American freeman and elector":

He was simple, he was profoundly ignorant, and he was the child of simplicity and ignorance from untold generations, inheriting simplicity and ignorance as he inherited the name of Bowen. He could not read; his father before him could not read; he was sprung from a race of illiterate low-downers; they, probably, from illiterate tramps or hinds in Old England. All the way back to the days of the Heptarchy, it may be; all the way back to the pirate keels of Hengist and Horsa; all the way through the Germanic forests and the Scythian steppes; all the way back across to the Indo-European cradle in Aryana; there is no certainty that a Bowen of this stock ever did read — no certainty that a Bowen of this stock was ever anything but illiterate and stupid. With the inherited, accumulated, and concentrated ignorance of so many generations in his brain and his very marrow, how should Selnarten fail to be the bubble of every high-toned gentleman who chose to puff him out with a breath of nonsense, and shake him loose for folly or mischief?

Selnarten's kinsman in *Kate Beaumont*, Redhead Saxon, becomes the bubble of Armitage.

Though his official duties ended before Reconstruction fastened what a Northern correspondent called a huge system of brigandage upon South Carolina, De Forest saw enough to assault its misrule. He had always fought separationism and remained the Independent who as late as 1876 wrote letters in support of Hayes, for he feared the election of Tilden would "hand over our national policy to the South." But he respected the honesty personified in a Poinsett, a Legaré, or Perry who "could handle the pitch of political life and not be defiled." Like his Vance Fosbrooke, he rued the superseding of the Rutledges, Pinckneys, and Huggers by the parvenu Rhetts. In the *Nation* (12 March 1868) he pleaded in this first year of President Grant that American government needed the Southern aristocrat who

> like his predecessors of Greek, Roman, and feudal days . . . demanded a high place in public affairs, caring little for the stealings of office, but much for its honor and power. . . . Unlike the shy scholars of New England and the fastidious millionaires of New York, he did not mutter that politics are too low for a gentleman and pass over his claims for Congress to showmen and pugilists. . . . And the republic was all the stronger and grander for this large ambition of his until cotton turned his brain and blinded him to the necessities of the age.

An impeccable Peyton Beaumont could defy the lobby. We believe him when he tells his son that the Beaumonts look only to honor. "Money! You can't turn my head by talking money. I know the value of the thing. But, by heavens, I wouldn't swerve a hair for the sake of it. I'd blow my brains out first." But the bemused freedmen send to the Capitol a Pompey from Alligatorsville ("The Colored Member,"

Galaxy, March 1872). Though his daddy was raised by the Beaumonts of Hartland — "Hoo! *dey* was quality," — Pompey is no match for carpetbaggers like that "late convert from New York city democracy," Jack Hunt.

As De Forest's civilian career gathered momentum he began to form all the Southern years into fiction. Mr. Vance Fosbrooke, "A Gentleman of An Old School" (*Atlantic,* May 1868), is as well known in Charleston as the chimes of St. Michael's. Like Major Lawson he has "lived himself into social distinction by sheer dint of deportment." A widower at 36, Fosbrooke buys a handsome quadroon woman who bears him four children; they give their father more joy than the all-white son of his marriage, a spendthrift who carouses on Sullivan's Island — a place which intrigued De Forest as it had Poe. At the onset of war Fosbrooke escapes North with his octoroon children and remains there dependent upon their unfailing charity.

De Forest returned to New Orleans in "The Taillefer Bell-Ringings" (*Atlantic,* August 1869), with a setting of "venerable oil paintings, mainly of the Spanish and Italian schools, such as are to be found in New Orleans in greater number than in any other American city," a gentleman who prides himself on using Addisonian diction — "as is the case with our Southern gentry," and a selfish woman who ends as depraved as Becky Sharp. (A reviewer of *Miss Ravenel* in 1867 thought the marriage of Colburne to the widowed Lillie came out of Thackeray's Captain Dobbin and Amelia. "The Duchesne Estate" (*Galaxy,* June 1869), illustrated by Winslow Homer, is a tale of the struggle for thousands of well-tilled Louisiana acres.

Memories of his chosen province moved into the larger fiction published at the start of the 1870's. In "Annie Howard" the steamboat *Isaac Newton* carries a "miraculously dirty" mulatto, a low-downer, a semi-chivalrous deputy sheriff, and Mr. Pinckney Hayward. To *Overland* (1871), the novel of a trek from Sante Fe to San Diego, he gave a Greenville bushwhacker named Texas Smith who loathes "the high-toned gentlemen who used to overawe his childhood." By the time *Kate Beaumont* began to appear in *The Atlantic* in January 1871, the New Englander had earned a reputation with critics — if not the public — as a Southern writer.

On 24 May 1871 the New York *Tribune* wondered if the swift visit of Trollope in search of new characters would end in stale generalizations: a gentleman who "rises to orate" between each mouthful of potato and squirts tobacco juice between each glass of champagne; a young lady who addresses her friends as "You ass." The *Tribune* suggested a surer way to authenticity — the use of the Englishman's technique by native writers:

> It will be better for American fiction . . . when it . . . adapts the Trollope school of art; when the novelist, instead of using his *dramatis personae* as characterless puppets to embody or preach his favorite dogmas, or harrow the reader's soul by mysteries and murders most foul, simply contents himself with photographing the people and scenes about him. Mere reproduction is certainly legitimate art, if not the highest; and it assuredly is the most successful. What service Holmes has rendered in this way to New-England, Bayard Taylor has given to Pennsylvania, Harte to California, and De Forest, almost unnoticed, is now bringing back the South as it was before our recollection with a few powerful but inimitable touches.

IV

All that De Forest thrust into the opening chapters of *Kate Beaumont* worried him and led to revision. Like the ill-fated *Mersey* steaming west from Liverpool (Cooper used the same frame in *Homeward Bound*), the narrative under the weight of diverse cargo almost goes down before reaching Charleston. There is the start of the shipboard romance between Frank, who looks like a young Washington, and 18-year-old Kate, as pure as Santa Cecilia. Through the choric merchants from Hartland Village come hints of mystery and then the revelation that Frank is a McAlister, hereditary enemy of the Beaumonts. The "old difficulty," the feud which has victimized three generations and left its survivors as scarred as Ahab, comes between the lovers. So does Mrs. Chester, Kate's aunt.

An older Mrs. Larue, she is of the sisterhood De Forest provided throughout his fiction as proof that infatuation and sexual desire are not exclusive attributes of youth. (Elsewhere he quotes Michelet to the effect that the best of women "occasionally have moral vertigos.") Mrs. Chester's "fancy for young fellows . . . almost a mania with her," developed during an unsatisfactory marriage. Now on the verge of a

{ 23 }

bizarre and uncontrollable phase she pursues Frank who is twenty years younger and would rather study High Dutch scientific books to further a career started at Oxford and Göttingen.

Some aspects of South Carolina show early. The subservience of the captain and merchants to the three Beaumonts on the *Mersey* indicates a caste-conscious "old-time" society. To Mrs. Chester her own class is the "untitled nobility"; she is as proud of the feud as of a "family heirloom, unmistakably aristocratic." Tom Beaumont, Kate's younger brother, spends his time "talking horses . . . to boozing companions," but flares in anger when Mrs. Chester hints that he is not a gentleman. She retracts. Only the peril to the ship and his inherited code force Tom to stop his cocktails. "If I'm to drown, it's more like a gentleman to drown sober. Going down drunk all very well for a common sailor. But our sort can look the thing square in the face."

Before De Forest lands his passengers he subjects them to a mutinous crew and a night spent in a crowded small boat. The saving of Kate's life by Frank transcends the misery.

"You have come home to lift us poor South-Carolinians out of the slough of ignorance and conceit," an old friend tells the would-be scientist. Major Lawson is an amateur litterateur and professional flatterer whose manner is "like warm olive oil, poured over your head. . . . As for his thin, genteel figure it was so lubricated with constant bowing and gesturing, that it was as supple as an eel." There on the huge piazza of the Charleston hotel, waving his cambric handkerchief to herald the birth of an idea, he prophesies that Frank's heroism will lead to a pastoral version of *Romeo and Juliet* with a joyous ending. From now on the narrative is assured of continuity. The parallel with the immortal lovers of Verona pulls the reader to Hartland District where the local Tybalts wait.

Out of shadow and transplanted reality De Forest created his enclave, his Barsetshire. Somewhere between Columbia and Greenville, on neutral ground, he placed two plantations only four miles apart. Within easy ride are the establishments of the patriarch Kershaw and the Devines. They own hundreds of slaves but no overseer — the word never appears — leads them from streets of cabins to work the fields. There is a single glimpse of cotton whitening, but no mention of harvest — except of flowers for the mantel bouquets. The author's view is within the high post gate through overgrown shrubbery rather than out over weeded acres. And he sees no stereotype of Drayton Hall, no great pillars and salons splendid with marble and crystal, but "a plain, widespreading, mass of wood-work . . . the white paint of the building itself rather rusty, and the green blinds not altogether free from fractures and palsy."

Hartland Village is as solid as the tobacco-stained, pitch-pine floor of the courthouse now scrubbed into a "speckled cleanliness" for the church fair. The all white throng — "the slave population is to have an evening for itself" — enjoys the alcoves of greenery, the festooned walls, the tables tended by pretty girls, and the antics of that hardy folk hybrid, the Howling Gyascutus. Then Jenny Devine, "sparkling with black eyes, glistening with white teeth and one shoulder poked high out of her dress for a temptation," aligns a Beaumont against a McAlister. Wit is taken for innuendo, an incendiary epithet is hurled, and the carnival like the one that rolled through the Corso in *The Marble Faun* becomes the "emptiest of mockeries." A challenge follows and the feud is out of hand again.

Without citing Preston Brooks' caning of Senator Sumner, De Forest could counter easily the charge that he exaggerated Southern belligerence. According to T. B. Thorpe, "It was difficult to find one's self in a group of six or eight prominent citizens without soon learning that one or more of them had been an actor in a duel." Governor Perry had received half a dozen challenges and killed a man. The famous William L. Yancey went to jail for shooting a Greenville physician in a manner reminiscent of the way in which Armitage hits Kershaw. Thackeray wrote his English friends of the killing of a Richmond editor; and the author of *The White Rose of Memphis* died violently on the street at the hands of a former associate — Colonel Falkner himself had stood trial twice for murder.

Southern novelists from Tucker and Caruthers to Cooke and Cable placed scenes in Duelling Oaks; it was part of the young gentleman's itinerary to maturity — or the grave. *Russell's Magazine* for May 1857 not only defended the duel but found something "noble and elevated" in its ritual. A Charleston printer the next year issued John Lyde Wilson's definitive *Code of Honor; or Rules for the Government of Principals and Seconds in Duelling*. The text was needed, Wilson indicated in his preface, because duelling "will be persisted in as long as a manly independence, and a lofty personal pride in all that dignifies and ennobles the human character shall continue to exist. . . . The severest penal enactments cannot restrain the practice . . . and their extreme severity in this State, the more effectually shields the offenders." The Beaumont sons, like their minister, the Reverend Arthur Gilyard, share this faith in the *code duello* as an adjunct to civilization. They abhor the rencontre — the "accidental single combat" or impassioned assault without protocol — the Grangerford-Shepherdson ambushes — as little better than gouging and biting. And like Judge Driscoll of *Pudd'nhead Wilson,* they seek a pistol rather than a court of law. (Twain listed *Kate Beaumont* in his 1882 notebook.)

The less militant McAlisters rate the custom as disagreeable as wearing a hot black beaver. Frank dramatized the refutation by William J. Grayson in *Russell's* for August 1857, that the duel is a barbarism incompatible with Christianity, "fostered by bad passions — by vanity and revenge, the ape and tiger of the human heart. . . . We can no more think of St. Paul as assisting at the duel than as preaching, in Ephesus, at the altar of Diana." To the enlightened, the formal manslaughter of the code was no different from informal murder.

As De Forest remembered, in that "land of romance" he found Uncle Toby, Squire Western, Sir Pitt Crawley, Colonel Newcome, Mr. Pickwick, and Eugene Sue's criminal, Le Chourineur. His bid for entry into this gallery is the Honorable Peyton Beaumont whose first sound is a savage grunt; his first gesture a reaching for morning brandies — two on weekdays, three on Sundays; his first association with his valet Cato. No languid St. Clare and Adolph colloquy like that in *Uncle Tom* ensues. The slaves are well fed and clothed; not even the younger Beaumonts may birch them. But "broken sleep, an inflamed alimentary canal, and gout" irk a wilful temper and Peyton throws a boot at the grinning boy.

It is while his iron-gray chin is shaved in a swamp of lather that Peyton learns of the McAlister insult. Satisfied that his oldest son, Vincent, knows the duties of a gentleman, he goes to breakfast. A widower who has buried two wives, he is the indulgent father to his five children but responds when provoked. Poinsett, "a fat, tranquil, pleasantly spoken and talkative fellow of perhaps twenty-five," complains of local dullness and the lack of conversation like that of Europe.

"We do speak; there is much monologuing, and I perform my share of it; but as for talking, quick interchange of ideas, fair give and take, we are on a par with Cooper's noble savage."

"Why the deuce don't you go to work, then?" burst out Peyton Beaumont. "Here you two fellows are as highly educated as money can make you. You are a lawyer, graduated at Berlin. Vincent is a doctor graduated at Paris. And yet you do nothing; never either of you had a case; don't want one."

"Ah, work! that is dull too," admitted the smiling, imperturbable Poinsett. "Idleness is dull; but work is duller."

Target practice is interrupted by the arrival of Kate who tells of their debt to a McAlister, and joined with her grandfather pleads for peace. As "pale and mild as a saint newly taken to glory" she is more successful than Starbuck with Ahab.

All through the writing of *Kate Beaumont* De Forest worried that the plot was "elephantine." The "great question of course is — is the story *interesting?*" he asked Howells on 27 May 1871. To span the quiet days after the "once hostile digits were intermingled," he resorted to the device of the magazinist and flogged the narrative lest readers of *The Atlantic* complain like Tom, "what was the further use for Beaumonts in this world since they were no longer to fight Mc-Alisters." He returned Mrs. Chester to her pursuit of Frank. By now like Holmes' Elsie Venner there is a snaky glitter in her eyes as she fills visitors with madeira and cognac.

The mercurial schemer succeeds only in creating what her author called a sentimental muddle. In desperation Peyton summons from the upcountry his older daughter, Nellie Armitage, who comes with her "beseeching air" and the face of a woman hiding a "stirring and trying heart-history." As she works to secure a happy marriage for Kate we sense her domestic grief. She rejects Frank because he is a McAlister, but recognizes his stature when he talks of a career: "Nobody hereabout sympathized with his tenderness for chemistry and his passion for metallurgy; sometimes he thought he should have to drop his science and go to sleep upon cotton, like the rest of South Carolina." Nellie cannot resist him and gives her tacit blessing.

This interlude also contains Mrs. Chester's house servant Miriam, who tells her mistress, now withdrawn into girlish fantasy, that she is altogether too old to be "friskin' roun' a young feller like Mars Frank McAlister. He ain't a gwine to wanter frisk back, an' you can't make him."

De Forest saw early that it was the "tyranny" of slavery that caused the Southern community to be distinctive, but nowhere could he find "extant nephews" of Uncle Tom. Nor did he place the Negro in Dr. Cartwright's category of the lowest of human species — "a creature with a servile mind . . . almost void of reflective faculties, and consequently unable to provide for and take care of himself." His Cato is sly; Quash is fit only to carry his drunken master; Miriam is more humane than her mistress and the minister for she brands the duel as Satan's work. In other fiction Ham Irvine is brutal and lustful, "lamming" his successive wives with his wooden leg. Harkles (Hercules) is a tower of devotion, Jehu is a monkey, parrot, and grasshopper; Major Scott's count of the Commandments reaches the Seventh only under duress. Jane is a lazy blackamoor; Pompey is "as ignorant, as heavy-brained, and as morally degraded as the vulgarest peasant of Europe." But all are casualties of evolutionary malice, Darwinian illustrations of tragic stress:

This man and brother [he wrote in "The Colored Member"], had been a slave; he was descended from men and brethren who had for two hundred years been slaves in a land of strangers; he was further descended from men and brethren who for thousands of years had been slaves, savages, idolators, and cannibals on their own native soil. Since the hoariest cycle commemorated by history, there had not been a year when somebody was not "getting after" these men and brethren, hunting them for the mere artless pleasure of killing them, making them work when they didn't want to, and for purposes which were not to their profit, taking their wages out of their hands and their bread out of their mouths, tattooing their backs with cat-o-nine tails and their shins with boot-toes, and, in short, giving them a hard, mean, degrading life of it. On Egyptian granite and in Greek and Roman marbles and Venetian canvases, and in more modern picture-books, their woolly heads and prognathous [Cartwright's term] jaws and cucumber shins had been painted and sculptured and printed in every attitude expressive of subjugation, servility, poltroonery, helplessness, and ridiculousness.

Men like Clarence Gordon and Howells recognized the truth in this angle of vision, wider than the abolitionist's or the racist's. "Hitherto," wrote Howells in *The Atlantic*, March 1872, "Southern character has been treated almost always in direct reference to slavery, and Mr. De

Forest gains an immense advantage in refusing to deal with slavery except as a social fact. In this way we are brought nearer to his Southerners as men and women, and enabled to like or dislike them for purely personal reasons; though any one who supposed him indifferent to the question in abeyance would singularly mistake him, and would lose half his meaning."

For the second time fate favors the mating of the Titan and the flower girl. But into the "severely furnished" McAlister parlor walks a *deus ex* Washington, an emissary sent by the Democratic caucus. The South led by a "phalanx of fire-eaters" has reacted violently to David Wilmot's Proviso urged in early August 1846 upon Congress by the Pennsylvanian who sought to bar slavery forever from Mexican War territory. To save the party and the country, leaders pursue a strategy of electing moderates like Judge McAlister rather than extremists. But to oppose the incumbent Peyton Beaumont is to reopen the feud. Personal ambition long frustrated at the polls, praise that prods his vanity, and money for campaign expenses force Judge McAlister to rationalize an acceptance.

When Peyton learns of the candidacy he breathes "nothing but brandy and gunpowder from ten minutes after he woke up to two hours or so after he went to sleep." His ire is contagious and soon Tom shoots at Frank who counters by tying the young drunk with a bed cord, "like Laocoon in his serpents." When the other Beaumonts confirm the ungentlemanly rencontre they insist upon a duel.

"I am like a spirit in hell, seeing paradise afar off," cries the disconsolate Frank. He refuses to aim at his opponent and both leave the oldfield untouched despite one of the seconds, General Johnson, who is as experienced as Thackeray's Major MacMurdo. This "seedy old grandee" with his tears intermingling "a thin drizzle of tobacco juice," his savage reminiscences, and his anxiety for decorum "even in homicide" is De Forest's happiest moment with the code.

Another mark in the pattern of South Carolina life, as obvious as the duel according to De Forest, was the use of liquor beyond gentlemanly appreciation of vintages, cellaring, and bottling. In one of his short pieces, alcoholic breath identifies a stranger's home state. In another, Captain Horsfall's diet is mainly "double-enders." Senator Pickens Rigdon of *Playing The Mischief* is never without a bottle of Stubbs white wheat. Two of the Beaumonts, like Fate Ferguston, "destroy a pile of whiskey." The cronies who gather of an evening in Duffy's become so mellow they say grace with every round.

Once again De Forest could defend himself against the *Southern Magazine* and others who charged exaggeration. He himself was no teetotaler; one of his verses begins:

> *I mind me sitting in a Tuscan town*
> *Beside a flask which turned the world to rhyme.*

The male tippler became as standard a character in his novels as the Mrs. Chesters, with origins as varied as Virginia and New York in *Miss Ravenel,* and Massachusetts in *A Lover's Revolt* (1898). There is no single compulsion. Colonel Carter drank to save himself from the suicidal boredom of army posts or because he found himself in Cairo, Illinois. Tom Beaumont gave a host's reason:

> As to America, I hurrah for it, of course. We can whip the world, if we could get at it. But when it come to palaces and picture-galleries and that sort of thing, by Jove, we're in the swamps; we're just nowhere. We haven't anything to show. What can you take a man round to when he travels amongst us? The only thing we can offer to pass the time is just a drink. Show him up to a bar; that's what we have come to. And that's the reason, by Jove, that we're always nipping.

The most fervent of all social reforms was temperance, with Neal Dow's success in Maine matched by other Northern states. Colburne's Barataria is so abstemious that it may outlaw the raising of rye! Pleas for sobriety came from pulpits like Lyman Beecher's or tales like Hawthorne's "A Rill from the Town Pump." Groups of artisans called the Washingtonians paraded out of Baltimore in the 1840's singing their joy in dashing to the earth the flowing bowl. They converted multitudes to water and enlisted a young journalist, Whitman, to write of the fate of the inebriate. In Cincinnati, Dickens looked down from his hotel window and saw a Washingtonian procession, one of the few national sights to please the tourist. Among the souvenirs de Tocqueville placed in his trunk was a temperance tract.

There was no comparable success in South Carolina, though its Sons of Temperance cheered Father Theobald Mathew, and its Bible societies bewailed the "excessive use of ardent spirits." Randolph Armitage answered with mock piety while sharing a jug with Redhead

Saxon, "This is what kills us and we love it. We are good Christians; we love our worst enemy."

Summoned by her husband, Nellie takes Kate ten miles beyond Brownville to the mountain home with its scaled paint and broken windows. The Apollonian Armitage entertains Kate who cannot rid herself of the fear that the place is "haunted by mysteries, if not by misery." The weeks go by while her host continues to be charming and sober. But Armitage is not out of Augusta Evans Wilson's *St. Elmo.* The night comes when he must "break bounds, he must run away, he must go wild, he must have a spree." With Redhead Saxon he rides to the cracker ball at Nancy Gile's. The girls in "calico, limp with dirt; others in narrow-chested, ill-fitted scant-shirted gowns of the coarsest white cotton" and the lank men in stinted gray or butternut are already drinking and dancing. It was "his presence which turned mere vulgarity into vice and gave the scene its finishing touch of degradation."

As a traveller De Forest observed dissipation in the Latin Quarter of Paris. His Tom Mallory (*Harper's,* September 1865) knows *grisettes,* watches the "extravagant pranks of the cancan," and frequents the "Cyprian gardens." Here he rendered sin into local idiom.

In the morning the two women stand over Armitage where he lies after a debauched night. Nellie's lines anticipate the terror of waking brutality and the end of the marriage. "He prides himself on not being ruled by his wife. It is so much more manly, more chivalrous, more high-strung to be ruled by a jug!" The sisters flee to Hartland.

Peyton's Washington duties are as vague as his management of the plantation. But thanks to a "violent adherent," John Stokes, we see him as a campaigner. Unlike his ponderous adversary who needs coach and four horses "to go an' ask poo' men for their votes," Peyton rides to the cabin on horseback.

He walks in square an' strong, like he was to home. He straddles out before the fire, an' parts his coat-tails behind him, an' hollers for his tod of plain whiskey, an' chaws an' spits like one of the family. *He* don't make no mistakes betwixt the old man an' the old woman. He knows other folks as sure's he knows himself. He knows the name of every voter in this part of South Carolina an' the name of that voter's dog. He's that kind of man that rouses your entuzzy-muzzy. He's a man that South-Carolinians will take a heap of trouble for.

But neither man electioneers with total abandon. Peyton, as tender as a mother to his daughters, burdened by Nellie's tragedy and Kate's luckless choice, devotes more time to comforting them than to carrying Calhoun's banner through the district. Nellie at last forces him to accept Frank by insisting that "there are plenty of Armitages who don't bear the name." To ensure peace, Peyton proposes to withdraw from the race. In an extraordinary session his sons and General Johnson, who is master of the popular spread-eagle style of eloquence, argue that Peyton is not only a father but champion of States Rights and Southern principles: "Beaumont, if our Alexander is to turn his back in the very moment of crossing the Granicus, what is to become of us?" Regional pride, General Johnson's evocation of sacred names — Moultrie, Eutaw Springs — and the *Tribune's* inopportune hurling of its "weightiest Free-Soil thunder" keep Peyton at the hustings.

It is Judge McAlister who makes the gesture to withdraw, for neither science nor Jenny Devine can comfort his son. But now De Forest's metaphor of the feud and the love affair as a seesaw becomes apt again. In a wild skirmish started by Randolph Armitage the one casualty is Kate's grandfather, Kershaw, that "colossal statue erected to physical beauty and moral goodness, grown venerable." Because the Hartland voters blame the McAlisters for the death, Peyton wins the election overwhelmingly.

A reader of the *Memoirs of Vidocq* and the author of a mystery novel, *Seacliff* (1859), De Forest clears the accused clan through a ballistics probe which shows the fatal bullet marked with the letter A — an "ugly hieroglyphic for us," observes a Beaumont kin.

There will be other pages of anguish, brawls, challenges, and courtship by a new suitor. "We cannot tell the *whole* life, even of a country village," De Forest noted in a letter to Howells. "We must choose some characters for our painting and shut our eyes to others." Hartland is richer for the late inclusion of the Reverend Arthur Gilyard whom not even Whittier would call a clerical oppressor. De Forest heard his prototype preach from a text dear to defenders of slavery, St. Paul's Epistle to Timothy: "And they that have believing masters, let them not despise them, because they are brethren."

At last Major Lawson's prophecy must prevail. The Capulets and the Montagues gather and sing no elegy but an epithalamium.

V

Sectional sensitivity to historic truth rather than to aesthetic value dominates criticism of *Kate Beaumont*. Readers of the novel published seven years after Appomattox inevitably analysed the era before Sumter.

The *Galaxy*, proud that it printed *Overland* and shorter pieces by "the cleverest writer of American fiction," accepted *Kate Beaumont* as a lesson of character and social influence that "found expression in our great socio-political revolution — the war of 1861. If we had ever doubted the fact which began to dawn on the popular consciousness some four decades ago, that the phrase 'Southern chivalry' was neither pleasantry nor satire — but literal — that Southern society was in a large sense medieval and feudal — the present work would have remedied the doubt." The logical comparison followed:

No one, not even Mrs. Stowe, has drawn so clearly, because so simply and frankly, the physical courage and impulsiveness, the haughty punctilio, the class arrogance and prejudice, the blind wilfulness and animal appetite or passion, which makes the 'high-strung gentleman' of the Carolinas such an antithesis to the . . . self-contained product of Northern cultivation. Not even in *Uncle Tom* can we find a better picture of the Southern 'Cracker,' or read with such terrible clearness the degradation and brutality which must crush down the lower orders under the rule of color and class legislation. We would gladly do all honor, too, to the virtues which Mr. De Forest, by implication, would have us believe spring from this somewhat heated soil.

Howells told readers of *The Atlantic* that the whole effect of the narrative was so lifelike that he was "persuaded to believe it the first full and perfect picture of Southern society of the times before the war; certainly it is the most satisfactory." Years later he placed Nellie in his *Heroines of Fiction*, and reiterated the belief that *Kate Beaumont* was not only De Forest's shapeliest work but one "worthy of the greatest novelist living in any country." This tribute moved De Forest to cry out of his obscurity and illness, "Can it be, by some chance, that I was a great man once for a little while, and missed knowing it and letting a whole passing generation know it?"

In a judgment filled with striking phrases, the official organ of the

Southern History Association offered praise and blame. "The picture is a caricature, the story is a libel; but withal the thing is excellently well done, and we must pronounce *Kate Beaumont* to be by long odds the most interesting tale of Southern life that we remember to have read." The reviewer accepted the accuracy of De Forest's portraits, but argued

> The libel lies in the *composition* of the picture, in the assembling of these various characters upon one canvas as a representation of the *average* life of South Carolina — a life whose motive power is brandy and bitters, whose pivot is murder and sudden death, whose amenities are duels and "cracker-balls." A state of things that could not exist in Albania nor the Abruzzi, that would be intolerable in the rudest and newest settlements of Texas and Arkansas, is represented as the normal and unexciting condition of affairs in the refined circles of Carolina, among the best and noblest people of the coast and upland regions.

After its defence of a world De Forest never attacked, the *Southern Magazine* turned to technical limitations and found the novelist "is not a very dramatic writer; he has missed a great many 'situations.'" More than in his later major fiction De Forest shattered scenic intensity and continuity by intermittent shuttling to new settings without adequate motivation: "Back to the Beaumonts one must now hasten to learn how they received the apology." Nor did he add to dramatic tension with his frequent auctorial comment: "We shall know in due time what success Kate had in pleading with Vincent to withdraw his challenge." (He cut some of these in his final revision.) He placed a heavy burden upon today's reader with a device he admired in *Bleak House* and practiced in *Overland*: chapter endings contrived to force a new sequence of excitement. "My God, this is a mutiny." Or, "By the flicker of a candle dying in its socket she saw Randolph holding his wife down on the pillow with one hand, while with the other he brandished a long knife." The mutiny ends; Randolph wants corn liquor, not blood.

In the criticism of two Northern magazines we may have the explanation for the failure of Osgood to exhaust the first edition of *Kate Beaumont*. *Harper's* found subject, place, and time repugnant. "Is it not better to forget the dead past than to keep it remembered?" The *Nation* insisted that the author had slighted the "sentimental reader" who demanded that "the study of the human heart, the same from Maine to Texas, should not be sacrificed to the 'local color.'" The novel, concluded the critic, "is not unlike a play in which the scenery is admirably painted, and all the subordinate characters are excellently represented; they know their parts perfectly, they fight with a blood-thirstiness that cannot be too highly commended; the blue and red fire blazes at the proper moment, but the hero and the heroine do not come upon the stage."

There are, however, rounded encounters from the first sight of Peyton to his farewell, as no longer steeped in brandy or "hot with his chronic pugnacity" but mellowed by Kate's joy he greets the wedding guests. "He had on a blue dress-coat with gilt buttons, a buff vest also with gilt buttons, and buff kerseymore trousers tightly strapped under the instep. . . . The strong colors, so suggestive of military uniform, perfectly became his bold, trooper-like officer-like expression and the dark ruddiness, almost as deep as mahogany, of his complexion."

Because De Forest did not restrict to one area his plan to speak "with severe truthfulness, and without regard to the proud illusions of Hartland District," the historian of *The Southern Poor-White*, Shields McIlwaine, cited the pioneer use of this class in the "treat" night. The entire Saxonburg section, with the later visit of Mrs. Chester to Bentley's "old rookery" supports the validity of Howells' comment that De Forest was "a realist before realism was named." Other readers lauded Peyton's waking, the family parliament in the long parlor, the hesitant journey of the peace makers, and the meeting of the Judge and Mr. Choke as they prepare for one of the crucial elections of the 1840's: "Divide the voice of this State, and you split disunion everywhere." Those like Gordon (*The Atlantic*, November 1873), who sought that Victorian requisite, the death bed, found the last hour of Kershaw as poignant as the one with Huldah in *Playing The Mischief*. In fact Gordon listed the novel just under the high place held alone by Hawthorne.

Kate Beaumont is not only a lament for a land on the far side of the bloody chasm and for the Peytons who now live in a world the novelist called an almshouse. When he compared the girl of thirty years ago and the girl of today, as he did in 1868, he conceded that a Josie Murray read *The Newcomes* and *The Atlantic* rather than Kate's fare of *Thaddeus of Warsaw* and the *Lady's Book*. Josie heard better music than "The Battle of Prague." But the Murrays and the Olympia Vanes were extravagant clothes-worshippers, predatory passengers rather than crew members. His admiration went out to the open, candid Beaumont sisters though to Nellie he gave emotional scenes and language denied the frailer Kate. "Bear it as I do," she tells her father as they pace the garden after he hears of the long soilure.

De Forest's audience, so humiliatingly small in comparison to that of a Wilson or a Southworth (whose two score volumes were all reissued in the collected edition denied him), expected and found specimens of his wit. Redhead Saxon's mock duel, according to *Galaxy*, was the funniest thing since Dickens. "When a man can't hit a house standin' inside on't, he'd better quit shootin'." That "red-eyed destiny," General Johnson, whose admirers credit him with flights of eloquence in which he takes leave of intelligibility, is of the same tall stock as Twain's Dauphin. And even the *Nation* enjoyed his "little side remarks — the sort of indication of the writer's reflection," such as the filling of manor houses with professionals who never practice their medicine or law. "By the way, it is perfectly amazing how many medical gentlemen there are in the South. A literary friend tells me that, during a six months' experience among the smaller towns and ruder taverns . . . he slept with nearly a hundred doctors."

De Forest ended his earlier strictures on fiction with the prayer that a "true Southern novelist may arise, for he will be able to furnish us vast amusement and some instruction. His day is passing; in another generation his material will be gone; the 'chivalrous Southron' will be as dead as the slavery that created him." A degree of fulfillment came with *Kate Beaumont*.

JOSEPH JAY RUBIN
The Pennsylvania State University

ACKNOWLEDGMENTS

I wish to thank the Yale University Library for permission to examine and reprint its De Forest manuscripts and letters, and for photostating the novelist's corrected copy of *Kate Beaumont* and the Charleston letters. The Pennsylvania State University continued to support the research first started with *Honest John Vane* and *Playing The Mischief*. Its Fred Lewis Pattee Library offered facilities and materials; and Charles W. Mann, Curator of the Rare Book Room, obtained an Osgood *Kate Beaumont* and other De Forest items. Harvard University Library made available copies of De Forest's letters to Howells. The quotations from the letters of Howells are printed with the permission of his heirs; further use may not be made by others without express permission. The University of South Carolina Library, the Library of Congress, and the Library Company of Philadelphia answered numerous inquiries. Gordon N. Ray identified the subject of Thackeray's Charleston lectures. My colleague, Richard B. Gidez, shared his knowledge of nineteenth century American fiction. Professor Alfred S. Reid of Furman University proved that the courtesy De Forest encountered in South Carolina still prevails.

Once again it is a pleasant duty to record gratitude to Harrison T. Meserole for his many hours of editorial help.

TEXT

The text of *Kate Beaumont* printed here is the third and final state. The novel first appeared as a magazine serial in *The Atlantic,* January-December 1871. The next year James R. Osgood of Boston, publisher of *The Atlantic,* issued a book set from corrected sheets of the installments. Then came De Forest's "retouching" of his own copy as he made abortive plans to reissue his major works. (See the Preface to the Monument Edition of *Honest John Vane.*)

His marginal changes, like those in *Playing The Mischief,* are often no more that the switching of a verb, the turn of a phrase, the clarification of a tag line. But beginning with the Osgood there is a surprising bowdlerization by change of epithet or excision. *The Atlantic* "God," "Devil," "damn," and "drunk" become "G-d," "dickens" or "doose," "blasted," and "tipsy." (The one arbitrary change in the Monument text is the return to "God.") In the last version he inked out some of the analysis of Bentley's love of liquor, the steward's "being slightly beery," and Nellie's domestic dilemma. Duffy swallows three glasses a day, not the original three horns. "Nasty" crackers are elevated to "vulgar"; "bummers" to "topers"; "a young rough of an Antony" — unfortunately — to "a young totally indifferent Antony"; the lover's whisper is no longer "tremulous with passion."

In the attempt to increase the pace of the narrative — "to quit the eddies and head down stream" — and to honor changing fashion, De Forest abandoned some of the auctorial intrusions. As though wary of providing critics with easy quotes, he never restored this part of Frank McAlister's *Atlantic* censure of American culture:

> Even in novels, — one would think we might do something there, we have a wealth of strong incidents and curious characters, — but what is the result? The American novelist either can't draw a character, or he can't make a plot. In general he is dry and dull as a school geography.

One of the "curious characters," Mrs. Chester, loses years in successive stages: from an "elder lady" nearly fifty, to a "riper lady" of forty-four and forty. To the considerable toll taken by the duel De Forest added five "valuable lives." Sensitivity to the charge that "the weak point" in all of his novels was "general immateriality in the heroine" made him delete the first paragraphs of the opening chapter and write a new description of Kate. The Judge's figure once exhibited "the outlines of an elephant when he stoops to pick up his hat."

The book Osgood produced had as little distinction as Harper's printing of *Playing The Mischief*: 165 double-columned pages, $9\frac{1}{4}$ by $5\frac{11}{16}$, set in eight-point type. Neither the green pebbled cloth with gold stamping and brown end papers nor the unsigned, full-length pen and ink illustrations lured enough buyers to exhaust the first edition.

Estes and Lauriat, the purchasers of Osgood's stock — the Boston firm was the fourth of De Forest's publishers to go bankrupt or suspend publication — made clear to him on 17 April 1877 that the fiction Howells named "one of the best American novels ever written" had no place in a future list:

> We have not sold the copies of *Kate Beaumont* which we bought at that time. The sale for this class of book is very small at present. We were aware that you owned the copyright but we are doubtful as to whether it will ever pay to print again.

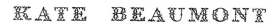

KATE BEAUMONT

CONTENTS

CHAPTER 1

In the days before the greatest of American wars, in those now all but incredible days when the planter was the grandest figure in American society, the long talked of and much advertised steamship *Mersey* set out on her first voyage across the Atlantic.

Charleston had been resolving for years back that it would not trade with abolitionists unless they lived in Europe; that it would no longer purchase its foreign merchandise through the fingers of New Yorkers and other northerners; that it would have shipping of its own and be the commercial emporium of planterdom. Accordingly it had established what it called a southern line of steamers between its own half rotted wharves and the gigantic granite docks of Liverpool. All South Carolina was in a state of exultation over the international event. Even remote Saxonburg, which consumed all its domestic productions, even to the last quart of its puckering and corrosive white whiskey, held a mass-meeting and swore to do its exportation by The Planter's Line. In Hartland District the Honorable Peyton Beaumont set up an immense banner labeled with the words, "Hartland Cross-Roads and Great Britain United," and kept the same flying for a week on end, and would have shot anybody who had laughed at it.

The first boat of this pattern southern line was the *Mersey,* fabricated in the Clyde, owned mainly by Scotchmen, manned by Englishmen, and captained by an Irishman. She left Liverpool at sundown; came to light next day in a storm of wind and driving rain; sailed for sixty hours on her lee-bulwark, or upsettingly near it; the steward and stewardess tumbling distractedly from stateroom to stateroom; only two passengers able to come up firmly to the rack of the sloping and heaving table; in short, sixty hours of such weather as would have sickened a viking. One marvelled if the very drove of porpoises who plunged like buffalos athwart the course of the ship did not feel uneasy about the midriff and disposed to forswear the sea.

At last the cyclone passed southward; the wind subsided to what mariners call a tawpsle breeze; the streaky and mottled waves flung but rare spits of clattering foam across the canted deck; the passengers resurrected and came forth, much engaged in mutual staring, never having seen each other before. Of course the two who had not been sick were out, leaning side by side against the port quarter bulwark, and smoking with that unendurable vaingloriousness which belongs to their kind. They seemed to be old acquaintance, for they hit each other familiarly in the ribs, and prefaced their remarks with, "I say, Duffy," and "I say, Bill Wilkins." There was some murmured bantering between them as to a young lady who stood braced in the sloping door at the head of the cabin stairway, looking timidly and yet wistfully at the unsteady freedom of the quarterdeck.

"Wilkins, go and offer your arm," exhorted Duffy. "Family trades at your shop."

"Oh, get out!" returned Wilkins, obviously scorning Duffy as a fellow who habitually joked at the wrong moment. "I know where to put myself, if you don't."

"I say, Bill, you don't like that," chuckled Duffy, puckering his flat doughy face into a simper which to Wilkins looked indescribably silly.

"Don't like what?" was the answer in a growl of scorn.

"Calling your bran-new store a shop."

"That's just like you, Duffy. I never knew you make a joke but what you had to explain it."

Duffy was silenced, but he kept on simpering while searching for a retort, as a stubborn artillerist keeps his battery in position while waiting for cartridges. Wilkins, a shrewd-faced, swarthy-complexioned man, with dusky and twinkling eyes and a good-humored expression, continued to glance sidelong at the young lady in the companion way. "She wants to get on deck," he muttered. "Somebody ought to give her an arm."

"Never saw you modest before," grinned Duffy, finding his repartee at last. "Must be somebody's threatened to give you a licking!"

Wilkins, scorning to reply, was about to step forward and offer the young lady his services, when the sight of a new comer checked him.

"Sail in, Bill," whispered Duffy with a scoffing dig in the waistcoat. "Bet you a hat you dastn't."

"Too late," said Wilkins. "Jehu! what a tall fellow! By Jehu, that man could wade ashore. Shut up now, Duffy; they are coming this way. Don't make a fool of yourself *all* the time. I can stand it, but most folks can't."

Duffy fell silent, and both men drew aside respectfully as the young lady passed them, her gloved fingers resting on the arm of a singularly tall young gentleman. But deferential as they meant to be, they found it impossible not to look at her fixedly. Her face was very beautiful, very interesting, and even very impressive. It was of the type which one expects to find in Italy, or more likely, in the Orient. The profile was gently aquiline, the complexion a medium brunette faintly flushed with rose, and the eyes of a dark lustrous hazel. But the expression was beyond painting, so sweetly pure was it, and so sweetly noble. One would have judged from it that she knew only the highest feeling and thoughts of which humanity is capable. There are such prophetic faces, which seem to utter a coming perfection of our nature, not to be attained perhaps on this sinful earth.

This young lady lifted her face shyly and yet with perfect self-possession toward the man whose arm supported her. It was obvious enough that she did not know him, and that she had only accepted his assistance because she needed it, and not with the slightest thought towards flirting.

"Do you wish to go aft?" he had ventured to ask as he passed her in the breezy house on deck which enclosed the companion-way. "I judged so by your looking out. May I offer you my arm and give you a seat?"

"I was waiting for my aunt," she replied. "But she does not seem to come."

Then, finding it very uncomfortable there, with the wind sucking through the door in a gale, she passed her hand over his sleeve, saying, "If you will take me to a seat, I will be much obliged to you."

"We have had a horrible time of it," he was remarking as they passed the respectful Duffy and Wilkins. "The weather has treated us like enemies and criminals."

"I am so glad to get on deck once more!" she said, her face lighting and coloring like an eastern sky under the rising of the sun. "O, how beautiful the ocean is!"

He looked down upon her with the dignified satisfaction of twenty-four admiring eighteen, and then remembering the limited duty which he had undertaken, he halted and placed a chair for her.

"Thank you," she said. "Don't let me trouble you further. I see my aunt is coming. You are very good."

Thus liberated, or rather perhaps graciously dismissed from his charge, the tall young man quietly touched his brimless cloth cap, turned on his heel with the dignity natural to giants, walked to the other side of the quarter-deck, leaned a yard or so over the bulwark, and watched the swift whirls of white and blue water, as they boiled out from under the paddle-box and raced along the ship's side.

The aunt, a stoutish lady, inviolably veiled, — clearly not disposed to be blown to pieces before fellow-passengers, — was in charge of a far stouter man, the captain of the *Mersey*. The captain got her a chair, slapped it down in a jolly way alongside the niece, and then planted himself bolt upright in front of the two, babbling and boasting louder than the weather.

"Yes, a fine ship, noble ship. Never commanded a better. Twelve, thirteen, fourteen knots. Make the passage before you could dress a salad. It's the beginning, ladies, of a great enterprise. At last our State will stand on its own feet, do its own business, put its money in its own pocket. Independent of New York? Of course we will be. It's high time. Don't you think so? I agree with you."

Captain Brien was born in Dublin, though only a baby at the time, as he loved to say, and raised in the American commercial marine. He was short and very thick; what our Southern mountaineers would call a chunk of a man; not protuberant nor blubbery, yet weighing his fifteen stone. His face was flat and nearly four-square, almost alarmingly ponderous in the jowl, with cheeks as hard and brown as smoked bacon. His complexion was a rich and curiously mottled mixture of sun-tanning and whiskey-tanning. He had the look of a bluff honest sailor, yet he habitually talked loud and bragged absurdly, partly because he was of Celtic blood and believed his own exaggerations, but partly also because he had found that passengers and especially women were cheered by trumpetings.

After three minutes of his hurrah-boys gabble, he felt that he had done his duty by the two ladies, and he prepared to leave them. It was time; he was running out of conversation; when he had shouted and huzzaed a little, he had done; such was Captain Brien as a member of society. So he glared at the helmsman; then he threw a glance aloft, as if he were still in a sailing-vessel and carried top-gallants; then, with a sudden lurch and a sharp shuffle, he was away. Next he was looking over the side, not far from the tall young gentleman, guessing at the ship's speed by the flight of the water. As he was about to move off — the uneasy, restless, hyena-like creature — the giant lassoed him with a question.

"Well, Captain Brien," he said, "how is the new line to succeed?"

"Succeed? Prodigious!" promptly shouted the skipper, in his loud cracking voice; a voice full of cheerful and almost frolicsome bluster; a voice which had an undertone of humbug. "Sure to pay. Pay right off. Keep paying. First great step in the right direction. Change the channels of trade in our country."

"It is not easy to change the channels of trade," observed the tall young gentleman. "It frequently takes centuries to do that. New York has an immense start."

A serious-minded person he seemed to be; one of those persons who love to speak veracities and to hear veracities uttered; who, perhaps, take offence when you offer them a mess of undisguisable claptrap.

Captain Brien looked up quickly at hearing his enthusiastic prophecies questioned. He did not frankly turn his face of bronze and mahogany; he merely slewed this gray, piggish, furtive, quick-glancing eyes. In an instant he had warned himself: "This man is not to be fooled with."

"You are right, sir," he said, dropping his brazen gasconading for a confidential, honest undertone. "New York *has* an immense start."

"Only two vessels in the line, I believe," continued the passenger.

"Only two," answered the captain briefly, not caring to continue the conversation, since he could not splash and spout and play the whale in it.

"And the other is not yet built?"

"Not yet built," softly admitted the captain. He began to look around him for duty: leaking at this rate was not agreeable nor wise.

The passenger saw that the subject was no longer a welcome one, and he dropped it. There was a silence of a few seconds, during which the captain glanced two or three times at the young man, as if trying in vain to call him to mind, or as if struck with his appearance. An imposing young fellow really; his height something quite extraordinary; certainly not less than six feet four. His face, too, notwithstanding its fine pink and white color, and notwithstanding the softness of his curling blond hair and long blond whiskers, was not such a face as one prefers to shake a fist at. Although the features were, in general, pleasing, the cheekbones were somewhat broad and the jaws were strong, showing a character full of pluck and perseverance. In expression it was charming; there was in it a wealth of both dignity and benignity; it reminded one of the early portraits of Washington.

"We have had rough weather," he said presently. "This is my first morning on my legs. Who are my fellow-passengers, may I ask?"

"All the right sort, sir," shouted the captain, for surely this was a subject that he might brag upon, without giving offence. "All of the right sort, and from the right spot. Such people as I like to carry. A most elegant lady, sitting over there just now, a perfect lady, sir. Her niece is one of the most charming, innocent, modest, — bless you, just the kind that we raise and brag of — just our own best kind, sir. Her brother Tom, too —" The captain stopped here, and looked at his helmsman, headstays, bobstays, etc. It seemed as if he had not so very much to say in favor of the brother Tom.

"What is the name?" inquired the tall gentleman, who doubtless had his reasons for wanting to know.

"The name is Chester; no, beg pardon, the aunt's name is Chester, — Mrs. Chester. The young lady's name is Beaumont. The Beaumonts of Hartland!" repeated the captain, proudly.

The tall young gentleman did not start; he merely looked as if he had heard before of the Beaumonts of Hartland; he also looked as if he were not pleased at meeting them.

"Ever been in Hartland?" inquired the captain. "Lovely village, — town, I should say."

"I have been there," was the brief and dry answer.

"Perhaps you have known the Beaumonts, then? I dare say they would be pleased to —"

"I never knew them," interrupted the youngster, more dryly than before.

"In a little company like this —" continued Captain Brien.

"I dare say I may make their acquaintance, at a proper time."

His intentions towards an immediate introduction being thus bluffed, the captain fell silent, and looked once more at his helmsman, bob-stays, jackstays, etc.

"How many days more of it?" inquired the passenger, after some seconds of grave meditation, his face meanwhile turned from the Beaumont group, as if he might wish to avoid recognition.

"How many days? Why that depends, you know. The weather comes in there. So does the newness of the engine. I shouldn't like to prophesy, Mr. McMaster."

The young man gave the captain a singular glance, and seemed about to speak, but checked himself. Could it be that his name was not McMaster, and that he had reasons for letting the error go un-corrected? After another meditation, he swung slowly away from the captain, his back still toward Mrs. Chester and Miss Beaumont, strode forward to the waist of the vessel, lighted a cigar, and smoked in deep thought.

Meanwhile Wilkins and Duffy, the latter with his narrow gray eyes constantly fixed on the tall passenger, were conversing about their own affairs.

"Duffy, how much do you suppose we've made by going to England?" queried Wilkins, puckering the corners of his mouth into satirical wrinkles.

"Made? How should I know? Foot it up at the end of the season. What do you think we've made, yourself?"

"Made blasted fools of ourselves."

"Oh, you'd better jump overboard, and done with it. You're always looking at the black side of things. How do you figure that out?"

"Well, figure it yourself; you can cipher, can't you? Expenses going and coming just four times what they would be to New York, taking in board at the St. Nicholas, a course through the theatres, and a blow out generally. It cuts down all my profits and eats into the capital. I think, by Jehu, we'd better let importing alone. It may do from a seaport; but hang me if I ever try importing into an inland village again. If we hadn't been as green as swamp meadows, we wouldn't have been got out of our little two-penny shops on any such business. And I believe the whole line will turn out a flam. Oh, it's all very well as a spree. That's it, a South Carolina spree. But you and I can't make fortunes on spreeing it."

At this moment the tall passenger passed them on his way forward to the waist. Duffy followed him with his eyes, then hurried to the companion-way, and took a long, sly look, then came back, staring inquiringly at his chum.

"I say, Bill Wilkins, how about that fellow?" he demanded.

"Big chap," returned Wilkins, turning his face away and surveying every point of the horizon.

"Yes, but who is he?" persisted Duffy.

"How should I know?" returned Wilkins, trying to look indifferent, but unable to conceal annoyance.

"Don't know him, eh?" continued Duffy, smiling and triumphant. "Ever live in Hartland?"

"Yes, of course I've lived in Hartland, twenty years or thereabouts. But he's no Hartland man."

"He may have been a Hartland boy, though."

Wilkins squared his back on Duffy, and walked aft; but Duffy would not be got rid of in this fashion; he followed, and continued his subject.

"Don't know him, hey? You know those people opposite, don't you?"

"What, Mrs. Chester and Miss Beaumont? Yes, I know who they are."

"And where they live?"

"Yes, and where they live."

"Well, you know the people on the other hill?"

"What other hill?"

"O, now make believe you can't understand anything," said the indignant Duffy. "Why, *the* other hill. Other side of the town. Straight back of your store. Two miles back."

Wilkins would not answer, and persisted in staring at every nook and corner of the weather, as if he did not hear his gabbling comrade.

"That's one of the —" began Duffy.

"Shut up!" broke in Wilkins.

"The youngest one," went on Duffy. "Been abroad eight years, studying and travelling. Changed wonderfully. I ciphered him out, though. I tell you, it's Frank —"

"Shut up, for God's sake," implored Wilkins.

"Yes, and you knew it all the while, and wouldn't tell me of it," complained the aggrieved Duffy.

"Yes, I *did* know it all the while," admitted Wilkins. "I recognized him the evening we came aboard. And I didn't tell you of it; and do you know why?"

Without answering or apparently noticing this question, Duffy pursued: "Yes, by jiminy, that's him. Sold him peanuts and candy many a time. I'll go and shake hands with him."

He started to go forward. Wilkins caught him by the skirt of his black swallow-tailed coat and dragged him back.

"Don't be a blasted fool!"

"Why not?" demands the innocent Duffy.

"Because it's ridiculous to be a blasted fool *all* the while, and because it makes mischief. Do you want to get up a muss on board? There are those Beaumonts, — that young doose of a Tom Beaumont. Don't you remember all the trouble between the two families?"

"Oh, exactly," returns the abashed Duffy.

"Oh, exactly!" scornfully repeats Wilkins. "Well, you see it now, don't you? *They* don't know him. He passes for Mr. McMaster on board. I heard the captain call him so, and he answered to it. He's quite right. It ain't best they should know him."

"If they should, there might be a dickens of a muss," observes the at last enlightened Duffy.

"I should guess so, by Jehu," mutters Wilkins, wrathful at Duffy for not having seen it all before.

CHAPTER 2

 If Mr. McMaster, as we will call him for the present, expected to keep at a distance from the Beaumonts during this voyage, he was disappointed.

After he was seated at the dinner-table the three members present of that family, the aunt, the niece, and the nephew, followed each other into the eating-saloon and took places opposite him, the young lady acknowledging by a slight inclination of the head her remembrance of his service in the morning. This was what he had not expected; in fact, this was just what he supposed he had guarded against; but the steward had misunderstood his five dollars, and thought he wanted to be close to the belle of the steamer. So there was nothing for Mr. McMaster to do but to return the girl's zephyr-like salutation, to glance rapidly at the faces of aunt and nephew, and then fall to eating in silence.

Meanwhile Duffy and Bill Wilkins, paired away farther down the table, looked on breathlessly out of the corners of their eyes. They expected, it is not best now to say precisely what, but clearly something remarkable. Duffy whispered, "That's curious, hey, Wilkins?" Wilkins responded with a grunt which signified as plainly as possible, "Shut up!" And when Duffy failed to understand, and so stated in an audible whisper, Wilkins hissed back between his teeth, "By Jehu! if you don't shut up, I change my seat." Whereupon Duffy, turning very red under the reproof, looked around fiercely at the listening waiter and called for a bottle of champagne, being a man who under such snubbings needed spirituous encouragement.

Presently Mrs. Chester began a conversation with the mysterious giant. Mrs. Chester was aristocratic; in fact, she was in a general way disagreeably haughty; not at all the sort of lady who habitually seeks intercourse with strangers. But the giant was — barring his too great height — decidedly handsome; and, what is more fascinating still to a woman, he had an air of distinction.

So Mrs. Chester astonished Duffy and Wilkins by saying to the tall gentleman, with that sweet smile which haughty and self-conscious people often draw out of their depths of condescension, "The sea is still a little troublesome, sir. It is safer on deck for a gentleman than for a lady."

The captain, seated in his Olympus at the head of the table, immediately thundered his introduction: "Mr. McMaster, let me present you to Mrs. Chester. Miss Beaumont, Mr. Beaumont, Mr. McMaster. We are all friends of the line, I believe; travelling comrades. Let's be jolly while we are at sea. Time enough to be solemn on shore."

No notice was taken of Duffy and Wilkins, nor of other persons around the foot of the table, all of whom Captain Brien knew by instinct to be of a different breed from the Beaumonts of Hartland.

"I think, madam, that we shall now have a quiet time, at least for a few days," said the so-called Mr. McMaster, in a full, round tone, and with a cultivated accent, very pleasant to hear. "The barometer seems to promise as much."

"Oh, does it?" smiled the lady. "I am so glad it prophesies smooth things. Well, we ought to be patient, even with a long voyage. It is homeward. It is towards our dear native country. I shall be so delighted to see its shores again! If you have been absent as long as we, you must be able to sympathize with me."

"I have been in Europe eight years, Mrs. Chester."

"Eight years!" exclaimed Mrs. Chester. "And I was gone only one year. How can an American stay abroad eight years?"

"I have been engaged in a course of studies which made the time pass very rapidly."

"Oh, I understand. My niece has been three years at school in England and France. We ran over after her, and took a year on the Continent. Europe is the best place, I suppose, for a thorough education. But eight years! Dear me! how glad you must be to return!"

"I can't quite say that. I leave great things behind me. Compared with America, Europe is a completed and perfect social edifice."

"Excuse me!" objected Mrs. Chester, quite sincerely and warmly. "I don't consider them our equals. Look at their hordes of brutal peasants. And even their aristocrats, I don't consider them equal to our gentlemen and ladies, our untitled nobility. Where will you find anything in Europe to compare with our best families?"

The tall gentleman waived the comparison of manners; he alluded, he said civilly, to art, and literature, and science.

"But look at our list of noble names," urged Mrs. Chester, pushing on from victory to victory. "The authors of the Federalist, — Legarè, Cooper, Bancroft, — Washington Irving."

The lady's lore, it will be perceived, was of early days; she had read "the books which no gentleman's library should be without."

Mr. McMaster obviously hesitated about contradicting a woman; then he seemed to find a reason for speaking plainly, even at the risk of giving offence.

"I admit those and a few others," he said. "But how few they all are! And we are a nation of thirty millions. We have been a civilized people a hundred years and more. I can't account for the sparseness of our crop of great intellects. I sometimes fear that our long backwoods life has dwarfed the national brain, or that our climate is not fitted to develop the human plant in perfection. Our painting can't get into European exhibitions. Our sculpture has only done two or three things which have attracted European attention. Our scientific men, with three or four exceptions, confine themselves to rehearsing European discoveries. Our histories are good second-class; so are our poems, the best of them. I don't understand it. There is only one poor comfort. It is not given to every nation to produce a literature. There have been hundreds of nations, and there have been only six or eight literatures."

Evidently this Mr. McMaster, or whatever his name might be, was a frank and resolute fellow, if not a downright wilful one. At the same time his manner was perfectly courteous, and his cultivated voice was even insinuating, though raised in contradiction. In spite of annoyance at hearing her native land criticised and her own importance thereby considerably depreciated, Mrs. Chester was confirmed in her opinion that he was a youth of good blood.

"How can an American attack his own country?" was her only remonstrance, and that sweetened by a smile.

"I beg your pardon; I don't call it attacking. If I should discover a leak in our vessel here, I should feel it my duty to tell the captain of it. How can we mend our imperfections so long as we persuade each other that we are already perfect?"

"By Jove, you're right there, sir," put in Tom Beaumont, a genteel but devil-may-care looking youth, perhaps twenty-one or twenty-two years old. "If I see a fellow going wrong, especially if he's a friend of mine, I say to him right off, 'Look here, old chap, allow me to tell you, by Jove, that that sort of thing won't do.' Yes, sir," continued Tom who had taken a cocktail before dinner and was now drinking liberally of champagne, "your doctrine suits my ideas exactly. As to America, I hurrah for it, of course. We can whip the world, if we could get at it. But when it comes to palaces and picture-galleries and that sort of thing, by Jove, we're in the swamps; we're just nowhere. We haven't anything to show. What can you take a man round to when he travels amongst us? The only thing we can offer to pass the time is just a drink. Show him up to a bar; that's what we have to come to. And that's the reason, by Jove, that we're always nipping."

It seemed as if Mr. McMaster thought that Tom had nipped too much that morning to allow of his conversation being profitable. He turned to the sister. He had, by the way, no business to turn to her. Even Mr. Duffy, though not very bright, was aware of that; he showed it by hitting his knee against the knee of his friend Wilkins; for Duffy could not endure to have an idea without letting some one know it. Nevertheless, a brief and rather shy conversation took place between Mr. McMaster and Miss Kate Beaumont.

Yes, she agreed with him, at least in part; she had been long enough abroad to like people abroad; the English she liked very much; the French not so well. The English were so frank and straightforward and honest! You could depend on them. It was strange that it should be so; but it seemed to her that life was more simple with them than with other people; they had less guile and pretence than other people. Perhaps, she admitted, she had seen the best side.

"Women are fortunate in being so situated as to see mainly the best side," said McMaster. "I have sometimes thought it would be an angelic existence to see all the good there is in the world and none of the evil."

Whether Miss Kate felt that there was a compliment in this, or whether she perceived that the young gentleman looked at her very steadily, she colored a little. He noticed it, and immediately stopped talking to her; he was astonished and indignant at his own folly; what right had *he* to be paying *her* compliments? The girl's face and air and manner had actually made him forget who she was.

Mrs. Chester once more grasped the reins of the conversation; and was allowed to have them, so far as her niece and the stranger were concerned; the genial Tom alone making an occasional clutch at them. It was noticeable that while this lady talked with Mr. McMaster, she was mellifluous and smiling; but from the moment her own family joined in the discussion, she acquired a sub-acid flavor. Nevertheless, all parties rose from the table on seemingly excellent terms with each other.

Once on deck, Mr. Duffy drew his friend aside and muttered in profound amazement, "Ever see anything like that, Bill Wilkins?"

The prudent Wilkins, looking as non-committal as a mummy, responded by an incomprehensible grunt.

"What would old Beaumont have said, if he'd happened in?" pursued Duffy.

Wilkins glanced cautiously about him: "Don't speak so loud, man. You'll split with it."

"I hain't mentioned the other name," declared Duffy.

"Yes, but by Jehu, you want to. I know you, Duffy. By Jehu, I'd rather trust a nigger mamma with a secret than you. I wish to Heaven you'd shut up on the whole subject till we get ashore. If you don't, there'll be a fuss aboard."

"Oh, you be hanged, Bill Wilkins!" retorted Duffy, walking away in great offence, and would not speak to his brother storekeeper again for half an hour.

Meantime the Beaumonts, clustered in a little group on deck, were discussing this Mr. McMaster.

"Seen him before, by Jove!" muttered Tom, bringing his fist down on the arm of his chair. "By Jove, Aunt Marian, I've seen him before. Where was it?"

"Tom, I wish you wouldn't by Jove it quite so constantly in my presence," replies Mrs. Chester. "You seem to take me for one of your own fellows, as you call them."

"By — I beg your pardon; there it pops again," says Tom. "I was going to say it wouldn't do at all among the fellows. Takes something stronger than that to make *them* look around."

"I care very little how you address them," retorts Mrs. Chester with peppery dignity. "What I do care for is how you address *me*."

"Well, all right. Beg pardon, as I said before. Catch another hold. Who *is* this tall chap?"

"He looks like so many young Englishmen," suggests Kate. "Only he is taller."

"So he does," nods Tom. "Perhaps that's it. Dare say I saw him in England and took him for a John Bull. Though, by — never mind, aunt — missed fire that time — try another barrel — what was I going to say? Oh! I can't for the life of me remember where I did see him. Was it in Scotland? Give it up."

"At all events, he is a gentleman," decides Mrs. Chester. "I didn't hear him by Joving it at us."

"Come, Aunt Marian!" said the young man, speaking with sudden seriousness and even dignity. "Allow me to suggest that that is going a great ways. Do you notice that you insinuated that I am not a gentleman?"

Mrs. Chester appeared to be struck by the protest; she looked up at her nephew with surprise and gravity.

"Tom, you are quite correct," she said, "I trust you will always repel that insinuation, from whomsoever it comes. I did not mean it."

"All right," returned the youngster, dropping back into the easy, good-natured tone which was habitual with him. "Now, if you don't mind it, I'll light up."

During this short tiff, Kate Beaumont glanced gravely and thoughtfully from one to the other of the pair. It was evident that she had been long enough away from her relations to forget their characters a little, and that she was studying them with an interest almost amounting to anxiety.

"So you like the English, Kate?" recommences Tom, with a bantering smile, — the smile of a good-hearted tease. "Honest, steady-going chaps are they? I wonder how you will like us. Seen any Americans yet that you fancy? What do you say to me?"

"You are my brother, Tom."

"Oh, that's all, is it. What if I wasn't? I almost wish I wasn't. What a fancy I would take to you! You'd have an offer this trip. Perhaps you will, as it is. This Mr. McMaster is looking a good deal your way."

"Nonsense, Tom!" And Kate colored as innocent girls do under such remarks.

"So I say," put in Mrs. Chester. "Tom, you talk like a school-girl. They babble about matches in that style."

"Do they!" wonders Tom. "News to me. Thought I'd suggested a new train of thought to Kate. But this Mr. McMaster —"

In short, there was much talk among the Beaumonts concerning this Mr. McMaster. For various reasons, and especially perhaps because of the mystery attaching to him, he was a favorite. On board ship any subject of curiosity is a delight, and any tolerably fine fellow may get the name of a Crichton. Even the fact that the young man did not seek the Beaumonts was rather a recommendation to people who were so sure of their own position. He was not a pushing creature; consequently he was a gentleman. Mrs. Chester sent for him to join in whist parties, and Tom clapped him on the shoulder with proffers of drinks and cigars.

As for him, he wished heartily that they would let him alone, until there came a time when he could not wish it, at least not heartily. In his first interview with them he had contradicted Mrs. Chester's glorification of America, not altogether because he did not agree with her and because it was his nature to be sincere and outspoken, but partly also to leave a bad impression of himself upon her mind, and so evade an awkward intimacy. It was awkward in more ways than one. His time was valuable to him; he had in his state-room thick German volumes of mineralogy and metallurgy which he wanted to master; and he had proposed to make this voyage an uninterrupted course of study. In the second place, there was between this family and his family a disagreement too inveterate and serious to be rubbed out by a chance acquaintance.

At times he regretted that he had not at first announced his name and individuality. He had not done it, from good motives; he despised and detested the old family quarrel; he did not want to be dragged into it personally; did not want a voyage of pouting and perhaps of open hostility. A momentary impulse, an impulse strengthened by the surprise of finding himself face to face with Beaumonts, had induced him to accept the false name which somehow had fallen upon him. Now that he had time to think over the matter coolly, was the impulse to be regretted? On the whole, no; notwithstanding that he hated to sail under false colors, no; notwithstanding that he was in a ridiculous position, no. As McMaster he could go through the voyage peaceably; and after it was over, he should never meet the Beaumonts again; although they lived within a few miles of each other, there was no chance of a meeting.

But if he voyaged with these people under a false name, he must not become intimate with them. On this, for the first two or three days, he was resolved; and on this, after two or three days, he was not so resolved. The temptation which led him into this change of feeling, the strongest temptation to which a man can be subjected, was a woman. If the youngster needs excuse, let us remember that for the last four years he had been studying with a will, and had had scarcely an idea or a sentiment outside of chemistry, mineralogy, and metallurgy. He had rarely spoken to a woman, except his elderly, hard working landlady, and the fat, plain daughter of his landlady. If there had been any pretty girls in the little town of Göttingen, he had failed to see them. For four years he had not been in love, nor thought of being in love. And, all of a sudden, here he was face to face with a young lady who was handsome enough and sweet enough to make a sensation in any society, and who, in the desert of the *Mersey*, with only Mrs. Chester and the stewardess for rivals, seemed of course the loveliest of women.

She was a mighty temptation. He could not help looking at her and studying her. If she needed helping from a dish within reach of his long arm, he must perforce anticipate the waiter. If she wanted to walk the deck, and her fly-away, devil-may-care brother was larking below among the beer-bottles and punch-glasses, he could not help saying, "Allow me." If she asked questions about life in Germany or about the studies in a German university, he did not know how to evade telling her many things, and so making an interesting conversation. Each link in this intercourse seemed in itself so unimportant! And yet the whole made such a chain!

Of course, this intimacy, so singular to those who knew all its circumstances, could not fail to draw the sidelong wonder of Messrs. Wilkins and Duffy. As the tall young man and the graceful young woman pace the quarter-deck in company, Duffy, clothing his flat face with puckers of deep meaning, pokes a spasmodic elbow into his friend's ribs and mumbles: "I say, Bill Wilkins, that's the queerest start out. That may be a love affair before we get home. What then?"

"Humph!" grunts Wilkins, — a grunt of contemptuous unbelief, — that fool of a Duffy!

"If it should," pursues Duffy, dimpling and simpering, "it might collapse the whole fight; put a complete stopper on it."

Wilkins utters another incredulous, scornful grunt and turns away; holding Duffy too much of a ninny to be listened to with any patience.

"I didn't say it *would*," explains Duffy. "I said it *might*. Old Beaumont himself wouldn't —"

"Shut up!" mutters Wilkins, grinding his teeth through his cigar, but looking innocently, diplomatically, at the foam in the steamer's wake. If that secret was to be divulged on board, it should not be the fault of the tongue, or face, or eye, of Bill Wilkins.

CHAPTER 3

 A long voyage. There was time in it for quite a little romance. And the time was not misimproved, for, if we should narrate minutely all that happened on board the *Mersey*, we should have a volume.

In the first place, there was Mrs. Chester's flirtation. She was nearly forty years, and yet she was not too old for coquetry, or at least she did not think so. More elderly people are thus minded than the young imagine; many a man well stricken in years has thoughts of captivating some chit of a girl; he not only wants to win her hand, but he trusts that he may win her heart; he actually hopes, the deluded senior, to inspire her with love. It is the same with some women; they cannot believe that they have passed the age of fascinating; they make eyes at young dandies who don't understand it at all; they would beggar themselves for a husband of twenty-two.

Mrs. Chester was well preserved; her complexion brunette, but tolerably clear, — from a distance; dark hazel eyes, still remarkably bright, — also from a distance; her hair very black, to be sure, but honestly her own, even to the color; her face long, but not lean, and with high and rather fine features; on the whole, a distinguished countenance. Her form had not kept quite so well, being obviously a little too exuberant, notwithstanding the cunning of dress-makers. What was repellent about her, at least to an attentive and sensitive observer, was her smile. It was over-sweet; its cajolery was too visible; it did not fascinate; it put you on your guard. Even her eyes, with all their fine color and sparkle, were not entirely pleasing, being too watchful and cunning and at times too combative. On the whole, it was the face of a woman who had long been a flirt, who had long been a leader of fashion, who had seen trouble without getting any good out of it, who had ended by becoming something of a tartar, and all without ceasing to be a flirt.

Mrs. Chester was a widow. A country belle in her youth, a city lady during middle life, she had lost her husband within the last six years, and found herself without a fortune, the pensioner of a wealthy brother. Disappointed woman; she thought she had not had her fair share of life's sweetness and was still uneasily seeking after worldly joys. Old enough to be Mr. McMaster's mother, old enough to matronize him wisely in society, she was unable to give herself the good advice to keep from flirting with him. She had courted his acquaintance at the table of the *Mersey* for his own sake. It was not because he had been civil to her niece; it was because she wanted him to be sweet upon herself.

Of course, he did not comprehend her. No man of twenty-four can have the least suspicion that an elderly or middle-aged woman wants him to flirt with her. Mr. McMaster (not his real name, please to remember) helped Mrs. Chester around the vessel in the innocence of ignorance. He did not want her company, but could not help getting it. "Mr. McMaster, will you oblige me with your arm up these stairs?" And then he was in for a long, prattling promenade on deck. "Mr. McMaster, will you please take me into the cabin?" And then he found himself caught in a maelstrom of whist. He had meant to keep away from the Beaumonts; but he could not manage it because of Mrs. Chester. The result was — the terribly pregnant result — that he saw a great deal of Miss Kate.

Pretty soon, say in about a week, there was a muddle. While he was talking to Mrs. Chester, and while Mrs. Chester supposed that she was his point of interest, he was really talking for the sake of Miss Beaumont. The aunt, as innocent of any such gentle purpose as a bald eagle, gathered these two chickens under her chaperonic wings and brooded in them thoughts of each other. Had she known what she was doing, she would have snapped at Kate, insulted Mr. McMaster, shut herself up in her state-room and had a fit of the sulks.

Results were hastened by rough weather. Mrs. Chester, losing her sea-legs once more, became to a certain extent bedridden, or lay about the decks inert. By this time our tall young friend was under a spell which promised pleasures and would not let him see dangers.

"Miss Beaumont, you need some one to assist you"; "Miss Beaumont, shall I annoy you if I walk with you?"

He cannot help saying these things; he sees the folly of them, no doubt, but still says them; resolves that he will do nothing of the sort, and breaks his resolution; a clear-headed youth, but getting ungovernable about the heart. Of course one likes him the better for this weakness, and would hardly have a man of twenty-four behave differently. But the result? The young lady, handsome by daylight, seems to him a goddess by moonlight. He experiences a pure, exquisite, almost unearthly pleasure in looking down at her bright, innocent face, and seeing it look up at him. He does a great deal of reading (not in chemistry) in the cabin, Miss Beaumont being always one listener, if not the only one. What a change has come over him, and how rapidly it has come! If this thing is to go on as it has begun, he will soon be indisputably in love. And then?

"Wonder if he ain't getting himself into a scrape?" thinks the diplomatic Wilkins, careful, however, not to utter the query aloud, lest babbling Duffy should repeat it and make mischief. "Well," he continues, still speaking in strict confidence to himself, "that's the way with all youngsters, pretty much. Women *will* get the better of them. They've tripped *me* pretty often." (Mr. Wilkins, now nigh on to forty, has not been badly tripped as yet, being still unmarried.) "*That* girl might upset me now, well as I know her breed. Pretty girl, devilish pretty girl, and looks like a good one, too, in spite of her breed."

There are moments when our tall fellow wonders at himself as much as Wilkins wonders at him. He is one of the wisest of youngsters; at least he has that reputation among his acquaintance; he has even had it at times with himself. Though of an impulsive race, and partly because he is aware that he is of such a race, he has proposed to himself to be practical, has set up practical-mindedness as his nirvana, and has stubbornly, self-repressively striven after it. For years he has not meant to do anything which was not worth while, nor even to do anything which was not the best thing to do. Many of his younger associates have considered him disagreeably well-balanced; have felt reproved, cramped, and chilled by his rational conversation and sound example; would have liked him better if he had had more emotions, enthusiasms, and whims.

And this sagacious youth has allowed his heart to draw him into a scrape; as the philosophical Wilkins puts the case, a woman has got the better of him. At the breakfast-table, no matter what may have been his resolves during the night, he cannot keep his eyes from bidding Kate Beaumont something kinder than good morning. If he sees her in need of a chair, he cannot help bringing her one. If he finds her pacing the unsteady deck alone (her aunt rolled in shawls, and her brother talking horse below to boozing companions), he must offer her his arm, or jump overboard. When Mrs. Chester, anxious in her least sickly hours to have him near her, proposes an evening family party of whist, he takes the cards. And, subsequent on the game, when the riper lady leans back in a corner, and, despite herself, falls into a series of dozings, how can he quit Miss Beaumont, or how be dull with her? One little weakness after another makes a whole day of unwisdom and wrong-doing.

Excuse him? Of course we can, and do it joyfully. We do not forget that pregnant saying, "A woman in the same house has so many devilish chances at a fellow"; and we remember that in a ship she has even more chances than in a house. Miss Kate had no rival young lady on board the *Mersey*. McMaster was like Adam alone when he first beheld Eve the unknown. The over-soul of his sex, the great necessity of loving some one of the other sex, the universal instinct which is too strong for any individuality, had begun to take complete possession of him, and to upset his boasted common sense, self-command, and so forth. A man may be upright and sensible; but a man's a man for a' that.

It was simple folly. He knew perfectly well who were the Beaumonts; he was informed, at least in a general way, of the long feud between them and his own family; he could not show for his conduct a ray of the excuse called ignorance. Before his mind's eye rose the two houses: the roof of the one visible from the roof of the other; separated by only four miles of God's blooming, joyous earth; yet never an act or message of friendship between them; rather a ceaseless interchange of wrongs and hate. It is one of the rare cases of a spite which has outlasted two generations, and which is so violent in its deeds and so loud in its words that all men know of it. It is a standpoint, a fixed fact; no one expects it to pass away. And yet, knowing all this bitter history, he has become surreptitiously intimate with Beaumonts, and has dared even to pay surreptitious courtship to a Beaumont girl.

On the twelfth day of the voyage, some time in the still, cloudy, sombre evening, this young man received a shock. The irrepressible Duffy, blind as a bat from coming out of the bright cabin on to the murky deck, halted a few feet from Mr. McMaster without seeing him, planted his back against the weather bulwark, rested his lazy elbows upon it, puffed gently at his cigar, and mumbled to Wilkins, "Seems to me that tall chap is getting himself either into a marriage or a fight."

The subject of the observation immediately stole away to meditate. This outside comment, this voice of the world at large, more potent than any of his own reflections, startled him into a terrible sense of his situation. What brought the comment more forcibly home to him was a suspicion, amounting almost to a certainty, that the speaker knew him. Duffy he had long since recognized, and Wilkins also; but he had believed until now that they did not remember him. Absent eight years; a boy when he left home; grown twelve inches or more since then, broad shoulders, side whiskers, mustache, and all that; — he must surely be changed beyond recognition. Now he believed that these two had found him out; and consequently he felt as if he were standing on a mine. Any day the Beaumonts might be informed who he was; and then what judgment would they pass upon him to his face?

"You a gentleman!" they would sneer, or perhaps storm. "Sneak among us and listen to our talk under a false name! Even if you were an indifferent person, such conduct would be shabby. As things are between our families, it is scoundrelly."

And then would arise the old, stupid, hateful quarrel, more violent perhaps than ever, and to some extent rational in its violence, because justified by his folly.

A young man has a vast power of repentance. When he sees that he has committed an error, he sees it in awful proportions. Our giant lay awake over his sin nearly all that night, and writhed in spirit over it all the following day. A gentleman sensitively a gentleman, what one might call chivalrous, what one might even call quixotic, yes, chivalrous in spite of his assumed name, quixotic in spite of his long struggle to be practical, he was tormented by remorse. How could a man of honor, who had caught himself falling by surprise into a dishonorable action, how could he do sufficient penance? Moreover, his blunder might lead to disastrous consequences; what chivalrous feat could he perform to prevent them? After a severe storm of emotions, after suffering spiritually more in one day than a nation of savages could suffer in a month, he hit upon one of the most irrational and yet perhaps one of the most natural plans that could be imagined. Only a young man could have devised it, or at least have decided upon it. The young are so wise and so foolish! They are such inspired idiots! Sometimes uninspired ones!

It was a moonlit autumn evening, strangely summer-like for the season, when he led Miss Beaumont on deck alone, ostensibly to take a walk with her, but really to carry out his plan.

We can imagine the hesitation and futility of his first steps toward a confession. There were two persons in him: the one intent upon being straightforward and prompt; the other shying and balking. All the young fellow's introductions seemed to lead in a circle and bring him back to where he had started. So hard is it to avow an error which is both intellectual and moral, when one is anxious to preserve the respect of the listener. It seems at the moment as if confession were a new crime, instead of a justifying virtue.

At last, out of patience with himself, Mr. McMaster (we will soon give his true name) made a direct plunge at his subject.

"Miss Beaumont, I beg your attention for a moment to a very serious matter."

A girl more experienced in society, or in novels, or in reveries, would have sniffed an offer of marriage. This one was ingenuous enough to be merely puzzled, to turn up her handsome face in the moonlight with calm wonder, to say with perfect simplicity, "What is it?"

"My name is not McMaster," he proceeded; then, after scowling a moment, "It is McAlister."

"I beg you will hear me out," he hurried on, anticipating that she would leave him, perhaps before he could begin his apology.

But Kate was as yet simply puzzled. Four years of absence from home, of far-away ideas and of hard study had rendered some of the notions and feelings of her childhood vague to her, so that the word "McAlister" did not at first rouse an association.

"I don't know how the captain got the idea that my name was Mc-Master," pursued the penitent. "Perhaps my illegible handwriting; I engaged my passage by letter. Never mind. He introduced me by that name. I thought — it was a great mistake — it looks like unhandsome conduct — but I honestly thought it best to let it pass."

"It was odd," hesitated Kate, feeling that she ought to say something, and not knowing what to say.

"You cannot blame me more severely than I blame myself," he added.

"I did not mean to blame you," Kate puzzled on. "If it was a joke? — Well, I don't know what I ought to tell you Mr. Mc —"

The moment she began to pronounce the name *McAlister*, she remembered the quarrel which it represented. She stopped; her hand fell out of his arm; she stood away from him and stared at him.

"I beg of you!" he implored. "Will you not do me the favor to hear my reasons? I appeal to you as a woman, who cannot sympathize with these old bitternesses, and who must wish for — at least not enmity. You had a brother on board. I did not want to resume the ancient quarrel with him. I hate the whole affair. It is a point of family honor, I know; it seems to be held a duty to keep up the feud. But I have learned other ideas. The quarrel appears to me — I beg you will excuse my frankness — simply barbarous. I have no more sympathy with it than I have with a scalp-hunt. Well, you can guess what I had in view. I wanted a peaceful voyage. I wanted not to be known to you or your relatives in any manner whatever. I assure you, on the word of a gentleman, that those were my motives for letting my name go unrevealed. Can you blame me for them?"

Kate, in spite of her astonishment and a certain measure of alarm, felt that she was called upon to be a woman, and she was capable of being one. After drawing a long breath to make sure of her voice, she said quietly, and with a really dignified firmness, "No, Mr. McAlister, I cannot blame you."

"I thank you sincerely," he replied, so greatly relieved that he was almost joyous. "I did not expect so much kindness. I only hoped it."

"I have lived away from home, like yourself," she went on. "I suppose I have lost some of the home ideas. But," she added, after a moment of reflection, "I am going home."

"Yes, I know what you mean," he said. "You cannot control your circumstances. I must give you up as an acquaintance."

Kate, looking frankly up at him, her handsome face spiritualized by the moonlight, nodded her head with a rather sad gravity.

"There is one thing more," he proceeded. "I am going to Hartland. I shall perhaps be seen there and recognized by some of your family. Then this deceit, this unhappy deceit of mine, will be discovered. And then the old quarrel may blaze up hotter than before."

"I hope not," murmured Kate, fearing however that so it would be.

"It is for that that I have told you what I have," he explained. "I have made my confession to you. I have begged your pardon. If you should say thus much to your father and brothers, they might perhaps be persuaded that I meant no insult. It would pain me horribly," he declared, stamping his foot slightly, and scowling at himself, "if I should find that I had rekindled the old spite."

Kate's head had drooped; it seemed to her that a heavy load was being laid upon her; she could not tell what to decide and to promise.

McAlister (we give him his true name henceforward) was also perplexed, and for a time silent. The weightiest part of his plan was still unfinished, and he was in great doubt whether he ought to carry it out.

"No; even that is insufficient," he broke forth, shaking his head. "There is still room to claim an impertinence, an insult. I am justified in telling you all that is upon my mind. Let me offer you one more reparation, Miss Beaumont. It is myself. I lay all that I am at your feet. I suppose you will refuse me. Never mind, I am sincere. I shall not change. You need make no reply now. But whenever you choose to speak, your answer shall be binding. Do not go. One single word. You can tell your family this; I wish you to tell them. All the consequences that may attach to this step I am prepared to take. I shall live and die by it."

Kate was stupefied. Wonderful as the interview had been thus far, she had not expected any such ending as this. While he (no flirt, be it understood) had supposed for days back that he was paying her unmistakable attentions, she was so little of a flirt that she had not guessed his meaning. The time had passed pleasantly; she had begun to respect and admire and even like this tall young gentleman; but that was all that had come into her heart or head. And now, bang! bang! one shot after another; here was a mask thrown off and a lover falling at her feet. She was not angry; she had no recollection just then of the family feud; she was simply amazed, and in a certain sense shocked. It was as if he had taken a liberty; as if, for instance, he had tried to kiss her; and he almost a stranger, a nine days' acquaintance!

The first words that she found to say were, "Mr. McAlister, I cannot talk to you. I think I ought to go."

And in her confusion and alarm she was about to leave him and traverse the staggering deck alone.

"Let me help you," he begged, offering his arm so gently and with such dignity that she took it. "Please allow me one word more. How may I address you during the rest of the voyage? As an acquaintance, I hope."

It was terrible to Kate, young as she was and inexperienced in the gravities of life, to be called on to decide such questions. She would consult her aunt; no, that would not answer at all; that might lead to great mischief. Her native sense — a wisdom which one might almost say was not of this world — enabled her to regain her self-possession and make a judicious response.

"We will speak to each other," she murmured. "But I must not walk with you alone any more. I will still call you Mr. McMaster."

At the top of the cabin stairway she left him, obviously in great trembling of body and agitation of spirit; so that, as he turned away, he was full of remorse at having given her such a shock.

Some minutes later he remembered that she had not answered his offer of marriage, and, walking hastily up and down the darkling deck, he fell to querying whether she ever would answer it.

CHAPTER 4

 When Kate Beaumont came to breakfast on the morning after that unexpected and astonishing offer of marriage, our friend McAlister saw, by the pallor of her face and the bluish circles around her eyes, that she had slept badly.

A smaller-souled man might have been proud of accomplishing at least thus much ravage in a woman's spirit, especially after she had not deigned to accept that offer which is the greatest of all man's offers, and had not even deigned to notice it. But this young fellow, we must understand once for all, had nothing petty about his soul any more than about his physique. A gentleman, a kind-hearted gentleman, full of respect for the girl whom he had terrified, and even to a certain extent loving her, he looked with humiliation and remorse upon his work.

"No sleep?" he gasped in his heart. "Was it I who kept her awake? I might have known it; shame on me for not having foreseen it! — a man who has looked into medicine, as well as other science! But have I not done for the best, in the end? Was it not incumbent upon me that I should say all that I did say? After insulting her — under the circumstances it was an insult — by forcing my forbidden company upon her, could I do less than place my whole self at her feet, to be spurned if she chose? Certainly not; I must be right there; every gentleman would say so."

So he saw it; looking at it, you observe, through the most chivalrous of spectacles; through spectacles, too, which, unawares to him, were colored by more or less of love's glamour. A young man who has been a little smitten is not to be trusted with reasoning about the lady who has moved him. He has fallen among the most amiable delusions, and is plundered of his wits without being aware of it. He is as much at the mercy of this one subject as a country greenhorn is at the mercy of a professional gambler. But we will not now judge the wisdom of Mr. McAlister's plan; we shall see in the course of time how it turned out.

No more walks and talks alone with Kate Beaumont. In lieu of her, Mrs. Chester; ocean being quiet again, *that* Venus rises from the depths; and finds plenty of chances to attract McAlister, or rather to grab him. It was, "Steward, please say to Mr. McMaster that we are making up a party of whist"; or, "Captain Brien, if you are going on deck, have the kindness to tell Mr. McMaster that we ladies are quite alone in the cabin"; or, "Tom, you walk so unsteadily that I should really be obliged if you would get Mr. McMaster to relieve you."

Velvet glove, though hand of iron, you see; a domineering soul, but gracious language. Indeed, it must not be guessed from any light-minded remarks of ours that Mrs. Chester was either vulgar or stupid. On the contrary, she was a woman whom most of us, if we should meet her in society, would treat with profound respect. What with some force of character, considerable experience in the ways of the world, and a high and mighty family position, she was a figure of no little dignity. Only men of a seared character laughed at her, and they only when by themselves. The laughter was mainly about her fancy for young fellows. It was almost a mania with her; it had grown upon her during her married life with a husband twenty years her senior; and now that she was a middle aged widow, she was fairly possessed by it. There was always a youngster dangling at her apron-strings, held there by Heaven knows what mature female magic, and making both himself and her more ridiculous than should be.

But our friend Mr. McAlister did not love to dangle. He was not of the dangling sort; modestly but intelligently conscious of his own value; tolerably well aware, too, that he could not dangle gracefully;

for one thing, much too tall for it. Moreover, although his liking for Kate Beaumont was sufficient to make him try to like every one who belonged to her, he could not fancy Mrs. Chester. He discovered in the lady, as he thought, a certain amount of hardness and falseness; and, gentle, sincere, frank almost to bluntness, he could not yearn after such a person. Besides, he was sore-hearted, anxious about the result of his late great step, and fearful lest his incognito might yet work mischief, so that he was not in spirits to bear the first woman who chose to take his arm. Accordingly he went heavily laden with Mrs. Chester, and, quite unintentionally, he gave her cause to suspect it. There was a slowness about joining her; there was a troubled absent-mindedness while convoying her; at times he excused himself from the whist parties on very slight grounds; at other times he was so busy with his books (scientific stuff) that he did not look up when she passed.

The annoyed Mrs. Chester, just like a conceited old flirt, suspected a rival. She watched the gentleman, noted his expression when his eyes fell upon her niece, and guessed the cause of his indifference to herself. Then followed some sly pumping of Kate: "A very handsome man, this Mr. McMaster."

"Do you think so, aunt?" replies the girl, who really had no fixed opinions as to the man's beauty, so little was her heart touched. "He is so very tall! Too tall."

Mrs. Chester, a veteran trickster, could not see through one thing, and that was feminine sincerity. She inferred at once that, because Kate had questioned the gentleman's handsomeness, therefore she did think him handsome. A good deal afraid of such a fresh rival, and also remembering her chaperonic duty towards her niece, she immediately uttered the warning cluck, "I wish we knew better who he is."

Kate, who did know who he was, and who had been thinking about the offer of marriage and the family feud, was by this time coloring sumptuously. New alarm on the part of Mrs. Chester; the girl already in love with this stranger, it may be; there must be an avalanche of chaperonic discouragement.

"We haven't the least knowledge of him," she broke out, almost spitefully, for her temper was quick and not easily held in rein. "He is the most singularly uncommunicative and even evasive person! I am half suspicious at times that we have done wrong in encouraging his advances." (Poor McAlister! he had made none.) "We may find that we have a — what do you call it in English? — a *commis voyageur* on our hands. Of course travelling companions can be got rid of. That is why I have allowed him to play whist with us, and so on. But even in travelling companions one wants a little less mystery."

"I thought you liked the mystery, aunt," remonstrated Kate, who, for some reason, perhaps only an emotion, had not been quite pleased to hear Mr. McAlister called a bagman.

"Oh, I have been interested by it a little," admitted Mrs. Chester, who had indeed been greatly interested by it, having gone so far as to suspect the youngster of being a German baron, and all because he read High Dutch scientific books. "Yes, the mystery has been amusing. Anything to pass the time at sea. But we must be careful about him."

After a moment's meditation, she added with sincere eagerness: "I really wish we knew something. Tom gets nothing out of him; doesn't try, I suppose. Has he never dropped a word to you, Kate, by which you could guess him out?"

Mrs. Chester's eyes suddenly became very sharp, and under them Kate colored again. The girl was grievously burdened with her secret; not accustomed to have an idea of such magnitude about her; acquiring womanliness under the pressure, but acquiring it painfully.

"Why should he tell *me* anything?" she asked, fairly driven into a hateful equivocation by her relative's reconnoissance.

Mrs. Chester was more or less informed and infuriated. Evidently, as she decided, this man had told Kate something about himself. If he had done that, if he had felt free or felt obliged to open his history to the girl, it was because he was in a state to open his heart to her. Engaged in love-skirmishes since her earliest teens, Mrs. Chester was always on the alert for love-skirmishes. Although she kept her self-possession under her discovery, she in the depths of her soul bounded with excitement. There were no more words on the matter; frankness was almost impossible with this woman, except in overpowering anger; but she resolved to keep a constant eye on Kate, and to ferret out Mr. McMaster.

An hour later, sitting on deck alone (a spider prefers to watch in solitude), she observed Messrs. Duffy and Wilkins engaged in muttered conversation, and discovered by Duffy's nods and jerks of the elbow that the talk referred to her man of mystery. She knew Duffy well by sight as a "store-keeper" in Hartland; why had she been so awkwardly haughty as not to recognize him heretofore? With the detective instinct of woman, she fixed at once upon Duffy as a subject for her catechism, rather than upon the diplomatic-faced Wilkins.

After a while her predestined victim dropped away from his comrade, and sauntered up and down the deck alone, hands in pocket, fingering his small change, and calculating his profits. The second time that he passed her, Mrs. Chester leaned suddenly forward in her chair, as if she had that instant remembered him, and called, " Mr. Duffy!"

He halted, his flat, doughy face coloring up to the eyes, and all his veins thrilling with excitement, under the honor of being addressed by Mrs. Chester.

"I am right, am I not?" asked the lady. "It is Mr. Duffy of Hartland?"

"Why, Mrs. Chester!" stammered the simple, modest man. "Just so. Mr. Duffy of Hartland. Had the pleasure of selling you goods now and then, ma'am," he added, wishing to show an agreeable humility. "How have you enjoyed your voyage, Mrs. Chester?"

Before continuing the conversation, the lady signed to him to take a chair beside her, sweetening and enforcing the invitation with a smile. Lifting his hat and feeling as if he ought to remove the shoes from off his feet, Duffy seated himself.

"The voyage has been fairly pleasant," resumed Mrs. Chester. "A little lonely, I must say, — such a small company! I should have claimed your acquaintance before, Mr. Duffy, if I had recognized you. Why didn't you speak to me? Hartland people ought not to be strangers, especially when they meet away from home."

"Beg pardon," smirked Duffy, quite abashed at his error. "Didn't feel exactly sure you would recall me. You see, Mrs. Chester, I never had the pleasure of speaking to you except across the counter, and that ain't always a claim."

"Ah, yes! we live so far from the town!" said the lady, in sidelong apology for not having invited the shopkeeper to the Beaumont mansion. But Duffy needed no such apology; he had never expected to be asked into that "old-time" society; he felt himself more than well treated in being spoken to once a year by Mrs. Chester. Still, he was so far encouraged by this graciousness, that he ventured to cross his legs and thus put himself more at ease on the small of his back.

"Been on the Continent, Mrs. Chester," he proceeded, slightly rubbing his hands.

"Ah, indeed?" she replied. "And how did you like the Continent?"

"No. *I* haven't been there. Beg your pardon. I meant *your* party."

"O yes. A delightful tour. And have you only seen England? Really, Mr. Duffy, you should have given a month or two to the Continent."

"Couldn't, Mrs. Chester. That's the way with a business man; he has to go where he has to; always on his muscle — I mean business. I went over to look into importing, and it took up every snip of time that I could spare from home."

"I am so sorry. However, I ought not to regret it, except for your sake. Your business is of the *greatest* consequence to Hartland. You men of enterprise are our — our main-stay. I hope, Mr. Duffy, that you met others of our townsmen abroad, engaged in profiting by the new line."

"None that I know of. O, yes; Mr. Wilkins here; but we went together."

"And how few Hartland people we have on the steamer," added Mrs. Chester, by way of closing this preliminary prattle and gliding on to the subject of her man of mystery. "Only you two gentlemen and my party."

"N-no, — y-yes," stammered Duffy, glancing uneasily at McAlister, just then pacing the midships, his lofty blond head plainly visible. Mrs. Chester had also seen the young man there, and she now noted the merchant's singular glance towards him.

"Do you know that gentleman?" she asked, as quick as lightning and with telling directness.

"N-no. Ah, yes. That is. Let me see. What *is* his name?" was the blundering response of the entangled Duffy.

Mrs. Chester would not help him; she might have suggested that the name was McMaster, but she was too sly to do it; she had guessed that Duffy knew something about the youngster, and she was resolved to make him tell it; if he would not, he must do his own lying, without assistance from her.

"I see," she added. "To tell the truth, I have had my suspicions all along. Can't you put me out of doubt? It would be quite a favor."

Duffy was scarlet; he looked about for Wilkins; did not see him and gasped.

"That, Mrs. Chester," he began, leaning forward and speaking in a whisper. "Well, I've been wondering all the while you didn't recognize him. Thought perhaps you did. Couldn't tell what to make of it. Why, it's Frank, the youngest. Been in Europe eight years. Changed as much as ever I saw a feller."

"Oh!" responded Mrs. Chester, who was still quite in the dark, not knowing much of the McAlisters. "So it's the youngest? Frank?"

"Yes. And they do say he's the best of the lot," continued the pacificatory Duffy, anxious to prevent a "muss." "I do suppose, if there's a decent fellow on that hill, a fellow who don't want to make trouble for nobody, it's this same Frank McAlister."

At the word "McAlister" Mrs. Chester came very near bursting out with an amazed and excited "Oh!" It cost her all her strength as a social gymnast to enable her to catch her breath, bend her eyes to the deck with an expression of remembrance, and say in a quiet tone, "So it is Frank McAlister. He has been called, I understand, Mr. McMaster," she presently added.

"Well, yes — McMaster — McAlister — some mistake perhaps," suggested the gentle-minded Duffy. "May be, too, that he let it go so, not wishing to be unpleasant to you. Beg pardon. You know the old difficulty. Excuse me for mentioning it. I forgot myself, Mrs. Chester."

"No offence, Mr. Duffy," replied the lady, proud of the feud as of a family heirloom, unmistakably aristocratic. "The thing is a matter of public notoriety, I believe."

She changed the conversation; there was some talk about the fine sights of London; presently Duffy perceived that he had stayed long enough and went.

"I'll bet you one thing," whispered the scoffing Wilkins when they were alone together. "You've been letting out everything to Mrs. Chester."

"No, sir," weakly replied the conscience-stricken and abashed Duffy. "Hang me, if I tell her anything of that," he tried to bluster. Then, under pretence of wanting a cigar, he went below in great bitterness of spirit to get a drink, mentally cursing himself, Wilkins, Mrs. Chester, and women generally. "Bla-ast the women!" groaned the humble telltale. "They always will bore things out of a feller."

But Duffy is of no account, and we must lay him aside like a sucked orange, just observing that the secret was worth nothing in his bosom, while now it is where it may bear fruit. It makes a difference with a coal of fire whether it is in a potato-bin or a powder-magazine.

The nature and history of the quarrel between the Beaumonts and the McAlisters will be told in due season. Just here it is only necessary to say that Mrs. Chester, notwithstanding her twenty years of marriage, was what she called "Beaumont all through," keeping up family prejudices and grudges with the family loyalty of a woman, and, for instance, abominating the McAlisters as her father had abominated them before her. A sly and spiteful breed she thought them; people whose strength it was to strike when you were not looking; people always ready to take a mean advantage of the noble Beaumonts. What could such a woman think when she learned that Frank McAlister, son of that old fox (as she called him) Donald McAlister, had been palming himself upon her as a stranger, accepting her pettings under a feigned name, allowing her to pinch his arm (if she did pinch it), and — well, and so on? A trick, she decided; a mean and dastardly trick; perhaps a piece of espionage; perhaps a studied insult. One or the other; it was some one of these things; and whichever it was, it was an outrage.

"I'll teach him!" she muttered, as she remembered pretty phrases which she had murmured to the young man, and suspected him of having laughed at them in his sleeve. "Playing his jokes on a lady!" gurgled this vain, excitable, easily angered, and not so easily pacified woman. "An insult to our whole race!" was another stinging reflection, envenomed by a family pride as strong as corrosive sublimate. People of average unsuspiciousness and mild temper will find it hard to imagine how entirely this elderly baby looked at the offensive side of the discovered deceit, and how suddenly furious she had become over it. Not a supposition crossed her mind that McAlister had meant no harm, or had meant only good. She instantaneously imputed hostility to him, and in return she was instantaneously hostile.

Well, what was she to do about it? Cut the man, of course; but that was not enough for good old Beaumont hate, inflamed by a new wrong; he must be visited with a more efficacious punishment. Revenge, however, was easier to wish for than to devise, even with spiteful Marian Beaumont Chester, the cause heretofore of more than one quarrel between man and man. To be sure, if she should tell her harum-scarum nephew what had happened, he was just the youngster to drink a pint of whiskey, break out copiously in profane language, make a scandal at all events, and pick a fight, perhaps. But Tom, adroit and audacious as he was in squabbles, did not seem to her a match for this cool-headed giant. Furthermore, Mrs. Chester remembered that all the responsibility of an immediate disagreement would rest upon her, and did not find herself quite willing to shoulder it alone. Had the whole family been here, had there been some weighty soul at hand to set her on, or even to hold her back, how promptly and loudly would her voice have been raised for war! As it was, responsibility, man's special burden, how should she endure it?

Not a word did she whisper to her niece, nor had she a thought of consulting her. So simply and single-mindedly angry was she, that she had actually forgotten her suspicion that Kate knew or guessed who this man was, as well as her other suspicion that there was some small matter of heart intelligence between the two. She merely remembered the girl as a child, quite incapable of feeling or deciding properly concerning such a grave situation as this, and no more to be consulted as to the family honor than if she were still a denizen of cradles and trundle-beds. It is generally difficult for old heads to conceive that young heads have lost their pulpiness, until the junior craniums knock it into the senior ones by dint of vigorous butting.

Late in the evening (no whist after tea that day) Mrs. Chester's load of wrath became so intolerable that she manfully resolved to bear it alone no longer. She sent for Tom to her state-room, saying to herself that here was business for masculine muscle, and that it was high time for her nephew to show himself a chip of the old Beaumont timber.

But the McAlister firebrand, notwithstanding that it had dropped into Mrs. Chester's powder-barrel of a temper, was prevented from producing an immediate explosion by a deluge of still more tremendous intelligence.

When the nephew presented himself, he looked surprisingly sober for the time of day, and evidently had something very serious on his mind.

"Tom, come in and shut the door," began Mrs. Chester. "I have something very important to tell you."

"Yes, and, by Jove, and I've got something to tell *you,* and, by Jove, I may as well tell it," responded the youngster.

"What is it?" asked the lady, suspecting that her secret was out, and half disappointed at not being the first to publish it.

"The ship is on fire," said Tom. "Yes, by Jove, on fire, as sure as you're born. Yes, it is."

CHAPTER 5

 The news that the *Mersey* was on fire drove the Mc-Alister affair as clean out of Mrs. Chester's head as a cannon-ball could have done.

That was Mrs. Chester; capable of emotions as fiery as ignited gunpowder; but capable of holding only one charge at a time. Moreover, there was a certain restricted sense in which this worldly and spunky woman was naturally religious. I do not say that she was satisfactorily devout; nor do I undertake to remember whether she was or was not a church communicant; my whole statement amounts to this, that she believed heartily in the other world, and was afraid of it. Not that she thought of it profitably or often; she only trembled at it when it seemed near at hand. If she was possessed of a devil, as most of her enemies and some even of her relatives asserted, it must have been that devil who, when he was sick, a monk would be.

For the present the secret of the incognito was not divulged, and Tom Beaumont was not st'boyed at the foe of his family. In fact, not ten minutes had elapsed before Mrs. Chester, having flown to the captain for consolatory assurances, and got nothing which satisfied her, was looking up into the grave, calm, benignant face of Frank McAlister, and asking of it news of life or death.

"I believe," said the deep, mellow voice of the young man, "that the fire has been discovered in the hold; or rather, it has been suspected there. Investigations are going on now which will let us know whether there is any real cause for alarm. If there is fire, it is in the cargo; probably a case of spontaneous combustion; badly stored chemicals, it may be."

"What a shame!" burst forth Mrs. Chester, trembling with anger as well as fear. "Whoever put such things on board ought to be hung."

"They are not mine," he observed, in answer to her sudden glare of accusation. "Indeed, I don't know as yet that there is anything of the kind below. Only, it seems likely. Otherwise, how account for the fire?" added this investigator.

"I shall go and see what *is* there," she cried, making a rush in her dressing-gown towards the stairway.

"It is of no use, madam," ventured Mr. Wilkins, who had just come below. "Can't get near the place. They're taking out cargo, and the deck is all littered up; the Devil's own mess — beg pardon. Nothing to be seen but smoke coming out of the hatchway. I don't see, by Jehu, how those sailors can stand it down there. O, I s'pose it'll all come out right," he concluded, noting the terror of Mrs. Chester.

At this moment Duffy arrived, with an air of bringing a glass or two of grog to the rescue, inside his jacket.

"The Spouter!" he said, apparently continuing a conversation with Wilkins. "I say, Bill Wilkins, the Spouter'd cool her off in no time."

"What is the Spouter?" eagerly asked Mrs. Chester.

"Our fire-engine, Mrs. Chester. Hartland fire-engine. I'm cap'n of the comp'ny. 'Member, Mrs. Chester, how Hutch Holland's store got fire, 'n' we put the m'chine at it? Had the m'chine out 'n' on the spot in five minutes. Took up posish at the corner —"

Mrs. Chester, totally uninterested in the prowess of the Spouter, since it could not help her, turned her back impatiently on the some- what tipsy Duffy, while Wilkins grasped him by the arm and led him to the other end of the cabin, saying, "Here, tell *me* about it."

Serious hours passed. Now and then a male passenger went on deck, crawled as near as he could to the lumbered hatchway, tried to peer through the boiling whirls of smoke, came back to the anxious ladies, and reported — nothing. Tom Beaumont, by this time as tipsy as Duffy, and much more noisy in his liquor; was back and forth continually, talking unreportable nonsense.

"Oh, why can't you find out something, some of you?" was the cry of the angered and terrified Mrs. Chester. "Where is that Captain Brien? I want him to come here and tell me what is the matter. I want to give him a piece of my mind. How dare he load his ship with combustibles! He hasn't heard the last of this. Not if he gets us ashore, he hasn't heard the last of it. I'll follow him up. I'll ruin him."

"Cap'n Brien 'sh all right," declared Tom. "Cap'n Brien 'sh a gentleman. He's up there, workin' like a beaver. Don't y' hear him holler?" Here a ludicrous idea struck the young gentleman, and he repeated with an exasperating smile, "Nigger in a wood-pile, don't y' hear him holler?"

"Tom!" implored Kate Beaumont, who seemed even more moved by her brother's condition than by the common danger.

"Oh yes, — all right," laughed the youngster. "Got little too much aboard. Go on deck again 'n' cool off. All right pretty soon."

"Oh, what a miserable set!" gasped Mrs. Chester, stamping with impatience. "Is there no clergyman on board? I never will go to sea again without a clergyman on board. Is there nobody here who can pray? I would give all I'm worth for a prayer-meeting. I wish I had brought old Miriam. *She* could pray for us."

She glared around upon the men, angry that none of them could pray for her. Kate Beaumont turned away gravely, walked with bended head to her state-room and closed the door upon herself. Was it to lift a supplication to Heaven for deliverance, or for resignation? McAlister hoped so, believed so with inexpressible tenderness of spirit, and sent his soul after her.

"I think we had better make some preparations," he presently said to Mrs. Chester, as she paced the cabin with clasped hands and lifted eyes. "The coast cannot be far off. We may reach it in boats, if it comes to that. May I advise you to make up a little package of such things as you must save, and to tell Miss Beaumont to do the same? I hope it will not be so bad as that. But we had best prepare."

Mrs. Chester gave him a stare, and then hurried to her room. The young man had decided that, as for himself, he was ready; he wanted nothing but his overcoat and the life-preserver which hung over his berth; it was folly to think of cumbering a boat with books and baggage. He now fell to pacing the cabin quietly; and in so doing he approached Wilkins and Duffy.

"I *say*," called Duffy, looking up with a fixed, absurd smile, and striking his fist hospitably on the table in front of him. "Take seat, Mr. Mc — McAlister. Know you. Knew you ten days ago. Sit down over there. Talk about Hartland."

"Oh you drunken blatherskite!" growled the disgusted Wilkins, leaning back as if to rise from the table.

"Hold on, Bill Wilkins," said Duffy, grasping his friend tightly. "Mr. Wilkins, Mr. Mc — McAlister. Both Hartland men. Talking about Hartland."

"Beg your pardon, sir," muttered Wilkins, addressing McAlister. "He's always that way when he takes a spoonful. He hasn't had but two glasses under him, and here he is higher than any other man would be on a quart."

"Only two glasses," declared Duffy, trying to look sober. "Not tight. Just trying to cheer the — the occasion. You see, Mr. McAlister —"

Wilkins squinted a look of apology towards the young gentleman.

"Never mind," muttered the latter. "Disguise is probably of no importance now. I had my reasons."

"Certainly," nodded Wilkins; while the eager and smiling Duffy, who had not noticed this aside, went on with his babble.

"You see — talking of Hartland — 'member the fire there four years ago? Oh, you wasn't there, excuse me. Hutch Holland's store. 'Member *me* — Duffy — keep store there — right opposite Wilkins? Cap'n of the fire-engine. Spouter! Had her out in five minutes. Hose busted. Took out a length. Busted again. Took out 'nother length. Rammed her close up to the ole shanty. Let drive into the cellar — ten tons of cold water — cleaned cistern all out. Well, couldn't stop the blasted thing. Why? Well, here't is — petrolem afire — don't ye see? Filled the cellar full of water, 'n' histed the pe-tro-le-um," slowly this time, resolved to pronounce it. "Went on blazing 'n' ripping 'n' roaring just the same. Floated — rose to the top, 'n' burnt like fury — didn't care how much water there was. More water the better. How should I know? Nobody said petrolem — pe-tro-le-um, hang it! If I'd known 'bout petrolem, I'd 'a' pitched in sand, 'n' smothered it. But water! kept me slinging water on to petrolem. Wouldn't stay on it. Petrolem rose to the surface 'n' burnt right straight along. Caught the floor at last, 'n' sailed up like sky-rocket. That's the way the ole shanty went. None of my fault. Nobody said petrolem — pe-tro-le-um."

He paused a moment; his friend Wilkins smirking slightly, notwithstanding a gloomy under-thought about the fire in the hold; and McAlister surveying him gravely, reflecting on what he had said, rather than noticing how he said it.

"Well, what was I driving at?" resumed Duffy. "What was it, Bill Wilkins? Didn't stop with Hutch Holland's burn-out. Told ye that before."

"I should think so," growled Wilkins. "Forty times. Full load every haul."

"Oh, I know — petrolem down there," continued Duffy, jerking his head toward the forward part of the ship. "That's the reason water won't catch hold. Want sand. Won't bring about anything till we get some sand. An' where's sand? Bottom of the ocean. Bound to bust — that's what's the matter — settled to bust — bet yer pile on 't. Let's have some more whiskey. I'll go 'n' hunt the steward."

As he rose, Wilkins caught him by the arm and jerked him down again, more effectually than tenderly.

"No, no, Duffy! *We* don't want any. And you're drunk enough for the whole ship's company."

"But Mr. McAlister wants whiskey," insisted Duffy. "Let go of me, Bill Wilkins."

"Nothing for me," objected McAlister, raising his voice a little, and awing the fuddled man into his seat.

"Well, all right, then," assented Duffy. "If you say so, that settles it. I only drink myself on these occasions. Wilkins here ought to take some. He's scared, Wilkins is. I say, Wilkins, ain't you scared?"

"Yes, by Jehu, I am," confessed Wilkins. "I wish to gracious I was ashore."

"Want to live, don't you, Wilkins?" continued Duffy, still keeping up his fixed, silly smile. "Find it pleasant world, don't you, Wilkins? Like to catch 'nother hold on't?"

"Yes, I'd take a contract to live five hundred years," said the frank Wilkins, not apparently a frightened man, either. "I like it. I've had a good time here. I don't feel sure that I shall ever be let into another world that'll be so pleasant to me. I'd take a contract for five hundred years, and after that I believe I'd be willing to take another."

"An' be shipwrecked!" asked Duffy, still simpering.

"Yes, and be shipwrecked."

"An' fail, Wilkins? Bust up 'n' fail, now 'n' then?"

"Yes, throw in as many failures as you like, and all sorts of other bothers."

"Well, Wilkins," said Duffy, speaking with extreme gravity, as if he were really called on to decide something, — "well, Wilkins, don't know but I 'gree with you."

"Wilkins wouldn't like it in Heaven," he added, turning to McAlister. "Not a 'ligious man. Now, I'm 'ligious; had advantages. But Wilkins, let him have his own way, 'n' Wilkins wouldn't go to Heaven, — not till all the other places was shut up."

At this moment Tom Beaumont slid like an avalanche into the cabin, got up with much rubbing of his back, berated the brass edges of the stairs, and began to beat aft.

"Another of 'em!" muttered Wilkins. "By Jehu, here's what's a going. I can't stand so much blathering when I'm sober myself."

Leaning forward, he whispered in Duffy's ear, "Shut up about that name, will you, now?"

"Name? Oh yes, McAlister. Keep shady. Secret of a gentleman, — word of a gentleman, I mean."

And as Tom approached the table, Wilkins and McAlister left it together, proceeding towards the deck.

"Those two fools!" muttered Wilkins. "They'll get water enough in their rum, by Jehu, if they're not looked after. They'll be so drunk they couldn't jump into a boat if it was as big as a continent. Hope you'll excuse Duffy, sir. He's not that way often. It only takes a thimbleful to capsize him. Good, peaceable, well-meaning fellow. Don't know a better intentioned man. I like him, though he is a doughhead, especially when he's tight."

Meeting the steward, he whispered hurriedly: "Look here. Close up your gin palace, and lose the key. Some people on board have crowded themselves too full already. Lose the key right off."

"You don't seem to be alarmed out of your wits," said McAlister.

"Oh, I can stand this sort of thing so so. I've had adventures before now. Still I was honest in what I said to Duffy; I don't mean to die as long as I can help it; don't want to die a particle. Hang me if I see anything gay in it."

On deck they perceived, by the light of the stars and a deck-lamp or two, that no more smoke was curdling up from the hatchway. The captain, too, instead of being forward superintending the struggle with the fire, was standing near the helmsman, looking now at a chart and now at the compass.

"All out, Captain?" asked McAlister, drawing a deep breath of relief. "Shall I tell the ladies?"

Raising his heavy-lidded eyes, red and watery from the effects of the smoke into which they had been peering, the skipper gave his two passengers a sullen, noncommittal stare.

"What! not out?" exclaimed Wilkins.

"Confound it, no!" in a growl of wrath and impatience.

"Captain," said McAlister, in his calmly authoritative way, "it seems to me that in such a state of things you had better tell the passengers plainly what to look for. It may save a panic when the crisis comes."

"Well, the case is just here," returned the captain, slowly and sadly. "We can't get at the fire. It's low down in the hold, and yet water won't flood it. Can't unload enough to reach the spot. No man can stay below a half-minute. I don't know what the deuce is burning down there. It sends up a smoke that no human being can face. It's chemicals, or some kind of oil, and yet there's nothing of the sort on the freight-bill. Well, if it's oil, water will only do harm; raise the stuff, you see, and set the deck afire; then we're gone. What I've done is to batten down the hatches, to keep out the air and smother the flame. If only the stuff will burn out without catching the ship! We're heading now for the nearest land."

"Shove her right along and run her high and dry," assented Wilkins, cheeringly.

"That's all that can be done," groaned the captain.

"How far to land?" queried McAlister.

"About three hundred miles. The boat is going her very prettiest. If we can only keep in her twenty-four hours!"

"Had you not better say all this below?" insisted McAlister. "Passengers will take a captain's word for everything."

"I'll come down. But my God! isn't it horrible! First ship I ever lost, gentlemen; and I fifty-five! By heavens, I'd rather have died than seen this day. I hate to face those women. There's that girl. I had a daughter once. I hate to meet that girl."

And Captain Brien, all bluster and humbug swept out of him, wiped away honest tears of misery.

"By Jehu, yes, we must save that girl," struck in Wilkins, energetically.

"Yes!" said McAlister with solemnity.

A few minutes later, the dozen or so of passengers were gathered in silence about the captain in the cabin. He told his story, much as he had told it on deck, and then added, in a business-like way, as if he were issuing directions for an ordinary disembarkation: "Now for *your* duty. Make up your little packets for the boats. Get some ship-bread about you. And then keep cool and stand by. When I want you, I'll call for you. I'm very sorry, ladies and gentlemen. It's not my fault. I didn't stow the ship. That's all."

And, glad to get out of the cabin, glad to escape from those blank faces which all seemed to reproach him, the captain slowly wheeled his short, solid body towards the stairway, to go on deck and resume his sleepless watch.

"Oh you wretch!" Mrs. Chester burst out in a tremulous scream. "Oh you worthless, villainous —"

"Hush, Aunt, hush!" begged Kate Beaumont, seizing her elder relative around the waist, and trying to draw her towards her state-room.

"What's that? What's the row?" called Tom Beaumont, now half crazed with liquor. "Who's a fightin'? Who wants to fight? Let me in."

"Never mind," whispered Wilkins, hurrying the captain towards the stairs. "The woman's hysterical, and the boy's drunk. You get on deck, captain. It's all right."

Tom meanwhile has rushed up to Kate, his face full of maudlin affection, and his right hand under his coat skirt. "Anybody insulted you? say, sis?"

"No, Tom," cried the girl, full of shame and terror. "Oh, *do* try to be quiet!" And here she burst into tears.

Wilkins ran back, caught the young lunatic by the elbow, and walked him aft with a confidential air, whispering, "Tell you all about it. It's nothing but your aunt's got the hysterics."

"Oh, that's it?" drawled Tom, falling back from him to the length of his arm, and staring with head on one side. "Let her have 'em!"

"Yes, that's it. But we must get to work; make our little bundles for the boats. There," pushing him coaxingly on to a settee; "you lie down out of the way, won't you? Let me strap up your duds. Want your overcoat?"

And so on, — the adroit and self-possessed Wilkins! — thoroughly accustomed to tipplers! In three minutes the wretched youngster was asleep, leaving Wilkins at liberty to make his preparations for him, and then to go about his own.

All the crew were up all night getting ready to quit the ship at a moment's notice. There were men enough to manage four large boats; and these boats were sufficient to carry thrice as many passengers as there were, with stores sufficient for a fortnight's voyage; so that, barring accident or tempest, there was every probability of getting all hands safely to land. Kegs of water, boxes of hard-bread, cases of preserved meats, etc., were ranged along the deck, ready for embarkation. Captain Brien's variegated face gleamed and reddened every few minutes in the light of the binnacle lamp, or in the glow which poured out of the doors of the furnace-room. The firemen and the engines kept each other hard at work. So far as McAlister could judge (and he was not, of course, easy to please in the matter), everything was being done that could be done.

"How goes it?" he asked, meeting the skipper in one of his trottings back and forth between the engine and the wheel.

"Beautiful!" The captain was almost gay, his doomed boat was running so gamely. "That engine is charming. It's like a young lady dancing. Fourteen knots! Never saw the beat of it in a boat of this size. Isn't it too hard!" he exclaimed, striking his clubs of fists together and stamping his fat feet, as short and broad as a bear's paws. "Here's this little angel of a boat gone to smash! And all for some blasted cargo — the Davy Jones knows what — that oughtn't to have been shipped, and wouldn't have been if I'd done the stowing. Oh — by — jimmy!"

And, lowering his head like an angry bull, the captain butted on toward the helmsman.

Going below and traversing the cabin, McAlister overheard Tom Beaumont snoring whole nightmares in his state-room, and Mrs. Chester either whimpering or scolding in hers. As he passed the door of the latter, Kate Beaumont came out and began walking backward and forwards, apparently without noticing him. He looked over his shoulder pitifully at the pallor of the girlish face.

"Miss Beaumont," he thought he might say, "may I walk with you?"

She took his arm mechanically, and presently she raised her eyes to him, as if suddenly remembering who he was and what had passed between them. Well, it was no time for family feuds; it was no occasion for nice delicacy in choosing one's companions; she continued to walk by his side and lean upon him.

"I trust and believe this will end well," he said, longing to cheer her.

"You are very kind," she replied. "I am afraid I have not treated you well, Mr. — Mr. McMaster. I don't know. If I have done wrong, I beg you not to mind it."

"You have done everything right. I shall always respect you and thank you."

There seemed to be some comfort in this; of course not comfort enough for the hour.

"You are bearing this bravely," he went on, admiring her even then.

"I could bear it, if I only had help." And the girl, only eighteen, remember, sobbed. "Mr. McAlister, I want to ask one thing of you. We two women will be cared for. But who will care for my brother? Will — will you?"

"I pledge myself to it!"

"Oh, how good you are!" It was no time to reflect that she was placing herself under deep obligations to a man who had asked her hand in marriage. It is probable that, under the terrible circumstances of the crisis, she did not think of it. Standing on the verge of the other world, this world's entanglements were very vague.

"Could not you and I," he asked, "when we get home, put an end to this feud?"

"I don't know. It might be. I will try," she replied, with a feeling as if she were talking in a dream.

"Let us pledge ourselves here to try," he begged. "Will you do it?"

"Yes," she promised.

"And I," he added.

Then he insisted upon her lying down on one of the long settees of the cabin. "We may have a hard day to-morrow," he said, "and you must endeavor now to sleep. I will keep watch."

In such style passed the remainder of the night on board the slowly consuming *Mersey*.

CHAPTER 6

All next day the tame demon of fire and the wild demon of fire struggled with each other for the *Mersey*. The engines never relaxed the vehement jog of their highest speed; and the conflagration below never ceased its muttering, lapping, and gnawing.

"We're running for land like a man that's snake-bit running for a whiskey-mill," observed Wilkins, squinting with half-closed, calculating eyes at the racing bubbles alongside.

"By George, I wish *I* could run for a whiskey-mill," softly grumbled Duffy, who, having got sober overnight, was now in sustained low spirits. "Pretty time to close bar. Now's just the chance to hand round something cheering."

"Lord bless you, man! you don't want to go off by spontaneous combustion, do you? You'll catch fire soon enough and stay alight long enough, without troubling yourself to kindle up."

Wilkins seemed to be joking, but he was not; he had a way of saying his most serious things in this jester fashion; he was at this moment sincerely anxious to keep his friend from getting drunk and being drowned; nor was he at all unmindful of the gravity of his own danger.

"I don't want to get corned, no such thing," insisted Duffy. "I wasn't upset last night, though you thought I was. I can tell you everything I said."

"Lord! don't!" implored Wilkins. "Hutch Holland's store. Petroleum and sand. Know it all by heart."

"I'm going for that steward," resumed Duffy, after a minute more of dolorous meditation. "I can't stand this sort of thing without a drink."

"No use," said Wilkins. "They always lose the key of the spirit-room at such times. It's a thing that happens constant. He won't find it for you. Oh, come back! Look here I've got a little drop myself; there, turn up that flask."

"There's water in it," declared Duffy indignantly, after a long taste. "What the old boy did you go and put water in it for, Bill Wilkins?"

"Well, it was wrong, I know," grinned Wilkins, who had "thinned out" his whiskey of a set purpose and for Duffy's good. "Wrong as a general thing. Wrong in principle. But never mind. It won't be the water part of it that'll hurt you. There, that'll do; hand over."

Seeing Tom Beaumont come on deck, Wilkins snatched the flask from the sucking Duffy and hid it in his breast-pocket.

The youngster had slept all night, taken a late but hearty breakfast, and was now perfectly sober.

"How are you, gentlemen?" he nodded, in his free-and-easy, though graceful and not uncourteous way. "Not up all night, I hope. By Jove, I used my time; slept from one end to t'other."

"I think an eternity of sleep, yes, or an eternity of cat naps, would be right pleasant," said Wilkins.

"I'd go in for it," muttered Duffy, "under the circumstances."

"How are things?" asked Tom.

"Pretty hot amidships," was the bland reply of Duffy, who had begun to feel his whiskey.

"The doose!" growled Tom. "I understood down below that we would make land, sure. Hot, is it? By Jove, if the thing breaks through, we've got, by Jove, to wade into the boats and make a long pull of it."

"That's so," assented Duffy, gathering courage every minute, as the liquor clomb higher in his shallow head.

"Two hundred miles to skip yet; take us about sixteen hours," said

Wilkins. "That fetches us ashore somewhere near midnight. But, if we have to paddle, Davy Jones knows when we'll get there."

"H—ll!" is the compendious comment of Tom Beaumont, not frightened in the strict sense of the word, but realizing the situation.

In talk more or less like this, in occasional investigations as to the growing heat of the deck, in inquiries concerning the working of the furnace and the speed of the ship, and in much impatient walking or gloomy smoking, these gentlemen pass the day. We must however add, to the credit of Tom Beaumont, that he runs below every hour or two, to say a word of cheer to his aunt or sister. The dissipated youngster is brave beyond question, and not altogether lacking in the finer emotions.

"I do hope, Tom," says Kate, taking him by the arms and looking him sadly in the eyes, — "I do hope you won't drink one drop to-day. You took altogether too much last night. You made me ashamed and frightened. I thought, what if you should die in that state! And what help could you have been to *us*?"

"By Jove, sis, don't!" begs Tom, trying to laugh, but wilting a little. "It wasn't the correct thing; no, by Jove, it wasn't; and I beg your pardon, do, indeed. You see I was surprised into it, this thing coming on so sudden. All right to-day; not the first drop. In fact, can't find it. Steward got his wits about him and lost the key. By Jove, I came near giving him a welt; but he's right, and I know it; gave him a dollar. Told him to hold on to his key till I was ashore. If I'm to drown, it's more like a gentleman to drown sober. Going down drunk all very well for common sailors. But our sort can look the thing square in the face. Oh, don't *you* be anxious. You are not in danger. Every man on board is going to devote himself to saving you. I'll save you myself, by Jove, without any help. As for Aunt, there, that's different. I'm glad, by Jove, the old lady is getting a scare."

"Oh Tom!"

"Yes, I am. Hope it'll do her good about the region of the temper. What keeps her so still? Reading her Bible, hey? Time she did. 'Tain't often she makes eyes at the patriarchs. Reckon she must have forgotten where to look for them."

"Tom, stop! Our aunt is our aunt. You must not say such things about her, and I must not hear them."

"By Jove, sis, you'd go straight to heaven, wouldn't you?" exclaims the harum-scarum boy, staring at Kate in a kind of worshipping wonder.

A few minutes later the girl met Frank McAlister, and said to him hastily and with a touching shame: "I need not ask of you to-day what I did last night. My brother is capable of taking care of himself. You must take care of yourself. I thank you."

"I shall still have an eye to you all," he replied. "I shall do what I can," he added soberly, remembering how little it might be.

"I don't know how I could have asked such a thing of you," she went on, her mind reverting to the feud between the families.

"In such times as this all human beings are brethren. Besides, I had placed myself at your disposal."

She did not answer this last phrase, nor did she even color over it. In her trouble she perhaps did not hear it, or had for the moment forgotten his offer of marriage. The consequence of her silence was that he believed he had done wrong in alluding to the offer; and the consequence of this was, that he wished to make reparation for his fault by thinking only of her comfort and safety.

"Have you finished your preparations?" he asked.

"I have a little packet. I believe there is nothing more to do."

"How admirably brave you are!" he said, as he had said once before.

"Oh no! I am very anxious. I would give — Oh, what wouldn't I give — to be ashore."

"And yet you govern yourself!" he observed, wanting to kneel down and kiss her hand. "But you need more rest. Let me beg you to try to sleep as much as possible this morning. The day is better than the night for that. We can see the extent of our danger best by day, and you can be got to the boats the easier if it should be necessary."

"I will lie down in the saloon," she replied, after having made one step toward her state-room. The twin room was occupied by Mrs. Chester; and that lady's voice could be heard steadily reading the Scriptures, for she was in such a fright that she did not care if all the world knew it; resolved, at all events, that Heaven should know it.

Such was the life above and below on board the unlucky *Mersey*, as she made her desperate rush shoreward. All day there was a dreary watching and waiting; at times hope predominant, as if by infection, and every one expecting a safe deliverance; then again a sorrowful, paralyzing chill settling upon every spirit. The captain, who knew the situation best, and, like a wise officer, knew more than he told, chiefly dreaded two dangers. The fire might burn through the wooden sheathing, and let in a flood of water which would sink the steamer in a few minutes. Or the vessel, driving headlong toward a shore little frequented except by wrecks, and of which he knew nothing except by his charts, might strike some hidden rock or sandbar, and go to pieces far from land. No time was there for soundings; death, snarling and tearing below, was creeping nearer every moment; the hot breath of the imprisoned tiger was stealing thicker and thicker through the seams of the planking; the risk that there was in delay seemed greater than the risk that there was in speed.

Still, the bright morning passed safely; then a humid afternoon, full of sailing mists and shadows, came and went; and at last the *Mersey* was plunging over the sombre waters of a starless evening. All this while the wind held fair, balmy, and moderate, and the sea not too high for boats to be launched and to live.

At eight bells in the evening there were already high hopes on board the vessel; the lookout aloft was straining his eyes to catch an outline of land or a light; the captain, wearied to death, but constantly on deck, was rubbing his hands with a little air of cheeriness. At this moment there came a change; there was a different feeling under the feet; people thought, without saying so, "What is the matter?"

At first insensibly, but in a very short time quite obviously, there was a diminution of elasticity and a slowing of speed. Some of the passengers below had a sensation as if the ship were in port and coming quietly to dock. Others, who were on deck and could see no cause for this singular change, thought with sudden terror of the calmness of death stealing upon the convulsions of a man in delirium.

"What's all this?" called Wilkins, as Brien ran by him towards the waist. The captain stumbled on without answering, and the passenger hurriedly followed him, suspecting, with an awful sinking of the heart, that the end had come. Amidships they were met by men — stokers and engineers — rushing up out of the engine-room, some uttering curses, and others inarticulate cries of terror, while one, recognizing his officer, said sharply, "Water around the furnace!"

"Sure?" screamed the captain. Yes, there was no doubt of it; a strange hissing, a new noise on board the steamer, sent up its horrible confirmation; it was certain that the fire had let in the ocean, and that the two were fighting below for the mastery. It was a frightful struggle of the two giant elements as to which should destroy the creation of man's industry and exterminate the creator. The menagerie of natural forces had risen upon their tamer. The demons were in full and triumphant insurrection.

Meantime confused sounds of fright rang all over the dark decks; the panic reached below, too, and passengers ran up, demanding to know their fate.

"Sound the pumps," called the captain; and presently a voice answered, "Three feet in the hold, sir."

"Pump away, men," was the next order; and the thud and rattle of the pumps continued. Then pealed another voice, "Look out for an explosion," followed by a trampling of feet rushing towards the boats. The ultimate peril, long as it had been expected, had come at last, as death always comes, with paralyzing suddenness. Who could tell whether the now untended boiler would not explode? Who could tell how soon the water which was pouring in below would sink the vessel? Every one felt that there was no time to spare; nearly every one was wildly bent on saving himself.

Below decks the scene was different. The change in the vessel's movement had at first been imperceptible, and, even when noticed, did not for a minute or two create terror. Kate Beaumont went up to Frank McAlister with a face which expressed only a slight wonder, mingled perhaps with a little hope, and said, "What is it?"

"I beg pardon," he replied, starting up from a doze on one of the settees, "I did not observe anything."

"I — don't — know," she murmured, listening attentively between her words. "Something — singular."

Just then Mrs. Chester appeared, dropping her Bible at the door of the state-room, and running toward them joyfully.

"We are there!" she laughed. Oh, I knew it. I knew we should be saved. This horrible voyage! This horrible, horrible voyage! over at last! Oh Kate, I am so happy!"

The gladness of supposed escape had made a child of her; she was laughing aloud, and ready to dance, with her groundless elation.

"Oh, to think it is over!" she prattled. "What a horrible thing it would have been to drown at sea! Or to burn!" she added, with a shudder. "Oh, that was the worst. But it is all over. We are coming into port. How can we praise Captain Brien enough! The dear, good man! I could kiss him, black and blue and brown as he is. He has managed things so admirably! Really, if women might do such things, I am in a fit state to propose to him. — Not talk so, Kate? Why not? What a prim, cold little piece you are! Such escapes don't come once in a lifetime; no, thank Heaven! not once in a lifetime. I own it. I am half crazy with joy. What is *that?*"

The panic above had by this time broken out in a clamor which could not well be misunderstood. The startled woman turned short and stared anxiously at McAlister, who had delicately withdrawn to a little distance.

"Go on deck and see!" she ordered, forgetting who he was. "Go on deck and find out where we are. Oh, if I am mistaken!" she added, as he vanished. "It can't be. I won't have it. Oh, why don't they stop that horrible trampling and shouting? Let me alone, Kate. I *will* go up there. I *must* see."

McAlister returned, running down the cabin stairs, very grave and a little pale. Mrs. Chester extended her hands toward him with an agonized gesture of entreaty.

"Don't tell me!" she shivered. In the next breath she screamed, "Oh, *what* is the matter?"

"Get ready as quickly as possible," said the young man. "We must go ashore in the boats."

"The ship is sinking," wailed Mrs. Chester. "Oh, I feel it! That worthless, villainous captain!"

"Don't," begged Kate. "Do be calm. Oh, what shall we do?"

McAlister took the girl under his arm and hurried her toward the stairway, following Mrs. Chester, who was already rushing thither. In the confusion and hurry of the crisis all the little packets, as well as the life-preservers, were forgotten in the state-rooms.

Meanwhile matters had been made nearly desperate on deck by the misbehavior of the crew. A portion, at least, of the sailors and firemen had, it seems, got at the spirit-room during the day and supplied themselves with whiskey. Several were more or less intoxicated; moreover, they could be seen taking bottles out of their pockets and drinking; it was to be feared that the alcoholic mischief had only begun to do its work. Already there was a gang of these fellows around each of the larger boats, throwing in provisions and kegs of water after a reckless fashion, running against each other, cursing, pushing, and even striking.

"Hold hard there!" shouted the captain, as he saw some of them grasping the tackle falls. "No one gets into the boats without orders. Passengers first. Ladies first."

But the men kept at their wild, hurrying, bungling work, without answering him, and perhaps without hearing him.

"By Heavens!" groaned Brien. "It's a worse lot than I thought. Steward! Mr. McMaster! Some one hurry up those ladies. Avast, men. Don't let that boat go. Come out of her, every one of you!"

Finding them ungovernable, he ran below after his pistols; for he too had been caught unprepared by the sudden spring of the catastrophe. Coming back, he was caught on the stairway by Mrs. Chester, who clung to him in a sort of delirium of terror, at once reproaching and imploring, until he loosened himself by main force.

During this brief interval the crisis, aided by the drunkenness and panic of the crew, hurried along with the terrible swiftness which had marked it from the outset. One of the large midship boats had been let go by the run, and was dragging bottom-up and stove alongside, with two or three men drowning under it. Several planks in the waist had suddenly started and curled up, and the smouldering hell within the hull, finding vent at last, sent up tongues of flame, licking at its prey like a boa. The motion forward had ceased, and the ship, settling in a manner sensible to every one, wallowed with a sickly feeling among the waves. Its doom from the fire was imminent; but its doom from the ocean was still more threatening. The panic-mad sailors and stokers had gathered around the starboard boat and were preparing to send her down the side, some already crowding into her, and others loosening the falls. It was a lamentable and shameful exhibition of cowardice and drunken selfishness.

"We can't go with those scoundrels," cried the captain. "They would capsize us."

He was addressing McAlister and Tom Beaumont, who had brought up Mrs. Chester and Kate from below, and were taking them forward to the waist. Every one on deck, it must be understood, was now perfectly recognizable in the light of the hissing explosions of flame which shot up from the volcano below, only from time to time clouded by volumes of smoke.

"Come aft," ordered the captain. Next, raising his voice to a yell: "Every sober man aft! Stand by to let go the quarter boats. But keep out of them. I'll shoot the first one who steps in without orders."

Then, levelling his pistol at a fellow who had laid hands on the fall tackle of one of the small boats, he shouted, "Stand back there! My God, this is a mutiny."

CHAPTER 7

 The *Mersey* burning and sinking at once; a rabble of reeling sailors and firemen tumbling into the large boats; the few passengers, the ship's officers, and perhaps a dozen of the crew, huddled around the quarter-deck boats; the captain stamping, threatening, pistol in hand, directing the embarkation; — such was the disorderly and unpromising state of affairs.

Brien's pistol was not the only one flourished, for Tom Beaumont and Wilkins drew and cocked revolvers, and even the mild Duffy produced a derringer. Under the moral effect of this artillery, the getting of things and people into the boats began to go on as it should aboard an Anglo-Saxon wreck. "Heave in those water breakers"; in they went with a "Yo-hee-oh." "Now the bread boxes"; and the bread boxes followed. "Here, you, sir, man the starboard boat; Mr. Wilson, take charge of the other one." Two trustworthy men were now in each little craft, ready to cast off tackles on touching the water, and to make fast tow-lines. "Let go, slowly; ease away, men, steady; there she floats."

"Now then, ladies," and the captain turned to his passengers. "Mrs. Chester first."

Mrs. Chester, far more eager to go first than the captain was to have her, went down a rope in the grasp of a stout sailor, clutching him as if she meant to tear and devour him.

"Now, Miss Beaumont," was the captain's next call. "Look alive, there below. Haul up under the counter. Some strong man here for Miss Beaumont."

"I!" shouted Tom, pushing a sailor aside. "I'll take care of my sister. Hold on to me, Kate."

"O Tom! be careful," was the girl's prayer as she threw her arms around the young fellow's neck.

"Hold hard!" screamed the captain. But it was too late; the boy had missed his hold or lost it; and both brother and sister went into the dark ocean. There was a general groan, a rush to the bulwarks, and a hesitation. Who could swim? It is a notorious fact that sailors are seldom good swimmers. Now came another splash; it was our tall McAlister, who had gone under with a header; and then there followed an awful suspense.

"Here's one," shouted a sailor in the boat, leaning over and dragging in some wet object. It was Tom Beaumont, no more able to swim than to fly, and saved by the merest accident, happening to rise in the right place. His first words were, "Where is she?"

He had scarcely strangled this out, when there was a general cry of joy from all those staring men, standing as they were on a burning and sinking wreck. The light of the flames showed a head on the surface, twenty feet astern of the small boat, and under it, almost submerged by it, another head, this last being that of a man, while the first was that of a woman. It was McAlister, laden and almost borne under by the weight of the girl whom he was striving to save.

"Drop the boat astern," roared Captain Brien. "Give him a hand."

In another minute the two were drawn in board, the girl pale, cold, and nearly strangled still, the man breathless with his struggle under water. There was no time for changing of clothing; the steady sinking of the ship gave warning that the embarkation must hasten; and all that could be done for the wet ones was to bring them some blankets from the nearest state-room.

This was the only accident to the party on the quarter-deck. In twenty minutes or thereabouts from the springing of the leak every living soul had abandoned the vessel, and the crowded boats were pulling rapidly away to escape the flurry of her foundering. It was a gloomy and ill-promising voyage, that upon which they were now entering. The wreck, already low in the water, but blazing throughout its midships and sending up superb piles of flame from its paddle-boxes, only made the darkness of ocean visible. A considerable sea was running, tossing the small craft uncomfortably, if not dangerously, and sending in splashes of spray which soon made all equally wet. In a few minutes every one was chilled through, notwithstanding that the temperature was mild and almost summer-like. McAlister and Tom Beaumont combined in wrapping all the blankets around Kate.

"It is useless," she shivered; "I shall only be the wetter for them."

Mrs. Chester, sunk in discomfort and despair too deep for words, gave no sign of existence, except groaning.

"This is ugly, ain't it, Wilkins?" muttered Duffy.

"This is a big lot better than going clean under," returned Wilkins, his elbows on his knees and his head between his hands. "By Jove, the more miserable I am, the more I want to live. It's always so."

"Sick, Wilkins?" presently inquired Duffy.

"No, I just don't like to look at it. Show me land, and I'll sit up straight enough."

"We are all right now," struck up the captain from the sternsheets, falling into his characteristic strain of bragging and humbug, no doubt because he thought it would cheer the women. "It's only a little wetting. See land to-morrow, and tell our stories at home next day. In a month from now it will all be a good joke. We wouldn't have missed it for anything."

"Except me," he added to himself, remembering ruefully his damaged fame as a sailor, and his injured prospects as chief commander in the new line.

The unfortunates rowed due west, making what headway could be made. They had sailed for half an hour when of a sudden the broad flicker of light behind them vanished, and, looking backward, they could no longer see the *Mersey*.

"It seems like the death of a friend," murmured Kate. "I am sorry for the poor ship."

"That's so," answered Captain Brien, his heart warming more than ever towards the girl. "She was a beautiful boat, wasn't she?"

"I'm glad the miserable thing is sunk," mumbled Mrs. Chester, who never quite forgave anybody or anything which had caused her trouble.

Presently Kate Beaumont said in a low voice to Frank McAlister: "It was you who saved me. Was it not?"

"I was so fortunate," he replied in a tone which was like an utterance of thanksgiving.

"I knew it. But I have been so stupefied! I shall be indebted to you all my life."

"No," he said, and would perhaps have been tempted to try to press her hand, had it not been defended from him by wet blankets.

And so that conversation, meaning we will not undertake to say how much, came to an end.

But we must not prolong this voyage. It was an adventure which had nothing more to signalize it than what has been described. In the morning there was a cry of "Sail ho"; then came deliverance from danger and discomfort; then a short trip to Charleston, South Carolina.

In Charleston the Southern hotel *par excellence,* the house where the great planter of those days stopped when he returned from Europe, or when he came to the city with his family to do shopping and attend the races, was the Charleston Hotel. It was in the huge front piazza of this house that Frank McAlister, refreshed, newly attired, brushed, and anointed, encountered that ancient friend of his family, Major John Lawson, the descendent (so said the Major) of the De Lauzuns.

"Why, my dear fellow! Why, my de-ar fel-low!" cried the Major, smiling up to his eyebrows and shaking hands for a minute together, though gently, tenderly, Oh how affectionately! "Why, is it possible! why, is it paw-si-ble!" he went on, in a high, ecstatic soprano of wonder, somewhat as if he were talking to a child. "And so it is you, is it?" patting his shoulder. "Why, bless my body, so it is. I wouldn't have known you. What an amazing development!" and the Major fell back a yard to stare at the young giant with an air of playful, petting amazement. "Taller by three inches than your grenadier of a father! Why, if the old Frederick of Prussia had been alive, you would have been kidnapped for his regiment of giants. The Potsdam regiment," explained the Major, not a little proud of this bit of military history. "But no; you don't want to be told how you have grown; you have been at other and wiser business as well. Why, tell me all about it. Why, I could listen to you forever."

No words can describe the blandness and the unctuous flattery of the Major's manner. It was like warm olive-oil, poured over your head and flying all down your beard and vestments in an instant. No time was allowed you for resistance; before you could think, there was the Major letting it on from his inexhaustible cruet. His utterance was soft and cajoling, running through a wide gamut of affettuoso tones, a favorite close being high soprano or falsetto. His face was prematurely wrinkled with smirking and grimacing. It was haunted with smiles which appeared and vanished like fire-flies. Now one shone out on his cheekbone; now another glimmered on his forehead; now a third flitted along his wide mouth. Then again his whole countenance broke up into them, putting you in mind of the flashings of a shattered looking-glass, or the radiances of a breezy sheet of water in the sunshine. As for his thin, genteel figure, it was so lubricated with constant bowing and gesturing, that it was as supple as an eel.

Meanwhile there was a slyness in his gray eyes and humorous twinkling in the crow's-feet at their corners, which caused you to doubt whether he were not secretly laughing at you under his mask of flattery. The truth is that the Major did amuse himself with the simplicity of human vanity. He complimented upon principle; he had made a formula for his guidance in this matter, and he stuck to it in practice; as Talleyrand (was it?) said, "Lie always, something will stick," so he said, "Flatter always, something will stick." But we must not consider him as certain straight-forward, bitter persons did, a mere hypocrite. He was a good fellow; he really desired to make people feel comfortable; he offered them compliments, because he had little else to spare.

McAlister gave the Major a brief and plain statement of his life abroad. There had been four years at Oxford, three years at Göttingen, and one year in travel.

"You are a prodigy," grinned and fluted the Major, his voice quavering high into falsetto. "Why, you are a praw-di-gy. You must be a miracle of learning. There isn't another man in the State who has passed his life to such advantage. You have come home to lift us poor South-Carolinians out of the slough of our ignorance and conceit.

And the son, too, of my excellent old friend Judge McAlister! I am delighted beyond measure."

"There is much for me to learn, no doubt, as well as something to teach," replied Frank, in his manly, simple way, so different from the frisky, supple graces of the Major. "I do believe, however, that I shall have something to tell you, that is, in a year or two."

"Oh, but you have something to tell us now." And the soft Lawson fingers patted the huge McAlister arm. "You must begin at once."

"I suspect," continued Frank, "that there is wealth in the State which we know little about. There are mines to be sunk yet in our up-country. And this shore region, if I am not much mistaken is crammed with phosphates."

Phosphates! The word was beyond the Major's tether. He did not know what phosphates might be, and did not believe he should care. He proceeded to smother the youngster's learning with what he thought appropriate compliment.

"Ah, there comes out the old canny Scotch blood," he smiled. "Or is it Scotch-Irish? Ah, Scotch! A most intelligent and industrious people. The best practical race that we have in the State. Brave, too; brave as lions; what a race! The *perfervidum Scotorum* is world-wide famous. By the way, have you letters from your father? I haven't met him, bless my body! for months."

"Yes, I found letters here. My father, I thank you, is well. The whole family also."

"And you visit them soon, of course? Return to the paternal hearth? Do give my kindest regards, my most profound respects, to your father. Noble man! A pillar, sir! A pillar of society! And, by the way, — bless me, how could I forget it, — but what an escape! Saved from the sea and from fire! You must be a marked man, set apart for some wonderful fate. But the *Mersey* lost! Our steamer lost! *Our* steamer! What a calamity! *What*," and here the Major's voice fairly whimpered, " a ca-lam-i-ty! And, by the way," descending to a confidential whisper, "you had Beaumonts aboard. Your old — enemies. I hope nothing disagreeable."

"Embarrassments," answered the young man, slightly shrugging his shoulders.

"Dear me! I am excessively grieved. But nothing that will lead to a — a —?" inquired the old gossip, imitating the motion of raising a pistol.

"Oh no. At least, I trust not. I sincerely hope not."

"Let us hope so," said the Major, in a tone which reminded one of the formula, "Let us pray." "Why, it would be infamous," he went on. "In view of your noble behavior, it would be in the highest degree unreasonable. Saved the young lady's life, I understand. Ah! I surprise you; you had no idea that your fame would find you out so soon. Modest," — another patting here, — "modest, mod-est! But, you see, I met one of your Hartland business-men, — a nice sort of a commonplace fellow named Duffy, I believe, — and accidentally, quite accidentally, heard the story from him. And so you saved Miss Kate Beaumont's life? What a wonderful — providence, shall we call it? I told you truly, that you were a marked man, a man set apart for some extraordinary destiny. And Miss Beaumont? I haven't seen her since she was a mere child. How did you like the young lady?"

"An admirable girl," said the brave McAlister, not without a slight blush. "What I saw of her led me to respect her profoundly."

The Major's small, cunning gray eyes twinkled with the joy of a veteran intriguer, not to say matchmaker.

"Why, my dear fellow! why, my d-e-a-r fel-low!" he whispered, snuggling up to the youngster, and fondling his mighty arm. "If this should end in a reconciliation between the families, what an event! South Carolina could affort to rejoice in the loss of the *Mersey*. What a romance! Why not? Romeo and Juliet in the South? Bless me, my dear young friend, why not? Stranger things have happened."

"You forget the fate of Romeo and Juliet," replied McAlister, with a gravity which revealed how seriously he was taking this matter.

But the Major would not hear of carrying out the parallel; he guessed like lightning at his young friend's state of mind, and he prophesied smooth things; indeed, when did he ever prophesy any other?

"Oh no!" he laughed, waving away the suggestion of a tragedy. "Nothing of the sort, my dear Mr. McAlister. We shall see, if you only wish it, a better ending than that. Why, bless you, man, the Beaumonts are not barbarians of the Middle Ages. They — I remember the old feud — I respect your natural prejudices — but they, you will excuse me for saying so, are South Carolina gentlemen. They have the polish and humanity — you will surely pardon me — of the nineteenth century."

"I am sure that I wish to think well of them. I will tell you, moreover, that I only wait an opportunity to show them that I feel kindly towards them."

"An opportunity!" smiled and fifed the Major, — "an opportunity! It has come, and you have improved it. Improved it nobly, superbly, beautifully. Now it is their turn. You have saved the life of their daughter and sister. They must thank you. They must call upon you. They will. We shall see. Then, Romeo and Juliet, with a happy ending. Yes," closed the Major, fairly singing his hint for a pastoral, "Ro-me-o and Jul-iet in South Car-o-li-na!"

"They — the men, I mean — must call on me, of course or the matter is ended," observed McAlister. He spoke slowly and gravely; he was sincerely anxious to receive that peacemaking visit; he did not care how plainly the Major should perceive his anxiety; indeed, he scarcely thought of him at the moment.

"Certainly. They must. If they don't they are — Well, let us be charitable. But I can't conceive that they should not call. It is Tom, I believe, who is with the ladies. Well, Tom is young; but Tom knows what chivalry demands; born of one of our own good families; a race of gentlemen, — excuse me. Of course Tom Beaumont will make his bow to you before he leaves Charleston."

And the Major, in his excellent, gossiping soul, meant to call on Tom and flatter him into doing what was handsome. It must be understood that this man was by instinct a matchmaker; he liked women, liked to pay court to them, liked to see others do the same; and now, guessing that Frank was smitten with Miss Beaumont, he wanted him to woo her and win her. Besides, what a charming history, what an inexhaustible theme of conversation with ladies, what a subject to decorate all over with flowers from Shakespeare, would be this healing of an old family feud by means of a love-match! For the Major was a *littérateur*, in the amateur sense; he could quote eternally from standard authors, especially in verse; also he wrote a kind of poetical prose, much admired by some of the women to whom he read it.

But Major Lawson had other strong points. He did love — as what South-Carolinan of those days did not love? — to talk about fighting. Wars, duels, adventures with robbers, putting down of insurrections, and even family feuds, were all pure honey to him. He groaned over them, to be sure; but his lamentation was simple humbug; it was the merest rose-water philanthropy; in his soul he feasted on them. Next to love-making, and far beyond politics, he revelled in talking of combats. Not that he had ever had a fight; there was no man in the State more pacific. His title of Major did not signify war, nor even so much as service in the militia. He had been an aide-de-camp to a Governor; just an honorary aide-de-camp, with nothing to do; that was the whole sum of his martial life. His title, too, was really Captain, for he was only a Major by courtesy, familiar friends having breveted him at their dinner-tables.

Well, this peaceful creature must now turn to the old bloody feud between the Beaumonts and the McAlisters, and prattle of it with something like a licking of the chops.

"Terrible history!" he said, with the sorrow of a dog over a toothsome bone. "If we could only put an end to it! No less than nine valuable lives have been sacrificed to this Moloch since I came to the age of manhood, — four McAlisters and five Beaumonts; not to mention the side difficulties which it has brought about between friends of the two houses, — the Montagues and Capulets," he poetically added. "I well remember the excitement, the *furor*, which was raised by the — the meeting between your excellent father and Randolph Beaumont, the elder brother of Peyton. The State fairly shuddered with anxiety. Fairly shuddered!" And the Major shook himself in his black dress-coat. "Both men practiced for months, — for months, sir! Each knew it must come. Prepared himself, sadly and sternly, like a gentleman. Randolph declared that he would spoil McAlister's handsome face for him. Your father was a remarkably fine-looking fellow; not like you, who resemble your mother, — but still handsome. Indeed, he is so now; a king of men; a Saul! Well, sir, Randolph practised at the head; had a figure set up for that purpose in his yard; used it to hit the top of it with beautiful precision; really beau-ti-ful! Of your father's preparations I will say nothing. Perhaps the subject is unpleasant to you. But it was a stern necessity. He must take his precautions or he must forfeit his valuable life. Well, the day came; no preventing it. An admirable exhibition of courage. Two shots in quick succession. Randolph Beaumont sent a shot through McAlister's hair, and fell with a ball in his own heart. My God, what an excitement! The whole State shook, sir!"

McAlister had listened to this reminiscence with an amount of disrelish which surprised himself. It was not the first time that he had heard the story, and heretofore he had always heard it with interest. But childhood's ideas had more or less died out of him; during the last few years a passion for studies had dulled the combative instinct within him; and within the past week Miss Kate Beaumont had made him hate the family feud.

"I never heard my father allude to the tragedy but once," he said to the Major, rather coldly. "It was only a word, and I thought it was a word of regret."

The old gossip started. Had he made a mistake in chanting to the child the prowess of the parent?

"Oh, of course!" he hurriedly assented. "Your father is a wise, practical, humane gentleman. Couldn't look upon the matter otherwise than as a woful necessity, mere self-preservation. Certainly."

And so the Major suspended his raw-head and bloody-bones reminiscences. It was a disappointment to him, for there were still several nice joints to pick, and, dear me, how sweet they were! There, for instance, was the late duel between R. Bruce McAlister, our Frank's senior brother, and the present eldest son of the house of Beaumont. No deaths, to be sure; only a shot through a leg and another through an arm; but even so much was savory.

"Sad, sad business!" groaned the Major, bringing down the corners of his mouth decorously, as people will do at funerals and the like, even when they care not a straw. "All politics, — purely result of politics; not bitterness, I am glad to say. Simply a struggle between high-minded gentlemen, each of whom honestly and sadly believes the other mistaken. Opposition, as you are no doubt aware, between the supporters of the electoral system and the so-called parish representation. Your family, as original up-country gentlemen, naturally support the former. The Beaumonts, as original low-country people, are the extreme advance guard of the parishes."

"That is it, is it?" said Frank. "I never knew before what was the origin of the dispute. I was such a mere boy when I left home."

"That, and other things similar. Bless my soul!" and here the Major fluted his sweetest, "have I got to teach you the antiquities, the *fasti*, of your family? Why, the first McAlister of Hartland — your noble deceased grandfather — was one of the supporters of our grand old Horry — Marion's Horry — in his efforts to establish the common-school system in South Carolina. Naturally on the side of the people. A born Gracchus. And yet nature's gentleman, the truest of aristocrats."

"A supporter of education," said Frank. "Well, I thank him for that. I am of his party. Depend upon it, Major, that our State needs education, and that I shall do my poor best towards educating it."

"Amen!" pronounced the Major, solemnly, as if it were the thing that he had most at heart. "Well, my best wishes. Delighted to have seen you, — de-light-ed! Carry my respects to your family. And as for the Beaumonts," he added with a knowing, matchmaking, tender whisper; "they will call on you," in a lower whisper; "they will," almost inaudible.

And so, nodding and smiling, and, one might almost say, kissing his fingers, Major Lawson ambled away.

Would the Beaumonts call? Would Tom Beaumont come to say a civil word to the man who had saved his sister's life? Or would he, remembering only the ancient hostility of the two names, leave Charleston without a sign of friendship?

Such were the questions which chased each other through the brain of the young gentleman who paced alone the piazza of the Charleston Hotel.

CHAPTER 8

Let us skip on to Hartland, ahead of Mr. Frank Mc-Alister, and see what immediate chance he has for putting an end to the family feud.

Is there any possible reader of this story, who does not know what a church fair is? The Presbyterian church of Hartland has no steeple, except a little, undignified, rusty-white bob of a belfry, which puts irreverent people in mind of a parrot's cage. After having slumbered for years over the pointless state of their tabernacle, the members of the congregation have suddenly awakened to a sense of the absurdity of its appearance, and have resolved (as one old farmer expressed it) to grow a steeple. Every one of them has built imaginary spires in his soul, and has perhaps tumbled out of them in dreams. The result of all this longing is a church fair in the court-house.

The court-house is not only the *palais de justice* and the *hôtel de ville* of a Southernshire town, but is also its political club-room, its theatre, operahouse, lecture-hall, and coliseum. In it the party leaders shout, "Fellow-citizens, we have arrived at a national crisis," with other words to that effect. In it the scientific or historic or theologic gentlemen, who have been "invited" by the village lyceum, wipe their spectacles, look at their manuscripts, and begin, "Ladies and gentlemen of Hartland," or whatever the place may be. In it the musical concerts, tableaux vivants and charades of native talent unfold their enchantments. In it strolling actors, nigger or other minstrels, black-art magicians and exhibitors of panoramas, make enough to pay their hotel bills and get on to the next town. In short, the court-house is the academe of all exceptional instruction and amusement.

On the ground that the pews of the church will not give free circulation to the business of a fair, and on the further ground that the prosperity of every religious body is intimately connected with the public good, that crafty and potent seigneur, Judge McAlister, has secured the court-room gratis for the use of his society, notwithstanding much dumb jealousy on the part of Methodists, Baptists, etc. The greasy wooden seats have been "toted off"; the tobacco-stained floor has been scrubbed into a speckled cleanliness; there are plenty of gayly decked tables, with pretty girls smiling over them; there are alcoves of greenery, glowing with other pretty girls; the walls are fine with flowers, drapery, and festooned paper: it is a very lively and very pleasant spectacle. The squeezing, buying, prattling, laughing, and staring crowd enjoys the scene heartily. A decent and civil crowd it is, although far from being purely aristocratic, for it exhibits many plain people, many unfashionable garments and some homespun ones. No negroes, barring a few as attendants: the slave population is to have an evening by itself; then there will be goggling wonder and roaring laughter.

Even now there is plenty of noisy amusement, for the *Howling Gyascutus* is on exhibition, and what a funny beast it is!

"The howling gyascutus, ladies and gentlemen!" calls one of the junior managers from a stage at the upper end of the hall, — "the howling gyascutus!" he proclaims, leading out what seems to be a hairy quadruped, with very thick and long hind legs and very short fore ones. "I have the honor, ladies and gentlemen, to be the first to exhibit to the human race this remarkable animal. The howling gyascutus is the wonder of the age, — at least for the present occasion. He humps himself up to the dizziest summits of the persimmon-tree, and devours green persimmons by the peck without puckering, — a feat accomplished by no other living creature. He has been known to eat a pickaninny from wool to heel, as if he were a card of ginger-bread. His strength is supposed to be equal to that of Sampson, and he would pull down a temple of Dagon if he could find one, which he cannot in this virtuous community. His howl is the envy of auctioneers, deputy-sheriffs, and congressmen." (Here the nondescript roars in a manner which may be described as nothing less than human.) "It is not recorded that any other specimen of the breed has ever been captured. It is not believed that this one could have been overcome and brought here, but for his lurking desire to look at the beautiful ladies whom I see before me." (Loud applause from the dandies of Hartland, every one glancing at his particular Dulcinea.) " Such is the force of the howling gyascutus that he defies the unassisted power of the human biceps and other more unnamable muscles. If I should let him loose, you would see this magnificent court-house" ("Hi! hi!" from the bigger boys, appreciating the irony of the adjective) "disappear in his jaws like the bubbles that swim on the beaker's brim and break on the lips they're meeting. There would be a scene of destruction which the past cannot parallel, and which the future would look upon with a palpitation of the heart and other sentimental organs. I assure you, ladies and gentlemen, that, notwithstanding this enchanted chain and other favorable influences too numerous to be mentioned, it takes all my strength to hold him."

Here of course the gyascutus went into a paroxysm. He ran at the shins of his keeper; he stood five feet eight in his boots, and pawed the kerosene-lit air; he howled in his virile fashion until the blood of small urchins curdled with horror. A terrible nondescript; long gray fur, such as one sees in travelling-rugs; a head wonderfully like that of a stuffed bear; the tail of an alligator. After much roaring and clanking, and a good deal more of speechifying from his exhibitor, he was led away behind a green cambric curtain, followed by laughter, stamping, and clapping.

A little later, Wallace McAlister, one of Frank's two elder brothers, strolled out from unknown recesses, his pleasant, plain face unusually flushed, and his prematurely bald crown damp with perspiration.

"Oh Wally!" laughed his sister Mary, beckoning him to her alcove. "How could you make such a guy of yourself! But really, it *was* funny."

"Just to get it done," said Wallace, — a good-natured reason, which was quite characteristic of him. "Everybody else was afraid of being undignified. But, after I had volunteered to be gyascutus," he added, looking a little disgusted, "the fools put in Bent Armitage as keeper. I didn't know who was holding the chain till it was too late."

"Wasn't it stupid in them!" murmured Mary. "But never mind."

It must be understood that Bentley Armitage was a connection of the Beaumonts, and so not entirely to the taste of the McAlisters.

"Somebody had to be gyascutus and start the thing," continued Wallace, apologizing for himself. "A fellow must do something to get the fair along."

"Oh, it's very well," nodded Mary, cheeringly. "You howled to perfection. Now go and buy something. Do buy something of Jenny Devine, — won't you?"

Mary's eyes were very appealing. Jenny Devine was her friend, her pet, her wonder. It was an odd fancy too, or rather it was not at all odd, for Mary was quiet and very good, while Jenny was rather hoydenish and over-coquettish. There she was, peeping out of an alcove of hemlock a few steps farther on, a dangerous looking fairy, rather of the brunette order, sparkling with black eyes, glistening with white teeth, and one shoulder poked high out of her dress for a temptation.

"What does Jenny Devine want of *me?*" mumbled modest Wallace. "A bald old fellow like me!"

"You are *not* old," whispered Mary, coloring with sympathy for his mortification as he alluded to his defect. "Do go!"

For Mary wanted to bring about a match between this brother whom she loved and Jenny Devine whom she also loved.

"Stop! don't go now," she hastily added, "Vincent Beaumont is talking to her."

"Oh!" returned Wallace, casting a sidelong glance, rather watchful than hostile, toward the representative of the inimical race.

It may as well be explained here that at this period the men of the rival houses did speak to each other when they met by chance in society, but that they met as little as possible and their speaking was of the briefest description. As for their respective women folks, no communication ever passed between them.

Until Vincent Beaumont goes his way, and Wallace can find a chance to drop into the toils of Jenny Devine, let us amuse and instruct ourselves by studying Judge Donald McAlister. How bland and benignant this mighty personage looks as he paces grandly from table to table, and says a few no doubt fitting words to every lady, not to mention intermediate hand-shakings with every male creature! He a fighter of duels, a champion of a family feud, an obstacle to the millennium of peace! Why, bless you, he is obviously one solid chunk of goodness; his philanthropy shines out of his large face like a Drummond light out of the lantern of a lighthouse; his very accessories, as, for instance, his scratch and spectacles, beam amity. One would say, after taking a cursory glance at him, that here is an incarnation of the words, "Peace on earth and good-will to men."

His very figure has outlines which seem to radiate promises of tranquillity and mercy. It is not that he is corpulent, for although he weighs at least two hundred and thirty, he is so tall that he carries his avoirdupois well. But get behind him; notice the feminine slope of his shoulders; survey the womanly breadth of his hips. Is that a form, lofty and vigorous as it is, which one couples with the idea of pugnacity? It is the build, not of a gladiator, but of a "gentle giant," and that too of the female order. Even his walk is matronly; the great "second joints" wheeling slowly and with dignity; the large knees almost touching as they pass each other; the deliberate feet pointing tranquilly outwards; the coat-tails swinging like petticoats. Not that the Judge is ludicrous, unless it be to very light-minded persons, such as would "speak disrespectfully of the equator." He is not, — it must be emphatically repeated, — he is not fat nor clumsy. He simply has the form which is most common to tall men who have developed into a certain measure of portliness.

It is proper to state that he has a blander air than usual. His wife has managed the fair successfully, and he sympathizes with her satisfaction. His only daughter is looking her best amid the evergreens of her alcove, and Heaven has not been chary to him of the pride and love of a father. Furthermore (very characteristic, this) he has carefully calculated what the fair will cost him, and finds it barely one half of what he would have been expected to pay, had the expense of the steeple been raised by subscription. Finally, it is his ancient, deliberate, and judicious custom to look especially benignant upon public occasions.

But the Judge must not at this time be described fully. If we should attempt to do him justice, he would betray us into great lengths. An exhaustive study of him would fill a bigger volume than the pyramid of Cheops. We must let this monument go; we must open the door for him as he swings out of the court-room; we must turn to more manageable personages.

Great is avoirdupois," said Vincent Beaumont to Jenny Devine, as he watched the departure of the somewhat ponderous senior.

"What do you mean?" asked the young lady, suspecting one of Vincent's sarcasms and not willing to lose the full flavor of it.

"Character goes by weight. Every large man gets a certain amount of reverence which doesn't fairly belong to him. There is the Judge, for instance. Just because he is an inch or so over six feet, and has brawn enough to feed a tribe of cannibals, even I feel inclined to fall into his wake."

"He is a much finer man than you think," said Miss Jenny, one of those young ladies who rule by pertness.

"Thank Heaven!"

"And he is a much older man than you."

"Thank Heaven again!"

"What do you mean?"

"There is a chance that he won't last my time."

"Ain't you ashamed of yourself, Mr. Beaumont?"

It was a common phrase with Jenny, and she meant almost nothing by it. In reality Vincent's sub-acid prattle gave her vast amusement and pleasure. Sarcasm was the young man's strong point in conversation, causing a few to admire him immensely and a great many to dislike him. A born trait in him, the legacy perhaps of his French ancestors, he had greatly increased his proficiency in it by familiarity with a certain chaffing French society, for he had studied medicine in Paris. A doctor, by the way, he would not be called, for he had cut the profession immediately on returning home, and never prescribed unless for one of his father's negroes.

"And there is our downy friend, the gyascutus," he continued, glancing with a scornful languor at Wallace McAlister. "As he weighs eighty pounds less than his father, I suppose I may say a word about him."

"You may praise him as much as you like," said Jenny, an audacious coquette, who liked to play off one man against another.

Vincent was annoyed; not that he cared about Jenny Devine, but that he wanted her to care about him; for he too was a flirt, and a flintily selfish one. He could scarce forbear turning his satire upon the girl herself.

"I mean to praise him," he replied. "His humility in playing gyascutus deserves eulogium. And that he should accept my relative — the relative of a Beaumont, remember — for his keeper! I can't imagine a more graceful and delicate advance towards a reconciliation of the families. I should like to pat him on the head, as one does a fuzzy-crowned baby. Do you think he would let me?"

All this was nuts to Jenny, amused by the satire and delighted with the jealousy. Not a bad-hearted girl, she had something of the pet monkey in her brilliant composition, being fond of making a sensation and of playing the torment. Resolving now on a great blow for notoriety, she poked up one of her bare shoulders with a saucy air of power which a more experienced belle would not have ventured, and throwing out a rosy hand authoritatively, beckoned Wallace to come to her. What a triumph it would be if she could make a Beaumont and a McAlister stand side by side before her table and meekly play the rivals! No other girl in Hartland District had ever attempted such a feat.

The unwilling but fascinated Wallace approached. Vincent, anxious to avoid the meeting, was held fast by an idea that it would be ridiculous to go. It was like the nearing of two ships of war, each of whom is a stranger to the other's purpose, and is therefore silently clearing for action. Persons in the crowd looked on with anxious surprise, querying whether the young men were about to draw pistols, or whether the millennium were at hand.

"Mr. Beaumont — Mr. McAlister," said the triumphant, reckless, dangerous Miss Jenny.

The two men bowed; there could be no quarrelling before ladies: they were as courteous as if they were friends.

"I want you two to bid against each other for this pair of gloves," said the mischief-maker. Then the thought of the trouble that such a contest might cause dropped into her giddy head, and she hastily added, "The bidding is not to go above ten dollars."

"I bid ten dollars at once," calmly remarked Vincent, looking Jenny gravely in the face.

"So do I," said Wallace, his loose blue eyes wandering in a troubled way, for he thought all of a sudden that the girl might make a bad wife.

"Here, take each one," returned Jenny. "Five dollars apiece."

There was a moment of hesitation during which each man queried whether he were not bound to demand the pair. Then Wallace's good-nature put down his irritated sense of honor, and handing Jenny a five-dollar piece, he accepted a single glove. Vincent did the same, thrust his glove petulantly into a pocket, bowed in silence to the lady, and turned to go.

"Wait, Mr. Beaumont," called Jenny, who saw the eyes of fifty women fixed on her triumph, and was not willing to let it end so abruptly. "Trading is over, and we are about to talk. Both you gentlemen love to talk dearly. So do I. Let us have a delightful time of it. Mr. Beaumont, we are very much obliged to you for coming here. Considering that you are an Episcopalian, and don't believe that our church is a church, your conduct is very liberal, and we ought to thank you. Don't you think so, Mr. McAlister?"

"I do indeed," assented the much-enduring Wallace.

He said it to please the lady, but he said it stiffly and dryly, for the situation was not an agreeable one to him. Moreover he did not like the sneer which played around Vincent's flexible mouth. All the Beaumonts were unpleasant to him, and especially this would-be witty mocker.

"I have been exceedingly entertained," returned Vincent, with a slight, Frenchified bow, half a shrug. "Mr. McAlister here has been good enough to be very amusing."

The young Beaumont, it must be explained, had conceived an in-flammatory suspicion that these two were in combination to put him at a disadvantage, with the purpose of laughing at him after his departure.

Wallace colored at the reference to his undignified exhibition as a gyascutus.

"I had no special intention of troubling you to laugh, Mr. Beaumont," he observed in a rather too positive tone.

"We are often most amusing when we least mean it," was the snaky answer. "I have seen people who never knew how comic they were," added Vincent, his pugnacity rising as he tasted first blood.

Wallace, who was not quick at repartee (unless thinking of a retort next day can be called quick), simply stared his indignation. Jenny Devine noted the rising quarrel, and flung in some of her girlish prattle, hoping to make things pleasant again. But the mischief was done; the smouldering fire of the old feud had been blown to a flame; the two young men were in a state of mind to shoot each other. Jenny was so far alarmed that when Vincent again bowed himself away she did not detain him. She now talked to Wallace, with the intention of keeping him from following the other. But he was moody; he could not answer her, and hardly heard her; and at last, in a girlish pet, she let him go.

Knowing that he had been satirized, and feeling that he had been insulted, Wallace watched Vincent until he left the hall and then hastened after him.

"Mr. Beaumont," he called, when they were both in the moonlit street.

"Well, sir?" returned Vincent, facing about.

"I don't know exactly how to take what you have said to me," continued Wallace.

"I don't find that I am bound to assist you, sir," was the cool reply.

Wallace's hot temper immediately boiled over; he muttered some indistinct but evidently angry words.

"Perhaps you would be good enough to say something comprehensible," sneered Vincent.

"Yes, sir!" burst out Wallace. "I will be kind enough to say that I consider your style of innuendo not gentlemanly. Do you hear me, sir? Not gentlemanly!"

"I comprehend perfectly," replied Vincent, in a furious rage at once, but still preserving the clear even tone of his tenor voice. "I will send you my answer."

"Very good," said Wallace, and the two separated without another word, the one mounting his horse and riding away, the other turning to re-enter the court-house.

Meantime Mary McAlister had rushed at Jenny Devine, whispering, "Where is my brother?"

"I don't know," answered the flirt, suddenly very much worried, but trying to smile. "He is about somewhere."

"He isn't. What did you make him talk with that Mr. Beaumont for? Oh Jenny! I thought you were a friend."

Jenny rustled out of her alcove, caught Mary by the arm and hurried her towards the door, saying, "Let us look for him."

On the stairway they met Wallace, slowly ascending. He was very grave, but at sight of them a smile came over his homely, pleasant face, and he said cheerily, "What now? Do you want anything?"

Mary flew to him. "Is there any trouble, Wally?" she whispered. "You know how our mother would feel. Oh Wally, if there is any trouble, do stop it!"

"All right," laughed Wallace, putting his arm around her waist and helping her up stairs. "It's all right, Molly."

There was dire trouble, of course; but, as he believed, he could not stop it; and that being the case, he would say nothing about it!

CHAPTER 9

 "Hi! — Yah! — Ho! — Mars Peyt! — Gwine ter git up to-day?"

This incantation is heard in the bedroom of the Honorable Peyton Beaumont. It is pronounced by a shining, jolly youngster of a negro, seated on the bare clean pitch-pine floor, his legs curving out before him like compasses, a blacking-brush held up to his mouth for further moistening, and an aristocratic-looking boot drawn over his left hand like a gauntlet. The incantation is responded to by a savage grunt from a long bundle on a tousled bed, out of which bundle peeps a grizzled and ruffled topknot, and some portion of a swarthy face framed in iron-gray beard and whiskers. After the grunt comes a silence which is followed in turn by a snore so loud and prolonged that it reminds one of the long roll of a drum-corps.

The negro resumes his work, whistling the while in a sort of whisper and bobbing his head in time to the tune. Presently he pauses and takes a look at the bundle of bedclothes. "Ain't gwine ter wake up yit; mighty sleepy dis mornin'." More brushing, whistling, and bobbing. Then another look. "Done gone fas' asleep agin; guess I'll catch 'nother hold." There is a small table near him, with a bottle on it and glasses. A hand goes up; the bottle is uncorked and the liquor is decanted; very neatly done indeed. More brushing, whistling, and keeping time, just to lull the sleeper. The hand seeks the table once more; the glass is brought down, emptied, and set back in its place; no jingle. Then further brushing, and the job is finished.

His work done, the negro got up with an "Oh Lordy!" walked to the bedside, dropped the boots with a bang, and shouted, "Hi! Mars Peyt!"

"Clear out!" growled Mars Peyt, and made a lunge with a muscular hand, so hairy that it might remind one of the paw of an animal.

There was a rapid rectification of the frontier on the part of the darky; he retreated towards a doorway which led into what was obviously a dressing-room. At a safe distance from the bed he halted and yelled anew, "Hi! Mars Peyt!"

Mars Peyt disengaged one hand entirely from the bedclothes, seized the top of a boot and slung it at the top of the negro, who dodged grinning through the door just as the projectile banged against it.

"Hi! Yah! Ho! ho, Mars Peyt!" he shouted this time with an intonation of triumph, aware that his toughest morning job was over and pleased at having accomplished it without barking a shin.

"Now den, Mars Peyt, you dress youself," he continued. "When you's ready, I'll fix you cocktail."

"Fix it now," huskily growled the lord of the manor. "I'm dressing, — confound you!"

Such was the Honorable Peyton Beaumont; something like a big, wilful, passionate boy; such at least he was on many occasions. As for his difficulty in waking up of mornings, we must excuse him on the ground that he slept badly of nights. He went to bed on brandy; honestly believed he should rest the better for it; after two hours of travelling or fighting nightmare, woke up; dull pain and increasing heat in the back of his head; pillow baking hot, and hot all over; not another wink till morning. Then came a short, feverish nap; then this brushing, whistling, shouting Cato: — who wouldn't throw boots at him? But Cato was continued in the office of valet because he was the only negro in the house who had the impudence to bring about a thorough waking, and because Mr. Beaumont was determined to be up at a certain hour. He was not the sort of man to let himself be beaten, not even by his own physical necessities.

What was he like when he entered the dressing-room in shirt and trousers, with the streaky redness of soap and water about his sombre face, and plumped heavily into a high-backed oak arm-chair, to receive his cocktail and to be shaved by Cato? At first glance he might seem to be a clean but very savage buccaneer. It would be easy to imagine such a man grasping at chances for duels and following the scent of a family feud. His broad, dark red face, overhung by tousled iron-gray hair and set in a stiff iron-gray beard, had just this one merit, of being regular in outline and feature. Otherwise it was terrible; it was nothing less than alarming. Paches, the Athenian admiral who massacred the garrison of Notium, might well have had such a countenance. In the bloodshot black eyes (suffused with the yellow of habitual biliousness), in the stricture of the Grecian mouth, in the cattish tremblings of the finely turned though hairy nostrils, and in the nervous pointings of the bushy eyebrows, there was an expression of intense pugnacity, as fiery as powder and as long-winded as death.

In fact, he had all sorts of a temper. It was as sublime as a tiger's and as ridiculous as a monkey's. His body was marked by the scars of duels and rencontres, and the life-blood of more than one human being was crusted on his soul. At the same time he could snap like a cross child, break crockery, and kick chairs. Perhaps we ought partly to excuse his fits of passion on the score of nearly constant and often keen physical suffering. People, in speaking of his temper, said "Brandy"; but it was mainly brandy in its secondary forms, — broken sleep, an inflamed alimentary canal, and gout.

Meanwhile he had traits of gentleness which occasionally astonished the people who were afraid of him. While he could fly at his children in sudden furies, he was passionately fond of them, supported them generously, and spoiled them with petting. Barring chance oaths and kicks which were surprised out of him, he was kind to his negroes, feeding them liberally, and keeping them well clothed. As proud as Lucifer and as domineering as Beelzebub, he could be charmingly courteous to equals and friends.

"How you fine that, Mars Peyt?" asked Cato, when the cocktail had been hastily clutched and greedily swallowed.

"Devilish thin." Voice, however, the smoother and face blander for it.

"Make you 'nother?"

"Yes." Mellow growl, not exclusively savage, much like that of a placated tiger.

This comedy, by the way, was played every morning, with a variation Sundays. Mr. Beaumont, having vague religious notions about him, and being willing to make a distinction in days, took three cocktails on the Sabbath, besides lying in bed later.

The shaving commenced; the patient bristling occasionally, but growing milder; the operator supple, cautious, and talkative, slowly getting the upper hands.

"Now hold you head still. You jerk that way, an' you'll get a cut. How you s'pose I can shave when you's slammin' you face round like it was a do'?"

"Cato, I really need another cocktail this morning. Had a precious bad night of it."

"No, you don', now. 'Tain't Sunday to-day. Laws bless you, Mars Peyt, ho, ho! you's mos' 'ligious man I knows of, he, he! befo' breakfus. You'd jes like t' have Sunday come every day in the week, so's you could have three cocktails. No you don', no sech thing. 'Tain't good for you. There, liked to cut you then. Hold you nose roun', *dere.*" (Pushing the noble Greek proboscis into place with thumb and finger.) "Now then shut up you mouf; I'se gwine to lather. Them's um. This yere's fusrate soap. Makes a reg'lar swamp o' lather."

"Well, hurry up now," growls Mr. Beaumont, a little sore because he can't have his third cocktail. "Don't stand there all day staring at the soap-brush."

"What's Mars Vincent up to this mornin'?" suggests Cato, seeking to lull the rising storm with the oil of gossip.

"What *is* he up to?" demands Peyton Beaumont with a fierce roll of the eyes: — as much as to say, If anybody is up to anything without my permission, I'll break his head.

"Flyin' roun' greasin' his pistils an' talkin' softly with Mars Bent Armitage. Don' like the looks of it."

Mr. Beaumont uttered an inarticulate growl and was clearly anxious to have the dressing over. At last he was shaved; his noble beard was combed and his martial hair brushed upward; he rose with a strong grip on the arms of his chair and slipped his arms into his extended coat. He was much improved in appearance from what he had been; he still looked fierce, but not uncouth, nor altogether uncourtly. One might say a gentlemanly Turk, or even a sultan; for there is something patrician in the expression and port of the man.

In his long, columned piazza, whither he went at once to get a breath of the morning freshness which came in over his whitening cotton-fields, he met his eldest son, Vincent. The young gentleman was sauntering slowly, his hands in the skirt-pockets of his shooting-jacket, a pucker of thoughtfulness on his brow, and the usual satirical smile rubbed out. With dark, regular features, just a bit pugnacious in expression, he resembled his father as a fresh young gamecock resembles an old one tattered by many a conflict.

A pleasant morning greeting was exchanged, the eyes of the parent softening at the sight of his son, and the latter brightening with an air of confidence and cordiality. It was strange to see two such combative creatures look so amiably upon each other. Clearly the family feeling was very strong among the Beaumonts.

Instead of shouting, "What's this about pistols?" as he had meant to do, Mr. Beaumont gently asked, "What's the news, Vincent?"

Then came the story of the previous evening's adventure. It was related to this effect: there had been some ironical sparring between a Beaumont and a McAlister; thereupon the McAlister had said, substantially, "You are no gentleman."

"How came you to go near the clown?" growled Peyton Beaumont, his hairy nostrils twitching and his thick eyebrows charging bayonets.

"He approached *me*, while I was talking to Miss Jenny Devine."

Vincent did not think it the honorable thing to explain that the young lady was much to blame for the unpleasantness.

"The quarrelsome beasts!" snorted Beaumont. "Always picking a fight with our family. Trying to get themselves into decent company that way. It's always been so, ever since they came to this district; always! We had peace before. Why, Vincent, it's the most unprovoked insult that I ever heard of. What had you said? Nothing but what was — was socially allowable — parliamentary. And he to respond with a brutality! No gentleman! A Beaumont no gentleman! By heavens, he deserves to be shot on sight, shot at the first street-corner, like a nigger-stealer. He doesn't deserve a duel. The code is too good for him."

"That sort of thing won't do now, at least not among our set."

"It did once. It did in my day. You young fellows are getting so cursed fastidious. Well, if it won't do, then —"

Mr. Beaumont took a sudden wheel and walked the piazza in grave excitement. When he returned to face the young man, he said with undisguisable anxiety: "Well, my boy! You know the duties of a gentleman. I don't see that I am permitted to interfere."

"I have put things into the hands of Bentley Armitage," added Vincent.

"Very good. Do as well as anybody; — much better than his brother. Come, let us have breakfast."

At the breakfast-table appeared only these two men, and the second son, Poinsett. There was not a white woman in the house, though we must not blame Mr. Beaumont for the deficiency, inasmuch as he had espoused and lost two wives, and had been known to try at least once for a third. His eldest daughter, Nellie, was married to Randolph Armitage, of Brownville District; his only other daughter, Kate, and his sister, Mrs. Chester, were, as we know, in Charleston.

For some minutes Poinsett, a fat, tranquil, pleasantly spoken, and talkative fellow of perhaps twenty-five, bore the expense (as the French say) of the conversation.

"Our feminine population will be home soon, I venture to hope," he said, among other things. "Then, it is to be cheerfully believed, we shall come out of our slough of despond. American men, if you will excuse me for saying so, are as dull and dry as the Devil. They manage matters better in France, and on the Continent generally, and even in England. There, yes, even in England, common prejudice to the contrary notwithstanding, the genus homo is social. Conversation goes on in those countries. I don't say but that we Southerners are ahead of our Northern brethren; but even we bear traces of two hundred years in the forest. We do speak; there is much monologuing, and I perform my share of it; but as for talking, quick interchange of ideas, fair give and take, we are on a par with Cooper's noble savage. Let me hope that I don't wound your patriotism. I admit that I have an immoral lack of prejudices. But I want to know if you don't find life here just a little dull?"

"Why the deuce don't you go to work, then?" burst out Peyton Beaumont. "Here you two fellows are as highly educated as money can make you. You are a lawyer, graduated at Berlin. Vincent is a doctor, graduated at Paris. And yet you do nothing; never either of you had a case; don't want one."

"Ah, work! that is dull too," admitted the smiling, imperturbable Poinsett. "Idleness is dull; but work is duller. I confess that it is a sad fact, and painful to me to consider it. So let us change the subject. Most noble Vincent, you seem to be in the doldrums this morning."

"He has an affair on his hands," muttered the father of the family.

"Ah!" said Poinsett, with a slight elevation of the eyebrows, comprehending perfectly that a duel was alluded to.

"Another McAlister impertinence," pursued Mr. Beaumont, and proceeded to tell the story with great savageness.

"Wallace!" exclaimed Poinsett, "I confess that I am the least bit surprised. I thought Wallace an amiable, soporific creature like myself. But the spirit of the breed — the oversoul of the McAlisters — is too much for his individuality. We are drops in a river. I shall fight, too, some day, though I don't at all crave it. Vincent, if I can do anything for you, I am entirely at your service."

Vincent's smile was noticeably satirical. He was disagreeably amused with Poinsett's coolness over another's duel. And he did not believe that Poinsett could be easily got to fight.

"I suppose that Bent Armitage will do all that is necessary," he said.

"Let us hope that the loading of the pistols will be all that is necessary," replied Poinsett. "Let us hope that Wally will bend his stiff knees, and confess that we march at the head of civilization."

"By heavens, I want him shot," broke in Beaumont the elder. "I can't understand you young fellows, with your soft notions. I belong to the old sort. There used to be shooting in my day. Here is the most unprovoked and brutal outrage that I ever heard of. This beast calls a Beaumont no gentleman. And here you hope there'll be an apology, and that end it. I want Vincent to hit him. I want the fellow shelved; I don't care if he's killed; by heavens, I don't."

Mr. Beaumont was in a fit state to break glasses and overturn the table. His black eyes were bloodshot; his bushy eyebrows were dancing and pointing as if they were going through smallsword exercise; there was a dull flame of blood all over his dark cheeks and yellowish mottled forehead. Vincent, the medical graduate of Paris, surveyed his father through half-shut eyes, and thought out the diagnosis, "Temporarily insane." There was no audible response to the senior's good old-fashioned Beaumont burst of rage.

After some minutes of silence, during which Poinsett smilingly poured himself a second cup of coffee (holding that he could do it better than any waiter), the father recovered his composure somewhat, and added gravely: "Of course this is a serious matter. I hope, trust, and believe that Vincent will receive no harm. If he does" (here his eyebrows bristled again), "I shall take the field myself."

"We will see," smiled Poinsett. "My impression is that my turn comes in somewhere."

Here Cato, head waiter as well as valet, put in his oar.

"That's so Mars Poinsett. We all has our turn, fightin' these yere McAlisters."

"Why, what have you been at, Cato?" asked the young man. "Challenging the Judge? Or pulling the wool of his old mauma?"

"No, sah. Yah, yah, I don' go roun' challengin' white folks; knows my business better. An' when I pulls wool, I pulls he wool. Jes had a tackle yesterday with Matt McAlister, the Judge's ole man that waits on him. Matt he sets out, 'cause he's yaller, an' comes from Virginny, that he's better than we is, we Souf Carliny niggahs. So every time I sees him I sasses him. Yesr mornin', I meets him down to the sto' — Mars Bill Wilkins's sto', don' ye know? — kinder lookin' roun' for bar'l o' flour. 'So,' says I, 'Boss,' says I, 'how is things up to your ole shanty?' He's a kinder gray ole fellow, don' ye know? puttin' on airs like he was Noah, an' treatin' everybody like they's childern, rollin' his eyes out o' the corners kinder, an' crossin' his arms jes as the Judge does. So he looked at me, an', says he, 'Boy, who is you?' Says I, 'I'm Cato Beaumont.' So says he, 'I thought it mought be some o' that breedin'.' Says I, 'I was jes happenin' down here to teach you your manners.' So says he, 'Boy, my manners was learned befo' you ever heerd they was sech things.' Then I kinder tripped him, an' he kinder tripped me, an' then I squared off and fotched back, an' says I —"

"Why didn't you hit him?" roared the Hon. Mr. Beaumont, who had been listening with great interest. "What did you say another word for?"

"I was jes gwine to tell you what I said," returned Cato. "But now, 'fore gracious, you done made me forget it. I said a heap to him."

"And so there wasn't any fight after all," inferred the smiling Poinsett. "And nobody got hurt. Heaven favors the brave."

"It didn't 'zactly come to a wrastle," confessed Cato. "But I 'specs it would, for I was gittin' powerful mad: only jes as I was thinkin' o' gwine at him one o' Mars Wilkins's clerks come out, an' says he, 'Boys don' make so much noise'; an' so I quit."

Beaumont senior gave forth a mild growl of disapprobation, as deeply mellow as the anger of waters in caves of the sea-shore. "Cowardly niggers," was one sound which came from him; and yet, although he despised negroes for being cowardly, he did not blame them for it; he knew that chivalry, prowess, and the like were properly the business of white people.

Half an hour after breakfast pistol-shots resounded from an oak grove in the rear of the mansion. Vincent was practising on a board five feet eight inches high planted in the ground, hitting the upper part of it with fascinating accuracy. "Getting my hand in," he remarked to his father when the latter came out to look on; and presently the elder gentleman became interested, and made a few exemplary shots himself. The two men were in the midst of this cheering recreation when Cato came running upon them with frantic gestures and a yell of "Mars Peyt! Stage come! Miss Kate come!"

"What's that, you rascal?" roared Beaumont, his grim face suddenly transformed into the likeness of something half angelic, so honest and pure and fervent was its joy. Plunging a hairy hand into his pocket, he drew out a grip of coins, threw them at the negro, and set forth on a run which knocked him out of his wind in twenty paces. Then he halted, and shouted back, "Vincent, hide those pistols. Cato, if you say a word about this business, I'll skin you."

Then away again, on a plethoric canter, to meet his youngest daughter, his darling.

In the rear piazza of the house a tall and lovely girl rushed into his arms with a cry of "Father!" to which he responded with a sound much like a sob of gladness. There were tears of joy shed by somebody; it was impossible to say whether they came from Kate's eyes or from her parent's; but they were dried between their nestling, caressing cheeks.

"Why, Kate! what a woman you are!" exclaimed Beaumont, holding her back at arm's length to worship her.

Vincent and Poinsett already stood by waiting their turns for an embrace. It was clear enough that, whatever defects there might be in this Beaumont breed, the lack of family feeling was not one of them.

Meantime Mrs. Chester and Tom were coming through the house, the former chattering steadily in a high, joyful soprano, and the latter roaring his lion-cub content in slangy exclamations.

The scene contrasted with the pistol practice of the oak grove somewhat as paradise contrasts with the inferno.

Of the paradise and the inferno, which is to win?

CHAPTER 10

 "Why didn't you write that you had reached Charleston?" demanded Mr. Beaumont, when the first tornado of greeting had blown over. "I have been very anxious for the last few days," added this affectionate old gladiator.

"Write? Did write," answered Tom. "Sent off a three-decker of a letter. You'll get it in an hour or so. Came up in the same train with us probably. The mail service isn't worth a curse. But hain't you got your papers? So you don't know anything about the shipwreck? Shipwreck! Yes. Do you think I'd come home in Charleston store-clothes if I hadn't been shipwrecked? Trunks and steamer gone to the bottom of What's-his-name's locker."

And then came the story, Mrs. Chester and Tom telling it at once, the former in a steady gush of keen treble, and the latter in boisterous ejaculatory barytone. We will pass over this two-horse narrative, and come promptly to the amazement of Mr. Peyton Beaumont when he learned that there had been a McAlister on board the *Mersey*, breaking bread daily with his sister and his children.

"What the — Why the —" he commenced and recommenced. Then, like a pistol-shot, "How did he behave himself?"

His eyes began to flame and his phalanxes of eyebrows to bring down their pikes, in suspicion of some insult which he would be called upon to avenge.

"Didn't know him at first," explained Tom. "Didn't find him out till — till I got ashore. Played possum. Incognito."

"Incognito!" trumpeted Mr. Beaumont. "The scoundrel!"

"Incognito!" repeated Vincent and Poinsett, exchanging a look which also said, "The scoundrel!"

Kate flushed deeply; of course she remembered the offer of marriage and the salvation from death; but either she did not think it wise at that moment to speak in the young man's defence, or she could not muster the courage.

"And he dared to make your acquaintance under his incognito!" clarioned away the senior Beaumont. "I never heard of such infamous trickery, never! It's the most outrageous insult that ever our family was subjected to. By heavens, I am stupefied. I can't believe it. And yet it is so like a McAlister. A mean, sneaking, underhanded lot. Possums! Foxes! Ca-ts!" This last word in a hiss and with a bristling worthy of the most belligerent of old Toms.

"I say," began Tom. Then he turned to the two women. "Now look here. You two ought to tell how the thing went. It'll come best from a lady," explained Tom, who did not think that a male Beaumont ought to be a peacemaker, not at least in a matter of McAlisters.

"It certainly was very singular conduct," twittered Mrs. Chester. "I was excessively indignant when I first discovered the mystery. But —"

"But what?" broke in Beaumont senior. "What the d — dickens are you driving at?"

Kate, who was sitting on a sofa beside her father, slipped her hand around his neck, pulled his red-granite cheek toward her and kissed it. She remembered what a pet she had been in her childhood, and she had perceived within the last few minutes that she was a pet still, and she felt now that it was time to begin to use her power. Beaumont fondled her with his mighty arm, and uttered a chastened, not unmelodious growl like that of a panther at the approach of his favorite keeper.

"But the truth is," continued Mrs. Chester, "it is a very strange story, I am aware. It seems incredible, in one of that family. But I really believe the young man had good motives."

The truth further is, that Mrs. Chester had had a few pleasant words of explanation and of parting with "the young man" in the hall of the Charleston Hotel. Tom had not called on Frank McAlister; no, Tom could not shoulder the responsibility of such a move as that; he must leave the whole matter to the elders of his tribe. "Look here, now," he had said to Major Lawson, when the latter suggested the visit; "I ain't ungrateful to the chap for saving my sister's life; but then you know the bloody old row; he's a McAlister, you see." And then the Major had replied: "My de-ar young fellow, you are, I have no doubt, perfectly judicious; see your excel-lent father first."

But woman may do what man must not. Mrs. Chester, bewildered by some blarney of the Major's (who had told her that Frank raved — "Yes, my dear madam, fairly raved" — about her) had seized an opportunity to meet the handsome youngster in one of the passages. There he had explained the motives of his incognito, expressed his respect for the Beaumont name, and sagaciously added some incense for herself. Of course, too, he was wise enough not to say a word about his offer to her niece. The result of this conversation, and of some judicious remarks from Kate on the way up to Hartland, was that Mrs. Chester (very weak on the subject of young men, remember) was half inclined to forget the family feud and quite willing to say a good word for Frank McAlister.

"I at least acquit him of bad motives," she spunkily added, reddening under her brother's glare of angry amazement.

"Just so," put in Tom. "The chap did play possum, but I don't believe he meant any harm. Said he wanted to keep out of a quarrel, and I feel bound to believe him."

"Then he must be a coward," scoffed Beaumont senior.

"Scarcely," said Tom. "Didn't show that style. Tell him about it, aunt, or sis, one of you."

"Papa, he saved my life," whispered Kate, her voice failing at thought of that awful moment. "I went ten feet under water."

Her father caught her as if he himself were rescuing her from death.

"You went — ten feet — under water!" he gasped. And he looked for a moment as if he could cry ten feet of water at the thought of her danger and deliverance.

"And *he* saved her, after I'd lost her," added Tom, walking up to Kate and kissing her. "I tell you, I ain't a going to be very hard on a fellow that did that. He went clean under, slap into the middle of the ocean, right off the stern of the wreck."

"By heavens!" uttered Mr. Beaumont. It was almost a groan; his solid old heart was throbbing unusually; he felt as if he were going to have a stroke of some sort. Presently he looked up, his swarthy-red forehead wrinkled all over with perplexity, and gave Vincent a stare which said, "How about that duel?"

The young man's habitual smile of self-sufficiency and satire was gone. Respectably affected for the moment, he earnestly wished that the difficulty with Wallace had not happened, and queried whether he were not bound, as a gentleman, to fire in the air.

"But what is your opinion about this business, Kate?" asked Poinsett. "You have said nothing."

The girl threw off her beautiful timidity, and spoke out with beautiful firmness: —

"Of course, I am under the greatest obligations to Mr. McAlister. And, even if I were not, I should have nothing to say against him. I don't know whether he did right or not in concealing his name —"

"He didn't," Mr. Beaumont could not help muttering, while Vincent and Poinsett corroboratingly shook their chivalrous heads.

"But that began with an accident," continued Kate. "The captain made a mistake: he thought McAlister was McMaster; and then *he* let it go so. He said that he did it for the sake of peace; and I believe him. He seemed to be a gentleman. I believe every word he said."

"So do I," added Mrs. Chester, remembering how tall he was, and what a fine complexion he had.

"And I," confirmed Tom, rather hesitatingly, as if it were not quite the correct thing for a Beaumont to say.

"We are in what vulgar people call a fix," laughed that easy old shoe of a Poinsett. "My dear little Kate," playing with her chestnut ringlets, "if he hadn't saved you, we should have gone mad, every soul of us. No further use for our sanity. But since he has saved you, we are in sloughs of perplexity. My respected father and my much-esteemed brothers (descendants of the De Beaumonts of Yvetot and other places), we are threatened with the loss of our family institution, our race palladium. The feud with the McAlisters has been to us more than our coat of arms. I may almost call it the Beaumont established religion. It is impossible to conceal the fact that it has received a rude shock. Are we to drop away from the creed of our forefathers? Are we to have no faith? A merely human mind — such as I grieve to say mine is — recoils at the prospect."

Vincent, somewhat recovered from his first emotion, gazed through half-shut eyes at the joker, and inclined once more to fight his duel seriously. Beaumont senior got up, strode like a lion about the room, glared once or twice at Poinsett, and growled, "This is jesting, sir, on a very serious matter."

"I understand my brother," struck in Kate, with a clear, sweet, firm note, which sounded like a challenge from a cherub's clarion, if cherubs carry such an article. "Why shouldn't the quarrel end?"

All the men stared. Even Poinsett had not meant half so much. The words were audacious beyond any remembered standard of comparison. Words of such import had perhaps never before been uttered in the family.

Mr. Beaumont halted abruptly, and gave the girl a look of astonishment and inquiry which seemed to ask, "Have we a queen over us?"

Poinsett made a gesture of taking off a hat, and whispered smilingly, "Portia!"

Mrs. Chester rustled her skirts in perplexity, and Tom's eyes asked counsel of his father.

"My dear Kate, don't be flustered," said Poinsett, seeing that the child looked frightened at the sensation she had created. "What you have said was a perfectly natural thing to say, and, from the usual human point of view, a perfectly rational one. At the same time I suspect that we Beaumonts, not being of the ordinary human mould, are not fitted to discuss such a proposition without time for meditation. I apprehend that we had better lay it aside until our eyes have somewhat recovered from the first dazzle. Suppose you proceed, some one of you, or all three of you, with the shipwreck."

The counsel seemed to suit the feelings of every one. Mr. Beaumont stopped his walk, nestled down again by his daughter's side, and listened quietly to the threefold narrative. Not another word concerning the feud was said during the interview.

But, two hours later, the story of the duel got wind among the new-comers. Mrs. Chester, seated in her room amid old dresses which it was now necessary to make over listened to a stream of respectable gossip from her ancient maid and foster-sister, Miriam, a tall, dignified, and middle-aged negress, leaner and graver than is usual with her species.

"Laws, Miss Marian!" said Miriam, using the girlish title which she had always given to her born mistress. "Skacely a thing to wear! And all them trunks full of beautiful things gone to the bottom of the sea! Well, honey, it's a warnin' of the Lord's not to set our hearts on the vanities of this world. We oughter feel mighty grateful to him when he takes the trouble to warn us. The blessed Lord he's been powerful good to ye, Miss Marian. Mustn't forgit he's saved yer life, honey. Gin ye one more chance to set yer face straight for his city. An' perhaps he had other plans, too. Perhaps he saw ye was comin' to a time when ye wouldn't be able to wear the fine fixin's. We'se no idea gin-lly, how keerfully the Lord looks after us."

"What do you mean, Miriam?" demanded Mrs. Chester, pettishly. "Do you mean to say I'm getting old? I don't see it."

"Laws, honey, you's young enough. Never see no lady hold out better'n you do. Must say it: that's a fact. But I'se talkin' of somethin' more solemn than growin' old. You may be called on fo' long, if the Lord don't help in his mighty mercy, to put on mournin'."

"Who's sick?" demanded Mrs. Chester, more curious than anxious.

"It's Mars Vincent is sick. He's sick with sin an' wrath an' anger. Perhaps he's sick unto death. They's gwine to be another duel, Miss Marian."

Mrs. Chester looked up from her old dresses; duels had always been very interesting to her. She had been the cause of two, and they were pleasant remembrances. She liked to hear of such things and talk of them, as much as that non-combatant hero-worshipper, Major Lawson.

"They've been tryin' to keep it shet from you an' Miss Katy," continued Miriam. "Mars Vincent tole Cato he'd boot him, if he let on. But I'm gwine to tell of it, an' I'm gwine to bear my witness agin it. It's Satan's works, this yere duelling is, an' I'm gwine to say so. I don't care who hears me. Mars Vincent may boot me if he likes, I ain't afeard of bootin'."

"Vincent sha'n't hurt *you*," declared Mrs. Chester, with that feeling of loyalty towards an adherent which made a Southerner of old days fight for his slave, and makes a Southerner of these days fight for his dog.

"That's you, Miss Marian. I know'd you'd say jest that. But you needn't git mad on my 'count. The Lord he'll take care of me. Bless your soul, he allays does. But about this duelling. It's Satan's works, as I'se sayin' ever sence the Lord had mercy on me, though you don't think so. You has white folkses notions, all for fightin' an' shootin'. It's Satan's works, an' I've prayed agin it; prayed many a time there might never be another duel in this fam'ly; prayed for this poor blood-stained fam'ly, all covered with blood an' wounds; duels on duels an' allays duels, ever sence I can 'member; never hear of no sech folks for it. But 'pears like Satan's got the upper hands of my prayers, an' here's Mars Vincent led away by him, prehaps to his own destruction."

"But who is it with?" demanded Mrs. Chester, vastly more interested in the news than in the sermonizing which accompanied it.

"With Wally McAlister, that other poo' fightin' creetur, the Lord have mercy on his soul!"

"McAlister!" exclaimed Mrs. Chester, in sudden excitement, not at all pleasurable.

"Yes. Some mis'able chipper at the Presbyterian fair, not enough for two goslins to hiss about. Mars Vincent he kinder sassed Wally, an' then Wally he kinder sassed Mars Vincent, and now Bent Armitage he's been over with the challenge, an' it's to be some time this week. An' jes's likely 's not one o' them poo' silly creeturs 'll be standin' befo' the bar of God befo' 'nother Sunday comes roun'. Won't be able to call the Judge out there, if the judgment don't suit him."

Mrs. Chester had dropped her dresses. She had forgotten her usual gossiping interest in duels. She was leaning back in her arm-chair, reflecting with a seriousness which wrinkled her forehead more than she would have liked, had she seen it.

"Miriam, we must try to stop this," was her conclusion.

"Why, bless your darlin' heart!" burst out the negress. "Why, laws bless you, honey! Has the blessed Lord touched your sperit at last? Never heered you say that sort o' thing befo', never. Stop it? Why, we'll try, honey, hopin' the Lord 'll help us. But how's we gwine to work? Who's we to go at?"

"Go and call Miss Kate," ordered Mrs. Chester.

"Miss Katy? That poor, dear, little thing? Gwine to tell her about it, an' she jes come home this very day?"

"Go and call her," repeated Mrs. Chester, who cared little for any one's feelings, so that she compassed her ends.

Kate came in, hair down and shoulders bare, more charming than usual. Elderly Miriam devoured her with her eyes, but kept a discreet silence as to her loveliness, remembering "Miss Marian's" jealous spirit. The story of the duel was told.

"Oh dear!" was the brief utterance of Kate's vast sorrow and despair, as she seated herself on a stool and clutched her hands over her knees.

"Laws bless you, chile!" was the answering groan of Miriam. "I didn' want Miss Marian to go for to tell you. The Lord help this poo' fam'ly! Allays in trouble!"

"But do you think he'll be shot?" asked Kate.

"What, Mars Vincent? Dear me, chile, he may be. He's been shot twice."

"But can't it be stopped?"

"That is what I called you in for," said Mrs. Chester. "I don't believe this quarrel rests upon anything very important. I think it ought to be stopped. I do, indeed, Beaumont as I am, and Beaumont all over. But who's to stop it? What can *you* do?"

"Can't my grandfather do something?" suggested the girl.

"The very man!" shouted and laughed Miriam, jumping up from her squatting posture on the floor and raising her arms as if in benediction. "Jes the very man. Send over for Colonel Kershaw. Laws me, when I'se in trouble, I goes first to the Lord, an' he gen'rally sends me to Colonel Kershaw. Why didn' I ever think of him befo'? Specs I'se gittin old an' foolish."

"Yes, your grandfather will come into play very nicely," said Mrs. Chester, who did not fancy the old gentleman overmuch, principally because she was somewhat in awe of him.

"I'll cut right out an' start off a nigger after him," volunteered Miriam. "You, Miss Katy, you jes write him a little letter, askin' him to come right away to see you, jes saved from shipwreck, you know. Tell him not to fail on no account; you wants to see him powerful, this very day."

In ten minutes a mounted negro was galloping over the few miles of country which separated the Beaumont from the Kershaw plantation. Late in the afternoon the Colonel arrived, bringing with him our gracious friend, Major Lawson.

Colonel John Kershaw was one of those noble souls who look all their nobility. In his youth he had been a very handsome man, and at eighty he was venerably beautiful. His massive aquiline face, strangely wrinkled into deep furrows which were almost folds, was a sublime composition of dignity, serenity, and benevolence. You would have been tempted to say that a great sculptor could not have imagined anything better suited to typify an intelligent, good, and grand old age. Indeed, this head had been wrought patiently with both great strokes and tender touches by the mightiest of all sculptors. Perhaps no man ever looked upon it without feeling that it called for entire confidence and respect. Its moral grandeur of expression was heightened by the crown of nearly snow-white, though still abundant hair which rose from the deeply channelled forehead, and swept down over the coat collar.

Colonel Kershaw's countenance perfectly expressed his character. He was one of those simple, pure, honorable, sensible country gentlemen (of whom one meets more perhaps in our Southern States than in most other portions of this planet) who strike one as having a reserve of moral and intellectual power too great for their chances of action, and who lead one to trust that Washingtons will still be forthcoming when their country needs. For the readers of this story it is perhaps a sufficient proof of the weight and humanity of his influence, that, since his daughter had married a Beaumont, there had been only two duels between that race and the McAlisters, although there had been endless political differences and other bickerings. In doing thus much towards quelling the family feud, it was generally acknowledged that Colonel Kershaw had done wonders.

"How do you do, Beaumont?" he said in a deep, tremulous, mellow voice. "I have come to stay a day or so with you, and I knew you would be glad to see Lawson, who had just arrived to cheer me up. So Mrs. Chester, and Kate, and Tom have got home? Where are the dear people?"

There was a little scream and rustle behind him; it was the cry and the approach of girlish love. The next moment Kate, always a worshipper of her grandfather and still fanatical in the old faith, was in his arms.

"Why, my dear little child!" said the old man. "Why, my grand young lady!" he added, setting her back to get a fair view of her. "Ah, I never shall hold you in my lap again," he added, realizing that one more of the joys of life was gone. "Shall I? shall I?" he laughed when she told him that he would.

Next Major Lawson seized the girl, clinging to and patting her hand and staring at her face and smiling. "Beautiful creature!" he murmured. "Beautiful creature!" he whispered. "Beau-ti-ful creature!" he sighed into silence. But he was in earnest, not flattering purposely nor even consciously, being quite out of himself and quite sincere. "How like your mother!" he continued to flute. "Dear me, how like your grandfather! Colonel, your image! Your continuator. All your virtues and more than your graces!"

Notwithstanding the differences of sex and years, the resemblance between the two faces was indeed remarkable. Looking at the old man, you could see where the girl got her almost sublime expression of dignity, purity, and sweetness.

"Oh, go long, she's all Kershaw," soliloquized black Miriam, her arms akimbo, worshipping the pair. "An' her mother was, too, poor thing! Though how she could marry sech a tearer as Mars Peyt, beats me. Wal, women is women, an' they's most all fools, specially when it comes to marryin'. I s'pose it's for some wonderful good end, or the Lord he wouldn' make 'em so."

In short, the Colonel had an ovation from the whole household, male and female, white, black, and yellow. Beaumont senior was almost petulant with jealousy, as he often had been before on such occasions; for he, too, domineering and passionate as he was, desired to be worshipped, especially by his youngest daughter.

Presently the visitors were led away by grinning negroes to their rooms over the columned veranda, which ran along the whole front of the mansion. Half an hour later, when the Colonel had washed off the dust of travel and combed his noble mane of silver, there was a little tap at his door and a silvery call, "Grandpapa."

The old man started with pleasure; he had been wondering whether she would come to him; he had thought of it several times.

"Why, run in, my darling!" he laughed, opening the door for her, and leading her proudly to a chair.

"Do you want anything?" she asked. "I am housekeeper," she added with a smile, shaking a bunch of keys.

"And Mrs. Chester? I hope she is not discontented."

"Papa settled the thing himself. You know papa. But I don't think aunt cares for the trouble. So we are all pleased. But Oh, I am so delighted to see you! And you haven't changed; you are so like yourself. Isn't it nice that grandpapas don't grow? I am going to be silly with you; I am going to behave very little. You make me feel just like a child again. I want to sit in your lap as I used to do. Just this once, at any rate."

She installed herself on her throne, slipped a hand over his shoulder and smiled in his face.

"Isn't it doleful for you to live all alone? I wish our houses could be moved alongside each other. I hate to think of you all alone."

"I have my land and my people to take care of, dear. The time passes. Perhaps I am all the more fond of my friends for being a little lonely. Lawson was really very kind to come and see me. I was quite obliged to him."

"Grandpapa, I am going to trouble you," was the girl's next speech. Her face suddenly lost the petting, gleeful, childlike expression which had shone from it hitherto. It assumed womanliness; it ripened at once into a grave maturity; it was dignified, anxious, and yet remained beautiful; perhaps it was even more lovely than before.

"It is too bad in me, but I must worry you," she went on. "There are very serious matters passing here. There is to be a duel, grandpapa."

"A duel!" he repeated, his noble old physiognomy becoming still nobler with regret.

"It is a quarrel between Vincent and Wallace McAlister."

"The old story," murmured the Colonel, shaking his head at bloody reminiscences. "My child, tell me all you know about it. We may be able to prevent it."

"But first I must tell you something else," she said, blushing slightly. "There are special reasons why a duel between the families should not happen now. It would be, I think, a great scandal."

Then she hurried through the story of her salvation from death by Frank McAlister.

"My dear, Lawson told me this," said the Colonel. "Yes, as you think, a duel would be a scandal. It would be not only a crime, but a shame. I will see your brother. I will go at once."

"Oh, thank you! You will succeed," cried Kate, her face flushing with hope.

"Let us hope so. But I may not. This old, old quarrel!"

CHAPTER 11

 With slow, heavy steps Colonel Kershaw descended the stairs, seeking for some one who would aid him in preventing the duel.

Meeting the head of the family, he took his arm, led him out upon the lawn in front of the house, and asked, "Beaumont, when is this affair between Vincent and Wallace McAlister to come off?"

"Oh, so you have heard of it!" stared Beaumont. "I am sorry. Come off? I understand it is to be day after to-morrow."

"It is a very unfortunate business, Beaumont. Under the circumstances, doubly unfortunate. Only a few days ago Frank McAlister saved Kate's life. And now Frank's brother and Kate's brother are to shoot each other."

"Yes, by heavens it is unfortunate!" admitted Beaumont with loud candor, very creditable to him. "It's an ugly piece of business, under the circumstances. It is, by heavens, the awkwardest thing in my experience. I wish it hadn't happened. I wish — under the circumstances, you understand — that Vincent was honorably out of it. That insolent, boorish McAlister ought to apologize. A more villainous, brutal insult I never heard of. Calling a Beaumont no gentleman! Good heavens!" Here his eyebrows bristled, and he breathed short and hard with rage. "But, under the circumstances, I would say take his apology," he resumed. "Yes, Colonel, I've come to that. I have, indeed."

And Mr. Beaumont seemed to think he had come a long way in the path of peace and good-will toward men.

"But, if no apology arrives, then what?" gravely inquired the octogenarian.

"Why then, I don't see — what *can* Vincent do? He's pinned. No getting out of it. Must go out. Good heavens! *I* don't want him to fight. But a gentleman can't accept such language. You know as well as I do, Colonel, that he can't."

"Yet under the circumstances," persisted Kershaw, not domineeringly, but meditatively.

"Yes, I know, — the circumstances," almost groaned Beaumont. "We *are* under obligations to those people. First time, by heavens! But so it is. And, as I said, I'd like to have the thing settled, of course honorably."

He was not a little in awe of the old gentleman. Kershaw had long ago fought duels, and moreover, he had served gallantly in the war of 1812; thus he was a *chevalier sans reproche* in the eyes of fighting men, and even Beaumonts must respect his record. Such a gentleman, too; he could no more counsel an unworthy deed than he could do it; it was not supposed that he could so much as conceive of anything dishonorable. And here he was meditating, how to stop the duel, and so keeping his son-in-law on the anxious seat. At last came his decision, uttered in the impressive tones of old age, — tones which gave it the weight of an oracle.

"I think, Beaumont, that, considering what we owe to the McAlisters, Vincent might honorably withdraw the challenge, assigning our obligation as the cause of the withdrawal."

"You don't mean it!" gasped Beaumont. "Withdraw the challenge! Why, Colonel, — why, good heavens!"

All his respect for the old man (and he did respect him above any other being that he knew) could hardly keep him from exploding with anger.

"That is my advice," proceeded Kershaw, gently. "You know who I am and what my opinion is worth. I solemnly believe that, in withdrawing the challenge on that ground, Vincent would not only do a gentlemanly thing, but would do the very thing that a gentleman in his position should do."

Beaumont was cowed by this great authority, and, after some further ejaculations, lapsed into perplexed silence.

"Are you willing, my dear Beaumont, that I should advise Vincent to this step?" inquired the Colonel.

"Well, well, have it your own way," returned the other, a little impatiently. "You ought to know what is right; of course you do know. I put the whole matter in your hands. You have my consent, if you can get Vincent's. But for God's sake, Colonel, remember that the honor of the family is in your hands."

He writhed as if he were handing over his whole fortune to be the gage of some more than doubtful speculation.

"If the step is taken, I will make it known that it is taken by my advice," promised Kershaw.

"Ah!" breathed Beaumont, much relieved.

"Who is Vincent's second?" asked the Colonel.

"Bentley Armitage. And there — speak of the Devil, you know — there he comes. Well now, you won't mind my quitting you; you won't take it hard, Kershaw? I don't object to your proposition; but I don't want to be responsible for it."

"I thank you, Beaumont, for letting me assume the responsibility."

And so they parted, the Honorable dodging shamefacedly into the house, and the Colonel advancing to meet Armitage.

"Colonel, good evening," was the young man's easy salute. "Glad to see you looking so hearty, sir."

"You are well, I hope, sir?" bowed Kershaw. "And your brother and his wife?"

"All peart, I thank you. Never better."

Bentley was a tall young man, rather too slender to be well built, with a swinging, free-and-easy carriage. He had a round face, a moderately dark complexion, a deep and healthy color, coarse and long chestnut hair, and a small curling mustache. The smile with which he spoke was a very curious one, being marked by a drawing up of the right corner of his mouth into the cheek, which gave it a quizzical expression. There was something odd, something provincial, or one might say old-fashioned, in his tone of voice and pronunciation; but you were disposed to infer from his manner that this peculiarity was the result of an affectation, rather than of a lack of habit of good society. It was evident enough that he used such rural terms as "peart" and "hearty" in the way of slang.

"Excuse me, Mr. Armitage, for being direct with you," said Kershaw. "I understand that you are the second of Vincent in this affair with Wallace McAlister."

"Just so, Colonel," replied Bent, striding along beside the old man, and speaking as composedly as if it were a question of possum-hunting. His gait, by the way, was singular, his right foot coming down at every step with a slap, as if it were an ill-hung wooden one. This was the result of a shot received in a duel (he generally spoke of it as his snake-bite), which had caused a partial paralysis of the lifting muscle.

Kershaw now repeated what he had said to Beaumont, advising and urging that Vincent should withdraw his challenge.

"I don't think that cock would fight, Colonel," coolly judged Bentley. "I allow due weight to the motive which you suggest. It is a hefty one. But withdrawing a challenge, without a previous withdrawal of the affront, is a step which has no sufficing precedent, at least so far as I know. I presume that, if it were left to my principal, he would not consent to it."

"I am speaking with the knowledge of Mr. Beaumont senior," continues the patient and persevering peacemaker. "Have you any objection to my discussing this point with Vincent in your presence?"

"Not the slightest, Colonel. Walk this way. We'll nose him out in the oak grove, I reckon. You see, Colonel, aside from other considerations, this move might be taken advantage of by the McAlisters. They might do bales of bragging over it. Just imagine old Antichrist blowing his trumpet."

"Who?" inquired the elder, with a puzzled and rather shocked stare.

"I beg your pardon. I mean Judge McAlister. It's a poor joke which pleases our friend, Mr. Beaumont. — It's a compliment to your mas'r, anyway," he added with a smile, addressing Miriam, who was just then passing the couple.

"Ah, Mars Bent!" replied the pious negress. "You bes' quit that kind o' jokin' befo' you gits into t'other world. You may laugh on t'other side o' your mouf yet, Mars Bent."

Bentley took his reproof good-humoredly, curling up his odd smile into the dimple of his right cheek, and nodding pleasantly to Miriam.

"There's Vincent," was his next remark. "Hul-loo, there! Hold your horses. — Colonel, excuse me for yelling. My clapper doesn't work well to-day. I mean my right foot; it flops more than usual. I call it my clapper, and the other one my clipper."

"Can't that trouble be cured?" inquired Kershaw, with honest interest.

"Don't suppose it. In fact, know it can't. I am doctor enough to know that."

Yes, Bentley was a physician; had graduated at Philadelphia. By the way, it is perfectly amazing how many medical gentlemen there are in the South. A literary friend tells me that, during a six months' experience among the smaller towns and ruder taverns of the slave States, he slept with nearly a hundred doctors. Concerning Bentley it is almost needless to add, that, being a planter of considerable means, he never prescribed, except for his own negroes.

"I should be very glad to obtain your influence on the side of peace in this affair," continued Kershaw. "We are both connections of the family."

"Exactly, Colonel," answered Bentley, remembering with the utmost *nonchalance* that his brother Randolph was the husband of Peyton Beaumont's eldest daughter. "Well, I will say this much, that I've no objection to any course that my principal will accept."

Half displeased with this cool youngster, Kershaw pushed on in thoughtful silence, and soon met Vincent.

"A proposition," was Bentley's brief introduction to the matter in hand. "The Colonel has something to suggest which I approve of his suggesting."

Vincent, his habitual ironical smile dismissed for the present, bowed respectfully, and listened without a word until the old man had stated his proposition. When he spoke it was with a perfectly calm demeanor and a bland finish of intonation.

"It appears to me that I am called upon to subordinate myself too entirely to the — we will say duties of the family. After I have obtained my personal reparation from Mr. Wallace McAlister, I am willing to enter into an expression of our common obligation to Mr. Frank McAlister. What does my second think?"

"Just to oblige the Colonel," explained Bentley, "I agree to throw the affair entirely out of my hands, and replace it entirely in yours.

That is, with your permission, you understand. So why not play your own cards, Vincent?"

"Come into the house, gentlemen," begged the Colonel.

"Why so?" asked Vincent.

"The affair *is* a family affair. I must beg leave to insist upon that view of it. It is so complicated with family obligations and proprieties, that it cannot be treated separately. Such is my opinion and such will be public opinion. Let me beg of you to discuss it in family council. I ask this as a personal favor. I ask it as a great favor."

If Kershaw's request was a strange one, and if he supported it by neither precedent nor sufficient argument, it must be remembered that he was very old and very good, and was, in short, the most venerable being whom these two young men knew. After a brief hesitation, Vincent nodded an unwilling assent, and the three walked back to the house. Passing the door of the dining-room, Bentley Armitage, who was lagging a little behind the others because of his "snake-bite," was arrested by a vision. Kate was looking out upon him, beautiful enough to fascinate him and eager enough to flatter him.

"Mr. Armitage," she called, — in her anxiety it was a whisper, — an unmeant, but intoxicating compliment.

"Miss Beaumont." And Bentley bowed in the stiff way common to men with "game legs." "My relative, I venture to put it. I haven't had the pleasure of meeting you before in five years."

"Yes, and I have grown and all that," replied Kate, trying to laugh and look cordial for she was eager to please him.

"Mr. Armitage, after five years, the first thing is that I want a favor of you."

"To hear is to obey," said Bentley, quoting from the "Arabian Nights," — favorite reading of his.

Desperation made Kate eager, audacious, and straightforward.

"I know all about this duel," she went on. "I don't know whether you consider it proper for me to talk about it. But I must. Do you think, Mr. Armitage, that I like to come home and find my brother on the point of risking his life?"

Bentley wanted to say that he was not responsible for the duel, but he did not feel that the code of honor justified him in such a speech.

"It wouldn't be natural," he admitted. "I don't suppose you do like it. Very sorry for the whole affair."

"It makes me miserable." (Here there was a quiver of the mouth which moved Bentley to his fingers' ends.) "If you can say anything, — and I am sure you can say *something*, — do say it. Do give me your help to make peace. I am sure you can find a word to say, I don't know what. You will oblige me so much. You will oblige my grandfather. You will do right. I know it must be right to stop this duel. Won't you, Mr. Armitage, can't you, do me this great favor?"

There was no resistance possible. There was a hand laid upon Bentley Armitage stronger than the code *duello*. He promised that he would throw his influence — or, as he slangily phrased it, drop his little ballot — on the side of peace. Kate gave him a smile which suggested a better world, and sent him on his way a softer-hearted man than he had ever been before.

A few minutes later there was what might be called a family parliament in the long parlor. Mr. Beaumont, his three sons, Colonel Kershaw, and Bent Armitage sat as gravely as Indian sachems in a council.

"We ought to have calumets and wampum belts," whispered Bentley to Tom; but the youngster, reverent of the code *duello* and of the family honor, declined to smile.

"Gentlemen, this is an extraordinary occasion," said Colonel Kershaw, rising as if to address the United States Senate.

"It is, indeed," burst out Vincent, unable to control the excitability of his race. "I believe I am the first gentleman who ever had his family called in to prevent him from demanding reparation for an insult. It is a most extraordinary and embarrassing situation."

"You're right, old fellow," declared Tom. Tom was young, and he was boyish for his age; like all boys, he felt it necessary to take the warlike side of things; it seemed to establish his courage and make a man of him. "I'd like to have this thing blow over," he continued. "I was mightily in favor of having it blow over. But after the challenge has been sent, don't see how you can withdraw it. That's where I draw my line."

"You are interrupting the Colonel," said Vincent, who felt that everybody was interfering with his business, and so was petulant with everybody.

"I understand that my principal assented to this council," put in Bent Armitage, seeing that things were going against peace, and remembering his promise to Kate.

Vincent stared. Was his second to be against him? Was Bent Armitage going to turn peacemaker?

"I did assent," he muttered, fixing his half-shut eyes on the floor, and softly clutching his hands to keep down his irritability.

"Gentlemen," resumed the patient Kershaw, "I have but a few words to say. I do not propose to attack the code *duello*. Although it is repugnant to my feelings, at least in these latter years, I do not propose to ignore it. I know how thoroughly it is fixed in your views of life and in the habits of our society. I consent, though not with satisfaction, that you should in general be guided by it. But the code does not include the whole of human duty and honor; you will admit thus much. There are other proprieties and gentilities. Now on this extraordinary occasion it seems to me that these other proprieties and gentilities are more imperious than the demands of the code. You, Beaumont, have had a daughter saved from death by a McAlister. You, Vincent, have had a sister saved from death by a McAlister. Under the circumstances, is it right for Beaumonts to shoot McAlisters? I put one duty against another. I say that the obligation of gratitude overbalances the obligation of vindication of gentility. What I propose, therefore, is this: withdraw the challenge, because of the debt of gratitude; make that debt the express ground of the withdrawal. If Mr. Wallace McAlister does not then retract his epithet, he will, in my opinion, prove himself ungentlemanly, stolid, and brutal, and we can afford to despise his comments. What do you say, my dear Beaumont?"

"By heavens, Kershaw! By heavens!" stuttered Beaumont. "It's puzzling, by heavens. Well, if you must know what I think, I admit that you have made a strong point, Kershaw. A very strong point indeed, Kershaw. We don't want to go before the world as ungrateful and that sort of thing. That isn't gentlemanly. On the whole, Kershaw, — well, on the whole, I say, taking into view all the circumstances, you know, — I don't see any valid objection to your proposition. Hem. I don't object. That's just it; I don't object."

With these words, Beaumont bowed his bristling head in great perplexity, wondering whether he had done right or wrong. Colonel Kershaw and Bent Armitage both glanced anxiously at Vincent. The curious Lawson, who had been dodging about the hall and had overheard most of the proceedings, peeped through a door-crack to get a view of the same young gladiator. The fat Poinsett nodded his large head two or three times, as if in assent to the peace proposition, but said nothing. Tom, overwhelmed by his father and the Colonel together, stared vacantly at the floor.

"I venture to say that I see no valid cause for objection," observed Bentley Armitage, remembering Kate.

"I do," burst out Vincent, looking up angrily at Armitage. "I wish it understood that I am as grateful as I ought to be to Mr. Frank McAlister for his act of common humanity. But when it comes to withdrawing a challenge, — good heavens! I had abundant provocation, and I have it still. Let Wallace McAlister withdraw his epithet. He is at full liberty to do so. That is where peace should begin."

Major Lawson left his post near the door, and skipped across the hall into the dining-room. In ten seconds more Kate Beaumont, as pale and mild as a saint newly taken to glory, came out of the dining-room, crossed the hall, and entered the awful family council. Bentley Armitage rose and offered a chair. Poinsett smiled with an amused look, and beckoned her to his side. Kershaw held out his hand, and Vincent turned away his head. Mr. Beaumont said, in a tone of much wonder and faint remonstrance, "Kate!"

The girl, without noticing any of the others, advanced upon Vincent, seated herself beside him, looked eagerly in his averted face, and seized one of his hands.

"Oh Vincent, this is my first night at home in four years," she said in a trembling voice. "I shall not sleep to-night. I shall do nothing but see my brother brought back —" She could not finish this sentence. "And my first night at home! You could make it such a happy one, Vincent! Don't you think anything of my being saved from death? There was no hope for me, if it had not been for this man's brother. I had bid good by to you all."

Here her father's grim face had a shock; he twisted his mouth oddly, and rolled his eyes like a lunatic; he was trying to keep from blubbering. Colonel Kershaw clasped his wrinkled hands suddenly, as if returning thanks to Heaven, or praying. Lawson, listening in the hall, capered from one foot to the other as if he were on hot iron plates, and drew his cambric handkerchief.

"I don't want such a duel as this," Kate went on. "It does seem to me so horribly unnatural. Not this time, Vincent; don't fight this time. Do make this my first night at home a happy one. Oh, I will be so grateful to you; I will be such a sister to you! Dear, can't you answer me?"

Mr. Beaumont rose abruptly and got himself out of the room. He did not fully want his son to do what he still considered not quite chivalrous; and yet he could not bear to hear him refuse Kate this great and passionately sought-for boon. One after another, Kershaw, Bent Armitage, Poinsett, and Tom followed him. The pleading sister and the sullen brother were left alone.

CHAPTER 12

 We shall know in due time what success Kate had in pleading with Vincent to withdraw his challenge.

While the girl aided by her grandfather, was resisting the demon of duels in the Beaumont house, Mr. Frank McAlister was maintaining an equally dubious contest with the same monster under his paternal roof-tree.

We must hurry over the scene of his arrival at home. There had been a pleasant family drama; there had been warm welcome for the returned wanderer. The deliberate and solemn Judge was not the kind of man to fly into a spasm of emotion, like his excitable enemy, Peyt Beaumont; but he had a calm sufficiency of the true parental stuff in him, and he was proud of his gigantic, handsome son, full of all the wisdom of the East; he gave him a vigorous hand-shaking, and looked for an instant like kissing him. Mrs. McAlister, a tall, pale, gray, mild-eyed woman, took the Titan to her arms as if he were still an infant. Mary worshipped him, as girls are apt to worship older brothers, at least when they are big and handsome. Bruce, the eldest son, was all that a South Carolina gentleman should be on such an occasion. Wallace at once gloried in Frank's grandeur and beauty, and wilted wofully under a sense of his own inferiority.

The story of the shipwreck was told to affectionately breathless listeners; and then came, of a necessity, the saving of Miss Beaumont from a watery grave.

"I have some hope," added Frank, with the blush of a man who feels far more than he says, "that the incident may pave the way to a reconciliation of the families."

"Heaven grant it!" murmured Mrs. McAlister, her face illuminated with hope of peace and perhaps with foresight of love and marriage.

"Amen!" responded the Judge in a perfunctory, head-of-the-family, not to say beadle-like, manner. One of those model men who set an example, you perceive; one of those saints who keep up appearances, even at home.

"By George, it ought to," muttered Wally, conscience-stricken about his duel. "It ought to bring about a reconciliation. But, by George, there's no telling."

Then, at a proper moment, when only the three brothers were together, came the story of the quarrel with Vincent. It must be understood that among the McAlisters duels were not such common property, such subjects of genial family conversation, as among the Beaumonts. The McAlisters fought as promptly as their rivals; but, Scotch-like and Puritan-like, they treated fighting as a matter not to be babbled about; they drew a decorous veil over their occasional excesses in the way of homicide. When a McAlister boy got into an unpleasantness, he never mentioned it to father, mother, or sister, not even after the shots had been exchanged. The Judge believed that duelling was sometimes necessary; but he did not want to have the air of encouraging it: first, because he was a father and cared for his sons' lives; second, because he had a certain character to maintain in the district. Mrs. McAlister, a religious and tender-hearted woman, looked upon the code of honor with steady horror. Mary tormented her brothers by crying over their perils, even when those perils had passed and were become glories.

We can imagine Frank's disgust and grief when he learned that there was to be another Beaumont and McAlister duel. He pleaded against it; he inveighed against it; he sermonized against it.

"Frank, you make me think of converted cannibals coming home to preach to their tribe," said Wallace, smiling amiably, but unmoved and unconvinced.

{ 154 }

"Who is your second?" asked Frank, hoping to find more wisdom in that assistant than in the principal.

"Bruce," replied Wallace with a queer grimace, somewhat in the way of an apology.

"Bruce! Your own brother?" exclaimed the confounded Frank. "Why, that is horrible. And isn't it something unheard of? It strikes me as an awful scandal."

"It *is* unusual," admitted Wallace. "But Vincent Beaumont makes no objection to it, and, moreover, he has chosen his own connection, Bent Armitage. Besides," he added, looking at his elder brother with an almost touching confidence, "Bruce will fight me better than any other man could."

Bruce McAlister was a man of about six feet, too slender and too lean to be handsome in a gladiatorial sense, but singularly graceful. Although not much above thirty, his face was haggard and marked by an air of lassitude. He was a consumptive. Perhaps the disease had increased the charm of his expression. His large hazel eyes, sunk as they were in sombre hollows, had a melancholy tenderness which was almost more than human. His face was so gentle, so refined, so gracious, that it charmed at first sight. There was no resisting the sweet smile, the flattering bow and petting address of this man. He put strangers at ease in an instant; he made them feel with a look that they were his valued friends; he so impressed them in a minute that they never forgot him in all their lives. It would not be easy to find another man who had such an appearance of thinking altogether of others and not at all of himself.

"It *is* an unusual step, Frank," said Bruce, in a mellow, deep, and yet weak voice. "It was of course not ventured upon without the full consent of the other party. I accepted the position solely with the hope of diminishing Wallace's danger."

"Well!" assented Frank with a groan. "And now, Bruce, tell me the whole thing. What is the exact value of the provocation?"

In a quiet tone and without a sign of indignation Bruce related the story of the difficulty.

"Beaumont's manner and words were irritatingly sarcastic," he concluded. "Wallace naturally resented it."

"Still, all that he said was — was parliamentary," urged Frank. "Wallace, I don't want to judge you; but it does seem to me that you might have spared your reply; it was terribly severe. Couldn't you apologize? If I were in your place, I would. I would, indeed."

Wallace stared, rubbed his head meditatively, and then shook it decidedly.

"And for this you mean to fight?" pursued Frank. "Actually mean to draw a pistol on your fellow-man? The whole thing — I mean the code *duello* — is a barbarity. I was brought up to reverence it. From this time I abjure it."

"Fight? Well, yes," returned Wallace, again rubbing his prematurely bald crown; not quite bald, either; simply downy. "Of course I will fight. Not that I admire fighting. It's the reasoning of beasts, sir. And as for the *duello*, well, I look on it as you do; I consider it out of date, barbarous. But society — our society, I mean — demands it. If society says a gentleman must — *noblesse oblige* — why, that settles it. If it says a gentleman should wear a beaver," lifting his hat and gesturing with it, "why, he must get one. Disagreeable thing; ugly and uncomfortable; just look at it. Look at my head, too. Bald at twenty-eight! That's the work of a black, hot beaver. But since it's the distinguishing topknot of a gentleman, I submit to it. Just so with the *duello*. I think it's blasted nonsense, and yet I can't ignore it. As for the Beaumonts, I don't want to be shooting at Beaumonts. Just as willing to let them alone as to let anybody else alone. But when a Beaumont ruffles me, and society says, 'Let's see how he takes it,' why I take it with pistols. Very sorry to do it, but don't see how I can help it. I suppose my position is a weak one. Logic don't support it, and God won't approve it. Know all that. Not going to fool myself with trying to prove that I don't know it. And, by George, I wish I could make my reason and practice agree. Wish I could, and know I can't."

"Would you mind leaving this matter to our elders?" asked Frank, the idea of a family council occurring to him as it had occurred to Colonel Kershaw.

"Oh Lord! don't!" begged Wallace. "You couldn't beat me out of it, but you'd bother me awfully. You'd have mother on your side, sure, and she's an army. Yes, by George, she's one of those armies that are marshalled by the Lord of hosts," declared Wallace, stopping to meditate upon the perfections of his mother. "She *is* a peacemaker," he resumed. "I've heard her say that she almost regretted having a boy;

if her children were only all girls, this feud might have died out. By George, I wouldn't mind being one of the girls. I might have been handsomer. I might have kept my hair, too; not being obliged to wear a beaver." Here he rubbed the "fuzzy" summit of his head with rueful humor. "By heavens! bald at twenty-eight! It's an ugly defect."

He was so cheerful and resolute, notwithstanding the shadow of death which lay across his to-morrow, that Frank was in despair.

At this hopeless stage of the conversation a negro brought in word that "Mars Bent Armitage wanted to see Mars Bruce."

Bruce went to another room, received Armitage with an almost affectionate courtesy, talked with him for a few moments in a low tone, and waited on him to his horse as tenderly as if he were a lady. When he returned to his two brothers there was in his usually melancholy eyes something like a smile of pleasure.

"I am the bearer of remarkable news," he said calmly. "The duel can now be honorably avoided."

"How?" demanded the eager Frank.

"What!" exclaimed the astonished Wallace.

"Hear this," continued Bruce, opening a letter. "'On behalf of my principal, Mr. Vincent Beaumont, I withdraw the challenge sent to Mr. Wallace McAlister. The sole motive of this withdrawal is the sense of obligation on the part of Mr. Beaumont and his family toward Mr. Frank McAlister for saving the life of Miss Catherine Beaumont.' Signed, Bentley Armitage."

"By George!" exclaimed Wallace, and continued to say by George for a considerable time. "I owe him an apology," he presently broke out. "If I don't owe him one, I'll give him one. Bruce, write me an apology, won't you? By heavens, I never thought a Beaumont could be so human. Anything, Bruce; I'll sign anything. This is new times, something like the millennium. What would our ancestors say? Frank, by George, this is your work, and it's a big job. In saving the girl's life you have saved mine, perhaps, and Vincent's. Three lives at one haul! How like the Devil — I mean how like an angel — you do come down on us! By George, old fellow, I'm amazingly obliged to you. I am, indeed. Is that thing ready, Bruce? Let's have it. There! Now, Bruce, if you'll be kind enough to transmit that in your very best manner — By the way, old fellow, I'm very much obliged to you for standing by me. I'm devilish lucky in brothers."

"I do hope that this is the beginning of the ending of the family feud," was the next thing heard from Frank.

"Well, I don't mind," agreed Wallace.

"You ought to say more than that," urged Frank. "One friendly step deserves another. You have been fairly beaten so far in the race of humanity by this Beaumont."

"Yes, he has got the lead," conceded Wallace. "For once I knock under to a Beaumont. The fact confounds me; it fairly takes the breath out of me. But will he last? *Can* the blasted catamounts become friendly?"

"Try them," said Frank. "I propose a call on them."

"Wallace has apologized," observed Bruce. "The next advance should come from the Beaumont side."

"We ought to give more than we receive," lectured Frank. "It is the part of true gentlemen, as the word is understood in our times, or should be understood."

"It is worth considering," admitted Bruce; "it is worth while to suggest the idea to our father."

"And mother," was Frank's energetic amendment, to which Bruce did not think it best to reply. The honor of the family was very dear to him, and he did not believe that women were qualified to judge its demands, much as he respected the special good sense of his mother.

Back to the Beaumonts one must now hasten, to learn how they received the apology. Vincent glanced through Wallace's letter without changing expression, nodded as a man nods over a compromise which is only half satisfactory, read it aloud to his father and brothers (with a sister listening in the next room), and then filed it away among his valuable papers, all without a word of comment. Beaumont senior was gratified, and then suddenly enraged, and then gratified again, and so on.

"Why, Kershaw, the fellow *has* some streaks of gentility in him," he admitted, with a smile of wonder and satisfaction, walking up and down with the pacific, manageable air of a kindly, led horse. But presently he gave a start and a glare, like a tiger who hears hunters, and broke out in a snarl: "Why the deuce didn't he say all this at first? He ought to have apologized at once. The scoundrel!!"

After some further thought, he added in a mild growl: "Well, it might have been worse. After all, the blockhead has made it clear that he doesn't mean to take advantage of Vincent's magnanimity. Yes, magnanimity!" he trumpeted, looking about for somebody to dispute it. "By heavens, Vincent, you have been as magnanimous as a duke, by heavens!"

Here the magician who had wrought thus much of peace into the woof of hate came smiling and glowing into the room, slipped her arm through that of her eldest brother, and whispered: "So it has ended well, Vincent. I am so much obliged to you! I am so happy!"

Next she glided over to her father and possessed herself of his hairy hand, saying, "Come, your man-business has gone all right; come and show me where to put my flower-beds."

She was bent, — the audacious young thing, it seemed incredible when you looked at her sweet, girlish face, — but she was bent upon taming these fine, fighting panthers; and she was bringing to bear upon the work a beautiful combination of tenderness, of patient management and gentle imperiousness; she was inspired to attempt a labor far beyond her years. The trying circumstances which surrounded her had matured her with miraculous rapidity, and brought into bloom at once all her nobler moral and stronger mental qualities. She was like those youthful generals who have performed prodigies because they were called upon to perform prodigies, and did not yet know that prodigies were humanly impossible. No doubt it was well for the girl that Heaven had given her so much beauty and such an imposingly sweet expression of dignity and purity. A plainer daughter and sister, no matter how good and wise and resolute, might not have accomplished such wonders.

On the following day two horsemen left the mansion of the Beaumonts and rode towards the mansion of the McAlisters. They rode mainly at a walk, the reason being that one of them was over eighty years old, while the other, although not above fifty-five, was shaky with pains and diseases. Several times during the transit of four miles the younger suddenly checked his horse and turned his nose homeward, saying, "By heavens, I can't do it, Kershaw. No, by heavens!"

"Come on, my dear Beaumont," mildly begged the venerable Colonel. "You will never regret it. It is the noblest chance you ever had to be magnanimous."

"Do you think so, Kershaw? Well, magnanimity is a gentlemanly thing. By heavens, that was a devilish fine thing that Vincent did. It put a feather in his cap as high as the plume of the Prince of Wales. Moral courage and dignity! By heavens, I am proud of the boy."

"So am I," said Kershaw.

"Are you?" grinned the delighted Beaumont. "By heavens, I'm delighted to hear you say so. I was afraid you didn't appreciate Vincent. But I ought to have known better; every gentleman would appreciate him. The man who now doesn't appreciate Vincent, he's — he's an ass and a scoundrel," declared Beaumont, beginning to tremble with rage at the thought of encountering and chastising such a miscreant. "Well, Kershaw," he added, "let us go on."

After a little he added in a tone of apology, "Some people might say that this errand is the business of a younger man. But my sons are not related to Kate as you and I are. The girl springs directly from your veins and mine; and consequently we are the proper persons to thank the man who saved her life. Don't you think so, Kershaw?"

"Certainly," replied the patient Colonel, who had already advocated that view with all his eloquence.

Presently they discovered the McAlister mansion, and here Beaumont came to another halt. This time his resistance was more obstinate than before; it was like the struggle of an ox when he smells the blood of the slaughter-block.

"Kershaw, I can't go to that house," he said, his face and air full of tragic dignity. "That house is the abode of the enemies of my race. There is a man in that house who has my brother's blood on his hands. I can't go there; no, Kershaw, by God!"

His voice trembled; it was full of anguish and anger; it was a groan and a menace.

The Colonel made no remonstrance and no spoken reply. He took off his hat and bared his long white hair to the sun, as if in respect to Beaumont's emotion. In this attitude he waited silently for the storm of feeling to rage itself out.

"My father never would have entered that house," continued Beaumont. "No McAlister ever crossed my threshold. There has been nothing but hate and blood between us. It has always been so, and it must always be so. I am too old to learn new ways."

Still the Colonel sat silent and uncovered, with his long silver hair shining under the hot sun. The sight of this humility and patience seemed to trouble Beaumont.

"You can't feel as I do, Kershaw." he said. "Of course you can't."

"Let us try to make the future unlike the past," returned the Colonel, in a tone which was like that of prayer.

Beaumont shook his head more in sadness than in anger.

"This young man, Frank McAlister, has already begun the work," continued the Colonel. "Shall Kate's father and grandfather foil him?"

Beaumont began to tremble in every limb; he was weak with his diseases, and this struggle of emotions was too much for him; he held on to his saddle-bow to keep himself from growing dizzy.

"I don't feel that I can do it, Kershaw," he said, in a voice which had one or two embryo sobs in it. How, indeed, enfeebled as he was by maladies, could he choose between all the family feelings of his past and the totally new duty now before him, without being shaken?

"Beaumont," was the closing appeal of the Colonel, "you will, I hope, allow me to go on alone and return thanks for the life of my granddaughter."

"No, by heavens!" exclaimed the father, turning his back at once on all his bygone life, its emotions, its beliefs, its acts, and traditions. "No. If you *must* go, I go with you."

"God bless you, my dear Beaumont!" said Kershaw, his voice, too, perhaps a little unsteady.

After some further riding Beaumont added: "But we will see the boy alone. Not the Judge. I won't see the Judge. If I meet that old fox, I shall quarrel with him. I can't stand a fox when he's as big as an elephant and as savage as a hyena."

A little later he asked: "You're sure Lawson thinks well of this step?"

"He approves of it thoroughly," declared the Colonel. "He considers it the only thing we can do, since the apology has been made."

"Well, Lawson ought to know what's gentlemanly," said Beaumont. "Lawson has always been a *habitué* of our society. By heavens! if Lawson doesn't know what's gentlemanly, he's an ass."

And so at last they were at the door of the McAlister clan.

CHAPTER 13

 The McAlister mansion was a very similar affair to the Beaumont mansion.

Speaking with severe truthfulness, and without regard to the proud illusions of Hartland District, it had no claim to be styled a mansion, except on account of its size alone. It was a plain, widespreading mass of wood-work, in two stories, with plenty of veranda and more than enough square pillars, the white paint of the building itself rather rusty, and the green blinds not altogether free from fractures and palsy.

Negro children, a ragged, sleek, and jolly tribe of chattels, ran grinning to hold the horses of Colonel Kershaw and the Honorable Mr. Beaumont. Matthew, the Judge's special and confidential servant, waited on them with dignified obsequiousness into the long, soberly furnished parlor, and received with jesuitical calmness (covering inward immense astonishment and suspicion) their request to see Mr. Frank McAlister. After delivering this message to his young master, he added in a whisper, "Better see your shootin'-irons is all right, sah. Them Beaumonts you know, sah."

"I never carry the cursed, barbarous traps," replied the young man, in noble wrath, and hurried off to welcome his visitors. He was calm, however, when he entered the parlor; he had a wise, delicate perception that it would not do to rush upon Beaumonts with an effusion of friendship; he must in the first place try to divine from the demeanor of these potent seniors how they wished to be treated. Moreover, it was his nature, as it is that of most giants, to be tranquil in manner. When the three met, it was Colonel Kershaw, outranking the others by reason of age, who spoke first.

"My name is Kershaw," he said with simple dignity. "This is my son-in-law, Mr. Peyton Beaumont. We have called to thank you for saving the life of our dear child, Catherine Beaumont."

"Yes!!" unexpectedly added Beaumont. He had forgotten where he was; for the moment he had no emotion but gratitude; his fervent "Yes" sounded like an amen!

There was so much feeling and such obvious sincerity in the speech of these men that Frank at once lost his Titanic serenity.

"Gentlemen, you overwhelm me," he burst out, wringing first one hand and then another. "You overwhelm me with your kindness. I can't express my obligations to you."

So catching was the young fellow's agitation, that Beaumont's combustible heart took fire, and he astonished the listening angels by saying, "God bless you, my dear sir! God bless you!"

"I would have lost my life willingly to save her," pursued Frank, hailing these friendly hearts with difficulty out of his storm of feeling. "I never saw another human being who seemed to me so pure and noble."

Kate's father was dazed with gratified paternal affection and pride; he had not a thought for the fact that it was a McAlister who uttered these compliments; nor did it even occur to him that the young man might be simply in love with the girl.

"By heavens, I thank you," he went on, while the hand-shaking, that mute, eloquent gratitude, also went on. "By heavens, sir, I am glad I came to see you."

Meantime he was dimly aware of, and unconsciously delighted with, the height, size, brilliant color, and noble expression of the youngster.

After a little further talk, all of this passionate, interjectional, truly meridional nature, Frank exploded a proposition which for the moment stunned Beaumont like the bursting of a shell.

"But, gentlemen, I am doing you injustice," he said. "The head of the family alone can properly respond to this compliment. Will you allow me to call my father to receive you? He would be gratified beyond measure."

Meet that enchanted wiggery, that elephantine fox, that diplomatic foe till death, that murderer of a brother, Judge McAlister! All Peyton Beaumont's breeding, all his consciousness that he was one of the representatives of South Carolina gentility and courtesy, could not restrain him from starting backward a little, with a leonine quivering of mustaches and bristling of eyebrows. He wanted to refuse; he looked at Kershaw to utter the refusal for him; and, like Hector seeking a spear of Pallas, he looked in vain. The old peacemaker had a sudden illumination to the effect that now was the time to bring about a reconciliation between the families.

"Mr. McAlister, you will do us a great favor," he said in his venerable, tremulous bass voice.

Beaumont broke out in a cold perspiration, made a slight bow, and awaited his fate in silence.

The Judge, sitting at that moment in his library, already knew of these visitors, and had decided how he would receive them, should he be called to that business. "Feud may as well fall to the ground, if it will," he had briefly reasoned. "No nonsensical sentiment about it on my side. If we were once friends with those tinder-heads of Beaumonts, we might contrive to manage them, and so always carry the district instead of almost never carrying it. Moreover, this girl being the probable sole heir of Kershaw, there is a fine match there for Frank. Finally, my excellent wife would be immensely gratified by peace, and her gratification is one of the many things that I am bound to live for." Such is a brief, unadorned, and therefore unjust summary of the reflections of the Judge.

But when he was actually summoned to meet his visitors, his politic thoughts changed to emotions. He remembered that duel of bygone days; remembered how he (then a young man) threw down his fatal pistol and burst into tears; remembered how he had mounted his horse and fled from his lifeless victim as he would not have fled from any living being. He trembled at the thought of meeting in kindness the brother of the Beaumont whose blood was upon his soul. For a few seconds he walked the library with such a rush of emotions in his heart that it seemed to him as if the seconds were years. Then he steadied himself; he rearranged his wig; he rearranged his countenance. He was once more the calm, dignified, gracious, smiling Donald McAlister, such as Hartland District had known for twenty years past.

And so, presently, the chiefs of the Montagues and Capulets of South Carolina were face to face and inclining their venerable craniums towards each other with a stiff, dignified courtesy, which made one think of kings bowing with their crowns on. There was a hesitation about going further; the McAlister hand advanced slightly and the Beaumont hand did not stir; it seemed as if unavenged ghosts would not let them exchange the grasp of friendship. But after a moment the instinct of hand-shaking was too much for them; they met as Southern gentlemen are accustomed to meet; the once hostile digits were intermingled.

To Frank the anxious lover, and to Kershaw the philanthropic peacemaker, it was a wondrous spectacle. A looker-on, unacquainted with preliminary tragedies, would, however, have seen and heard nothing remarkable. There were two grave, dignified gentlemen shaking hands with bowed heads and eyes dropped to the floor. Each said, "I hope I see you well, sir," and each replied, "I thank you, sir." No regrets over the savage past; neither reproach nor apology, not even by the most circuitous hint; not the faintest allusion, in short, to the family feud. The Judge was simply all that a gracious host in commonplace circumstances should be. He got out his blandest smile; with his own large plump hands he wheeled up arm-chairs for his visitors; he rang the bell and ordered refreshments. His mind settled by these little offices, he said as he seated himself, "Gentlemen, I am immensely indebted to you for this visit. It is one of the highest honors of my life."

"The old, palavering fox!" thought Beaumont; and replied aloud, "Judge, it is an honor to us. It is a matter of duty also," he added. "You are aware, doubtless, of our great obligations to your magnificent son here."

"I am most grateful that my son could be of service to your superb daughter," replied the Judge. "From what I hear of her I should say that no man would hesitate to risk his life on her account."

All of a sudden they were drifting towards each other at a most unexpected rate. This praising of each other's children was a sure method of touching each other's hard hearts. Insincerity? not a bit of it; not on this subject. Who wouldn't admire Kate? Who wouldn't admire Frank? Beaumont, whose judgment was the weather-cock of his feelings, ceased saying to himself at every breath that McAlister was a humbugging scoundrel and innocently marvelled at finding in him so much of good sense and goodness and truth. The Judge, though less easily cajoled than his visitor, was nevertheless so gratified with this call from his haughty old foeman, with the glimpse of that fine possible match for Frank, and with the vistas of desirable political combinations, that he was well lubricated with satisfaction. The habitually earnest and rather grim eyes of the two men were presently beaming in quite a human manner. The conversation gradually lost its tone of ceremony and became social. The serving of madeira and brandy introduced the subjects, so well known to antique South Carolina gentlemen, of vintages, cellaring, and bottling. In short, the Colonel and Frank aiding zealously, there was a comfortable unimportant talk of some twenty minutes.

This is the entire substance of that famous call of the Hon. Peyton Beaumont on Judge Donald McAlister, commonly believed to be the first friendly passage between them in their whole lives. We shall see in due time whether it came to so much in the millennial and matrimonial way as was doubtless hoped for by our gentle giant, Frank.

It was an astonishing event for the time. Beaumont rode home in a state of wonder over it, and filled his household with equal amazement when he told his adventure. Vincent, usually a prudently silent young man, stared at his father with much such an expression as he would have worn had the old gentleman confessed that he had been standing on his head. Tom wandered out of the house in a partially unsettled condition of mind, querying, perhaps, what was the further use for Beaumonts in this world, since they were no longer to fight McAlisters. Poinsett smiled and said to himself, "So my father has ventured among the enchanted wiggeries, and been somewhat deluded and humanized by them. Well, I ought to praise him for it." Which he did in his roundabout, jocose, adroit fashion.

"Yes, certainly, Poinsett," replied the reassured and gratified Beaumont. "The only thing to be done, under the circumstances. As for going any further, as for continuing to wave olive-branches, well, we'll see how these fellows behave themselves. By heavens, we'll wait and see."

But the great reward which the father received for his embassy of gratitude came from the charming little queen who had sent him on it. It was a score of kisses; it was a clinging of fondling arms; it was a rubbing of a satin forehead against his bull neck.

"Well, am I as good as grandpapa, now?" asked Beaumont, always a little jealous of the adored Kershaw.

"Yes," laughed Kate. "You have done ever so much more to please me than he could do. I comprehend perfectly, papa, what a sacrifice you have made for my sake. Jumped on your pride, haven't you? The old Beaumont pride! And the old Beaumont pugnacity, too! Oh, I comprehend it all, you dear, good papa! I am not a simpleton."

"Not a bit of it," said Beaumont. And thought to himself: "What an amazingly intelligent girl! I never saw a grown woman with half her intelligence; by heavens, I never did."

"And now, what else?" he asked aloud, growling a little bit, for she might demand too much.

"Papa, I think that if the McAlisters want to make friends on this, we ought to let them."

"Well, yes," assented magnanimous papa. "That is just what I was saying to Poinsett."

He felt as if a new career of greatness were being opened to him; as if it were well worthy of his character and position to let people make friends with him, if they wanted to; as if that kind of thing might be a fitting close to the life even of a chivalrous Beaumont.

In a day or two, delightful to relate, there came a call from "those fellows," meaning the Judge and Frank and Wallace. They were received in due state and with proper setting forth of refreshments by Beaumont senior, Vincent, and Poinsett; but the beneficent Kershaw being absent, somewhat of the shadow of the old feud seemed to fall upon the interview, notwithstanding Frank's best efforts at sunshine; and when the visitors departed it cannot be said that the hosts had any fervent desire to see them again.

Fortunately for the chances of the millennium, there were women of a truly womanly nature in each of these bellicose families. Pious and maternal Mrs. McAlister and brother-worshipping Mary McAlister longed for the holiness and salvation of lasting peace. Kate Beaumont, the sweet, first cause of all pleasantness thus far, had likewise her admirable reasons for wishing to see the feud buried forever. Mrs. Chester also desired harmony, for she wanted with all her coquettish old heart to resume communications with her handsome Titan, and she was the woman to go after what she wanted with the eager scramble of a terrier after a rat. By the way, we can hardly insist too much upon the fancy of this well-preserved lady for flirting with young men. It was a passion with her; some people said it was a monomania; others went so far as to think that she was insane on this point. What with her reckless imagination, her ancient habits of coquetry, and her excessive vanity, she had become thoroughly infatuated with the idea of getting Frank McAlister to dangle about her.

Accordingly, the following rose-colored sequence of events took place. Mrs. Chester, in her wild, impulsive way (such a mere child, as one kindly remembers), dropped in alone upon the McAlister ladies and prattled gleefully for two hours, denouncing the feud with the gayest of smiles and praying in the sprightliest manner that there might be no more bloodshed between the families. Hereupon Mrs. McAlister and her daughter made an immediate call at the Beaumont house, and were received with absolute festivity and pettings by the two females who there presided. The interview was all honest good-nature and gladness, unmixed with suspicion or ceremoniousness. The four ladies were in a new, spring-like state of emotion, fit to intermingle their hearts' tendrils and bloom into quick flowers of friendship. Mrs. McAlister and Mary on one side, and Kate on the other, fell in love at first sight. Mrs. Chester remained tender towards her Titan alone, but that of course involved amicable results, at least for the present. And the visit being thus joy-giving, it was quickly returned and was followed by others.

Thus at last we have, not only peace, but frequent and fond communings between the Montagues and Capulets of Hartland District. An amazing olive-tree surely, and more wonderful to its beholders than any supposable amount of bloody laurels. The orange-plant of the Indian juggler, springing from the seed and producing fruit inside of twenty minutes, would not have been half so much of a marvel to Messrs. Wilkins, Duffy, and their fellow-citizens. They were a little wild in those days; they felt as though the compass no longer pointed north; as though the Gulf Stream had changed its course. Moreover, where did Hartland stand now, with its famous family feud gone to Heaven, or otherwheres? The place had lost its monument; it had begun to resemble other middle-sized villages; there was an awful likelihood that it would become dull.

One result of the new order of things was that Frank McAlister, in one of his visits to the Beaumont house, had a *tête-à-tête* with Mrs. Chester, which the lady contrived to make very pleasant to herself. Another result was that on a second and happier occasion he met Kate Beaumont alone, some favoring fairy having sent the aunt off on a drive with Bent Armitage, and inveigled the brothers into a hunting expedition, and put the father to bed with the gout. It was the first time that the two young people had met without witnesses since the shipwreck. Naturally they talked of their great triumph, the reconciliation of the families.

"So we have won a victory," said Frank. "Or rather, you have. What wonders you have accomplished!"

"Don't overestimate me!" Kate blushed, remembering how much she had longed for this victory and how hard she had struggled for it. "Everybody has helped. I am so grateful to your father and brother and mother and sister for making the path of peace so easy to us. But my father and brothers have been amazingly good, too. You must praise them to me a little."

"I do," replied Frank, fervently. "I wish they knew how kindly I think of them. And your grandfather, — what a wonderful old man! what a god among men!"

"Isn't he?" said Kate, her eyes sparkling.

"He has the charm of a beautiful woman," declared Frank, enthusiastic about the Colonel on his own account and enthusiastic about him because he was the grandfather of Kate. "You have only to see him to worship him."

The girl was too innocent to suspect a compliment to herself, or to see an insidious advance towards love-making, in this talk about beautiful women.

"Mr. McAlister, I am glad you have found him out," she said simply. "I wish you would call on him. He would be delighted to see you. He has only Major Lawson with him."

"What an excellent-hearted man the Major is!" replied Frank.

"Isn't he?" said Kate, in her honest way, really liking the friendly, amiable Major.

There was not much sense of humor in these two young persons.

They were straightforward, earnest souls, mainly capable of seeing the interior goodness of other people, and not to be diverted from such insight by any external oddities. What they could discern in Lawson was, not his extravagant flatteries, his sentimentalities, and his flutings, but his quickness of sympathy, his warmth of friendship, and his gentle humanity.

Well, there was a long conversation, and it led to a promenade on the veranda, Kate's fingers resting lightly on Frank's arm. While they were thus pleasantly engaged, and presenting the prettiest prophecy possible of a walk together through life, there was a sound of horses' feet, and Mrs. Chester and Bent Armitage pulled up before them. It is not possible to paint in words the glare of suspicion, jealousy, and spite which shot from the aunt's eyes as she caught sight of her niece arm in arm with Frank McAlister. The next instant she regained her self-possession and put on a smile which might have melted platinum. In a minute more she was leading in the conversation, seemingly the gayest and happiest old hoyden that ever wore tight bootees. In another minute she had separated the two — shall we venture thus early to call them lovers?

An adroit creature was Mrs. Chester. Wonderfully clever ways had she of bringing about her foolish ends. She did not bluntly call Frank to herself, as a duller intriguer might have done. She beckoned Kate aside to listen to some trifling household matter; then she summoned Armitage to express his opinion upon the girl's decision; then, leaving these two together, she skipped over to Frank, apologized for deserting him, and trotted him away. The result, of course, was that the young man soon found that he had finished his call and must hasten home.

Now it was that Mrs. Chester turned upon Kate and scolded her for receiving Mr. McAlister alone.

"Where was your father? Gout? He ought to have got up, if he had forty gouts. He had no business to allow of such an interview. We are not on sufficiently familiar terms with that family. It is only yesterday that we spoke to them."

Kate looked so shocked under this attack that she immediately secured the sympathy of Bent Armitage, although he too had felt a twinge at seeing her alone with McAlister. He gave her one of his queer smiles, and rolled his eyes at Mrs. Chester in a way that said, "Never mind her." That lady did not see the smile, but she perceived that Kate had received encouragement from some one, and she turned sharply upon Armitage.

"What is your opinion?" she demanded angrily. "You seem to have one."

"My opinion isn't yours," answered Bent, in his odd, frank way.

"Oh!" gasped Mrs. Chester. She was in a rage, but she said nothing further, for at that moment a new idea struck her. This Armitage, she decided with the keenness of an old flirt, had defended Kate because he liked her. It was well; he should have the chit; he should take her out of the way. From that minute Mrs. Chester elected her niece to be the wife of Bentley Armitage.

CHAPTER 14

 "I begin to be afraid that Kate is a wild sort of girl," said Mrs. Chester to Bent Armitage, as soon as she was alone with him again.

"It's astonishing you never discovered it before," replied Bent, ironically smiling on the side of his mouth which was farthest from Mrs. Chester and hidden from her vision.

Kate Beaumont wild? Bent knew better, and Mrs. Chester ought to know better, and he believed that she did know better. But the lady was quite in earnest, for she had been scared by the fact of her niece receiving Frank McAlister alone, and her alarm had given rise to a sudden suspicion, almost amounting to a belief that the girl was a daring coquette.

"I have an idea that you like wild girls," continued Mrs. Chester.

"Well, I hang about you a good deal," answered Bent, one side of his face all seriousness, and the other full of satire.

"Oh, pshaw!" returned the lady, not however ungrateful. "I alluded to your fancy for that dreadful coquette, your cousin Jenny."

"Jenny is so happy in being my cousin, that she doesn't want to be anything nearer," said Bent. "And I am equally contented."

"Then you are pretty sure to fall in love with this other wild piece," pursued cunning Mrs. Chester. "Well, you might do worse. Kate has her good qualities."

Armitage turned grave; the lady had plainly broached a subject which to him was serious; and joker as he was, he had no jest ready for the occasion.

"Your brother married her half-sister," said Mrs. Chester, guessing that her batteries were beginning to tell. So they were; the young man was no longer laughing at her; he was listening to her eagerly and even anxiously; he was ready at the moment to look to her as a friend and counsellor.

"It would be so natural!" she went on. "I don't think any one would be astonished. She would not go out of the family."

Armitage was too profoundly moved, and we might even say disturbed, to be able to answer. The one thing that he had in his mind, or for the moment could have there, was this fact, that Mrs. Chester approved of his wooing her niece. He dropped away from her presently; in fact, he was encouraged to take his leave; and before long he was doing just what Mrs. Chester wanted him to do; that is, he was sauntering about the house to look for Kate. Not that he meant to propose to her; he knew that things were not by any means far enough advanced for that; but he wanted to be near her and to try to begin a courtship.

It must be understood that social matters were unusually lively in these days at the Beaumont place. Colonel Kershaw rode over often to take dinner or to pass the night; not a talkative man, for his good old heart was apt to utter itself mainly through his air of venerable benignity; his remarks being at once infrequent and admirable, like the rare opening of bottles of precious wine. With him always came Major Lawson, his puckered face and twinkling eyes beaming sympathy upon all, and his attuned voice fluting universal praises. (The ironical Vincent pretended to marvel that the Major did not have a slave stand behind him with a pitchpipe, like Tiberius Gracchus; and asserted that he was capable of paying compliments to the internal fires, apropos of earthquakes and other destructive convulsions.) Furthermore, the McAlisters, especially the women, and Frank, made their calls now and then, laboring to keep up the *entente cordiale*. Of other visitors, whom we have not time to know familiarly, a large proportion were dashing young fellows on horseback, attracted by the fame of a girl who was already reputed the belle of the district.

But no one was at hand so often or stayed so long as Bent Armitage. As we ought perhaps to have stated before, he was sojourning with his aunt, Mrs. Devine, whose plantation was only two miles away. He dropped in diurnally upon the Beaumonts, sometimes with, but oftener without, his coquettish cousin Jenny, talking his copious, light-minded slang serenely to all visitors, telling countless queer stories which were the delight of the master of the house, and paying more or less side-long, cautious courtship to Kate. Mrs. Chester helped him; she arranged traps which ended in *tête-à-têtes* between the two; she did her best to get the girl's head full of this admirer. In these days Mr. Frank McAlister was sometimes gloomily jealous of Mr. Bentley Armitage.

By similar managements and enchantments Mrs. Chester obtained various interviews with the handsome giant, about whom she had gone bewitched. If there is a human figure more pitiably ludicrous than an old beau crazy after fresh girls, who sack him and avoid him and giggle at him, it is surely an old belle angling for the attentions of young men who bear with her wrinkled oglings simply because she is a woman. But laughable as such a creature is, she may be very inconvenient. The courteous, kind-hearted Frank was as much in-commoded by his alert admirer as a horse by a gadfly. He could not shake her off; for in the first place he had not the unfeeling levity which enables some men to rid themselves of undesired amities; and in the second place he was instinctively eager to stand well with all Kate's relatives. But his patience under the load of Mrs. Chester did some damage by leading her to believe that he liked to hold her. So she gave him much of her company and of her gratitude, and one might perhaps say, speaking loosely, of her love.

We are driven to risk being tedious concerning this eccentric, this almost irrational woman. Amid the many callers, and especially the many young men who now frequented the Beaumont house, she disported herself as one who is in her element, darting and dodging and chattering like a swallow. All hospitality, she rang for refresh-ments at every new arrival, and seriously bothered several youthful heads with the Beaumont madeira and cognac. Her voice could be heard rising above all others, except when her brother struck in with his clangorous trumpet. Loud laughter, slappings with her fan, smart pattings on the floor with the toe of her bootee, and bridlings which imitated sweet sixteen, testified to her relish of the wit of the gentlemen. She was a woman who got intoxicated with conversation, especially when there was a flavoring of flirtation in it. She was capable of dignity; but that was generally when she was miserable or angry; in her good humors she was excited, mercurial, noisy. All day she was as busy as a bee; for when there was no company she prepared for it; shutting herself in her room to remodel and adorn old dresses; attending to the job personally in her own characteristic fashion; dashing breadths together awry, and then flinging them at Miriam to be set right, — being very proud of the rapidity with which she did things very badly. And out of all this hurly-burly she drew the only happiness that she knew.

Of course, specks of gloom would sail in among the sunshine. Once, when Mrs. Chester was perhaps a little unwell, Miriam found her shedding tears over the recollection of the trunks full of fine clothes which had gone down in the *Mersey*. At times she fell into great rages because certain wilful young gentlemen had showed plainly that they preferred to talk to Kate rather than to her. When sorrows like these crushed her she pouted in her room, snapped at Miriam, sniffed at her niece, and would not speak at table. It was amazing that the same woman could be at one time such a sunburst of hilarity and at another such a cloud of sulking and snarling. Vincent once lost his temper so far as to tell her that when she was not a cataract she was a dismal swamp. But see-sawing was her nature; she was nothing if not mercurial. Had some power suddenly blessed her with equanimity, she would have ceased to be Mrs. Chester.

This curious woman and her incommodious love affair had been a subject of study with Major Lawson. The sly, good-hearted old beau had had experience enough in flirtation to comprehend the sly, selfish old belle. He perceived that she was smitten with Frank McAlister, and he guessed that her ancient, made-over coquetries must be very embarrassing to the youngster, although the latter bore himself under them with the serenity and sweetness of a martyr. Moreover, the somewhat sentimental Major wanted to see his Romeo and Juliet drama played out happily; he wanted the Montagues and Capulets of Hartland District united in lasting peace by a marriage between

Frank and Kate. By Jove, what a delightful story it would be to recount to his lady friends in Charleston! And by Jove, too, sir, it would be a good thing, an eminently beneficent event, sir, a result that any gentleman might desire and labor for.

"My de-ar fellow, allow me," he at last said to Frank, drawing him mysteriously to one side and patting him tenderly on the sleeve. "You are injudicious — you really are — excuse me. Why, you shouldn't come here alone. A wise general does not advance all his forces in one column. He sends up a feint attack to draw the enemy's fire. He occupies the hostile attention by side movements while he delivers the real assault on the vital point. My de-ar fellow, you certainly will excuse me, you must try to excuse me. I am giving advice. It is an assumption. It is an offence. Promise me that you won't be annoyed. Well, confiding in your good nature, I venture to go on. When you call, bring an ally. Bring your brother Wallace, for instance. Let him ask for Mrs. Chester and talk to Mrs. Chester, while you ask for some one else and talk to some one else."

The young man had begun by blushing to his forehead, but he ended by bursting into a paroxysm of laughter. He laughed with the wonder and amusement of an unsophisticated countryman to whom some one explains the mystery of the pea under the thimble.

But the hint was not lost upon him. The next time he set out for the Beaumont house he was preceded by a feinting column in the person of the good-natured, self-sacrificing Wallace, fully instructed as to the stratagem which he was to execute, and grinning to himself over the same. On arriving, Wallace asked for Mrs. Chester, and immediately took that lady off on a drive. Twenty minutes later Frank made his appearance, and of course saw Miss Kate, "with no one nigh to hinder." This trick was played repeatedly; the brothers seeking to allay suspicion by coming sometimes separately and sometimes together; but the elder one always possessing himself of the aunt, while the other was assiduous about the niece.

"I say, Frank, this is rather heavy on me," Wallace at last remonstrated. "Sometimes the old girl is devilish sulky, and sometimes she is too loving. I don't know, by George, but what I shall have the misfortune to cut you out yet in her affections. I occasionally fear she'll make a grab at me, in spite of my bald head. (Bald at twenty-eight, by George!) I wish you'd hurry up your little matter. I don't feel as if I could stand above four or five more races with Mauma Chester in the saddle. She's a remarkably worrying jockey to go under, by George."

"Oh, hold on, Wally!" begged Frank, who was not making so much progress as he desired in his "little matter." Miss Kate, we have sentimental reason to fear, was in some respects an old head on young shoulders. She no doubt liked Frank better than any other young man; but she did not yet like him enough to risk all other means of happiness for his sake. Suppose she should become engaged to him, and perhaps go so far as to marry him; and suppose that then there should be another outbreak of that old, mighty feud, so full of angering memories? Where would she be with reference to her father and brothers and grandpapa? Separated from them? Their enemy? Not to be thought of!

Meantime Mrs. Chester, not quite a fool in a general way, and in love matters not easily imposed upon except by herself, made out to see through the cutthroat game of which she was the victim. For one whole night and the following forenoon she brooded over the discovery with alternate ragings and tears. In the afternoon, when Wallace McAlister called and sent up his compliments to know if she would ride, she had a spasm of desire to rush down stairs and pull out what hair was left him, and she with difficulty so far controlled herself as to send back regrets that she could see no one on account of a headache.

"Hurrah!" thought Wallace, and cantered away to call on Jenny Devine, totally forgetting to warn the coming Frank that Mrs. Chester would be at home. That infuriated lady watched him out of sight, and then watched for the appearing of his brother.

"Miriam!" she suddenly called. "There comes Frank McAlister to court my niece. I won't have this thing going on. Those McAlisters! Low, mean, vulgar 'crackers'! I won't have it. It's my duty to prevent it. Hurry down and tell him Miss Kate is out. Do you hear me? Hurry!"

Now Miriam knew two things: she knew, in the first place, that Miss Kate was at home; in the second place she knew her mistress's silly weakness for juvenile beaux.

"I don' go for to do it," she said to herself, as she walked away. "I don' tell no lies, an' I don' help out no foolishness. If Miss Marian is gwine to court young men an' gwine to hender true lovers, she may jess work at it alone. I'se a square woman, I is. I has a conscience, bless de Lord!"

As she passed Kate's room she opened the door softly, beckoned the girl to approach, put her finger to her lips, and whispered, "Come, Miss Katie. Come down to the front do', quick. I'se got suthin' to show ye."

Kate was of course curious; she glided down to the front door; the negress opened it; there was Frank!

"Can't tell him now she ain't to home," thought the conscientious Miriam; and walked back to her mistress with the truthful report. "Miss Kate was at the do' herself."

"Waiting for him!" almost shrieked Mrs. Chester.

"Didn' know he was thar," declared Miriam. "The dear chile was puffec'ly s'prised."

"I won't have this," asseverated Mrs. Chester. "I must interfere. I am going down."

"Laws, honey, you'se got a headache," said Miriam. "You jess better lie down."

In reply Mrs. Chester flew at her chattel, boxed her ears and drove her out of the room. Then, sobbing with rage, she threw herself on a sofa; got up presently, bathed her face and looked at it in the glass; went back to the sofa in despair and remained there.

On the evening of that day, having dragged her brother out into the moonlit garden, she began upon him with, "Well, Peyton Beaumont! You are managing things finely, I should say."

"Hullo! What's the row now?" demanded Peyton, scenting battle at once and charging with all his eyebrows.

"I'll tell you what's the row," continued the sister. "Here is this Kershaw estate going straight out of the family."

"What the devil is the Colonel going to do with his estate?" asked the alarmed Beaumont. "Not going to cut Kate off."

"Kate will be the heir of it, won't she? Well, Kate is being courted, and Kate will get married."

"I suppose she will, some day," sighed the father. "I suppose she will. Girls do. But how can I keep the Kershaw estate in the family! My boys can't marry their own sister."

"There is Bentley Armitage, the brother of your son-in-law. That would be in the family."

Beaumont uttered a sound between a groan and a grunt. As near as he could make out from what he heard, the brother of Bentley Armitage was not a model of husbands, and did not render his daughter Nellie very happy. Bent was a jolly fellow; he told hosts of capital stories; he was very amusing; he soothed the gout. But for all that, Beaumont did not find that he hankered after any more Armitages for sons-in-law.

"But you don't want a McAlister?" furiously remonstrated the lady.

"How a McAlister?" inquired Beaumont, with something like a shaking of the mane at the sound of the so long detested name. "What McAlister?"

"*Frank*," gasped Mrs. Chester, her naughty, sensitive old heart giving one great throb of tenderness over the monosyllable, mighty as was her jealousy and spite.

"Frank!" echoed the father, — "Frank!"

He broke away, walked a few steps in silence, turned back suddenly, and repeated in a gentle voice, "Frank?"

"Yes," trembled Mrs. Chester.

"Why, good God, Marian, he saved her life! Why, good God, what could I say to him?"

"Oh it hasn't gone so far as that," laughed the lady, a bit hysterically. "There is time yet to stop it from going so far as that. I don't think she cares for him yet. You can stop her from learning to care for him. You can send her off visiting."

Beaumont made no answer; he did not want to send her off visiting; he could not spare her from his sight.

"Would you make her miserable for life?" argued the aunt. "Suppose she should marry this man, and then the old feud should break out again?"

"Good God, I might lose my daughter forever," returned Beaumont, aghast. "Good God, I must send her away. Well, she must go to Randolph Armitage's. She must go to her sister."

"We can send her up under the care of Bentley Armitage," slyly added Mrs. Chester.

CHAPTER 15

 In the battle of life the new generation is always beating the old, outwitting it, outfighting it, outnumbering it, and driving it off the field.

Because Kate Beaumont was a child, she was too much for a father. When her bristly, grisly genitor, one of the most combative and domineering of men, propounded to her his notion of sending her on a visit to her sister, she at once dissipated it by saying that she would rather not go.

"Don't want to make Nellie a visit!" replied Peyton Beaumont, believing that he ought to insist, and doubting whether he could.

"Why, papa!" said Kate, in a tone of good-natured wonder and reproof. "Have you forgotten?"

"Forgotten what?"

"Don't you really know what I mean?" persisted the girl, a little chagrined.

"'Pon my honor, I don't."

"O papa! My birthday! Nineteen next Tuesday."

"Bless my body!" exclaimed Beaumont, looking uncommonly ashamed of himself. "Bless my body, how could I forget it! Well, of course I knew it all the while. It had only slipped my mind for a —" Here he recollected his conspiracy with Mrs. Chester, and fell suddenly dumb, querying whether his wits were not beginning to fail him.

"Of course I want to keep it here," said Kate.

"Of course you do," assented Beaumont, ready to knock down anybody who should object to it.

"Why shouldn't Nellie come to us?" asked Kate.

"She shall," declared Beaumont. "Write her a letter and ask her to come. Give her my best love, and tell her I insist upon it."

It was in vain that Mrs. Chester made assault upon this new disposition of events as soon as she heard of it.

"No danger, I tell you," interrupted Beaumont, his temper rising at her opposition, as a wave breaks into a roar and foam over a reef. "I tell you there's no danger whatever. Kate is not only a doosed brilliant girl, — yes, doosed brilliant, by heavens, if I do say it, — but she's a girl of extraordinary common sense. If I should hint to her the trouble which might come from her marrying a McAlister; if I should once say to her, 'Now, Kate, you see it might separate us,' she never would think of it. I tell you, I trust to her common sense. And by heavens," he added, his eyebrows beginning to bristle, "I want you to trust to it."

As Mrs. Chester had no efficient quantity of the grace in question, she did not believe in it as a motive of action with other people.

"Well, good by to the Kershaw estate," she replied, trying to bring the financial point of view to bear upon her brother.

"Good by to it and welcome!" roared Beaumont, indignant at this thrusting of filthy lucre under his honorable nose. "What the Old Harry do I care for the Kershaw estate? I am a Beaumont, and the descendant of Beaumonts. Who are you? I thought we looked only to honor, in our family. Money! You can't turn my head by talking money. I know the value of the thing. But, by heavens, I wouldn't swerve a hair for the sake of it. I'd blow my brains out first. And as for Kate's marrying against my wishes, you know she won't do it and I know it. There's no use in talking about it."

"No, there's no use in talking about it," replied Mrs. Chester, with what might be called a snapping-turtle irony.

Stung by her brother's charge that she was no true Beaumont, angered by his inconvenient obstinacy, and still more by his loud, overbearing voice, she suddenly and petulantly gave up her hopeless contest (as a child drops a hammer which has cracked its fingers), and marched off with short, spunky stampings, reminding one of that famous step between the sublime and the ridiculous. Her hips had become of late years an inch or so too wide to permit her to move thus with grace or dignity. They gave her skirts a quick, jerking swing, which, as seen from behind, was more farcical than majestic. The fat washerwoman or chambermaid of low comedy walks by preference in this manner. As Peyton Beaumont looked after her, he grinned with a kind of amused rage, and muttered, "By Jove, what a goose Marian can make of herself."

But after Mrs. Chester had got to her room, and had, so to speak, stuck out her lips behind the door for half an hour, she discovered some consolation and hope in the fact that Nellie Armitage was coming. She remembered Nellie as a "true Beaumont," full of the family pride and passion, the fieriest perhaps of Peyton's children. Was it not likely that such a woman would retain much of the feeling of the ancient family feud? Was it not almost certain that she would violently oppose a match between her only sister and a McAlister? Poor, bewitched, unreasonable, almost irrational Mrs. Chester plucked up her spirit a little as she looked forward to Nellie's arrival.

At last Mrs. Armitage came, bringing her two children with her, but not her husband. This young lady (then only twenty-four years old) bore a certain resemblance to her father. She was of medium height, with a figure more compact than is usual in American women, her chest being uncommonly full, her shoulders superbly plump, and her arms solid. Her complexion was a clear brunette, without color; her hair a very dark chestnut and slightly wavy; her eyes brown, steady, and searching. Barring that the cheek-bones were a trifle too broad and the lower jaw a trifle too strong, her face was a handsome one, the front view being fairly oval and the profile full of spirit. There was something singular in her expression; it was a beseeching air, alternating with an air of resistance; she seemed in one moment to implore favor, and in the next to stand at bay. To all appearance it was the face of a woman who had had a stirring and trying heart-history. You could not study it long without wishing to know what had happened to her.

She greeted her relatives with the quick, effervescent excitability of her Huguenot race. A minute or two later she was absorbed, indifferent, almost stony. It seemed as if something must have partly paralyzed the woman's affections, rendering their action intermittent.

"Kate has grown up very handsome," she quietly and thoughtfully remarked to her father, when she was alone with him.

"By Jove!" trumpeted Peyton Beaumont, unable to brag sufficiently of his favorite child, and falling into eloquent silence before the great subject, like a heathen prostrating himself to his idol.

"I hope she will have a happy life of it," added Nellie, with the air of one within prison-gates who wishes well to those without.

"Why shouldn't she?" demanded the father, lifting his stormy eyebrows as an excited eagle ruffles his feathers. "She has everything she can want, and we are all devoted to her. The baby, you know!" he explained, as if apologizing to his eldest daughter for so loving the youngest.

"It is all well enough now. But she may get married by and by."

"Ah!" growled Beaumont, glancing at her with an air of comprehension, half pitiful and half angry.

Mrs. Armitage revealed no more; if she was not happy in her own marriage, she was not disposed to say so; either she had been born with more discretion than was usual with Beaumonts, or she had acquired it.

"So the feud is ended," was her next observation.

"Well, yes; that is, you know — well, we get along," said the father. "We are allowing those fellows a chance to behave themselves."

He felt obliged to apologize to a Beaumont for having given up one of the antiquities and glories of the family.

"Of course you know best," replied Nellie, with that indifferent air which she had at times, and which made her appear so unlike her race.

"You see this young McAlister had the luck to place us under immense obligations to him," continued the old fighting-cock. "And doosed lucky it was for that blockhead his brother. Vincent would have shot him as sure as Christmas is coming."

"And how about Kate? Is she likely to marry this Frank McAlister?"

"Likely to marry the Old Harry!" snorted Beaumont, indignant at being spurred up to this ugly subject again. "Who the dickens told you that nonsense?"

"Aunt Marian wrote to me about it."

"Aunt Marian is a babbling busybody," returned Beaumont, thrusting his hands fiercely into his pockets, as if feeling for a brace of derringers.

"She told me not to tell you of her letter, and so I thought it best to tell you," added Nellie.

"By Jove! you know her," replied Marian's brother, bursting into a laugh. "By Jove, it's amazing how she lacks common sense," he added, as if his breed were famous for that characteristic. "In a general way, — I'm fairly obliged to own it, — whatever Marian wants done had better not be done. It's astonishing!"

"If there is any such courtship going on, I want it stopped," continued Nellie, somewhat of the family excitability beginning to sparkle in her eyes.

Peyton Beaumont, vain and self-opinionated and pugnacious as he was, would always listen to those privileged, those almost sacred creatures, his children.

"Look here, Nellie, I'm glad you came down," he said. "I want to talk to you about this very thing. Not that there is any danger, — Oh no," he explained, motioning away the supposition with his thick, hairy hand. "But then, if things should go on, there might be trouble. That is, you understand, the thing is just possible, — I don't say probable, mind, I say possible."

"It must not be possible," declared Nellie.

"You think so?" stared Beaumont, a little bothered. Considering his own weakness in the presence of Kate, was he absolutely sure that he could put the match outside of the possibilities, in case she should prefer to bring it inside?

"Certainly I think so," affirmed Mrs. Armitage, kindling in a way which left no doubt as to her being a true Beaumont. "See here, I want at least one woman in the world to succeed; I want Kate to have a happy married life. If she marries a McAlister, what are the chances for it? You know that family, and you know our own. How long will the two get on together? You know as well as I do that the old quarrel is pretty sure to come up again. Then where will Kate be? A woman who is forced to fight her own flesh and blood, God help her!"

She said much more to this effect; perhaps she repeated herself a little, as emotional people are apt to do; she was very much in earnest, and hardly knew how to stop.

"Well, of course!" neighed Beaumont, quite roused by her excitement, as one horse rears because another plunges. "The thing cannot, must not, and shall not be allowed. I'll see to it."

"You'll see to it!" repeated Nellie, amused in spite of her anxiety, and good-naturedly laughing him to scorn.

"What d' ye mean?" queried the father, trying to raise his bristles.

"You'll just see that every one of your idiots of children does exactly what he or she pleases," explained Nellie.

"Nonsense!" growled Beaumont, marching off with all his peacock plumage spread. To prove to himself that he possessed paternal austerity, he took advantage of the first opportunity to fall afoul of Tom, giving him a lively lecture for birching a negro. Only the lecture being concluded, he drew his cigar-case and presented the youngster with one of his costliest Havanas, the two thereupon smoking what might pass for the calumet of peace.

The case of Frank and Kate soon came up between Mrs. Armitage and Mrs. Chester.

"Of course not," haughtily affirmed Nellie, when her aunt had declared that the McAlister match would never do. "I have discussed the matter with papa. We will attend to it."

This was saying that the affair was none of Mrs. Chester's business; and that lady so understood the remark, and trembled with wrath accordingly. The two were treading on the verge of an old battleground which had been often fought over between them. Mrs. Chester, an advisatory and meddlesome creature, felt in all her veins and nerves that she was a Beaumont, and that whatever concerned any of that breed concerned her. This pretension, so far at least as it extended to the children of Peyton Beaumont, Nellie had always violently combated, even from infancy. One of her earliest recollections was of scratching Aunt Marian for trying to slap Tom. The fight had been renewed many times, the niece gaining more and more victories as she grew older, for she was a cleverer woman than Mrs. Chester, and also a braver. It need not be said that, while there was no outrageous and disreputable quarrel, there was no fervent love between them. But although Aunt Marian did not like Nellie, and was at the moment considerably irritated against her, she did not, under present circumstances, care to fight her.

"Of course you and your father will do what is proper," she said, putting on that air of sulphuric-acid sweetness which so many tartarly people have at command, and which profits them so little. You two are Kate's natural guardians," she further conceded.

"Certainly!"

She waited to hear something more about the match, but Nellie had no communications to volunteer, and there ensued a brief silence, insupportable to Mrs. Chester.

"Of course you never could give your approval," she ventured to resume, smoothing her niece's hair.

"No!" sharply replied Nellie, who would have answered more graciously if Mrs. Chester had kept her hot hands to herself.

Unamiably as this response was enunciated, the elder lady was so delighted with it that she lost her self-possession, and let out a gush of confidence which was imprudent.

"Kate will have plenty of offers. I know one fine young man who is desperately in love with her. I am sure that your husband's brother —"

Nellie turned upon her with sparkling eyes and quivering nostrils.

"Bent Armitage?" she demanded. "Is *he* courting her?"

"Oh no," responded Mrs. Chester, discovering her error and at once trying to fib out of it. "I was about to say that Bent, as you call him, told me that Pickens Pendleton was cracked about her."

Which was true enough as regarded Pickens Pendleton, only the tale of it had not come from Bent Armitage.

Well, each of the ladies had made a discovery. Nellie had learned, in spite of her aunt's prompt dodging, that Bent Armitage was wooing Kate; and Mrs. Chester had perceived without the slightest difficulty that such a match would be sternly disfavored by Nellie. Both being thus provided with matter for grave meditation, they found discourse a weary business, and soon separated.

The next important dialogue of this straightforward and earnest Mrs. Armitage was with her sister.

"How you have grown, Kate!" she laughed, turning her about and standing up to her back to back. "Pshaw! you are taller than I am. You ought to know more. I wonder if you do. What did you study abroad?"

"Oh, everything that is useful," smiled Kate. "Only I don't find that I use it. I think a good cookery-book ought to be the main class-book of every girls' school. I wish I knew a hundred receipts by heart."

"Well, send for a cookery-book, and go to getting them by heart."

"I have," said Kate.

"Pudding-making and love-making are woman's chief business," observed Nellie, shaping her course toward the subject which she had on her mind. "They are both important, but I think the last is the most so. Which do you like best of all the men who come here?"

"I don't like any of them," said Kate, for once driven to fib by an awful heartbreaking, and blushing profoundly over her — was it her guilt?

"Oh, what a monstrous lie!" laughed Mrs. Armitage.

"Then what do you ask such questions for?" retorted Kate, becoming honest again.

"Because I want to know," said Nellie, looking her earnestly in the face.

"When the young man speaks, I will come and tell you," was the evasive answer.

"But then it will be too late to tell me. Your mind will be already made up, and you will accept him or refuse him, and then advice will be useless."

"Oh, is that the way it goes?"

"That is the way it went with me."

"Well, you have never repented it," said Kate, who knew nothing of her sister's sorrows, if sorrows there were.

"Let me tell you one thing," answered Nellie, roused to fresh resolution by this remark. "Let me tell you whom not to marry. Neither Frank McAlister nor Bent Armitage. If you take the first, you will make trouble for yourself; and if you take the second, he may make trouble for you."

Kate struggled to retain her self-possession, but she was not a little disturbed, and her sister perceived it.

"You don't care for either of them?" demanded Nellie, imploringly. "I don't want it. Papa doesn't want it."

"I *won't* care for either of them," was the promise which dropped from Kate's lips before she realized its gravity. There was conscience and discipline in the girl; she instinctively and by habit respected and obeyed her elders; she did it naturally and could not help it. But the moment she had given her pledge she grew pale and tried to turn away from her sister.

"Look here, Kate, this costs you a struggle," said Nellie, slipping her arm around the child's waist and kissing her. "Which one is it?"

Kate made no answer, for she had as much as she could do to catch her breath, and she was for the moment beyond speaking.

"Not Bent Armitage?" begged Nellie.

Kate shook her head.

"The other?"

Kate bent her face.

"Oh Katie!" said Nellie.

After a moment Kate broke out, "But I don't care so much about him. Only you surprised me so. You worried me. You —"

"I know, Katie," whispered Nellie, all tenderness now. "I did put things at you too hard. Don't be vexed with me. I do love you. That is the reason. Well, you can't talk of it now. We won't say a word more now."

"Yes, I can talk of it," declared Kate, collecting her soul bravely. "What is the whole of it? What is it?"

"Suppose there should be another long quarrel with the McAlisters?" began Nellie.

"I know. I have thought of that. I will think of it."

"Oh, you are pretty sensible, Kate. Well, as for Bent Armitage —"

"You needn't tell me about *him*. It is of no consequence."

"I hope not," said Nellie, too anxious to be quite sure. "Well?"

"You have my promise," declared Kate, firmly.

"Yes," answered Nellie, meditatively.

"Do you suppose I won't keep it?"

"I wasn't thinking of that," replied Nellie, who, now that she had gained her point, had a sudden, natural, irrational reaction of feeling, and did not find herself positive that the promise ought to be kept. "I was thinking — but never mind now, dear. Another time."

CHAPTER 16

 Mrs. Armitage went through a variety of spiritual exercises with regard to this possible match between her sister and Frank McAlister.

At first she had been sternly opposed to it; then the contagion of Kate's emotion caused her to relent somewhat; next she reflected upon the matter by herself, and hardened her heart once more; at last she met the young man, and in consequence experienced a further change.

Although she was prepared to find him agreeable and handsome, she was rather surprised by his grand figure, his fine face, and pleasant address. His lofty stature did not seem to her objectionable or even very odd, for in the midland and back country of South Carolina, where she had passed her life, the human plant grows luxuriantly, six feet being a common height, and six feet four not unusual. Moreover, there are probably few women who do not find a certain massive charm in large men. "No wonder," thought Nellie, "that Kate likes this fellow, especially since he saved her life." Nevertheless, she would study him; she would see whether he were half as good as he looked; she would see whether he were good enough to make up for being a McAlister.

There was not much in their interview of the wandering small-talk which is apt to follow introductions; for both Mrs. Armitage and Frank were of that earnest class of souls who usually mean something and say it. The lady, too, had a fervent purpose at heart, and none too much time in which to carry it out.

"Are you going to live at home, Mr. McAlister?" she very soon inquired.

Frank colored; it seemed as if she were asking him whether he meant to live on his father, like so many other sons of well-to-do planters; and he remembered that he had been in Hartland several weeks without doing anything chemical or metallurgical.

"I haven't yet decided where I shall be," he replied. "But I hope before long to find some place where I can earn my own living."

Mrs. Armitage stared; a young gentleman of expectations who wanted to earn his own living was a novelty to her; she was so puzzled that she smiled in a rather blank fashion.

"And how do people earn their own living?" she demanded.

"I want to earn mine by making other people rich."

"I don't understand," said Nellie, more perplexed than ever, and beginning to query whether this McAlister were not jesting with her.

So Frank explained that he had studied metallurgy and commercial chemistry; that he proposed to test mines and phosphate beds, and decide whether they could be worked profitably; and that for such services he should expect a reasonable compensation.

"But will that get a living?" inquired Mrs. Armitage. Another reflection, which, however, she kept to herself was, "Is that work for a gentleman?"

"It may not for a time," laughed Frank. "Our people don't care much as yet for their underground wealth. Their eyes are bandaged with cotton. But I have an ambition, Mrs. Armitage. I want to open people's eyes. I want to develop the natural wealth of my State. I want to be a benefactor to South Carolina."

"Oh, that is right," admitted Nellie, thinking the while that, if he became famous as a benefactor, he might run for Congress.

"Yes, there would be little to do for a time," continued Frank. "So the other part of my plan is to obtain a professorship in some college."

Nellie frowned frankly; he seemed too grand a fellow to be a mere professor; she was already interested in him, and wished him well.

"If you really want a professorship, I should think you might easily get one," she said. "Your father has a great deal of political influence."

The serious young man was tempted to smile in the face of the serious young woman. Of course, scientific enthusiast as he was, he scorned the idea of getting a professorship through his father's wire-pullings, and trusted to earn one by making himself famous, desirable, and necessary as a chemist and metallurgist. But it was not worth while, nor perhaps in good taste, to try to render these matters clear to Mrs. Armitage.

"Well, you will not starve; your father will see to that," was her next remark, good-naturedly and smilingly uttered, but surely very discouraging.

His father again! It was almost provoking to have his high and mighty and respected parent flung at his head in this persistent manner. So far was Frank from looking to the paternal statesmanship and influence and acres for his bread and butter, that he at heart expected to gain pelf as well as honor by his sciences, developing untold wealth and sharing in the profits.

"Do you expect to find gold-mines in Hartland District?" was Nellie's next speech.

"No," patiently responded our scientist, not even marvelling at the depths of her ignorance, though he knew that auriferous ore out of Hartland was less possible than sunbeams out of a cucumber. "I shall have to run about after my work," he added.

He feared that he was damaging his chances as a suitor for Kate; but he was too honorable to tell anything less than the truth.

"Run about," repeated Nellie, quite decided for the moment that he should not have her sister; "I should think it would be pleasanter to stay at home."

Frank was discouraged; nobody hereabout sympathized with his tenderness for chemistry and his passion for metallurgy; sometimes he feared lest he should have to drop his sciences and go to sleep upon cotton, like the rest of South Carolina.

"You must excuse my frankness," said Mrs. Armitage, who perceived that she had dashed him a little. "It is so strange that I should be talking to you at all! It seems as if I were at liberty to say everything."

"There has been a prodigious breaking of the ice between our families."

"Yes; and you broke it. It was a great thing to do, and you found a grand way to do it."

"It was accident," said Frank, coloring under this praise from Kate's sister.

"I can't thank you enough for saving her," continued Nellie, a little moved. "It is useless to try to do it."

There was a short silence. The young man's spirit was beginning to burgeon and bloom all over with hope. The lady was meditating how she could tear up his hopes, without seeming to him and to herself outrageously ungrateful and hard-hearted.

"Yes, you did a noble thing," she resumed. "I hope you will never have occasion to regret it."

"How!" he exclaimed, in a sudden burst of earnest bass, at the same time starting up and pacing the room. "I beg your pardon," he almost immediately added, and sat down again.

"He is very much in love with her," thought Nellie. "What a dreadful business it is! What shall I say to him?"

She steeled herself with a remembrance of her duty to her sister, and added: "It might have been better if some one else had saved her."

The Chinese wall was broken down; the great subject of Kate Beaumont lay open before them for discussion; and the only question was, whether Frank McAlister could summon breath to enter upon it. For a moment he was like a climber of mountains, who should discover a barely traversable path leading to the longed-for summit, and should just then find himself turning dizzy. He had to make another excursion to the window and back before he was able to say, "Do you think I would take improper advantage of my slight, very slight claim to gratitude?"

"No, I do not," replied the impulsive Nellie, unable to help admiring him for his honesty and his beauty. "I am sure, Mr. McAlister, that you are a gentleman. But have you thought, have you considered? Oh, how hard it is to say some things! Well, I must speak it out. Here is my young sister under great obligations to you. And you are a McAlister. I know that there is peace now between our families. But how long will it last? Suppose it should not last? Would you like to have your name stand between your wife and her own father and brothers?"

Suddenly remembering that she had assumed that he cared to marry her sister, when he had not yet told her so, Nellie stopped in confusion. It was so like her to spring forward in that instinctive way; it was so like the emotional, headlong race to which she belonged.

"I hope it would never be as you say," groaned the young man, frankly acknowledging the purpose which had been imputed to him.

"Ah — yes," replied Nellie, with a sigh of sympathy. Her opposition was weakening; she found it very hard to withstand this good and handsome lover to his face; she was mightily tempted to get done with him by giving him her sister. Discovering her weakness, and deciding that it was her duty not to yield to it, she hastened to speak her mind while she had one.

"See here, Mr. McAlister. I ask you one thing. I ask it of you as a gentleman; yes, and as a friend. I beg of you that, if ever you should wish to say a word of love to Kate, you will not say it without the full permission of her father."

He came up to her with a bright smile, seized her hand, pressed it, and in his thankfulness kissed it.

Nellie's resolution was almost upset; she came very near saying, "Take her."

"I worship her," he whispered. "But before I say one word, you shall permit it. You and your father shall both permit it."

"Oh, it all amounts to nothing," returned Nellie, shaking her head with a slightly hysterical laugh. "Such things are said without saying them. If you love her, she will find it out, though you should never speak again."

"But you won't send me away?" begged Frank, his smile suddenly fading and his eyes turning anxious.

"No," said Nellie. "Every woman is a big fool on these subjects. I can't send you away."

Thus ended Mrs. Armitage's first attempt to prevent a match between her sister and Frank McAlister. It had been so far from a triumph that she had given the young man a tacit permission to continue some silent sort of courtship, and had at the bottom of her heart become little less than his partisan. She did not deceive herself as to the result of the onslaught; she admitted that one more such victory would beat her completely; and her sagacious decision was, "I won't say another word about it." It was a resolution, as certain metaphysicians inform us, easier for a woman to make than to keep.

In fact, Nellie was rather an aid than a bar to Frank in his researches after happiness at the Beaumont mansion, inasmuch as she kept Mrs. Chester from balking and worrying him with her venerable assiduities. It must be understood that the cracked old flirt had got over her wrath at the youngster for playing his brother upon her while he himself had walks and talks with her niece. She observed that in these latter days he never saw Kate alone; and, not knowing the true reason, she guessed that he had tired of her. Consequently she once more had hopes of — the gracious knows what; and with the return of hope came a resurrection of fondness for her Titan.

Now Nellie did not mean to smooth the course of Frank's love; impulsive as she might be, she was no such weathercock as that. But she had grown up in the habit of fighting Aunt Marian; and, moreover, she could not bear to see that venerable chicken make a fool of herself; for did not her absurdities more or less disgrace the family? As soon, therefore, as she perceived that Mrs. Chester was indulging in her time-worn vice of flirting with a man ever so much her junior, she prepared to open fire upon her. The two ladies were sewing by themselves in the breezy veranda, when Mrs. Armitage commenced her bombardment with "What a handsome fellow Frank McAlister is!"

How easily the slyest of us are humbugged when people talk to us about those whom we love! It was of no use to Mrs. Chester that she was a woman, that she was a veteran worldling, that she was an old coquette. The doors of her heart flew open at the sound of the name which was her open sesame; and with a throb of pleasure, with the sincere countenance of a gratified child she replied, "Yes, indeed!"

"He is trying to catch Kate, and I fear he will do it," added the cruel Nellie, sending a straight thrust at the unguarded bosom.

"It would be a most outrageous match," burst out the surprised and tortured Mrs. Chester.

"It would make more than one of us miserable," continued Nellie, turning the blade in the wound; and at the same time she gave her discovered, unhappy, ridiculous, irrational relative a glance of angry contempt. A woman who "loves not wisely" gets little pity from other women; they regard her as men regard a brother-man who loses his estate in silly speculations; perhaps, also, they look upon her as one who cheapens and discredits her sex.

All at once Mrs. Chester understood that Nellie had found her out and was openly flouting her. Exposure and a consciousness of "scorn's unmoving finger" are great helps to beclouded intelligences. Although this widow bewitched was half crazy about Frank McAlister, she could see somewhat of the absurdity of her position when another plainly pointed it out to her. She shook with shame and rage; her pale brunette cheek turned ashy; after a little her black eyes sparkled vindictively. But she had enough of self-control to go on with her cuttings and bastings, and to merely mutter, "Yes, the match would make plenty of trouble."

"He is enough to fascinate any woman, young or old," added Nellie, by way of completing her massacre of this mature innocent.

Wonders were accomplished by this short dialogue. Henceforward, so long as Mrs. Armitage remained at the plantation, Aunt Marian ceased making eyes at Frank McAlister, or trying to entrap him into moonlight strolls, or doing anything else that was lovelorn, — at least before witnesses. Her reformation was, however, only external; she was in reality fully possessed by that mighty demon, a heart-affair of middle life; she was reaping the reward of having passed twenty-five years in no other habit of mind, than that of love-making. She was so far bewitched with Frank McAlister that she would have rushed into the madness of marrying him, had he proposed it. The case may seem incredible to those who have not witnessed something similar. While we all know that elderly men sometimes fall desperately in love with girls, we are not accustomed to see elderly women get into hallucinations over youngsters. But the marvel sometimes happens; and it happened to poor Mrs. Chester.

In these days she passed much time in her room; sometimes lost in reveries which were alternately sweet and bitter; sometimes trying on dress after dress and ornament after ornament, not to mention perlatinas, etc.; sometimes studying herself in the glass and endeavoring to think herself youthful, or at least not old. Like Southerners in general, she found no embarrassment in the presence of a negro; and so her ancient maid, Miriam, had plenty of opportunity to observe these prinkings and prankings.

"Laws me!" muttered the indignant mauma. "Ef Miss Marian don't oughter have the biggest kind of a spankin'."

There was no reason why Miriam should not guess accurately what was the matter with her mistress. Mrs. Chester was one of those people who must have sympathy; she had always been accustomed to receive it from her faithful chattel; and she demanded it now with a curious frankness.

"I don't see why Mr. McAlister should avoid me," she would say plaintively. Then she would burst out with sudden vexation: "But in these days no woman can get any attention who is over twenty."

"Don't see nuffin perticlar 'bout Mars Frank," muttered Miriam, lying a little for her owner's good.

"Oh, he is so tall!" exclaimed Mrs. Chester, in naïve ecstasy.

So tall! Perhaps that was the key to her possession. The jaded flirt, famished after sensations, had been captivated by a physical novelty. Her next passion might be for a dwarf, or for one of the Siamese Twins.

"No woman over twenty has any chance of being noticed here in the country," she presently added, laying on the word *country* an accent of scorn and spite.

"Miss Marian, you's a big piece beyond twenty," exploded Miriam, losing all patience. "You's a young lookin' lady for your age. I allows it. But for all that, you ain't what they calls young no longer. I don' keer, Miss Marian, ef you doos git angry. I'se talkin' for your good, an' I'se gwine to talk a heap, an' I'se gwine to talk it out. You's jess altogeder too old to be friskin' roun' a young feller like Mars Frank McAlister. He ain't a gwine to wanter frisk back, an' you can't make him. Now you jess let him alone. He'll think mo' of you ef you doos; he'll think a heap mo'. An' so'll everybody. Thar! that's what I'se got to say; an' I've said it, thank the Lord; an' I'll say it agin."

Mrs. Chester's first impulse, under this benevolently cruel lecture, was to fly at Miriam and kill her; her next and victorious impulse was to cover her face with her hands and shed tears of humiliation and grief.

"Thar now, honey, don't," implored the suddenly softened Miriam. "Don't cry that way. I'se been mighty hash, I knows. The Lord forgive me for hurtin' your feelin's."

And then followed a strange, and almost pathetic scene of weeping on one side and coddling on the other, which only ended when the sorrowful Marian had taken a dose of chloroform and got to sleep. Coming out of her nap refreshed, she wandered through a thorny meditation concerning Frank, and struggled up to the top of an emotional Mount Pisgah whence she looked upon him with her mind's eye, giving up hope of possession. But this resolve left her in an angry state of mind towards him and his family, so that when she next met her bland and sympathetic friend, Major Lawson, she launched into an invective against the whole race of McAlisters.

"Dear me! Bless my soul!" said the Major, in his most soothing whisper. "I am excessively grieved that your feelings should have been hurt by — by circumstances unknown to me. What have those truly unfortunate people been doing? I trust nothing that an apology will not atone for. Do, my dear old friend, — may I not venture to call you so? — do confide in me. I will see them about it," he declared, grandly assuming an air of sternness, as Hector might have put on his helmet. "I will insist upon an explanation. By heavens I will, my dear friend."

"Oh, it is nothing of that sort!" returned Mrs. Chester. "There is nothing to have a quarrel about, I suppose. But —" and here she burst out passionately — "they are so — so ungrateful!"

"Un-grate-ful!" gasped the Major, seemingly horror-stricken. "Un-grate-ful!" he chanted, running his voice through four or five flats, sharps, and naturals. "You — you confound me, — you positively do, Mrs. Chester. Wh-at a charge! And they were supposed to be gentle-men. Claim to be such. Pass for such. Ah! — Well?"

And here he looked at her for further explanations, his hands wide-spread with mock sympathy, and his eyes full of real eagerness. In truth, the Major was very anxious, for he did not know but that some serious matter of offence had arisen between the families, and he trembled for his Romeo and Juliet romance.

"I have been as civil as I could be to Mr. Frank McAlister," began Mrs. Chester in a low tone, which was, perhaps, a little tremulous.

The Major's eyes brightened; so that was the whole trouble; the old flirt was jealous about attentions.

"I have certainly shown him all the consideration that a lady can properly show to a gentleman," she continued, her voice gaining strength, if her reason did not. "I have done it in kindness. His position here was peculiar. So lately introduced among us, and under such trying circumstances! I thought that he needed encouragement, and that some one was bound to give it to him. I have given it. And the result is" — here there was almost a choking in her utterance — "that he avoids me."

"Dear me! But no. It can't be possible. It isn't true," brazenly asserted the Major, alarmed by her evident emotion and fearing the worst results for Romeo and Juliet. "My dear old friend," getting hold of her hand and squeezing it tenderly, "you *must* be mistaken. Forgive me. I am in earnest. I am excited. This is enough to throw any man off his balance. Excuse me for speaking plainly: pardon me for contradicting you. But you *must* be mistaken. Why, it was only yesterday that I was talking with him, and the conversation fell upon yourself, my dear Mrs. Chester, and he was enthusiastic about you. Absolutely enthusiastic," repeated the Major as glibly as if he were telling the truth. "Nothing less than enthusiastic. Why, my dear friend, if he seems to avoid you, it must be attributed to modesty. He is afraid of wearying you, — afraid of wearying you," he reiterated, falling back and gazing at her respectfully, as if she were a wonder of intellect. "Afraid of wearying you," he added, reinforcing his air of deference with a tender smile. "Nothing else. Modest young man. Modest! Appreciative too. Knows your value. Highly appreciative. I happen to know that he appreciates you. Why I happen to know it, — I am his confidant. His confidant," insisted the Major, looking whole volumes of adoration, as if translating them from McAlister.

But we can give no idea of the mellifluousness, the sugar, and sirup, and molasses, of this wondrous flatterer. To appreciate his speeches it was necessary to hear them and to watch him as he exuded them. The petting, the coaxing, the adulation that there was in his voice and address beggared description. He was a band of music; he played successively on the harp, sackbut, psaltery, and dulcimer, flute, violin, and bassoon; he flew from bass to falsetto and back again with the agility of a squirrel scampering up and down a hickory. The repetitions in which he delighted were invariably distinguished by variations of pitch and manner. He said his impressive thing in barytone, and then he said it in tenor, and then he said it in soprano. He enforced it the first time with a stare, the second time with an arching of the eyebrows, the third time with a long-drawn smile. Nor did he weaken his effects by hasty or indistinct utterance; he was as deliberate and perspicuous as an experienced judge delivering a charge to an obviously stupid jury; he made a pause after each important statement, to give you time to swallow and digest it; and meanwhile he watched you steadily to see how you bore his dosing.

To some straightforward, hard-headed people, the flattering, pottering Major was very tiresome. But to Mrs. Chester and other souls, who could endure much complimentary serenading, he was more delightful than nightingales.

Well, he talked an hour, and he soothed his auditor. By dint of playing interminably on the same key, he produced in her what is known to lawyers who have to cajole jurymen as a "favorable state of mind." He made his female Balaam forget that she had come out to curse the McAlisters, and brought her to end the conversation by uttering their praises.

But in doing thus much good he unwittingly did some mischief, for he reawakened Mrs. Chester's foolish hopes with regard to her giant, and thus opened the way to further complications and furies.

CHAPTER 17

 So thoroughly deceived was Mrs. Chester by Major Lawson's inventions, that she resolved to come to an explanation with Frank McAlister, and give him to understand that his fears of wearying her with his society were groundless.

We will not detail the conversation that resulted; we will draw a partial veil over this awkward exposure of an unbalanced mind; we will skip at once to the finale of the discordant duo. Imagine the confusion and distress of our modest and kind-hearted Titan when Mrs. Chester, after many insinuating preambles, took his hand, pressed it tenderly, and said, "Let us be friends. Will you always be my friend? My best friend?"

What made his situation more pitiable was that her agitation (a mixture of anxiety, of womanly shame, and of affection) was so great as to be unconcealable.

"I have no intention of being other than your friend, madam," replied the unfortunately honest youth.

This answer, and especially this "madam," stunned her. She inferred that he would be no more than a friend, and that he looked upon her as an elderly lady. Had he slapped her in the face, he could hardly have stung her more keenly or repulsed her more completely than he did by that title of respect, "madam." Dropping his hand as if it were a hot iron, she recoiled from him a little and walked on in silence, her breast heaving and her lips very near to quivering.

"I hope certainly that we shall always be friends," hastily added Frank, perceiving that he had pained her, and deeply regretting it.

"Certainly," mechanically responded Mrs. Chester, for the moment pathetic and almost tragic. In the next breath she turned angry and continued, with a touch of hysterical irony, "Oh, certainly, sir! We understand each other, I believe! Well, I must go in! I am afraid of this damp air. Excuse me, sir."

And before Frank could say anything to the purpose, she had forced herself from him and was in the house.

"Upon my honor I don't understand it," muttered the stupefied chemist and mineralogist. "Is it possible that she *really* wants me to *really* flirt with her?"

Such a respect had he for womankind that he impatiently dismissed this supposition, as he had often dismissed it before. Because of his born chivalrousness, and still more because of his worship of Kate, he canonized the whole sex.

He was surprised out of his reflections by the apparition of Nellie Armitage from a small, thickly trellised grape-arbor close at his elbow. It was like the dash of a partridge from a thicket at one's feet; or rather it was more like the spring of a tiger from a jungle; at all events, she startled him roundly. He suspected at once that she had overheard his final words with Mrs. Chester, and he became almost certain of it when he came to notice her manner. Nodding without speaking, she took his arm and walked on rapidly, her nostrils dilated and her quick breath audible. It was evident that she was in a good old-fashioned Beaumont fit of wrath.

"Mrs. Armitage," he said, thinking it best to be at least partially frank, "I fear that I have vexed your aunt by an awkward speech of mine."

"I wish you had boxed her ears," broke out Nellie. "I wanted to."

He was enlightened: so Mrs. Chester was really making love to him; at least Mrs. Armitage believed it. He did not know what more to say, and the awkward promenade continued speechlessly.

"I was not in ambush," the lady at last observed. "I was dozing there — no sleep last night — hateful letters. Your talking waked me, and

I heard — Well, let us say no more about it. It is abominable. It is disgraceful. So ridiculous! Oh!!"

"I beg your pardon?" queried the anxious Frank. "I must ask one word more. You are not blaming me?"

"You are only too patient, Mr. McAlister. You are a gentleman. Let us say no more about it."

Emerging presently from an alley lined with neglected shrubbery so loftily grown that a camel would have been troubled to look over it, they came upon a little stretch of flower-beds and discovered Kate gathering materials for her mantel bouquets, while Bent Armitage stood at her elbow with a basket. Of the four persons who thus met, every one colored more or less with disagreeable surprise.

"I took the liberty of forcing my guardianship on Miss Beaumont," said Bent, looking apologetically at his sister-in-law. "The roses might have wanted to keep her, you know."

Mrs. Armitage gave Frank a glance which said as plainly as eyes could speak, "I confide in your promise."

Then, turning to Bent, she ordained: "You must leave your basket to Mr. McAlister. I want to see you about things at home."

Surrendering his pleasant charge to his rival, the young man followed Nellie, his lamed foot slapping the ground in its usual nonchalant style, and his singular, mechanical smile curling up into his dark red cheek, but his heart very ill at ease.

"Bent," commenced Nellie when they were alone, "I have nothing to say to you about your brother. There is enough to tell, but it is the same old story, and there is no use in telling it. The home that I want to talk to you about is my home here. What business have you strolling off alone with my sister? I told you not to do it."

"A fellow doesn't want to have the air of a boor," he muttered sullenly. "Just look at it now. A lady goes by with a basket to pick flowers. Can't a man offer to hold her basket? Isn't he obliged to do it? Would you have him tilt back his chair and go on smoking?"

"Oh, it's easy explaining," returned Nellie. "But I am not to be trifled with, Bent. You sha'n't court her. If you do, I'll tell my whole story to my father and brothers. Then we'll see if ever an Armitage enters this house again."

Bent was cowed at once and completely; the threat was clearly a terrible one to him.

"Before God, I don't take Randolph's part," he said. "I know you have cause of complaint enough. I wish to God he was —"

He stopped with a groan. His brother, as he comprehended the matter now in hand, was his evil genius, standing between him and Kate Beaumont. In his grief and anger he had come very near to wishing that that brother was dead.

"I don't sustain him," he resumed. "Besides, Randolph is not a bad fellow at heart. He is naturally a good fellow. You know what it is that makes him raise the devil."

"You are taking the same road," was Nellie's judgment. "You will be just like him."

"Never!" declared Bent with tears in his eyes. "You shall see."

She marched on with an unbelieving, unpitying face, and he followed her with the air of a criminal who asks for a remission of sentence, and believes that he asks in vain.

"Well, I must go, I suppose," he said, turning towards his horse as they neared the house. "If you see old Miriam, tell her to pray for me," he added with a smile of bitter humor. "What I want most is to break my neck."

"I am sorry, Bent," replied Nellie, just a little softened. "But depend upon it that I am doing what is best. Just look at it yourself. What sort of a state were you in yesterday? You were —"

She was interrupted by Mrs. Chester calling from her window to Armitage that she wanted to see Mrs. Devine, and would ride home with him.

"Delighted," grinned Bent. "I shall have somebody to cheer me. Misery loves company."

Just as Kate and Frank returned chattering and laughing to the house, the two people who adored them cantered hastily away, not sending a look backward.

Whether we want to or not, and whether we find it pleasant or not, we must go back to Mrs. Chester's heart-affairs, trusting soon to come to an end of them. We will not, however, try to analyze her present feelings; the matter is altogether too complicated and indiscriminate. As we value a clear head we must confine ourselves to her intentions, which were lucidly spiteful, mischievous, and full of the devil. It was not Mrs. Devine whom she wanted to see, but that lady's dangerous flirt of a daughter, Jenny; and before the day was out the old coquette and the young one were closeted in camarilla over Kate Beaumont's matrimonial chances.

"You ought to help your cousin," was Mrs. Chester's adroit recommendation.

"Can't he do his own courtship?" sneered Jenny. "You'll be asking me next to fight his duels for him."

"I want him to get her," pursued Mrs. Chester, too much engaged in her own train of thought to notice the sarcasm on her *protégé*. "It would be very pleasant for us all to have her married in the family, as it were. We shouldn't lose the dear child, you see."

Jenny stared and nearly laughed, for this phrase, "the dear child," struck her as both surprising and humorous, as she knew that Aunt Marian was not given to the family affections, nor even to counterfeiting them.

"Besides, it is so desirable to keep the Kershaw estate in the relationship," continued the eager and absorbed Mrs. Chester. "I must say that I wish poor Bent may succeed."

"And you want me to try to run off with Frank McAlister," laughed Jenny. "That's what you want, is it?"

The elder lady's eyes flashed; she was far enough from wanting *that*.

"I won't do it," added Jenny. "I believe Kate likes him."

"She doesn't," affirmed Mrs. Chester.

"Oh!" scoffed Jenny, incredulously.

"I tell you she doesn't. Besides, she ought not to. It would be the worst thing in the world for her."

And here came a long argument against a match with a McAlister, going to show that it would surely end in severing Kate from her family, and making her miserable for life.

"There is something in that," admitted Jenny. "Yes, you are right; no doubt about it. Well, take me over there and give me a chance. I don't mind trying to help Bent a little."

"Oh, do say a word or two for the poor fellow. As for Mr. McAlister, you needn't mind him much. Just talk to him now and then a moment, to keep him from getting in Bent's way. Not that he means to get in his way."

"Yes," answered Jenny, absent-mindedly. She was in a revery about this Mr. McAlister. Suppose he should fall in love with herself? Suppose she should fall in love with him? Would it be very bad? Would it be very nice? Oh dear!

The hospitality of the Beaumont house was illimitable, and nobody was put out when Mrs. Chester brought Jenny Devine to stay a fortnight. On the contrary, the little jilt was heartily welcomed, for she was a favorite with the young men of the family, while Peyton Beaumont still retained his archi-patriarchal fancy for pretty women. As, moreover, Wallace McAlister soon discovered her whereabouts, and two or three other stricken deer came daily to have their wounds enlarged, Jenny had more than beaux enough. But busy as she was with her own affairs, she found time to keep her promise to Mrs. Chester, and even to outrun it. On the very evening of her arrival she held a prolonged bedchamber conference about love matters with Kate Beaumont.

"And so there is going to be no wedding right away?" said Jenny, after some preliminary catechizing.

"No, indeed," replied Kate, with an ostentation of calmness.

"I think he is splendid," continued Jenny, trusting that her friend would be thrown off her guard and answer, "Isn't he!"

Getting no response, she added, pettingly, "So tall! Such a beautiful complexion! Come now, don't you like him? Don't you like him just a little teenty-taunty bit?"

"I like everybody as much as that," answered Kate, hurrying to a closet on pretence of hanging up a dress.

"Here, come to the light where I can see you," said Jenny, seizing her friend's bare arms and drawing her towards the kerosene lamp which was the Beaumont substitute for gas. "Oh, how you blush!"

"Anybody would blush, pulled about and catechized in this way," protested Kate. "How awfully strong you are! and impudent! Real impudent!"

"Oh, tell me a little bit about it," persevered Jenny. "Could you refuse him? If he should come and get on his knees, and make himself only five feet high, and say his little pitty-patty prayer to you, could you refuse him?"

"Yes, I could," declared Kate, amused and perplexed and annoyed all at once.

"Oh, yes. But would you?"

"I *would*," was the answer, uttered in a changed tone, somewhat solemnizing.

Jenny let go of Kate's hands, studied her suddenly sobered face for an instant, and believed her.

"Well, Kitty, it's awful," she said at last, with a mock-serious twist of her pretty mouth. "Somebody must console the poor man. I'll do it."

After a minute of meditation she added, "And there's my poor cousin cracked after you. Will you take *him*?"

Kate, who at the moment was ready to cry under such teasing, found a relief in answering this question with something like temper, "No!"

Jenny was so amused by this explosion from her usually quiet friend, that she burst into a shriek of laughter.

"Poor Bent!" she gasped. "Coffin number two. Will they drown themselves, I wonder, or take a cup of cold poison together? Poison, I guess. Mr. McAlister couldn't drown himself without going to the seaside. Just imagine them sitting down to arsenic tea and quarrelling for the first drawing."

"Jenny, what does all this mean?" demanded Kate, seriously. "Have you been sent here to pump me?"

"No, no, no, no, no!" chattered Jenny, "Why, wha-t an idea!"

"Excuse me," said Kate. "I must go now. Good night."

And, with an exchange of kisses which strikes us as sweetness wasted, the two girls parted and went to bed, the one to laugh herself to sleep over the interview, and the other to — well, she did not laugh.

The next day, believing that Kate cared little or nothing for Frank McAlister, and believing also that it would be well if she should never learn to care for him, Jenny watched eagerly for the appearance of that giant gentleman, and when he came, set her nets for him. She was fearfully and wonderfully successful; she got him away from her friend and got him away from Mrs. Chester; she made him take her to walk and made him take her to ride. She played backgammon with him, and euchre and high-low-jack, crowing over him defiantly when she beat him, and making pretty mouths at him when he beat her. It seemed for two or three days as if she only stayed at the Beaumonts' to receive his visits, and as if he only came there to see her. Something of a romp and a good deal of a chatterer, she had a thousand tricks for occupying and amusing men, and killed time for them without their being aware of it. The field was the more easily her own for two reasons: first, because Kate, mindful of her promise to her sister, had lately taken to holding the McAlister at a distance; and, second, because that young chieftain, discouraged at being treated with reserve and continually hampered by either Mrs. Armitage or Mrs. Chester, had come to a stand in his courtship.

The result of this seeming flirtation between the bothered Frank and the feather-headed Jenny was a sentimental muddle. Although Kate kept up a smiling face, she did not at heart like the way things were going, and she grew more reserved than ever towards her admirer. Mrs. Chester very rapidly became as jealous of Miss Devine as she had been of Miss Beaumont. Wallace detected the girl whom he loved best in making eyes at his handsome brother, and fell into a state of mind which was likely to rob him of what hair he had left. Nellie Armitage, now that she saw a chance of losing Frank as a brother-in-law, inclined to think that her sister might go farther and fare worse. From all that she could learn about him, she had come to admit that he was morally one of the finest young fellows in the district. He scarcely drank at all; he had never been known to gamble; he had never been engaged in a squabble. There were others, to be sure, as worthy as he; there were Pickens Pendleton and the Rev. Arthur Gilyard and Dr. Mattieson; but Kate could not be got to care about any of them. What if the child should throw Frank McAlister away, only to pick up Bent Armitage? In short, Nellie began to lose distinct recollection of the feud with the McAlisters, and to feel a little anxious, if not a little pettish, over this flirtation of Jenny Devine.

An explosion came; but of course it was neither Kate nor Nellie who brought it about; and equally, of course, it was Mrs. Chester. That sensitive young thing (only forty summers, please to remember) let her heart go fully back to Frank as soon as she saw him entangled with Jenny, and lived a year or so of torture in three or four days. It is perhaps impossible to write into credibility the almost insane jealousy with which she watched this girl of nineteen coquetting with this youth of twenty-four. But if you could have beheld the spasm which pinched her lips and the snaky sparkle which shot from her eyes when she discovered them together, you would have believed in the reality of her passion. Her emotions were so strong that her reasoning powers, never of any great value, were now not worth a straw to her. She forgot that she had done much to start Jenny on her present adventure, and thought of her as an unbidden intruder, impudent, cunning, false, and selfish. She secretly gnashed her teeth at her, and lay in wait to expel her. After a sufficiency of this firing up, she all at once broke through the crust and uttered herself like a volcano.

"I don't know what your mother would say to all this," she began abruptly. Not that she meant to be abrupt; in her excitement it seemed to her that much had been said already; that Jenny and everybody else must know what was upon her mind.

"All what?" demanded the young lady, her eyes opening wide at this sound of coming tempest. She knew, like all Hartland, that Mrs. Chester was a tartar; but she was, nevertheless, surprised by the lunge now made at her; in fact, Mrs. Chester was capable of surprising anybody.

"Oh, of course," sneered the old coquette, not to be foiled by the supposed arts of a young coquette.

"I don't understand you, Mrs. Chester," declared Jenny, drawing herself up with the hauteur of self-respect, and looking her assailant firmly in the face.

"Then it's my duty to make you understand," was the reply of a woman whose reason was dragging at the chariot wheels of her emotion. "I think that, considering you are not at home, you are flirting pretty smartly."

"You must be joking!" said the astounded girl. "Why, you brought me here to — what do you mean?"

"I mean what I say," returned Mrs. Chester, perfectly ready to quarrel and fit to go to a *maison de santé*. "You are flirting scandalously."

"Why, you old gossip!" exclaimed Jenny, suddenly and furiously indignant.

"Old! — gossip!" gasped Mrs. Chester, looking as if a strait-jacket would be a blessing to her.

"Where is Mr. Beaumont?" demanded Jenny. "I want to see Mr. Beaumont."

Mrs. Chester quailed as a lunatic might who should hear his keeper called for.

"He is not at home," she asserted, which happened to be the case, although she did not know it.

Jenny marched away with the swing of an insulted hoyden; called for her dressing-maid and had her trunks packed; evaded Kate's questions as to the cause of her departure; begged the loan of the Beaumont coach, and drove home. On the way she cried a little, and clenched her small fist a number of times, and laughed hysterically more than once.

Thus ended Jenny's visit to the Beaumonts; but short as it was, it had brought about one important result; it had led Kate's sister to see the value of Kate's lover. That very afternoon, even while Jenny Devine was having her wickedness borne in upon her by Mrs. Chester, Nellie had said to the young man, in her characteristically frank way, "How much have you changed in the last week?"

"Not one bit," was the earnest and honest reply.

"Then I withdraw my opposition," declared Nellie. "You may succeed, if you can."

"I shall speak to her now," returned Frank, his heart throbbing as if it were of volcanic nature and communicated with the internal earthquake forces.

"Oh!" gasped Mrs. Armitage, quailing a little under the suddenness of the thing, and wishing, as all women do, to prolong a spectacle of courtship. "Oh, so quick? But you must see my father first," she added, recollecting that obstacle, though likely, as she knew, to be but a frail one. "You surely will see him first?" she begged, feeling that she had no right to command a man who was invested with the great authority of love. "And he is not at home."

"I shall wait for his return," was the decision of a true lover.

CHAPTER 18

 While Frank waited for Mr. Beaumont, in order to ask him whether he might or might not propose marriage, he either walked up and down before Mrs. Armitage in absent-minded silence, or he talked altogether of Kate.

This behavior did not make him tiresome to the lady; on the contrary, she found him incessantly agreeable and fascinating. A man who has donned the cross of love, and set his adventurous face toward the holy city of marriage, is to a woman one of the most interesting objects that she can lay eyes upon, even though he looks for his crown to some other queen of beauty. To her mind he is bound on the most important and noblest of pilgrimages: the question of his success or failure impassions her imagination and kindles her warmest sympathies; she can hardly help wishing him good fortune, even though he is a stranger.

"But I must weary you, Mrs. Armitage," apologized Frank, not knowing the above-mentioned facts. "I must seem terribly stupid to you."

"No, indeed," returned Nellie, innocently, and continued to prattle away about her sister, telling every minute more of the subject than she meant to tell, and revealing through sparkling eyes and flushed cheeks her satisfaction with the state of things.

But this quarter of an hour of delightful expectation was a false portal, not opening to higher felicities. In place of Peyton Beaumont came his tropical henchman, Cato, riding up at the usual breakneck speed of darkies on horseback, rolling out of his saddle with the bounce of a kicked football, and holding forth a letter with the words, "Powerful bad news, Miss Nellie."

Mrs. Armitage read to herself and then read aloud the following note from her father: "Tell Kate — gently, you understand — that her grandfather is sick; you might say quite sick. On the whole, you had better send her over here to take care of him. I may stay here over night myself. Now don't scare the child out of her senses. Just send her over here at once."

"You see," said Nellie, looking up at Frank with something like a pout of disappointment at the postponement of the love business.

"I see," answered the young man, turning anxious and gloomy. "I must come another time."

He started soberly homewards; then, after going a quarter of a mile, he had a bright thought and returned to escort Kate over to Kershaw's; but, although he thus secured a half-hour with her, he proffered no manner of courtship, knowing well that it was no time for it. Finally, after seeing Lawson and learning from the troubled man that the good old Colonel was dangerously ill, he once more turned his back on his queen of hearts, the love message still unspoken.

Reaching home, he met in the doorway his evil genius, and politely bowed to him without knowing him. This fateful stranger, this man who, without the slightest ill-will toward Frank, or the slightest acquaintance with him or his purposes, had come to cross his path and make him dire trouble, was, in some points, a creature of agreeable appearance, and in others little less than horrible. His blond complexion was very clear, his profile regular and almost Greek, his teeth singularly even and white, and his smile winning. But he was unusually bald; his forehead was so monstrous as to be a deformity; his eyes had the most horrible squint that ever a scared child stared at; his expression was as cunning, unsympathizing, and pitiless as that of a raccoon or fox. His moderate stature was made to seem clumsily short by over-broad shoulders, thick limbs, and a projecting abdomen. It was difficult to guess his age, but he might have been about forty-five.

The Judge was escorting this visitor to his carriage with an air of solemn politeness and suppressed dislike, such as an elephant might wear in bowing out a hyena.

"I regret that you can't at least stay to dinner, Mr. Choke," he said, smiling all the way from his broad wrinkled forehead to his broad double chin. "As for the business in hand, you may rely upon me."

"I expect nothing less from your intelligence and noble ambition, Judge," replied Mr. Choke, with a smile so sweet that for a moment Frank failed to notice his squint.

Let us now go back an hour or so, and learn what was "the business in hand." Although this combination of beauty and the beast had come unexpectedly to the McAlister place, and had simply announced himself through Matthew as "Mr. Choke of Washington," the Judge had guessed at once what mighty wire-puller it was who waited in his parlor, and had thoughtfully stalked thither, snuffing the air for political traps and baits and perfidies. He, however, remembered his manners when he came face to face with his guest; he uttered a greeting of honeyed civility which at once set on tap all Mr. Choke's metheglin. Each of these remarkable men was by many degrees more polite than the other.

"I am delighted to welcome you to South Carolina, sir," said the Judge, with such a benevolent smile as Saint Peter might wear on admitting a new saint into paradise. "I have long known the Hon. Mr. Choke by reputation. Let us hope that you are prepared to stay with me for some weeks at least."

"You are exceedingly courteous and hospitable," replied Mr. Choke. "You are even more courteous and hospitable than I expected to find you. The South, Judge McAlister, is the land of hospitality and of courtesy. It should be. Heaven has lavished abundance upon it. What a soil, what a climate, and what men!" looking up reverently at the McAlister's lofty summit. "Even the water is a luxury."

It must be observed that these two men flowered out thus in compliments from very different causes. The host blossomed because he had grown up in doing it, and because all the people whom he knew expected it; while the guest, an extremely business-like man by nature, was merely talking what he considered the fol-de-rol of the country.

"We are unworthy of our gifts, and you do us too much honor, Mr.

Choke," chanted the Judge, when it came his turn in the responses. "I beg pardon. Excuse me for having forgotten your proper title. Judge, I believe, is it not?"

"No," returned the visitor, beaming out a smile of humility which was pure flattery. "I have not yet gained your eminence. I am merely an attorney-at-law, and of late a member of Congress. I have no claim to any address beyond plain Mister."

Merely a member of Congress! The Judge could not prevent the blue philanthropy of his eyes from turning a little green with envy. The title of "M. C." had been for more than a quarter of a century the mark of his ambition. To set those two letters to his name he had spent money, gushed eloquence, intrigued, entertained, flattered, bowed, grinned, lived, almost died, and all in vain. Ever since age had qualified him to run for that goal, the State party had been an overmatch for the Union party in his district, and it was always a Beaumont, or some other Calhounite, who had won the Congressional race. At last, two years previous to this interview, he had despaired of being called to save his country, had publicly announced his final withdrawal from politics, and declined a candidature.

But the disappointment rankled in his soul, and he still cherished wild dreams of success. His desire and hope were increased by his contempt and dislike for the men who had beaten him. In his opinion the Hon. Peyton Beaumont was nothing but a well-descended blockhead and rowdy. It was abominable that a man who had the rhetoric of a termagant and the logic of a school-boy should represent, year after year, a district which contained within its bounds the copious, ornate, argumentative, and learned Judge McAlister. A man who hoarsely denounced a spade as a spade had surely no claims compared with a man who blandly reproved it for being an agricultural implement. Moreover, Beaumont made few speeches in Congress, and those few excited bitter opposition. The Judge imagined himself as orating amid the echoes of the Hall of Representatives with such persuasiveness and suavity as to draw even the Senate around him, and to beguile Sumner himself into moderation. Yet he was not elected, and his inferiors were. It was horrible; like the belted knight who was overcome by the peasant, he cried, "Bitter, bitter!" and, in his revolt at such outrage, he could not believe that Heaven would be forever unjust.

Mr. Choke was an experienced detective of feeling. Looking modestly at the floor with his oblique eye, but studying his host's face steadily with his direct one, he perceived that he had won the game. The Judge was angrily envious; the Judge passionately desired to go to Congress; the Judge could be made use of. Suddenly dropping the conversational roses and lilies which he had waved hitherto, Choke entered upon business.

"Judge, we want you alongside of us," he said with an abruptness which wore the charm of sincerity. "We need just such men as you are in Congress. We need them terribly."

It was precisely McAlister's opinion, and he could not help letting his face express it, although he waved his hand disclaimingly.

"Now don't object," begged Mr. Choke. "I must be earnest, as I have been blunt. I must beg you to consider this matter seriously. I came here for that purpose; came here solely and expressly for that; hence my abruptness. Yes, I came here to beg you to take your proper place in the Congress of the United States."

"Oh, if I only could!" was the wish of the Judge's heart. But he controlled himself, wore his dignity as carefully as his wig, and pursed his mouth with the air of a Cincinnatus who does not know whether he will or will not save an ungrateful country.

"You are perhaps not aware, Mr. Choke, that I have withdrawn definitely from public life," he said, stroking his chin. This chin, we must repeat, was on a magnificent scale; it was even broader than the capacious forehead which towered above it; it gave its owner's face the proportions of an Egyptian gateway. It had development forward, as well as breadth of beam. It was one of those chins which proudly confront noses. From any point of view it was a great chin. There was plenty of room about it for rubbing, and the Judge now went over it pretty thoroughly, stirring it up as if it contained his spare brains.

"We understand that Beaumont is going to run again for the House," continued Mr. Choke, who did not believe that any old politician ever withdrew definitively from public life, and had no time to waste upon pretences to that effect. "We don't want him there. He is a marplot. He is a barking bull-dog who brings out other bull-dogs. Every word that he utters loses us votes at the North. If he and such as he continue to come to Congress and keep up their stupid howling there, the party will be ruined, and that shortly."

The great, calm, and bland Judge could scarcely help frowning. It did not please him to observe that Mr. Choke spoke only of the party. In connection with political matters the leader of the moderates of Hartland District always said, "The country!"

"We must get rid of these mules who are kicking the organization to pieces," continued the straightforward and practical Choke. "That is the object of my present tour. If we can bring into Congress twenty Southerners who will talk moderation, we are saved. It is all important to make a break in this phalanx of fire-eaters. It is almost equally important that the break should be made here in South Carolina. Divide the voice of this State, and you split disunion everywhere. Am I right?" inquired the Hon. Choke, perceiving that it was time to flatter the Judge, and stopping his speech to smile his sweetest.

"I entirely coincide with you," bowed McAlister, who, anti-Calhounite as he was, believed that South Carolina marched at the head of the nations, and that what she did not do would be left undone. He was a little out of breath, by the way, with following after the speaker. He was not used to such rapid argumentation and application. It was his custom to go over a subject with long chains of reasoning, staking them out deliberately, and often stopping to look back on them with satisfaction. Mr. Choke was rather too fast for him; had the air of hurrying him along by the collar; might be said to hustle him considerably. The Judge did not quite like it, and yet it was obviously his interest to listen and approve; it was clear that something good was coming his way.

"Well, we look to you," pursued Mr. Choke, with that bluntness of his which was so startling, and yet so flattering, because confidential, — "we look to you to beat Beaumont."

The Judge was like a woman on a sled drawn over smooth ice by a rapid skater. Unable to stop himself, he must hum swiftly along the glib surface, even though a breathing-hole should yawn visibly ahead. He had an instantaneous perception that running against Beaumont would reopen the family feud, and spoil Frank's chances for marrying the presumptive heiress of the Kershaw estate, besides perhaps leading to new duellings and rencontres. But how could he check his lifelong mania for going to Congress, while this strong and speedy Choke was tugging at the cords of it? The sagest and solidest of men have their weak and toppling moments. Unable to reflect in a manner worthy of himself, and incapable of restraining his ambition until Frank should have made sure of the Kershaw succession, he sprawled eagerly at full length toward the House of Representatives, and agreed to run against Beaumont.

"If you need help, you shall have it," instantly promised Choke, anxious to seal the bargain. "Our committee will furnish you with the sinews of war. The organization will go deep into its pockets to secure the presence of such a man as Judge McAlister in Congress. You can draw upon us for five thousand dollars. Do you think that will do it?"

"I should think it highly probable," bowed the Judge, virtuously astounded at the hugeness of the bribe, and unable to imagine how he could use it all.

"My best wishes," said Mr. Choke, taking off a very modest glass of the McAlister sherry. "And now allow me to wish you good morning."

"But, God bless my soul! you must stay to dinner," exclaimed the Judge, breathless with this haste.

"A thousand thanks. But I really haven't the time. I must gallop over to Newberry, arrange matters with Jackson there, and get on to Spartanburg by the evening train. A thousand thanks for your lavish hospitality. Let us hear from you. *Good* morning."

And Mr. Choke bustled, smiled, and squinted his way out of the McAlister mansion, leaving its master thoroughly astounded at the unceremoniousness and speed of "these Northerners."

But the chief of the Hartland conservatives was soon himself again. By dint of fingering that talisman, his broad chin, he rubbed out his emotions and restored his judgment. Once more in a reasoning, independent frame of mind, he coolly queried whether he should keep his promise to Mr. Choke, or break it for some patriotic reason. He had very little difficulty in deciding that he would hold fast to it. There, to be sure, was the family feud, certain to "mount" him if he ran for Congress; but it was a burden which lifelong habit had made easy to his shoulders. There, too, was the strong probability that his candidature might upset Frank's dish of cream. But if he should once beat the Beaumonts, if he should once show them that he was a rival to be feared, would they not be all the more likely to agree to an alliance, not only matrimonial, but political? As for the boy's heart, the Judge did not think of it. It was so long since he had been conscious of any such organ, that he had forgotten its existence. On

{ 216 }

the whole, he would keep his promise; on the whole, his word as a gentleman was engaged; especially as revenge and power and fame are sweet. But there should be discretion shown in the matter; until his trap was fairly set, nobody should know of it, excepting, of course, his trusted and necessary confederates; from the sight of even his own family he would hide it, as he knew how to hide things. Meanwhile, before the Beaumonts could so much as suspect what he was about, his son might lay an irrevocable hand on the heart of their heiress.

"Frank," he said next morning, "you ought to ride over to Kershaw's and inquire about the Colonel. If Miss Beaumont is still there, present her with my kindest regards and sympathies, and tell her I am distressed to hear of her grandfather's illness. Exceedingly distressed, you know!" emphasized the Judge, his brow wrinkling with an agony that stirred his wig.

So Frank rode over to Kershaw's, obtained an interview with Miss Beaumont, and spoke the speech which his father had dictated, but not the one which his father had intended. How could a sensitive, generous young fellow spring love-traps upon the woman whom he worshipped, while she was trembling for the life of her adored grandfather? This fruitless riding to and fro went on until the Judge became impatient and very anxious. Of the probability of Kershaw's death and the certainty that his estate would go to Kate Beaumont he talked repeatedly to his wife, hoping that she would be inspired to repeat these things to Frank, and that the boy would be led thereby to make haste in his wooing. At times, when it occurred to him that he might be ruining his son's chances of success and happiness, he was so far conscience-stricken and remorseful as to wrinkle his forehead and go about the house muttering. In those days guileless Mrs. McAlister could not imagine what it was that made her usually calm and bland husband nervous and waspish.

Frank, too, was in sore trouble; he wore a pinched brow, and grew thin. He afflicted himself with imaginations of Kershaw dying, and of Kate weeping by the bedside. In more selfish moments he cringed at the thought that funeral robes would prevent him for weeks or months from telling the girl what was in his heart! The longer the great declaration was put off, the more he feared lest it should be ill received. There were whole days in which he felt as if he were already a rejected lover. Even Mrs. Armitage could not keep up his spirits, although she was by this time keenly and obviously interested in his success, and talked to him daily in a very sweet way about her sister.

At last, unable to bear his suspense longer, he resolved that he would at least utter his gentle message to the father, trusting that some blessed chance would waft it on to the daughter. Anxiety and doubt walked with him to the interview; and his heart was not lightened by the contenance with which he was received. Peyton Beaumont, always sufficiently awful to look upon, seemed to be in his grimmest mood that morning. His very raiment betokened a squally temper. The neatness of attire which marked him when Kate was at home and saw daily to his adornment had given way to a bodeful frowsiness. He had dressed himself in a greasy old brown coat and frayed trousers, as if in preparation for a rough and tumble. Apparently he had slept badly; his eyes were watery and bloodshot, perhaps with brandy; his voice, as he said good morning, was a hoarse, sullen mutter.

"Mr. Beaumont, I have come to ask a great favor," began Frank, with that abruptness which perhaps characterizes modest men on such occasions. "I ask your permission, sir, to offer myself to your daughter."

Beaumont was certainly in a very unwholesome humor. His optics had none of the kindness which frequently, if not usually, beamed from their sombre depths when he greeted the savior of his favorite child. Even at the sound of that tremulous prayer of love they did not light up with the mercy, or at least sympathy which such an orison may rightfully claim. They emitted an abstracted, suspicious, sulky stare, much like that of a dog who is in the brooding fit of hydrophobia.

"I don't understand this at all," he replied, deliberately and coldly. "Your father and you — between you — I don't understand it, I don't, by heavens! It looks as though I was being made a fool of," he added, in a louder and angrier tone, his mind reverting to McAlister perfidies of other days.

"I beg your pardon, — I don't comprehend," commenced Frank, utterly confused and dismayed. "I should hope that —"

"Isn't your father preparing to run against me for Congress?" interrupted Beaumont, his black, blood-streaked orbs lighting up to a glare.

"I don't believe it!" was the amazed and indignant response.

The elder man stared at the younger for, what seemed to the latter, a full minute.

"Mr. Beaumont, do you suppose I am deceiving you?" demanded Frank, his face coloring high at the ugly suspicion.

After gazing a moment longer, Beaumont slowly answered, "No — I don't, — no, by Jove! But," he presently added, his wrath boiling up again, "I think your father is humbugging us both. I think, by heavens —" He had been about to say something very hard of the elder McAlister's character as to duplicity; but, looking in the frank, manly, anxious face of this younger McAlister, his heart softened a little; he remembered how Kate had been saved from death, and he fell silent.

"It is useless now to ask an answer to my request," resumed Frank, after a pause.

"Yes," said Beaumont. "Things don't stand well enough between our families. What you propose would only make worse trouble."

"I will go home and inquire into what you allege against my father," continued the young man, with a sad dignity. "Meantime, I beg you to suspend your judgment. Good morning, sir."

He held out his hand. Beaumont took it with hesitation, and then shook it with fervor.

"By heavens! I don't know but I'm a brute," he said. "If I have hurt *your* feelings — and of course I *have* hurt them — I beg your pardon; I do, by heavens! As for what you propose, — well, wait. For God's sake, wait. Good morning."

More miserable than he had ever been in his life before, Frank rode home to call his father to an account.

CHAPTER 19

 Words are a feeble, undisciplined rabble, able to perform little true and efficient service. Even the imagination is an uncertain general who gets no full obedience out of wretched soldiers, and sees not how to marshal them so that they may do their best duty. It seems, at times, as if there were nothing real and potent about the human being, except the passion which he can feel and which he cannot describe.

Here is a man full of love, — full of the noblest and far the strongest of all passions, and this passion so intensified by anxiety and disappointment that it is near akin to frenzy, — riding furiously homeward to encounter his father with a face of white anger, and to ask hoarsely, Is it true that you have made me wretched for life? So far as feeling is concerned, the figure is one of high tragedy. The youth is mad enough to break his neck without recking, mad enough to commit a crime without being half conscious of it. He is so possessed by one imperious desire, that he cannot take rational account of the desires of others. Flying over the slopes between the Beaumont house and his home, he is impatience and haste personified. He comes in upon his father with the air of an avenger of blood. Well, have we described him in such a way that he can be seen and comprehended? Probably not.

"Is it true, sir, that you are running for Congress?" were his first words.

The Judge dropped back in his large office-chair, and stared over his spectacles at this questioning, this almost menacing apparition. It was the first time in his life that he had been frightened by one of his own children. For a moment he was too much discomposed to speak. It was really a strange thing to see this large, sagacious, cunning face, usually so calm and confident and full of speculation, reduced to such a state of paralysis.

"Is it true, sir?" repeated the young man, resting his tremulous hands on the back of a chair, and sending his bold blue eyes into his father's sly gray ones.

"Why, good heavens! Frank," stammered the Judge, "what *is* all this?"

Frank said nothing, but his face repeated his question; it demanded a plain answer.

"Why, the fact is, Frank," confessed the Judge, with a smile of almost humble deprecation, "that I have been badgered, yes, I may say fairly badgered, into trying my luck again."

Uttering a groan, or rather a smothered howl of anger and pain, the young man sat down hastily, his head swimming.

"But, good heavens! Frank, is there anything so extraordinary in it?" asked the father.

"Mr. Beaumont charged you with it," said Frank, dropping his face into his hands. "I didn't believe it."

"Charged me with it!" repeated the Judge. "Is it a crime, then?" he demanded, feeling somehow that it was one, yet trying to be indignant.

"It reopens the old account of blood," the youth muttered without looking up.

"Not at all. I don't see it," declared the Judge, glad to find a point on which he could argue, and grasping at it.

"It breaks my heart," were the next words, uttered in a whisper.

All notion of an argument dropped out of the Judge's head. A world suddenly opened before him in which no ratiocination was possible. He became aware of the presence of emotions which were as mighty as efreets, and would not listen to logic. He was like a man who has denied the existence of devils, and all at once perceives that they are entering into him and taking possession. He was so startlingly and powerfully shaken by feelings without and feelings within, that for the first time in many years his healthy blood withdrew from his face. His cheeks (usually of a red-oak complexion) flecked with ash color, he sat in silence, watching his silent son.

For some seconds Frank did not look up; and if he had lifted his eyes, he would not have seen his father; he was gazing at Kate Beaumont and bidding her farewell.

"That is all," he broke out at last, rising like a denunciatory spectre, and speaking with startling loudness and abruptness, so little was his voice under command. "I have nothing more to say, sir."

"See here, Frank," called the Judge, as the young man strode to the door.

"I beg your pardon," muttered Frank, just turning his discomposed face over his shoulder. "I can't speak of it now."

He was gone. The Judge looked at the closed door for a minute as if expecting to see it reopen and his son reappear. Slowly his eyes dropped, his ponderous chin sank upon his deep chest, and he slipped into perplexities of thought. For a long time he emitted no sound, except a regular and forcible expulsion of breath through his hairy nostrils, which was a habit of his when engaged in earnest meditation. At last he said in a loud whisper, "Good heavens! He really likes her. Loves her."

Then he tried to remember his way back thirty-five years and pick up something which would enable him to understand clearly what it was to be in love. In the midst of this journey he found himself on a platform before a crowd of his fellow-citizens, explaining to them his very eminent fitness for a seat in Congress. Next, after another plunge toward the lang-syne of affection, he became aware of the offensive propinquity of Peyton Beaumont, and gave him just for once a plain piece of his McAlister mind, calling him an unreasonable old savage, a selfish, greedy brute, etc.

"Ah!" gasped the Judge, angrily, recurring to his loud whisper. "Must I quit running for Congress because *he* demands it? What business has he to domineer over me in this fashion? By the heavens above me, I will run and I'll beat him. I'll be master for once; I'll bring him down; I'll smash him. Then we'll see whether he won't beckon my son back. I'll make him glad to accept my son. I'll make him jump to get him."

Of course he was greatly pleased with this idea. It laid hands on the goal of the Capitol, and humiliated the life-long enemy, and secured the Kershaw estate, and made Frank happy. Perhaps no man, however judicial-minded by nature or habit, is entirely lucid on the subject of his ruling passion. The Judge felt almost sure of winning his seat in the next Congress, and quite sure that that success would make all other successes easy. After some further loud breathing, he resumed his whispering.

"I can help Frank. I can do better for him than he can do for himself. If I give up, and he gets the girl by that means, he will be a slave to the Beaumonts for life. But let me once lay her father on his back, and he can make his own terms. Beaumont will be glad to come to terms with a family that can beat him. Beaumont will jump at the marriage. The girl will jump at it. Frank will have reason to thank me."

Then came more expulsions of breath, and then calmness in that mighty breast. The Judge was tranquil; he had reasoned the matter clean out; he had reached a decision.

Somewhat of these meditations he revealed to Frank at their next interview, taking care, of course, to deal in delicate hints, so as not to hurt the boy's feelings.

"I have no right to stand in your way, sir," was the cold, hopeless reply.

"Why no, of course not," was the feeling of Judge McAlister, although he failed to say it. It did not seem to him, now that he had had time to reflect upon the matter, that any human being, not even his favorite son, had a right to stand in his way, especially when that way led to the House of Representatives. At the same time he repeated to himself, that neither would he stand in the boy's road, but, on the contrary, would help him mightily.

"It will be all right, Frank," he declared blandly and cheerfully, meanwhile looking at the ceiling so as not to see the youngster's gloomy face. "You will find that your father is right."

Thus it was that the Judge's candidature went on, and that as a consequence the old feud blazed out volcanically. Any one who could have studied the two families at this time, would have judged that they hated each other all the more because they had stricken hands for a few weeks. The Beaumonts raved against McAlister duplicity, and the McAlisters against Beaumont imperiousness and insolence. The Hon. Peyton breathed nothing but brandy and gunpowder from ten minutes after he woke up to two hours or so after he went to sleep. His boys, even to the fat and philosophic Poinsett, oiled their duelling-pistols, wore revolvers under their shooting-jackets, refreshed their memories as to the code of honor, and held themselves ready to fight at a whistle. The McAlisters, a less aggressive and fiery people, but abundantly capable of the "defensive with offensive returns," made similar preparations.. The women of the two houses were blandly but firmly warned by their men that they must not call on each other. There were no advocates of peace, at least none in a state to intervene. The good gray head of Kershaw was tossing on a sick-pillow; and the pure, sweet face of Kate was always hovering near it, her soul so absorbed by his peril, that she scarcely heard of other troubles. Nellie Armitage, bewildered by the sudden reflux of the traditional hate, and believing with her father, that Judge McAlister had shown himself the most punic of men, had not a word to say for her sister or her sister's lover. In the rival house the women were silent, obedient to their male folk, as was their custom. Frank, not at liberty to speak against his father, not at liberty to plead the cause of a heart which nobody seemed to care for, was voiceless, helpless, and miserable. *He* wore no revolvers; he wanted to be shot at sight.

The village of Hartland was charmed with this fresh eruption of its venerated volcano. Men, and women, and boys were in as delightful an excitement over it as ever were so many physicists over a convulsion of nature. There was no end to the discussions, and the predictions, and the bettings. But we cannot listen to all these crowding talkers; we must select some little knot which shall sufficiently chorus to us public opinion; and perhaps we cannot do better than incline our ears to our old-time acquaintance, Wilkins and Duffy. Every evening, after trading hours were over, these two friendly rivals in merchandise had a meeting, sometimes in the "store" of one and sometimes in that of the other, and discussed the Beaumont-McAlister imbroglio with the aid of other village notables. These little reunions were very interesting to Wilkins and at the same time very provoking. His ancient crony was much in liquor at this period of Hartland's history. The excitement which filled the district had been too much for Duffy.

Duffy had taken to drink to quiet his nervousness, and his head as we remember, being uncommonly weak, the remedy had increased the disease. He rushed into the imprudence of three glasses a day, and consequently he was more or less flighty from morning to night.

"I tell you, Wilkins, it's all right," he affirmed in the course of one of these parliaments. "All come out right in the end. Make up an' marry yet. Bet you a hat they will. Bet you a hat, Wilkins. Any kind of a hat. Black hat or white. Broad brim or narrow brim. Bell crown or stovepipe. Bet you a hat, Wilkins."

"Now don't be a blasted fool!" implored Wilkins, for perhaps the tenth time that evening. "I don't want to win your hat. I don't want your bet. Just shut up about your hat and listen to reason."

They were in the little room in rear of Duffy's "store"; the room where he kept his double-barrelled shot-gun and revolver; the room where he slept. It was nearly midnight; buying and selling were long since over; several of the village gossips had been in for an hour; there had been much talking and some drinking. General Johnson, a little, meagre, pale-faced, gray-headed man, attired in a black dress-coat, black satin vest, and black trousers frayed around the heels, stood with his back to the Franklin stove, his hands behind him, his coat-tails parted, apparently under the impression that he was warming himself, although there was no fire and the weather was stifling. Colonel Jacocks, a plethoric young lawyer with a good-natured flabby face, and a moist, laughing eye, sat on Duffy's bed, his fat thighs spreading wide, and his fat hands in his pockets. Major Jobson (the partner of Jacocks), a slender, very dark and sallow young man, with piercing black eyes and an eager, martial expression, marched up and down the room like a sentinel, striking the floor with a thick black cane, the handle of which was evidently loaded. Duffy, very soggy with his last little drink, was astride of the chair, holding on by the back and staring argumentatively at Wilkins. Wilkins, his leathery and humorous face much more in earnest than usual, was gesturing at Duffy.

All these men, excepting the prudent and strong-headed Wilkins, were solemnly and genteelly the worse for liquor. Jacocks, notwithstanding that he sat there so quietly, was to that extent elevated that he had insisted on saying grace over the last "drinks around," taking off his broad-brimmed hat, and raising his fat hand for the purpose. General Johnson had been so far from seeing any impropriety in the act, that he had reverently bowed his head and dropped a tear upon the floor, muttering something about "pious parents." But tipsy as the gentlemen were, they could remember that they were gentlemen, and keep up a fair imitation of sobriety. Even the jolly Jacocks, although he had fallen from his religious exaltation into a spirit of gayety, was only blandly merry.

"Go on, Duffy," he said, winking at the fierce Jobson. "No man who can sit astride of a rocking-chair can be beaten in an argument. Hold fast by your opinion. Only don't bet hats; bet drinks for the crowd. The crowd will then stand by you."

"I will," responded Duffy, with obvious thickness of speech,—speech as broad as it was long. "I'll bet drinks for the crowd, an' I'll bet hats for the crowd. I say those two families'll make it up yet; shake han's all roun' an' make't up; make't up an' marry. Bet you those two families'll make't up. Bet you they will. Bet you drinks for the crowd. Bet you hats for the crowd. Bet you they'll make't up. Bet you they will."

"Oh just hear him now!" exclaimed Wilkins, driven to desperation by such persistent unreason. Then walking up to General Johnson, he whispered confidentially, "That's the way he always is, if he takes anything. Only had one horn since supper, and here he is drunker than you or I would be on a quart. And those two fellows are putting him up to make a fool of himself. I don't call it the square thing."

"Allow me, Mr. Duffy," interposed the General, thus incited to remonstrate. "And you my dear Colonel Jacocks, excuse me for disagreeing. Knowing as I do the characters of these two families, and having been intimately familiar with them from my youth up, I venture to say that I unhappily see no reason to believe that there can be any lasting amity between them, especially in view of the political differences which have lately arisen, or rather which have always smouldered beneath their intercourse. My impression is, and I cannot tell you how much I regret to insist upon it, that the Beaumonts and McAlisters, incited by a family history without parallel in the chronicles of time, are destined to remain enemies for many years to come, until circumstances, more potent than have yet been developed, shall arise to soothe the passions which boil betwixt them, and lead them irresistibly into one common bond of friendship cemented by interest and new methods of thought and feeling."

General Johnson had a disputed reputation as an orator. He could talk in a diffuse, inconclusive, incomprehensible manner for hours together. His admirers, among whom was young Jobson, gave him credit for "flights of eloquence"; these flights being the passages in which he took leave of intelligibility altogether. On the present occasion, as the reader must have observed, he came very near a flight. Jobson looked at him with ebony eyes of intense admiration, glanced about the company to call attention, and tapped his cane smartly on the floor. But Duffy was neither entranced, nor convinced, nor even interested. He had simply his own ideas about the subject in hand, and he was bent solely on uttering them.

"That's so," he declared, just as if the General had agreed with him. "Always told you fellahs they'd come together. Told you two so months ago. Told you they'd marry an' put an end to the fight. You know it, Bill Wilkins. Told you so on board the *Mersey*. That's what I said. I said they'd marry an' put an end to the fight. Don't ye mind how I said so?"

"Oh — blast it!" groaned Wilkins.

"Well, blast it, if you want to. But don't ye 'member it? Don't ye 'member I said so?"

"Yes, I know you said so. But they haven't done it. That's the point. They haven't done it.

"But they're goin' to," persisted the infatuated Duffy. "Bet you hats for the crowd. Bet you they'll make it up an' marry. That's what I bet on. Bet you they will."

"Oh thunder!" responded Wilkins, driven to wrath. "Well, you may lose your hats, if you will. Yes, I'll bet five hats with you. Time, one year from to-night."

"And drinks for the crowd," amended Jacocks.

"Yes, drinks for the crowd," agreed Wilkins.

"And now, Duffy, tell us about Hutch Holland's store," grinned Jacocks.

"Took up posish at the corner," commenced Duffy, with a muddy idea that there was humor in the repetition of the old story.

"Oh, stop," implored Wilkins. "If you go over that confounded bosh again, I'll quit."

"But seriously, gentlemen," interrupted Major Jobson, perceiving that his favorite orator and great man, General Johnson, did not enjoy this trifling, — "seriously, gentlemen, I believe that this feud between the Beaumonts and McAlisters is fuller of earthquake throes than in the times of old. I believe that we shall shortly behold tragedies which will make even sturdy old Hartland recoil with horror. I believe that before the election is over blood will flow in torrents."

"Oh, not torrents," objected Jacocks, who accused his partner of a tendency to Irish oratory, and habitually laughed at him about it. "Say drops."

"Well, drops then," responded Jobson, with a fierce roll of his great blazing black eyes. "But drops from the heart, gentlemen. Drops of life-blood."

"Meetings are sure," declared General Johnson, thinking how easily he had got into a number of meetings during his life, and feeling not unwilling to assist at a few more.

"Oh, hang it! I hope not," groaned the humane and pacific Wilkins. It must be understood, by the way, that had not General Johnson been a rather seedy old grandee, not given to paying his bills, and much addicted to accepting treats, Wilkins would not have been so free and easy with him. To a Peyton Beaumont or a Donald McAlister this modest and sensible storekeeper would have been far more reverent.

"Your feelings, sir, on this subject honor you, and honor our whole species," melodiously began the frayed and threadbare General. "But, sir, you will pardon me, I hope, for suggesting —"

He was interrupted by the sound of unsteady steps in the darkness of the long outer room. Southerners, when not over-excited by liquor or anger, are fastidious about giving offence; they are more prudent than non-duelling peoples, as to letting their opinions reach the wrong ears. The General stopped talking, assumed a diplomatically bland expression of countenance, and waited for the unknown to show himself. His caution was well timed, for the visitor was Tom Beaumont.

"Good evening, gentlemen," said the youngster, courteously, although he was clearly in liquor. "Thought I should find somebody hanging up here. We wo-n't go ho-me till morn-ing."

"Duffy is in for a night of it," whispered Major Jobson to Wilkins. "I shall vamos."

"I must see Duffy out," the faithful Wilkins muttered in reply. "If I don't keep watch over him, he'll say some blasted stupid thing, and then Beaumont'll mount him."

Meantime Tom advanced to a couple of whiskey-bottles which stood on the stove, found a gill or so of liquor in the bottom of one of them, poured it out, and drank it pure. He was as confident and superior as if he belonged to a higher scale in creation than these other men. He even seemed to patronize General Johnson, reverend with eloquence and honors, and seedy with noble poverty. Moreover, the respect which the youngster demanded was accorded to him. There was a silence about him as of courtiers. To Wilkins and all the others he represented a great name, the name of a long-descended and predominant family, the name of the Beaumonts. They were not humiliated, but they were deferential; he was not insolent, but he was confident. There was a sort of calm sublimity in the juvenile toper, notwithstanding his thick utterance and ridiculous reeling.

"We wo-n't go ho-me till morn-ing," sang Tom. "Who says he will? Duffy, more whiskey. I treat. Here's the cash. Roll in the whiskey. None of that, Wilkins," plunging at the door to prevent the exit of the person addressed. "Over my body, Wilkins."

"Somebody in the store," returned Wilkins.

"Bring him in," laughed Tom, and flung the door wide open.

To the horror of Wilkins the light from the back room disclosed the lofty figure of Frank McAlister, who had entered for the purpose of buying some small matter, and without a suspicion that he should stumble upon a Beaumont.

"Ah!" shouted crazy Tom. "There's the tall fellow. I'll take him down a story. I'll razee him."

Whiskey, the family feud, the pugnacious instinct of his race, made him forget that he owed this man lifelong gratitude. He had not an idea in his buzzing head but the sole stupid idea of rushing to the combat.

"For God's sake, get out of this," whispered Wilkins, springing forward and pushing Frank toward the door. "He's as crazy as a loon. Get out of this, if you don't want mischief."

Our gentle giant certainly did not want mischief with one of Kate's brothers; but in his surprise and indignation he stood his ground, softly putting Wilkins aside.

The next instant the long room rang with the report of Tom's pistol, whether fired by accident or intention no one could afterwards tell, not even the lunatic young roister himself.

CHAPTER 20

 If Tom fired purposely, then it must be that Frank looked to him about ten feet high, for the ball went a yard or two over the head of the latter, entering the wall only a little below the ceiling.

Wilkins took the hint and dodged into some invisible nook of safety. He was a cool, brave man, and he was pretty well accustomed to this sort of thing, but he had a rational dislike to being shot for some one else. General Johnson, that bland, yet heroic *habitué* of duelling-grounds, advanced speechifying through the half-darkness, but fell over a pile of ropes and cords, with his hands in his pockets, and lay for some seconds helpless. The somnolent Jacocks did not stir from his seat on Duffy's bed; and Duffy, smiling straight whiskeys, remained astride of his rocking-chair. The martial-eyed Jobson hastily pushed the door to with his loaded cane, and then intrenched himself behind the projecting fireplace, remarking, "This is cursed ugly."

The hereditary enemies had a free field to themselves for a fight in the dark.

"Where are you?" shouted Tom, so completely bewildered by drink and the obscurity that he turned his back upon the foe, and fired a couple of barrels into Duffy's calicos. Frank plunged toward the flashes, wound his long arms around his slender antagonist, pinioned him, disarmed him, and threw the pistol over a counter.

"Let go of me," shouted the struggling Tom. "I say, who is that? Is it you, McAlister? Let go of me."

"Will you be quiet, you idiot?" demanded Frank, who had forgotten that he wanted to be shot, and fought instinctively to keep a whole skin, as other men do.

"Oh, it's you, is it?" returned Tom. Then came a string of ferocious threats, and of such abuse as cannot be written. But it was useless for the madman to scold and scuffle; he was thrown across a chair with his face downward, and held there; he was as helpless as a mouse in the iron grasp of a trap. At this point Wilkins, judging that the pistol-firing was over, came out of his unknown hiding-place, and, throwing open the door of the back room, let in light upon the battle-field. General Johnson now saw his way clear to disentangle himself from the coils of rope on which he had made shipwreck, and in so doing kicked a loose bedcord within reach of the combatants. Frank perceived it and instantly grasped it.

"Will you give me your word of honor to keep quiet?" he demanded.

"No, I won't," gasped the captive, still struggling. "Take your hands off me."

"Then, by heavens! I'll tie you," exclaimed Frank, beside himself with anger for the first time in this history.

In half a minute more Tom was wound from head to foot in the bedcord, like the Laocoön in his serpents.

"Merciful God!" whispered General Johnson to Wilkins. "Tie a gentleman! I never heard of such a thing in the whole course of my experience."

"Let's get out of here," said the martial-eyed Jobson, when he became aware of what was going on. "Beaumont might hold us responsible."

And, raising a window, he leaped into Duffy's back yard, followed the lead of a scared cat, made his way into the street, and hastened homeward with his face over his shoulder. Meantime Jacocks, Duffy, and Wilkins gathered behind the General, and stared speechlessly at the pinioned Beaumont, as much confounded at his plight as if they beheld him paralyzed by the wand of an enchanter. Probably the oldest inhabitant of Hartland could not have remembered seeing a "high-tone gentleman" subjected to such treatment. But then the inhabitants of Hartland, meaning those of the masculine gender, rarely lived to be old. A good many were carried off early by whiskey, and a considerable number "died in their boots."

"I wish to prevent him from disgracing himself," said Frank, recovering somewhat of his self-possession, as he remembered that his captive was Kate's brother. "A rencontre is not gentlemen's business."

"Mr. McAlister, I approve of your sentiments," murmured General Johnson, growing more cheerful as he saw a duel in prospect. The honor of Hartland and the chivalrous repute of its race of patricians were dear to the noble old militia-man.

"I shall go now," added Frank, after setting Tom in a chair and giving him a last knotting to fasten him in it. "When he comes to his senses you will please explain the matter to him. His pistol is behind the counter. Mr. Duffy, I came in to purchase something; but it doesn't matter now. Gentlemen, good evening."

"Good evening, Mr. McAlister," replied the General, touching his seedy beaver, while the other three simply bowed without speaking, so fearful were they of drawing upon themselves the wrath of the high and mighty Beaumonts.

"Untie me, won't you?" roared Tom, as his eyes followed Frank out of the street door. "I tell you, by ——! untie me."

"Yes, yes," assented the pacificatory Wilkins, pretending to pick and pull at the bedcord. But he was so judiciously slow and bungling that before he had half finished the disentanglement the gallop of a horse was heard outside; and when Tom at last seized his pistol and rushed howling into the street, no McAlister was in the neighborhood.

"That's just as right as can be for the present," observed Wilkins, peering out cautiously. "But it isn't, by gracious, any too right for the future. There'll be a duel sure. Duffy, you've lost your hats."

"Bet you, I haven't," returned the imperturbably smiling Duffy.

"Oh, you go to bed and sleep off your quarter of a thimbleful of whiskey," advised Wilkins, as he marched homewards.

This adventure between Tom Beaumont and Frank McAlister sent all Hartland into spasms of excitement. For three days hardly any business was transacted in the little borough. Duffy, who had seen a little of the fight, told a great deal; and Jobson, who had not seen "the first lick" of it, told much more. General Johnson narrated and lectured, and prophesied on every corner; and, being invited into various barrooms repeated himself until he grew pathetic over "those two noble young men, by gad, sir"; meanwhile leaning his shining elbows for support on the sloppy counter and letting his tears mingle with a thin drizzle of tobacco-juice. The only spectator of the "unpleasantness" who could not be got to remember anything about it was the sagacious Wilkins; blandly intent upon saying nothing which should offend either mighty Beaumont, or doughty McAlister, and also pleased to go on with his trading while others entertained the topers; whereby he got into temporary disfavor with the chivalry of Hartland, a race scornful of prudence and of finance.

If the village was thus excited, imagine the tempest at the Beaumont place. It must be understood that Tom got home without breaking his neck, fell a slumbering in a heap while unbuckling his spurs, was found and put to bed by a helot accustomed to such duties, and in the morning related his mishap to his father, at least so far as he could remember it. Such, by the way, was the candid habit of the junior Beaumonts; they always went to the head of the family with the tale of their disagreements. The father was proud of this frankness, looking upon it as the behavior of true-born gentlemen, and contrasting it favorably with the managements of other youngsters, who, as he said, sneaked into their duels.

Peyton was utterly astounded by the story of the tying, and could not bring himself to believe it on Tom's unsupported testimony, half suspecting the boy of *delirium-tremens* or other lunacy. But the insult being at least possible, he rode over to the village in search of General Johnson, and obtained a full, finished, and flowery statement of what had happened at Duffy's. When he got home he was in such a fit of rage as nobody could be in but an old-time Beaumont. He drank a pint of brandy that forenoon without feeling it.

"Vincent, this is perfectly awful," he said, drawing a gasp of horror, as he thought anew of the hitherto unheard-of indignity which had been inflicted upon a Beaumont. "I really don't know what to do, Vincent," he added almost pathetically.

"Tom will have to fight him, of course," replied the eldest son of the family, his face perfectly calm over this terrible announcement. "The old obligation is more than cancelled."

"Cancelled! Of course it is," exclaimed Beaumont senior. "An insult cancels any obligation. Of course, Tom must fight. He couldn't stay in the State if he didn't. But how? I never heard of such an outrage. What sort of fighting will avenge it? — Ah!"

This "Ah" was a whispered confession of fearful pain. At that moment one of the most dolorous of Peyton Beaumont's diseases gave him a twinge which it seemed to him would separate soul from body. He straightened himself, threw his head slowly backward, grasped the arms of his chair with both hands, and remained silent for a few seconds, his forehead beaded with perspiration, and his eyes fixed in agony. As the transport passed he drew another low sigh, this time a deep breath of relief, and resumed the conversation. Not a complaint, not an explanation, not even a groan. If the old fellow was something of a savage, he at all events had the grit of a savage, and he was for a moment sublime.

"Does it seem to you, Vincent," he calmly asked, "that Tom ought to insist upon any peculiar terms? Fighting over a handkerchief, for instance?"

"I don't see it," put in Poinsett. "Tom's own story is that he fired his revolver, and that the other man did not fire. Tom has already had his shot."

"Suppose you have your shot on the duelling-ground, and then your antagonist rushes on you and pulls your nose?" returned Vincent.

"Yes; there is your case," said Beaumont senior, turning upon Poinsett. "There is McAlister's behavior. A most beastly business! Just worthy of a nigger."

"I beg your pardon, but I can't see it," declared the clear-headed Poinsett, educated to law and logic. "There was no duel here. Tom passed an insult and fired a pistol, all without immediate provocation. I don't excuse the tying, understand. After McAlister had disarmed Tom, he was at liberty to kill him, or to leave him. The tying was superfluous and insulting. But at least, a part of the wrong of it is removed by the fact that Tom had taken the initiative and forced the rencontre. I don't believe that we should be justified in demanding any unusual proceedings. A duel simple is all we can ask."

After a long argument Poinsett's judicial mind prevailed over the fiery brains of the other Beaumonts, and they decided to demand only a duel simple.

Does the inhabitant of a more peaceful district than Hartland find himself horror-stricken and incredulous over this tremendous family council? The Beaumonts were not inhabitants of a peaceful district; they were the most pugnacious brood of a peculiarly pugnacious population; for generation after generation they had had an education of blood and iron. A Quaker, a New-Englander, or even an ordinary Englishman could not easily comprehend their excitable nature. Two centuries, perhaps seven or eight centuries, of high feeding, high breeding, habits of dominion, and habits of fighting, had made them unlike the mass of men. They were of the nature of blood-horses; they had the force, the courage, the nervousness, the fiery temper, and the dangerousness; they were admirable, and they were terrible. There was not one of them, old man or boys, not even the lazy Poinsett, who would not have fought to the death, rather than submit to what he thought dishonorable. They had a morality very different from the morality of the hard-working, law-abiding bourgeois. It was utterly different, and yet it governed as strictly. They would no more have fallen short of their ideas of honor than Neal Dow would break the Maine liquor law, or Charles Sumner would trade in niggers. If we want to find a parallel to the Beaumonts in some other land, we must, I think, go to the Green Erin of one or two hundred years ago, and resurrect the profuse, reckless, quarrelsome, heroic O'Neills and O'-Learys and O'Sullivans.

Tom's challenge found our usually pacific Frank McAlister in a pugnacious state of mind. He was pale and haggard in these days; he ate little and slept scarcely at all, and fretted continually over his troubles; the consequence was that his nerves were shaky and his temper insurgent, and his reason far from clear.

"Look at that," he said, handing the cartel to his brother, Robert Bruce. "Did you ever hear of such an unreasonable, malignant little beast? I disarmed him and tied him to keep him from committing simple murder and bringing himself to the gallows. The young brute ought to thank me on his knees. And here he wants to fight me. By heavens, if it were not for one thing, I don't know but I would; yes, I would — kill him. But that is nonsense," he added, after a moment's pause. "I would do nothing of the sort. I am not bound to fight him, and I won't fight him."

Bruce, meanwhile, his habitually thoughtful and melancholy eyes fixed on the ground, was considering the affair from the point of view of the code. His conclusion was precisely the same with that of the logical Poinsett.

"You had a right to disarm him," he said. "And you had a right to kill him. But the tying was an insult. The challenge is *en régle.*"

"What!" exclaimed Frank, astonished by the argument, and at the same time beaten by it. "So, according to the code, I owe a shot to the man whom I would not let murder me? What barbarity!"

"If you had simply disarmed him, he would not have had a foot left to stand upon," said Bruce. "I am sorry you tied him."

"It was an awful outrage!" returned Frank with bitter irony. "I served him right, and committed an outrage. It won't answer among madmen to be rational."

"What will you do?" asked the elder brother, after a full minute of silence.

"Look here, Bruce," Frank burst forth. "I don't care one straw for your cursed code of honor. It is a beastly barbarity; I hate it and despise it. But I want to be shot. I want this very man to shoot me. He saw me save his sister from death when he had lost her. He is the very man to shoot me; don't you think so? If I want to be shot, — and I do with all my heart and soul, — let *him* do it. You know what is the matter with me, don't you? I love his sister more than my life. I love her and I have lost her. No use living. I stopped this cursed quarrel for a while; I stopped it, as I thought, forever; and here it is again. It will never end in my time. I give up to it. It has beaten me. Even she has joined in it. I have dared to write to her, and have got no answer. I never can marry her; and even if I could, it would only be to make her miserable; and I would rather die than that. Oh my God, how I love her! And she, — she won't give me one line, — won't say that she does not hate me — like the rest of her family. And for all that I love her. Bruce, I wonder if you or any one can understand it. I wonder if any man ever so loved a woman before. I can call up every expression of her face. I can see her now as plainly as if she were here. Oh my God, what a heaven I can make around me! But it is a delusion. I am like a spirit in hell, seeing paradise afar off. There is a great gulf fixed. My father fixed it. Her brother helps. All the power of this damnable old feud goes to widen it. There is no crossing. There is no hope at all. Not the least. I wish I was dead. I want to die. Yes, let him fight me; let him shoot at me as much as he pleases; let there be an end of it. I sha'n't fire back. Understand that, Bruce. I sha'n't fire at *her* brother. Not at Kate Beaumont's brother."

His voice broke here and his gigantic frame shook with sobs; he did not try to conceal his agony, for he was not ashamed of it; indeed, he rather gloried in confessing that he suffered for her; it was a strange consolation, and it was his only one. Shall we impute to him the force of his passion as a weakness, and the greatness of his power of suffering as a littleness? It would be an error; the nobility of a soul is gauged as much by its emotional, as by its intellectual strength; the being who feels is as sublime as the being who thinks.

Bruce could make no response to his brother's outburst of anguish. There was a silence similar in motive to that which men often keep in the presence of those who lament the dead. It was the speechlessness of sympathy and awe, incapable of giving help, and conscious that there is no comfort.

Shall we who do not fight duels, condemn the young man for accepting the challenge to the field of honor? We must remember the education of his childhood, the spirit of the society in which he now lived, and the irrationality of overmuch misery. But although he would hazard his life in a way which our reason and his own reason condemned, he would go no further in the path of bloodshed. He persisted in declaring that he would receive Tom's fire, and that he would not return it. On this point he would not listen to argument.

"Then," said Bruce, his own voice trembling a little at last, — "then I will have nothing more to do with it. You must seek some other adviser."

"I shall choose General Johnson," replied Frank.

"The old wretch is murderous," remonstrated Bruce. "He will get you both killed, if possible. He will keep you standing there all day to be shot at."

"So much the better," was the desperate response of one of those rational men, who, when they do go mad, outpace all others' madness.

Old and shaky as General Johnson was, he no more quailed before the task of seeing Frank through his "difficulty" than a fashionable dowager shrinks from matronizing a young belle through a party. One result of this strange choice of a second was that Tom Beaumont made a still more singular one.

Our sociable friend Major Lawson, riding over to the Beaumont place with news of Kershaw and Kate, heard with horror of the projected encounter. How should he stop the duel, save the life of Frank McAlister, close up once more the abyss of the feud, and bring to a happy ending his poem of Romeo and Juliet? Should he apply for aid to Kershaw or to Kate? Alas, the old man was but just convalescing from a perilous illness, and the shock of such news as this might sweep him back to the borders of the grave! As for the girl, she was worn out with watching; moreover she had received mysterious letters which paled her young cheeks; she had written answers, and then had torn them up suddenly, as if under a sense of duty; she was evidently wretched and evidently ailing. Clearly she was in no fit condition to wrestle with fresh troubles, and it would be both cowardly and wicked to drag her into an arena of gladiators. Next the Major had thoughts of appealing to Frank, and begging him to prevent the duel by an apology. But the Beaumonts were obviously infuriated to that degree that no pacific act of satisfaction would serve which was not a degradation. Thus baffled wheresoever he looked for aid, our peacemaker took a desperate leap into the darkness of the untried, and resolved to offer himself as Tom's second, with the hope of effecting an arrangement. Knowing nothing of duels except by report, and abhorring them with his whole gentle nature shrinking from participation in them, his impulse was an inspiration of true heroism.

"My God, my dear Tom!" said the Major, drawing that warlike youngster to one side, and speaking with such earnestness that he forgot to play his usual vocal variations. "This is a dreadful business; more dreadful than I had expected. I knew of the political misunderstanding. I knew that the Judge had been unwise enough to reopen the quarrel with your excellent father. But I did hope that things might get on without bloodshed. Excuse me. I mean no reflections. My remarks have no personal bearing. I was simply speaking from general considerations of humanity. But allow me. Permit me a friendly question or two. I feel deeply interested in your welfare," protested the Major, who in reality wished that Tom would drop down dead. "May I ask who is to be your second?"

"I wanted Vincent," said Tom, with abominable frankness and calmness. "I thought McAlister would take his brother Bruce; then I could have had Vincent, who knows these things like a book. But he has chosen old Johnson; and that knocks me out of Vincent, of course; and, in fact, I suppose I ought to pick out some other old cock. That's what fellows would call the correct thing."

"Take *me*," begged Lawson, turning pale as he made his great plunge. "My dear young friend, I am quite at your service, Take *me*."

We must do Tom Beaumont justice. When he was in liquor he was a brute; but when he was sober he was a gentleman at all hazards; that is, as he understood gentility. Knowing full well that Lawson was no fit man to take charge of a duel, and profoundly astonished at his audacity in proposing so to do, he instantly and politely accepted his offer. In five minutes more, still trembling from head to foot with excitement, the Major was off to discuss the terms of the meeting with General Johnson.

"What!" exclaimed Vincent, when Tom informed him of his choice of a second. "That old imbecile! He doesn't know anything about it."

"How could I help taking him when he offered?" answered the heroic young roister.

"I don't know," admitted the puzzled Vincent, after long consideration.

Peyton Beaumont was equally amazed and displeased when he heard who was to manage for his son on the field of honor. But on learning that Lawson had himself proposed the arrangement, his mouth was stopped at once; and though he had seen Tom at the brink of death through the Major's inability to load pistols, he would not have opened it. It must be admitted that these Beaumonts, domineering and uncomfortable as they were, had their admirable points.

CHAPTER 21

 Major Lawson cherished hopes that he should be able to palaver General Johnson into some peaceful accommodation of the difficulty between Tom Beaumont and Frank McAlister.

But the General had an instinctive feeling, which he had greatly strengthened by venerable sanguinary experience, to the effect that accommodations not preceded by gunpowder are a disgrace to high-toned humanity, and not to be agreed to by any right-minded second. In duelling matters he was on his familiar hunting-grounds, and easily an overmatch for a novice in the intricate, tremendous chase. Moreover, one babbler is, as a rule, quite able to take care of another; and even the Major was not a longer winded creature than the old stump orator. Thus the latter had his own sweet will, courteously balked all attempts at effecting a reconciliation, and serenely brought the two parties face to face.

An "oldfield," — that is, a deserted clearing, a plot of land once alive to humanity, and now dead, a few acres gone utterly barren except for weeds, bushes, and dwarf pines, — an oldfield, some four or five miles from the village, was the place of meeting. Anxious for decorum even in homicide, and perhaps more especially in homicide, the

General had made the arrangements with able secrecy, so as totally to baffle the curiosity of the loungers of Hartland. The only persons present were the principals, the seconds, Dr. Mattieson, a Dr. McAuley, two negro coachmen, and two negro servants; these four last, by the way, being as cheerfully interested in the occasion as if they were full-blooded white men of the highest toned origin and habits. The rising sun was just beginning to steal through the stunted trees and burnish to splendor the drops of dew upon the starveling grass. The ground was so staked out as that the life-giving light should not dazzle the eyes of either of the men upon whom it now shone for perhaps the last time.

Major Lawson, looking very ghastly and piteous, as if he were about to plead for his own existence, walked hastily up to that red-eyed destiny, Johnson, and muttered a few words in such an agitated tone that they were incomprehensible.

"I beg your pardon?" inquired the tranquil General. "I am obliged to reply that I did not catch your meaning, — my hearing, Major," explained the polite old fellow, whose senses were as acute as those of a young squirrel.

"Hem!" uttered the Major, vehemently clearing his throat, for he was both ashamed of his agitation and eager to be understood. "I was taking the liberty, my very dear General, to suggest that it is not too late to — in fact to prevent bloodshed. To prevent bloodshed," he repeated, trying to soften Johnson with a smile and an inflection.

The General, in spite of his habitual urbanity, looked frankly annoyed, not to say disgusted.

"Major, have you anything to propose on the part of your principal?" he asked dryly.

"In case of regrets — of a sufficient apology," stammered Lawson, not knowing how to proceed, and fearing lest he had already said more than the code justified.

"Bless me, no," smiled the relieved General, who had absolutely feared a withdrawal of the challenge, although the scandal did not really seem possible. "My dear Major, I am happy to say — I mean I am sincerely and singularly grieved to state — that I have no authority to offer an apology. As for submitting the idea to my principal, I should not dare do it at this late moment. In my opinion it would be trespassing upon his liberty of action. But, bless me, Major! why, you

are suffering, you are pale. Don't trouble yourself to explain. I understand it all. You are weighed upon by your sense of responsibility.
Cheer up, sir," exhorted the friendly General, nobly taking Lawson's
hand. "You have done your whole duty as a gentleman and a Christian.
Your philanthropic and humane conduct claims and obtains my sincere
admiration. Let me assure you that you may make your remaining
preparations with a conscience as clear as heaven's own azure." After
gazing for a moment with blear-eyed ecstasy into the blue ethereal
above, he added briskly, — "Well, let us hasten. These suspenses are
trying. Moreover, we must avoid interruptions; they are always causes
of scandal. Receive my thanks, Major, for your humane suggestion,
and my regrets that I cannot avail myself of it."

With a profound bow the Major tottered away, muttering to himself, "Bloodthirsty old beast!"

Altogether the most excited, anxious, and alarmed man on the
ground was John Lawson. He was face to face with a monstrous
event, with the grandest ceremony of the knightly society in which he
had been bred, with an instant question of life and death. He felt as
if he were being presented at court, and also as if he were about to
commit murder. Great responsibilities and duties weighed upon him;
he must fight his man well, and he must load a pistol. These things,
too, these tremendous courtesies, and this momentous business, he
must undertake for the first time; and, to complete his embarrassment,
he must undertake them in the presence of a man who knew everything, while he knew nothing. Every step that he took, however carefully premeditated, might be an outrageous blunder in the eyes of
that critical, cool, abominable old Johnson.

But Lawson's greatest trouble was lest somebody should be shot. If
that happened, how could he ever sleep again, or be happy while
awake? Especially if Frank McAlister should fall, never more to rise,
how would matters stand with social, soft-hearted John Lawson?
Would his pet, Kate Beaumont, or even his old friend Kershaw, ever
forgive him? The Major would have given his worldly estate to have
the loading of both weapons, so that he might charge them with
nothing but the downiest wadding. He wished that he had the courage
to submit to his principal that it would be well to fire over the head of
the other principal. Meanwhile he was loading his pistol with great
difficulty, for his eyes were dim with lack of sleep the night previous,

and his hands were so shaky that he dropped several caps before he got one on the nipple.

"Rough business being roused out so early in the morning, isn't it, Major?" said Tom Beaumont in such a cheerful, cheering voice, that Lawson turned to stare at the youngster.

Tom appeared as a Beaumont should on such an occasion; he lounged easily about, and he had a pretty good color in his cheeks. He had come to the field in a proud spirit, determined to do himself and his family honor. So fearful he had been that he should look pale at the scratch, that he had washed his face repeatedly in cold water before leaving home, and finally had given it a rubbing with spirits of hartshorn.

But although Tom was resolved to behave manfully in this his first duel, he somehow did not find himself bloodthirsty nor even very pugnacious. The near prospect of death had softened his spirit, and made him almost forgive his antagonist. He had come to remember with gentleness and with something like gratitude the family obligation to this Frank McAlister. By moments he considered the propriety of firing at least one shot in the air, and very nearly decided that he ought so to do. This gentle change in his feelings he only revealed to others by a single phrase, which was so ill understood that it was afterwards credited to him as a jest.

"By heavens," he muttered, glancing with a troubled smile at his tall antagonist, "if I wanted to shoot over his head, I couldn't."

Frank McAlister never once looked at Tom. The lofty, grand monument of a fellow stood perfectly quiet, with his arms folded, his head bent, and his eyes on the ground. He was engaged in an obstinate struggle to fix his mind entirely, steadily, and to the last on Kate Beaumont. He had passed the night mainly in carrying on this struggle. He had not slept, except in brief dozings. On awaking from each, his first thought had been the duel; no, it had not been so much a thought as a vague foreboding, — an uncertain, sombre consciousness of peril. In the very next breath came a recollection of Kate and a renewal of the effort to settle his soul upon her alone. She had not answered his letters; she had doubtless condemned him because of his father and his family; she had condemned him, without a hearing, to be separated from her forever; he knew, or thought he knew, all that. Never mind; he would love her still, making her the whole of what life remained to him; he would think steadily of her and of nothing but her. Thus he had passed the night, striving to reach her through enemies and circumstances; and now, in the near presence of death, he was continuing the same pathetic, agonized battle. His constant pleading was, "Let me die, conscious of her alone."

Of a sudden the sun, stealing under the branches of a young pine, smote upon his eyes and summoned him to face another thought. In spite of his wrestling to cling to the beloved object which was to him nearly all of earth, he remembered and realized the awful solemnity of that transit which he was near to making. He felt that he must appeal for strength and comfort to a higher power than any human being. Wrong as he was, he dared to pray, or rather he dared not refrain from praying. An irresistible pressure was upon him, and all in the direction of prayer. It did not command him to repent, but merely to ask forgiveness and help. It was the hurried instinct of a swimmer overwhelmed by billows and dragged deathward. Without a lifting of the eyes or even a moving of the lips, there passed through his mind something like the following words:—

"Oh Father in heaven, I am here by my own folly and wickedness. But I am broken-hearted, and long to die. Give me strength to bear the deserved stroke; strength to bear wounds, suffering, and death. Pardon me for rushing upon my fate. Thou knowest what a burden has fallen upon me. Forgive me for sinking under it. Grant me mercy here and hereafter."

His prayer uttered, he felt strengthened. It was a moment incredible to such as have not passed through similar trials. He calmly advanced to meet death by the help of a woman whom he had lost and a Creator whom he had disobeyed. Impossible though it was, these two sustained him, as he took the loaded pistol from his alert, uncomprehending, heartless second.

There was a short silence. Lawson, trembling visibly all over, turned away his face and then shaded it with one hand, longing to cover it altogether. The steady old Johnson, in a firm, clear, shrill voice, called: "Gentlemen! Are you ready? One, two, three. Fire!"

Two reports answered. Each of the combatants kept his position. The tragedy had crashed by harmlessly.

At the sound of the pistols Major Lawson wheeled as quickly as if he had been hit, and made a step or two toward Frank McAlister.

Then, remembering himself and seeing his favorite standing, he hurried to his own principal.

"What the deuce did he fire in the air for?" at once demanded Tom.

"Did he?" inquired the amazed Major. "Why, of course he did," he immediately added, recovering his presence of mind. "The ball passed thirty feet over your head."

"I didn't hit him?" were Tom's next words, in a tone of inquiry.

Lawson glared over his shoulder in alarm, and then said with a sigh of undisguisable relief, "It appears not."

"There's no pluck in firing at a man who won't fire back," Tom quickly added.

Lawson silently grasped the youth's hand and pressed it warmly.

"It seems a little like mere murder," continued Tom. "What do you say?"

"Noble young man!" murmured the Major. "Noble, gallant, chivalrous young man!" he continued, with real and profound feeling. "Mr. Beaumont, you honor your race. Shall I say — shall I have the great pleasure of saying — that you demand no further satisfaction? You may properly direct me to say it. My dear, noble, distinguished young friend, you may feel entirely justified in directing it."

"Ye—s," drawled Tom, after a moment of reflection which was torture to Lawson. "Only I won't shake hands. I'll have another fire first. He may go this time, but I won't shake hands."

"Noble young man!" sang the Major (though with less fervor than before), as he turned to meet General Johnson.

That veteran swashbuckler did not look gratified, nor hardly amiable. He had noted with dissatisfaction that his man had fired in the air and he was in chivalrous anxiety lest the duel might be closed by that mistaken act of magnanimity, unparalleled in the history of his own personal combats.

"I have the honor to inquire whether your principal demands any further satisfaction?" he said with a succinctness and grimness quite foreign to his Ciceronian habits.

"We demand nothing more, sir," replied Lawson, bowing and smiling, exasperatingly sweet. "The magnanimous and chivalrous conduct of your principal induces us to terminate the combat."

The General was somewhat mollified. A compliment to his principal was precious to him; it was a flattery which he had a right to share.

"Allow me to express to you my admiration for the gallantry and the knightly bearing of your principal," he responded in his stateliest way. Then, in a more familiar tone, "Noble young fellows, both of them, Lawson. Noble boys, by gad."

"Certainly," coincided the Major, warmly. "Johnson, we are honored in serving them. Honored, General, honored."

"Yes, sir," affirmed the General, with an emphasis rarely equalled, at least in this world.

"My principal only ventures to claim one reservation," added Lawson, apologizing for the claim with a bow and smile. "He declines a formal reconciliation, — the usual shaking of hands, General, — nothing but that."

"Ah, indeed," replied Johnson, smiling also, for he saw a chance to continue the duel. "Excuse me, my very dear Major, but that is a matter which requires consideration."

"The political antagonism of the families, you remember," ventured to suggest the newly alarmed Lawson. "Reasons of state, if I may venture to use the expression. No personal feeling, I assure you. Dear me, no."

"I shall take great pleasure in laying the matter before my principal and requesting his decision," returned the diplomatic Johnson.

Frank McAlister, expecting nothing less than another exchange of shots, had resumed his struggle to think of no other thing on earth than Kate Beaumont, and was standing with arms folded, brows fixed, eyes dropped, unconscious of all around him.

"Shake hands?" he said dreamily, when he at last caught the meaning of the General's elaborate statement of the fresh difficulty. "Of course I don't require it. I shall never touch a hand of that family again."

"Allow me to observe that you have already shown immense forbearance," suggested the discomfited Johnson.

"That is my part," quietly answered Frank. "I came here for that."

"My God! these are new notions," thought the gentleman of an old school, as he marched back to make his pacific communication. "In my day men fought till something happened. What the deuce is to come of all these Quakerly whimwhams?" he concluded, with a notion that good society might not last his time out.

But the astonishment, and we might say the grief, of the hoary hero were fruitless; for once a duel between a Beaumont and a McAlister ended without bloodshed; in a few minutes more the oldfield was left deserted and without a stain.

Tom Beaumont dashed homeward on horseback, and on the way met his father, also mounted. Although the grim old knight had been able to send his son to meet death, he could not help suffering keen anxiety as to his fate. He did not know that he had the gout that morning, nor could he drink brandy enough to raise his spirits. After passing two hours in patrolling his garden, lighting and throwing away a succession of cigars, and roaring to Cato every few minutes for juleps, he called for his fastest horse, thrust his swollen feet into the stirrups, and galloped off to meet the carriages. The father and son encountered each other unexpectedly at the angle of a wood.

"Ah, Tom!" exclaimed Peyton Beaumont, grasping the young fellow's hand. "All right, my boy?" Then, impelled by a strange mixture of emotions, "God bless you, my boy!"

Next followed some straightforward, business-like inquiries as to the circumstances of the meeting.

"You did well, Tom," was his brief comment. "On the whole, taking into view the previous circumstances of the case, you did well to let him off."

In a subsequent conversation with Lawson he expressed himself much more fully on this point of the "letting off" of Frank McAlister.

"By heavens, Tom is a trump!" he said proudly. "I knew no son of mine would do anything in bad taste. Tom did right in sparing the fellow. And, Lawson, I am more pleased with the fact than you can imagine. Lawson, by heavens, it's a strange thing, but I liked that tall fellow. I absolutely felt an affection for him; and what's more, I can't quite get over it; I can't, by heavens! It's a most astonishing circumstance, considering that brutal insult. Why, just think of it; just think of it, Lawson. Tied my son! Tied him like a thief, like a nigger! Consider the outrage, Lawson; how *could* he do it? I wouldn't have thought he could tie one of my sons, or tie any gentleman. I wouldn't have believed it of him. I had a high opinion of that fellow. I almost loved him. He had the making of a gentleman in him. If he had been born in any other family, he would have become as fine a fellow as you could wish to see. Well, badly as he has behaved to Tom, I'm glad he wasn't hurt. I can never forgive him, never. But I didn't want him killed. No, Lawson, no."

"He may do well yet," suggested the cunning Major. "You know, I suppose, my dear Beaumont, that he fired in the air."

"Yes. Tom told me. Of course Tom told me everything. It speaks well for the fellow, shows that he has good instincts," admitted Beaumont, magnanimously. "Ashamed of his brutal insult, you see," he explained. "Willing to take the legitimate consequences of it. On the whole — by heavens! Lawson, I wish we had never met, or never quarrelled."

From Peyton Beaumont we return to Frank McAlister. He would have been glad to ride away alone from the duelling-ground, but he had not expected to leave it an able-bodied man or even a living one, and had therefore neglected to bring a horse. The result was that he made his journey back to Hartland in the same carriage with his second. It was a singular *tête-à-tête*, an interview of gabble with revery. The old fellow tattled in his unconsciously ferocious way about the duel, and about other duels, a long series of chivalrous horrors, as ghastly and bloody as so many ghosts of Banquo. The young fellow heard not, answered not, and thought only of Kate Beaumont. It was not rational meditation; he did not, for instance, query as to what might be the feelings of the girl concerning this meeting between himself and her brother; he was in no state to marshal facts or to draw conclusions. His condition was consciousness, rather than intelligence; and his consciousness revolved only about the idea that he loved.

How he had met her; how she had looked on this occasion, and that, and the other; what had been the tone of her voice, the expression of her eyes, the meaning of her gestures; — these things and many more like them thronged through his spirit. Nor were they mere remembrances; they were tableaux and audiences; she was in his presence. She advanced, and passed before his face, and went sweetly out of sight, only to come again. Except for an under voice of deepest despair which whispered, "Lost, lost!" the revery was indescribably delicious.

"I *have* been happy," he said in his soul. "I thank her for the purest happiness that I ever knew. No one, no event, no lapse of time, can rob me of the fact that I once knew her and was daily near her. I am still bound, and always shall be bound, to owe her greater gratitude than I can utter. She created me anew; she has made me nobler than I was; she lifted me up like a queen out of mere egotism. Until I met her I did not know that I had the power in me to love. She has made me worthy to be on the earth. Thanks to her, I have no shame for myself; I am perfectly wretched, but I possess my own respect. It is proper and beautiful to exist only for another. She has ennobled me."

At this point he vaguely understood the General to say: "Yes, sir. A man ought to shoot his own brother, sir, if that brother gives him the lie. He ought to shoot him, as sure as you are born, sir. By gad! that's my solemn opinion, as a gentleman, sir."

The next moment the young man was lost again in his revery. "I have lived, for I have loved," he repeated from Schiller. "To her beautiful soul be all the praise for my redemption from selfishness. Thanks be to Heaven also that she has been worshipped in a manner worthy of her. It may be that no other woman was ever honored by such an adoration. Thank Heaven that I have been deemed fit to confer upon her this great distinction of entire love. Merely in laying the whole of my heart at her feet, I have honored both her and me. Perhaps no other man was ever permitted so to worship such a worshipful being. My reward is sufficient, and it is more than I deserve. I have lived to high purpose, and I am content to die."

Here again he caught a few words from the interminably prattling General: "The truth is, that old Hugh Beaumont, the father of Peyton, you know, shot your great-uncle, Duncan, quite unnecessarily. In my opinion you would have been justified in remembering that fact to-day, and acting accordingly. Not to mention," etc., etc.

Notwithstanding this savage reminiscence, Frank remained in his lovelorn abstraction. His mood was more potent than mere revery; it rose to an exaltation which was almost mania; he was as irrational as those are who love with their whole being. His passion was a possession, the object of which had usurped the place of himself, so that he was not only ruled but absorbed by her. The power which she exercised over his spirit was a matter of pride with him. He wished to be known as her adorer, her infatuated idolater, her helpless slave. It needed all the natural gravity and dignity of his character to prevent him from babbling of her constantly to his friends. In riding or walking he had wild impulses to stop people, even though they were perfect strangers, and say, "I am nobler than you think me, for I love Kate Beaumont."

Let us not jeer at him; let us study him reverently. If any man is clean of the world, it is the lover; if any man is pure in heart, it is the lover. There is no nobler state of mind, with regard at least to merely human matters, than that of a man who loves with his whole being. The wife's affection is equal; so is the mother's. There is no diminution of honor in the fact that this sublime and beautiful emotion is in a measure its own reward. It is also its own pain; think of the sorrow of rejection! think of the agony of bereavement!

Nearing home, Frank met one of his father's negroes on a horse which he had been taking to the smith's. Muttering an indistinct farewell to Johnson, he sprang out of the carriage, mounted the animal and set off at full speed toward Kershaw's, not even remembering to send word of his safety to his brother Bruce. He was wild with impatience to look once more upon the house which sheltered Kate, even though he might not enter it. Fortune granted him more than he hoped, for he met the girl in the Kershaw barouche. She had that morning heard of the duel, and she was hurrying home to prevent it.

In his exaltation, his little less than madness, Frank dashed up to the carriage and stopped it.

CHAPTER 22

 So haggard and pale had Frank become since Kate last saw him, that guessing all at once that the duel had taken place, and that he was wounded or that Tom was killed, she screamed, "What is the matter? Why do you speak to me?"

He had *not* spoken as yet; and he could hardly speak now. It was the first time that he had ever heard such a voice from her, or seen such an expression of agony, terror, and aversion on her face. In amaze, and scarcely knowing what he said, he replied, "Your brother is well."

"It isn't true," she gasped, scared by his hoarseness and pallor, and shrinking from him. "Oh, is it?" she demanded. Then, seeing the answer in his face, she reached towards him, her rich cheeks flushing, her hazel eyes sparkling, and her small mouth quivering with joy. "Oh, thank you, Mr. McAlister," she whispered. "Then you have not fought."

"I wanted him to kill me," was Frank's confession. "I wanted him to, and he would not."

"Oh, how could you?" she answered, falling back from him with a look of reproach which seemed like anger. "Cruel — wicked man!"

The coachman, a grave and fatherly old negro belonging to Kershaw, judged that he had heard the last words that could ever pass between these two, and softly drove on. Had he not done so, there would surely have been explanations and pleadings on the part of Frank, and Kate might at once have pardoned, or even more than pardoned. But the uncomprehending slave, acting the part of a deaf and blind fate, divided them before they could think to forbid it.

Frank remained behind, speechless and paralyzed. The first word of harsh reproach which we receive from one whom we dearly love is an avalanche. For a time it puts out of mind all other calamities and all other things whatsoever. To Frank there seemed to be nothing in the world, nothing past or present or future, but those words, "Cruel — wicked." His eyes were on the retreating carriage, and he did not move until it was out of sight. Then he rode away at full speed, directing his course toward a wood near the Beaumont place, his sole purpose being to reach a stile over which he had once helped Kate to pass. Finding it, he dismounted and stood for a long time contemplating the worm-eaten rail, repeatedly kissing the spot on which he remembered that her foot had rested. After an hour in this place, an hour made heavenly as well as wretched by passing pageants of her form and face, he found himself faint with hunger and fever and rode slowly homeward.

We must return to Kate. She had scarcely been driven past the sight of the man whom she had called cruel and wicked, ere she longed to call him to her side. "Why does he drive on?" she thought, glancing helplessly at the slave, who would have stopped had she bidden him. Next she turned in a useless paroxysm of haste, and looked back at Frank through the rear window of the carriage, querying whether he would follow her. "What did I say to him?" she asked, sure that she had uttered something bitter, but not yet able to remember what. In great trembling of body and spirit, and finding life a woful perplexity and burden, she was taken home.

The first of the family to meet her was Tom. She drew him to her, kissed him on both cheeks, and then held him back at arm's length, looking him sadly in the eyes and saying, "Ah, Tom! How could you?"

The next instant, remembering those words, "I wanted your brother to kill me, and he would not," she threw herself into the boy's arms and covered his face with kisses and tears of gratitude. This staid, simple, pure girl, her eyes humid, her cheeks flushed to burning, and every feature alight with unusual emotion, was at the moment eloquent and beautiful beyond humanity. There never was a finer glow and glory on anything earthly than was then on her exquisite young face. Just in this breath her father came to the door, and stood dazzled by his own child. Steeped in brandy and hot with his chronic pugnacity, he forgot at the sight of Kate everything but Kate.

"Ah, my daughter!" he said, taking her into his short heavy arms and pressing her against his solid chest. "How I have neglected you for the last few days! What have I been about?"

"Father, was it fair —?" she began, and stopped to recover control of her voice.

"No, it wasn't fair," answered old Peyton, understanding in a moment and repenting as quickly. "No, by heavens, it wasn't fair. Tom, we ought to have told her. She's a Beaumont, and she's my own dear daughter, and she had a right to know everything we did. Kate, we have behaved, by heavens, miserably."

"Well, it is over, and safely," sighed Kate, laying her head on her father's shoulder. "I thank God for it," she added in a whisper.

"So do I, Kate," replied Beaumont. "I do, by heavens. I'm a poor, savage, old beast; but I am thankful, by heavens. I'm glad Tom is out of it safe, and I'm glad the other is out of it safe."

"Father, I must go to bed," said the girl, presently. "I am very, very tired."

"Not sick?" demanded Beaumont, staring at her in great alarm.

He assisted her up stairs to her room; he would not let anybody else do it; he forgot that his feet were masses of gout. When he came down, he said to Tom, "Ride for a doctor; ride like the devil. Don't bring any of those d—d surgeons who were in the duel. Bring somebody else."

During that day and the next he haunted the passages which led to his daughter's room. Indifferent to pain, merely cursing it, he regularly hobbled up stairs to carry her food with his own hands, affirming that no one else knew how to wait on her properly, and denouncing the incapacity and stupidity of "niggers." When she was awake and able to see him, he sat for hours by her bed, holding her hand, looking at her, and talking softly.

"My God, how I have neglected you!" he groaned; "I don't see how I could have done it. I ought to have known that you would run yourself down. I ought to have interfered."

Such was Peyton Beaumont: he passed his life in sinning and repenting; and he did each with equal fervor. As to the cause of Kate's shattered condition, he had grave suspicions that it was not merely watching over Kershaw, and not merely the shock of the news of the duel. At times he regretted bitterly the renewal of the feud, and blamed Judge McAlister very severely for having brought about the untoward result, being, of course, unable to see that he himself was at all responsible therefor. "Unreasonable, incomprehensible, hardhearted, selfish old brute!" he grumbled in perfect honesty, meaning McAlister, and not Beaumont. Well, there was no help for it; the only thing to be done was not to speak of that family in Kate's presence; above all, she must not once hear the name of Frank. This wise decision he communicated distinctly to Nellie, and vaguely, but with great energy of manner, to Mrs. Chester. As for his boys, he trusted to their sense and delicacy as gentlemen, and he trusted not in vain.

The result was, that, when Kate came down in a day or two to table, anxious to learn all about the quarrel, and to hear the name of McAlister incessantly, she got never a word on those subjects. It was very uncomforting; it was like being shut in prison. Open utterance of hate against the McAlisters would have been more tolerable to her than this boding silence with its attendant suspense. Kate had self-command and dignity of soul; she would not allow her face to show anxiety or sorrow; there was nothing uncheerful in it, save a pathetic lassitude. But at times it seemed to her as if her heart must absolutely break bounds and demand, "Will none of you speak of him? Is it not enough that I shall never see him more? Must I not even hear his name?"

She could not relieve herself by struggling against the feud. She had fought it once when fighting it seemed to be a matter of simple humanity and of affection for her own race. But now, her soul more or less laden with Frank McAlister, she could not demand peace without having the air of suing for a lover. Indeed, she dared not introduce the subject of the family warfare, lest her face should reveal the secret of her heart, and even suggest more than was thus far true. For she maintained to herself that as yet she was not quite in love with this man. To love him, especially to confess it to others, when he had not openly asked for her affection, would be shameful; and the girl was calmly resolved to endure any suffering rather than descend below her own respect or that of her family. So for several days there was silence in the Beaumont prandial and other general conclaves concerning Frank McAlister and all his breed.

"I think Kate is getting on very well," remarked Peyton Beaumont to his married daughter. It was not an assertion, but a query; he did not feel at all certain that Kate was getting on well; he wanted a woman's opinion about a woman.

"If saying nothing, and growing paler every day, is getting on well, you are right," answered Nellie, in her straightforward, business-like, manly way.

"You don't mean," stammered the father, — "you don't mean that she cares for —"

"Don't mention his name," interjected Nellie. "That man, I absolutely hate him. I did want him shot. He is intolerable. Do you know, father, I sympathized with that man and showed him that I did? To think that after that, no matter what the provocation, he should tie my brother! Grossly insult my brother! It was not an outrage upon Tom only; it was an outrage upon me and upon Kate."

"The scoundrel!" growled Beaumont, his eyes flaming at once, and his bushy eyebrows working like a forest in a hurricane. "Nellie, why didn't you say this before? Tom would have shot him, sure."

"Ah, — well. On the whole I did not want to. I had liked him so well, that I could not quite say the word to have him — hurt. I had really liked him; that was it. And perhaps it is as well; yes, perhaps it is better. He behaved well in the duel, father?"

"Yes," assented Beaumont, a tiger who had been tamed by his children, and easily followed their leading. "He stood up to the scratch like a man."

"And he didn't fire at Tom."

"That's true. He showed penitence. He behaved well."

"Let him go," added Nellie, after a moment of revery. "But Kate must not be allowed to meet him again."

"Of course, she won't meet him again," declared Beaumont, lifting his eyebrows in amazement. "How the deuce should she meet him again?"

"Shall I take her away with me for a few weeks?" asked Mrs. Armitage.

"No," returned the father, promptly. "Why, good heavens, she has just got home. I can't spare her yet. But you are not going now," he added. "What do you want to go for?"

"My husband has written me to come," answered Nellie, with that strange look, half imploring and half defiant, which so often came over her face.

Beaumont walked up and down the room, muttering something which sounded like, "Hang your husband!"

"Besides, Aunt Marian quarrels with me every day," pursued Mrs. Armitage, forcing a smile.

"Oh, never mind Aunt Marian! She quarrels with everybody and always did and always will. She can't help it. She grew up that way. And really she isn't so much to blame for it. She was a spoilt baby. My father couldn't govern his only daughter, and my mother wouldn't have let him if he had wanted to. The consequence was that Marian always behaved like the very deuce, just as she does now. Yelled, scratched, fought for sugar, bounced away from table, called her mother names, sulked by the twenty-four hours, grew up that way and stayed so. Come, Aunt Marian is too old to cure; she is a fixed fact. No use quarrelling with her. Let her alone and never mind her."

"I don't mind her much," said Nellie, coolly. "I rather think she gets the worst of it."

"I rather think so," the father could not help laughing, pleased that his daughter should overmatch his sister.

"It's a shame, isn't it, that people shouldn't govern their children?" continued Nellie with a smile.

"A shame? It's downright wickedness," declared Beaumont, who had not a suspicion that he had failed to rule his offspring properly.

Nellie laughed outright.

"Still, I must go," she resumed. "I have been here nearly a month; it is so pleasant to be here! But it is time that I got back and set to work. There are the autumn suits for our niggers to be cut out and made up."

"Oh! answered Beaumont, seeing something to the purpose in this statement.

"And I want Kate to help me."

"Pshaw! You don't want her."

"She ought to learn that sort of thing."

Beaumont uttered a growl of discontent: he could not spare his favorite.

"I shall leave it to Kate," declared Nellie, as she closed the interview, somewhat queening it over her father.

In the same spirit of benevolent imperiousness she went off directly to lay the question of the visit before her sister. She had not heretofore meditated her plan; she had thought of it while talking with her father, and immediately resolved upon it; and she was now as much prepared to urge it as if she had had it in view for weeks. She meant to suggest it to Kate; and, if it was opposed, to argue for it; and, if necessary, quarrel for it. It was one of those cases of instantaneous consideration and decision for which women, and indeed all emotional people, including Beaumonts, are noted.

Kate, however, was not altogether womanish or Beaumontish; there was something manly, there was something of the Kershaw nature in her; she was thoughtful, judicial, deliberative, and a little slow. In her aquiline face, delicate and feminine and beautiful as it was, there was a waiting, holdfast power, like that in the face of Washington.

"Don't you mean to go?" demanded Mrs. Armitage, excitedly, and almost angrily, after advocating her plan for ten minutes.

"Yes," replied Kate. "Thank you, Nellie. I shall be very glad to go."

"Then why didn't you say so?"

"I was thinking," said Kate, dreamily.

About the corners of her small, pulpy, rosy mouth there was a slight droop which Mrs. Armitage comprehended at once and translated into a long confession of trouble. She rustled forward, put one of her large arms around the girl's waist and kissed her in an eagerly petting way, as a mother kisses her baby. Not a word of explanation passed between the two; and when Nellie spoke again it was only to say, "Now go and get ready."

"Have you asked papa about it?" demanded Kate.

"I told him I should leave it to you," replied Nellie, in her prompt, decided way. "I will let him know that you are going."

"He and grandpa Kershaw must both be consulted," said Kate, with tranquil firmness.

The next day, all relatives consenting, willingly or unwillingly, Mrs. Armitage carried her sister from the scene where she had found weariness and sorrow. Some hours of travel in rattling, reeling cars, over a rickety railroad, brought them into the mountainous western corner of the State, and left them at sundown in the straggling borough of Brownville.

"We shall perhaps find Randolph here," said Nellie, as they neared the lonely, rusty station-house. "He wrote me that he should come every evening until I appeared." Then she added with a somewhat humbled air, "But I don't much expect him."

It was a wife's imbittered confession of the fact that her husband has learned to pay her little attention.

The Armitage equipage, a shabby barouche attached by a roughly patched harness to two noble horses, was at the station; but the only human being about it was a ragged negro coachman; there was no Randolph.

"He would have come if he had expected you," was Nellie's too frank comment. "Husbands are fond of novelty. Wait till you get one."

"I am sure you are unjust to him," said Kate. "Of course he has his business."

"Oh yes, of course," replied Nellie, hiding the wound which she had been indiscreet enough to expose. "We women demand incessantly, and demand more than can be given. I only thought it worth while to warn you not to expect too much."

"What is that?" asked Kate, anxious to change the subject of the conversation, and pointing to an axe and a coil of rope which lay on the driver's foot-board.

"Dem ar is to mend the kerridge with, case it breaks down, miss," grinned the coachman.

"You don't know our Saxonburg fashions," laughed Nellie. "Family coaches will get shaky if they are kept long enough; and we up-country people almost always keep them long enough."

"I don't object to old things," said Kate; "excepting old family feuds," she added, unable to help thinking at every moment of the troubles at home.

In an hour the high-spirited bays halted champing at the door of Randolph Armitage's house. It was a strange-looking residence, which had obviously not been created all at once, but in successive parts, as the means of the owner increased, and without regard to aught but interior convenience. Two stories in height here and one story there, with one front facing the south and another the southwest, it appeared less like a single building than like an accidental collection of buildings. If three or four small dwellings should be swept by a flood, and beached together without further disposition than that of the random waters, the inchoate result would resemble this singular mansion. It was, in fact, the nest where the Armitages had grown up through three generations from backwoods rudeness to their present grandeur, if grandeur it might be called. There was evidence in the building that prosperity did not yet haunt it overflowingly. The white paint which had once decked the miscellaneous clapboards had become ragged and rusty. In a back wing, constituting the kitchen and servants' quarters, several window-panes were broken. The wooden front steps were somewhat shaky, and the enclosing fence fantastically dilapidated.

The adorning light of a summer day in the hour after sundown fell upon Randolph Armitage as he came out to greet his wife and children. Kate had not met him since she was a girl of fourteen: but she perfectly well recollected the glamour of his personal beauty, — a beauty which was so great that it fascinated even children. In the exquisite mild radiance of the hour he seemed faultlessly beautiful still. He wore an old loose coat of gray homespun, but the shapeliness of his form could not be hidden. His long black hair, matted and careless as it was, offered superb waves and masses. There yet was the Apollonian profile of old, the advanced full forehead, the straight nose nearly on a line with it, the delicately chiselled mouth, the small but firm chin, the straight and smooth cheeks, the many-tinted brown eyes, and the clear olive complexion. He still seemed to Kate the handsomest man that she had ever seen; handsomer even than that grand and good giant, Frank McAlister.

"So you have come at last!" were the ungracious first words of this Apollo.

Kate knew nothing of the domestic troubles of her sister. On hearing this reproving growl, she suspected only that Nellie had wrongly delayed her return home; and before even she got out of the carriage, she tried to take the blame upon herself. She called out, "I dare say it is my fault, Randolph."

"What!" he exclaimed, his face changing from sullenness to gayety. "Is it Kate?" he asked, helping her down the step and gazing at her with admiration. "What a beauty you have grown!" and he kissed her cheek caressingly. "Why, my dear little sister, you are a thousand times welcome. So my wife waited to bring you? She is always doing better than I suspect."

He kissed his wife now, and she calmly returned it. Kate of course could not divine that the embrace was on her account. How should she, whose heart yearned to love and be loved, guess easily that husband and wife could meet without pleasure.

"And here are my youngsters," said Armitage, turning away from Nellie with singular suddenness. "Willie, did you have a nice long visit? And you, Freddy? Did you both play with grandpapa?"

He lifted them successively, hugged them with a graceful air of fervor, and set them down promptly.

"And now, Kate," he added, offering her his arm gayly, "let me escort you into my house for the first time. It is a great honor to me and a great pleasure."

All the evening his manner to his guest was most caressing and flattering. Moreover, he dressed in her honor, laying aside his slovenly homespun and coming to the table attired in a way to show his fine figure to advantage. Yet as the hours wore on, and as Kate's spirits turned to depression under a sense of homesickness and fatigue, she seemed to perceive something disagreeable, or at least something suspicious, under this brilliant surface. She was like one who, after gazing with delight on a tide of clear sparkling water, should half think that he discovers a corpse in the translucent abysses. The light of the lamps showed her that Randolph's face was not all that it had been in other days; the fervid color had faded a little, and there were bags under the still brilliant eyes, and a jaded air as of dissipation. Was it true, too, that there was a shadow of reserve between husband and wife, as if neither were sure of possessing the other's sympathy? What did it mean, moreover, that they occupied separate rooms?

In spite of the girl's efforts to believe that all went well in this family which was so near and dear to her, she retired that night with a vague impression that she was in a household haunted by mysteries, if not by misery.

CHAPTER 23

 What blessed restoration there is in the sleep and in the health of youth! Palaces of hope and happiness which had tumbled to ruin at eventide are rebuilded ere morning by these beneficent magicians.

When Kate came to breakfast, after the refreshing slumber which even troubled hearts may know at nineteen, she had forgotten the bodings of the night before, or remembered them only to scout them. All went aright to her eyes in the Armitage dwelling that day and the day following and for many days after. Sincere, amiable, unsuspecting of evil, anxious to think well of others, she was the easy and contented dupe of a skilful though wayward enchanter.

On certain holy festivals good Mahometans turn their jackets inside out, and go all in green, the color of the prophet. In like manner Randolph Armitage had a garment of deportment which he could turn according to the circumstances of time or company, the one side being of the color of the Devil and his angels, while the other might please the eyes of saints, or pure women. The silver lining of this sable cloud it was now his pleasure to wear outward. Kate was young and beautiful, and it was one of his amusements to charm young and beautiful women; moreover, the girl might be expected to bear witness of him among the Beaumonts, should he misbehave during her visit; and if he feared anybody on earth, it was his puissant relatives by marriage. So for weeks he controlled the seven capital devils who inhabited his soul, suffering none of them to issue forth and disport himself in her presence. He was a fond father, a gentle husband, an amiable brother-in-law, and a merciful master to his slaves. He astonished his wife, and almost rewon her heart. He fascinated Kate.

It was not a difficult matter for him to be thus delightful. He possessed that mighty glamour of excelling beauty which sheds attractiveness over even indifferent, even misbecoming behavior. So sweet and so fair to look upon was his smile, that mere young girls, mere rude boys, mere untutored crackers, were glad at winning one from him, and never forgot the pleasant sight all their lives after. Hundreds of people who knew him not had stared wonderingly in his face as he met them, turned to look at him after he had passed, and eagerly inquired his name. All through Saxonburg District, and in the rough surrounding region, he was known as Handsome Armitage. A mountaineer from East Tennessee had once stopped him in the street, and said: "Stranger, excuse me; but you be certainly the puttiest man I've seen sence I come to Sou' Carline. Mought I ask what you call yourself?"

But, in addition to his beauty, Randolph had the charm of a flexible character, apt to take the bent of his society. It was his nature to be hail fellow well met with Satan or with the archangel Ithuriel, according as he found himself in the company of either. He had intelligence to perceive at once, and to the full, both the purity of Kate Beaumont and the innate grossness of the vilest low-down harridan in the district. He was as much in place, so far as his behavior went, with the one as with the other. The result was, that, as Nellie divulged nothing concerning her husband, Kate believed him to be good, and knew him to be charming. She walked with him, rode with him, tried her hand at fishing under his guidance, learned games of cards of him, read him the letters which she received from home, talked with him about the feud, and made him little less than a confidant. Of course he agreed with her in all things; caring little about the family quarrel, it was easy for him to condemn it; despising politics, it was easy for him to bemoan the election difficulty. He had the coinciding amiability of indifference and hypocrisy. Thus it was that this stainless and unsuspicious girl found in this thoroughly corrupt man a friend whom she valued and almost reverenced.

"You don't half appreciate your husband," she reproached her sister.

"Yes, I do," replied Nellie, making an effort of repression which was truly sublime, and withholding her ready tongue from all confession or complaint.

"You should be very sweet to him, if only on my account," added Kate, with a smile of perfect incomprehension and innocence. "How kind he is to me!"

"I *am* obliged to him, on your account," said the martyr-like wife. "I have told him so."

"I don't believe it," laughed Kate. "I want you to tell him so in my presence."

Just then Randolph entered the room. It was one of his handsomest moments; his cheeks were flushed, his eyes bright, his air elated; moreover, he had dressed himself carefully and becomingly. His wife settled her eyes upon him with such an expression as if she were dazzled against her will.

"Randolph," she said, her voice wavering a little, perhaps with recollection of the tenderness of other days, "Kate wants me to thank you again for your kindness to her. I do so with all my heart."

Armitage smiled, that smile that said so much; he just moved his lips, those lips that were so eloquent without speaking; then lightly and gracefully he advanced to Nellie, lifted her hand, and kissed it. For a moment the wife was much moved; she drew his hand to her and pressed it against her heart. Kate rose, in her eyes a glistening of tears, in her heart one of the high-blooded impulses of her father's race, and stepping quickly up to her brother-in-law, kissed his cheek.

"Thank you, my dear, good child," he said, turning upon her with a flush of sincere gratification. "You almost tempt me, you two, to stay at home this evening. But," he added, without the least difficulty, and in the same breath, "I have an engagement. Don't sit up for me."

After he had gone Kate said to Nellie, "I *must* tell you. You have delighted me. When I came here, — when I first came, — I thought that you two were — indifferent. I beg your pardon, both of you."

"Ah, Kate!" replied Nellie, "you are capable of falling in love. If you were not you would not care for these things so. You can love, and I am sorry for it."

Hours passed after this scene, and Armitage did not return. As the evening wore on towards midnight, Nellie's brow grew darker and darker with an expression which was not so much anxiety as something sterner. She looked at last like one who is receiving blows, not in a spirit of angry retaliation, but with sullen defiance. Her air was so gloomy and hard that it disturbed her sister.

"Had you not better send out for him?" asked Kate. "Do you know where he has gone?"

"He sometimes stays out in this way," said Nellie, calmly. "We won't sit up longer for him."

"But hadn't we better?" urged the younger woman.

"No, no," replied Nellie, almost imperiously. "I would rather you would not. I wish you to go to bed."

Leaving the two to find such sleep as is the lot of anxious women, let us follow Randolph Armitage and see how he was passing the night. On the morning of that day this "high-strung" gentleman had risen to find himself under the spell of a mighty impulse; an impulse which had come to him he knew not how, and which he could not account for, nor analyze, nor control; an impulse common with men of dissolute lives, and forming the main-spring of their characteristic actions. He must break bounds, he must run away, he must go wild, he must have a spree. He was no more capable of philosophizing upon the possession than a horse is able to state why he snorts, flings out his heels, and dashes headlong over his pastures. His brain, his stomach, his arterial structure, or some other physical organ, had gone mad, either with boisterous health or with inflammation, and demanded the relief of violent activity; whether noble or vicious was indifferent, only that his habits of life almost necessarily directed the outburst towards immorality. In the horsy language of his favorite companions, lewd fellows of the baser sort, and mostly of low-down birth, "he had got his head up for a spree."

While in this state of mind he met Jim Saxon, widely and unfavorably known as Redhead Saxon, a "low-flung" descendant of the rude family which had first settled the district of Saxonburg, and served as the mean origin of its name. It was with this coarse, gaunt, long-legged, hideous desperado and sycophant in homespun that he had made the engagement which took him from his home during the evening. He had gone straight from the exquisite scene with his wife and Kate Beaumont to a cracker ball.

Three miles from his house, in a region of sand and pines and scrub-oaks, there was a clearing which had once supported a settler's family, and which, as the soil became exhausted, had degenerated into an oldfield, overgrown with bushes and long weeds. In the centre of the oldfield was a log-cabin, the clay fallen from its chinks, the boards on its roof warped and awry, its windows without glass, and closed by rude shutters, the chimney a ruinous, unshapely mass of stones and mud, the outer air free to enter at numberless crannies. This cabin was the residence of two "lone women," who held it rent free of its charitable owner, a wealthy physician of the village. The eldest was Nancy Gile, thirty years old, but looking thirty-five, yellow-haired, white-faced, freckled, red-eyed, dirty, ragged, shiftless, idle, a beggar, and otherwise of questionable life. The youngest was Sally Huggs, a small, square-built, rosy-cheeked, black-eyed girl of not more than seventeen, who had run away from her mother to secure larger liberty of flirtation. Nancy Gile had two illegitimate children, and Sally Huggs was herself an illegitimate child. The reader can guess at the kind of morality that adorned the household existence.

There are no outcasts. People who are not in "our society," and not in the circle below that, and not in any circle that we deem society, have still a surrounding of more or less sympathetic humanity, and even perhaps a following of admirers. Nancy Gile and Sally Huggs, poor and ignorant and degraded as they were, had an environment of friends whom they wished to hold fast, and of enemies whom they desired to propitiate. Consequently, when they one day came into unexpected, almost miraculous possession of five dollars more than was necessary to buy bacon and hominy for the morrow, they resolved to raise their standing and enlarge their popularity by "giving a treat."

A pound of tallow candles for illumination, and three gallons of white raw whiskey for refreshment, summed up their purchases. As for supper, they trusted, as any other host of the oldfields would have done, that each guest would provide his or her own, and eat it before coming. For music there was Sam Tony, a youth of piny woods extraction, as lean and yellow as his own fiddle, and a gratuitous scraper on such occasions. The invitations had been spread by word of mouth at the previous "sale-day" in the village, and had gathered in every young Saxonburg loafer or cracker who was not in open hostility with the household. Even those tramps, the Bibbs, who had no abiding habitation, but slept sometimes in brush cabins, and sometimes in the sheltering corners of warm fences, had sent one representative in the shape of a ragged, dirty girl of eighteen, trim and slender and graceful in figure, but yellow and ghastly with exposure and lack of proper nourishment. When handsome Armitage and hideous Redhead Saxon rode into the benighted tangle of the oldfield, Nancy Gile's cabin was humming like a huge beehive with the noise of dancing and laughing low-downers, and flaming from every door and window and chink with tallow-dip splendor.

"It looks like a storming old blow-out," said Armitage, as he tied his horse's bridle to the drooping branch of a tree. "Quash," he added, addressing a negro whom he had brought along, also mounted, "stay by these beasts. Come on, Redhead."

He was already heated with liquor. His manner and voice had become strangely degraded since that pretty scene at his home. In place of his make-believe, yet gracious gentility and tenderness there was a wild, reckless, animal-like excitement. Perhaps it was more than animal; it may be doubted whether any beast is ever a rowdy; we have heard that even a drunken ape has decorum.

The one room of the cabin, eighteen feet or so by twenty-five, was crammed. In the centre eight couples were jostling and elbowing through a sort of country dance. Crowded between them and the log walls, and filling the two doorways, and covering the shaky stairs which led to the loft, was a mass of young men and girls, applauding, yelling, chattering, laughing, or staring with vacant eyes and gaping mouth. Even the wide-open doors and windows and chinks and the broad chimney could not carry off all the mephitic steam generated by this mob of unclean people.

To a New-Englander or a Pennsylvania Quaker fresh from the pacific, temperate, educated faces of his birth-land, it would not have seemed possible that these visages were American. The general cast of countenance was a lean and hardened wildness, like that of Albanian mountaineers or Calabrian brigands. There were no stolid, square, bull-dog "mugs"; everywhere you saw cleverness, or liveliness, or at least cunning; but it was cleverness of a wolfish or foxy nature. The forms, too, were agile, most of them tall, slender, and bony, the outlines showing sharply through the calico gowns or homespun suits.

Four or five plump and rosy girls, looking all the plumper because of sunburn, were exceptions to the general rule of mere muscle and sinew. All the men, through early use of tobacco, and constant exposure to hardship, were figures of displeasing lankness.

The stinted, graceless costumes increased the general ungainliness. Some of the girls were in calico, limp with dirt; others in narrow-chested, ill-fitted, scant-skirted gowns of the coarsest white cotton, such as was commonly issued to field-hands; others in the cast-off finery of charity, worn just as it had been received, without remaking. Nearly all the men had straight, tight trousers, insufficient vests, and short-bodied, long-tailed frock-coats of gray or butternut homespun.

Scarcely one of these faces had been illuminated or softened by the touch of civilization. If they were less stolid than the countenances of so many Indians, they were not much less savage. Not that the savagery was perfectly frank and open; there was an air of slyness about it and even of sycophancy; it was the ferocity of a bloodhound, waiting to be set on. While these people knew how to commit deeds of blood, they could go about them best at the command of a "high-tone gentleman." But even to their masters they must have looked a little untrustworthy. It was evident that human life, no matter of what dignity and descent, would be held by them in light esteem. After all, valuing their own lives little, they were not despicable. In spite of law-abiding prejudices, it is impossible not to accord some respect to a hearty willingness to give and take hard knocks. The best intentioned members of society cannot look down with unmixed contempt upon a man who fights like the Devil, although they may find him inconvenient and proper for suppression. Born to be proud of my countrymen, reposing a loving confidence in their pugnacity and their knack at firearms, I would adventure the population of this hive in any part of the Abruzzi, sure that they would make their frontiers respected and perhaps lay Fra Diavolo under contribution. In fact, I should rejoice to colonize them in those regions, trusting that the drama of the Kilkenny cats might be re-enacted.

Into this genial mob bounced Handsome Armitage with a sense of satisfied sympathy and without the slightest consciousness that it was his presence which turned mere vulgarity into vice and gave the scene its finishing touch of degradation.

"Hurrah, Nancy!" he shouted, seizing the mistress of the house and whirling her round in an extemporized waltz, much to the confusion of the country-dancers. "Bully for you, old girl! This is a glorious blow-out."

"Square, I'm right glad to see ye," returned Nancy Gile, her white face reddening with pride and pleasure. "I said you mought come. Sally said you wouldn't."

"Where is she?" asked Armitage.

"Thar she is, Square, dancin' along with Sam Hicks."

"Sally, come here," called the high-toned gentleman. "Come here, and let's have a look at your cheeks."

"Can't," laughed Sally, hot and gay with exercise and attentions, for she was the belle of the ball. "Got to dance this through. Then I'll come."

"Who the deuce is Sam Hicks?" demanded Armitage.

"He's a Dark Corner man," explained Nancy. "He met up with her last sale-day, an' took an awful shine to her. Talks like he was goin' to marry her. Mebbe he will."

"Mebbe he won't," laughed Armitage. "Well, give us some whiskey. I haven't had a drink for half an hour. Redhead, try it."

"After you, Square," returned the respectful Redhead, filling a glass for his superior. "It's the same old spring I reckon. Pickens whiskey, fresh from the mill, clar as water, an' strong as pizen. Reckon that'll warm you, Square, to the toes of yer boots."

Armitage took the little tumbler, half full of pure spirit, put its sticky brim to his handsome mouth, and sipped at the contents.

"Nasty," he said. "But never mind; it does its work. Redhead, this is what kills us, and we love it. We are good Christians; we love our worst enemy." Then, a recollection of his college reading coming upon him, he raised the glass on high and invoked it in the words of the gladiators, "Ave Cæsar! morituri te salutant."

"That's tall talk, Square," grinned the admiring Redhead.

"Taller than you could understand if I should tell you what it means, you cursed ignoramus," returned Armitage, as he tossed off the poison.

At this moment the country dance ended, and the dancers made a rush toward the whiskey. Sam Hicks sought to keep possession of his rosy-cheeked little partner by passing one butternut-clothed arm around her waist while he poured out for her a half-tumbler of the Pickens District nectar.

"Ladies first," said Armitage, pushing him back with a jocose, contemptuous roughness.

"I was gwine to help a lady," replied Hicks, sulkily. "Sally here wants a drink."

"I'll give her one myself," persisted the high-flung gentleman. "Do you mean to keep her all the evening? Stand out of the way!"

"Let go, my boy," counselled Redhead Saxon, gliding behind the mountaineer and whispering over his shoulder. "Mought get a welt acrost yer snoot. Let go to catch a better holt."

Sam cast a pleading look at his girl, then an angry though cowed one at his imposing rival, and gave back grumbling. Armitage mixed a drink for Sally, insisted upon her swallowing the whole of it, took her roughly under his arm and marched her away.

"You little wretch, why didn't you come to me at first?" he scolded, half in jest and half in alcoholic earnest. "What do you stick to that booby for? Why don't you stick to me?"

Sally looked up in his face with an expression which might be described as vulgar shyness or low-bred modesty. She was dazzled and awed by the handsome, fine gentleman who had taken possession of her; and at the same time she hankered after plain homespun Sam Hicks, who wanted to marry her.

"I don't know jest what you're up to," she blurted out spunkily and yet timorously.

"And what the deuce is *he* up to? Going to marry you, is he?"

Sally made no reply, but she colored a coarse blush, and threw a glance at the faithful pursuing Hicks.

"You can't go to him," said Armitage. "You must dance the next set with me."

And dance he did, playing pranks which raised shouts of laughter in the rough crowd, throwing fondling grimaces at his partner and threatening ones at his rival. The dance ended, he let Sally go back to Hicks, only to claim her again as soon as he had taken another glass of whiskey. A couple of hours passed much in this way. Armitage seemed possessed to get drunk, to pay a rude courtship to Sally Huggs, and to torment Sam Hicks. That he could enjoy the coarse farce seems incredible; and yet the stupid, low-lived fact is that he did enjoy it. It was a monotonous, uninteresting, disagreeable, degrading exhibition; and we only describe it because it dramatizes in brief the character of the man when in his cups. Intoxication had turned him into an insolent, quarrelsome savage; and when we add that it always affected him thus, we can understand the habitual expression of his wife's face; we know how she came to have that strange air of half pleading, half standing at bay.

Let us hurry. About midnight, Armitage, wild as a madman with drink, tore Sally Huggs away from her lover for perhaps the tenth time, and gave the latter a blow which laid him prostrate.

"Quit that, Sam!" shouted Redhead Saxon, rushing upon Hicks and stopping his hand as it sought the inside of his homespun coat. "Now get out of here, Sam, before mischief is done," continued the faithful henchman of Armitage. "Don't go to fightin' with high-tone gentlemen. They're too hefty for you, my boy."

Sam Hicks was not an ordinary low-downer, educated in the depressing vicinity of great estates, and subservient to the planting chivalry. He was a mountaineer, as independent and fierce and lithe as a wild-cat, and disposed to fight any man who trespassed upon his rights or person. He tried to get at Armitage, and struggled violently with Saxon and three or four others who held him, his long yellow hair thrown back from his thin and sunburnt visage, a fine though coarse figure of virile indignation. But at last, overcome by numbers, he became sullenly quiet, and suffered himself to be led out of the cabin. Tranquillity was the more easily restored because Armitage was too drunk to care for the raving of the mountaineer, or even to notice that Sally Huggs soon slipped out of the revelry in pursuit of her betrothed.

Half an hour after this "unpleasantness," Saxon succeeded in persuading his intoxicated patron to mount and set out for home. The path led the length of the oldfield, then through a wood of young pines and stunted cedars, then across other oldfields and some natural barrens, and then down a lane lined by forests, at the end of which it touched the high road. For a time the party moved slowly, there being only starlight, the ground uneven and tangled with vines, and Armitage reeling in his saddle. As they entered the lane Saxon fell back alongside of the negro, and muttered, "Quash, when we strike the road, we'll try a gallop. You keep on one side of him, an' I'll keep on the other."

At this moment there was a pistol-shot from the dense underwood of the forest which overhung the lane.

"Sam Hicks, by thunder!" growled Saxon, feeling for his revolver. "Bile ahead, Square!"

Instead of pushing onward as directed, Armitage turned his horse toward the spot where the flash had showed, and put him straight at the fence which separated the narrow path from the wood. But the animal floundered in a swampy drain, and, unable to rise to the obstacle, pitched against it.

"Hold on, Square," called Saxon, dismounting and taking post behind his horse as behind a breastwork. "Don't go in thar. He'll pop you, sure."

But the warning was useless; the crazy man, shouting with rage, dismounted and began to climb the fence; in a moment, drunk as he was, he had reached the top of it. Just then there was another report, coming from the black recesses of the wood; and in the same breath Armitage toppled over the fence and fell to the ground; there was a single groan, followed by silence.

"Oh Mars Ranney! Mars Ranney!" presently whispered the negro, shaking with grief as well as terror.

"Guess your boss has gone up," muttered Redhead Saxon, after a moment of listening.

"Oh, I'se feared so, I'se feared so," whimpered Quash. "Oh Mars Saxon, what'll we do?"

"Dunno, though," continued Redhead. "That last ball whistled by like it hadn't hit nothin'. So did the first one perhaps, though I didn't notice."

After further hearkening he resumed: "We must git him out of thar. Quash, I'll hold the hosses. You sneak in an' feel for him."

The negro trembled and hesitated, fearing another shot from the hidden assassin; for life is as dear to slaves as to freemen; perhaps dearer.

"Start in, you black cuss," commanded Redhead, turning his revolver on Quash.

"I'se gwine," quavered the demoralized chattel. "Wait till I catch my bref. I'se gwine."

Crawling on his hands and knees through the mud and water of the drain, Quash slowly approached the fence, displaced a rail, and slid through the aperture.

CHAPTER 24

 Asleep, comfortably, and for the time unwakably asleep, lay Randolph Armitage on the damp mossy turf of the forest, not a scratch upon him from Sam Hicks's bullets, both gone astray in the deceiving moonlight.

He was gathered up, borne to his horse, set astride behind Quash, tightly bound to him, and thus taken home. Transportation of this sort being naturally slow, it was two or three in the morning before Redhead Saxon got clear of his responsibility, stealthily depositing this senseless lump of humanity in its usual place of storage, and then hurrying away on guilty tiptoes after the fashion of boon-companions who bring home drunkards. All this time nothing could waken Armitage; he would open his eyes under shaking, and keep them open, but he still slumbered on; he was a limp, inert, inconvenient mass of stupor. The moderately affectionate and immoderately lazy Quash simply laid him on a sofa and covered him with a shawl. Then, with the thoughtlessness of discovery and of consequences characteristic of slaves, at least when they are negroes, he stretched himself on the bare floor and went to sleep, without so much as locking the door.

In this state the two were found at six in the morning by Nellie Armitage, who could not altogether repress anxiety to know whether

her husband was alive. She gave him one glance, guessed with sufficient accuracy how he had spent the night, turned from him in quiet scorn, and awoke the blackamoor with her foot.

"Where have you been with him?" she asked.

"Hain't been nowhar," responded Quash, lying without a moment's thought and with infantile awkwardness, as "niggers" do.

"How dare you tell me that? Leave the room."

As Quash crept out Kate Beaumont glided in, asking, "Has he returned? Is he hurt?"

Mrs. Armitage, shaken by a night of sleeplessness, lost control of herself in this emergency; the weariness, the sorrow, the shame, and the scorn that were in her face turned at once into red-hot anger, demanding utterance; and though she at first raised her hand instinctively to check her sister's advance, she immediately dropped it.

"Come on," she said. "It is time to tell the truth. I have hidden my misery long enough. Come here and look at him. There is a husband; that thing is a husband. What do you think of it?"

Armitage lay perfectly quiet; indeed there was a look about him as if nothing on earth could move him; he was the image of utter helplessness and clod-like insensibility. One eye was partly open, but there was a horrible glassiness and lifelessness in it, and it was obvious that he saw nothing. His face was colorless, except a faint tinting of bluish and yellowish shades, as if it were the countenance of a corpse. Yet in spite of this shocking metamorphosis, his features were so symmetrical that he was handsome still.

Kate, trembling from head to foot, stared at him without speaking. She had never before seen a man in the last stage of intoxication; and in spite of what Nellie had said, she did not fully comprehend his condition.

"Oh!" she gasped. "What is the matter with him? Is he — dying?"

"He is dead, — dead drunk," replied the wife.

"Oh no, Nellie!" implored Kate.

"To think how I have loved him!" Nellie went on. "That man has had all the good, all the best that was in my heart. He has had it and trampled on it and wasted it till it is gone. I can hate now, and I hate *him*."

Kate joined her hands as if pleading with her sister to be silent.

"No man ever had greater love; no man ever despised greater love," continued Nellie. "I have seen the time when I could kneel and kiss the figures of the carpet which his feet had rested upon. I worshipped him; even after I began to find out what he was, I worshipped him; I passed years in forgiving and worshipping. Once, when he came home drunk, yes, when he came home to abuse me, I would watch over him all night in his stupid sleep, and forgive him the moment he spoke to me in the morning. Oh, how handsome he was in my eyes! He fascinated me. That was it; he was beautiful; I could see nothing else. How I did love him for his beauty! And now see how I hate him and despise him. I can take a mean and cowardly revenge on him."

She suddenly advanced upon the senseless man, and slapped his face with her open hand.

"Oh, you woman, what are you doing?" exclaimed Kate, seizing her and drawing her away. "Nellie, I won't love you!"

"Yes, I am hateful," replied Nellie. "Do you know why? I can't tell you half the reasons I have for being hateful. Look at that scar," pointing to a mark on her forehead. "I have never revealed to any one how I came to have that. He did it. He struck me with his doubled fist, and that gash was cut by the ring which I gave him."

Kate sat down, covered her face with her hands, and shuddered.

"It was not the only time," pursued Nellie. "He had struck me before, and he has struck me since. And there have been other insults; I would not have thought that I could have taken them; but from him I have learned to take them. Oh, if my father and brothers knew! They guess, but they don't know."

"They would kill him, Nellie," whispered Kate, looking up piteously, as if pleading for the man's life.

"I know it. But that is not all. I have become so savage, that it seems to me I would not mind that. What I care for is exposure. If they shoot him, people would learn why. It would be known that I had failed; that Nellie Beaumont could not live with her husband; that she could not lie on her bed after making it; that she had failed as a wife and a woman."

Kate dropped her hands and looked up as if to speak. But she said nothing; she was dumb in the presence of this immense misery; she merely stared at Nellie as one stares at a drowning man who cannot be saved.

"I cannot even ask a separation," continued the wretched wife. "I shall stay and fight it out here until I can fight no longer. But I wanted some one's sympathy. I wanted at least to tell my own sister how miserable I am."

She stopped, fell on her knees, laid her head in the girl's lap, and broke out in violent crying.

After a minute she rose, lifted Kate to her feet, embraced her passionately, and said in a voice which had suddenly become calm, "This is my first cry in two years. My heart feels a little less like breaking. Let us go."

"Do you suppose he has heard?" asked the younger woman, glancing at Armitage.

"Heard?" answered Nellie with a hard laugh. "He couldn't hear the last trump, if it should be blown in this room. Isn't he horrible — and handsome? My darling, that is an Armitage. Don't marry one of them. Promise me. You won't?"

"Never," answered Kate.

"I must tell you a great deal," continued Nellie, when she had reached her own room. "My heart is open and I must let it run."

During a large part of the day she talked about her husband, detailing with painful minuteness the outrages of his periods of orgie; how he had upset tables, thrown food out of the windows, broken dishes, furniture, mirrors, beaten the servants and children; how he had fallen down and slept all night in his dooryard, or had been brought home half dead from accidents or fights.

"Sometimes it is ridiculous," she said. "I have actually laughed to see him lying among the ruins of chairs and crockery. It seemed so absurd that any human being could become demented enough to beat and belabor inanimate things till he gasped with fatigue and wore himself out, that I could not help laughing. Of course I had lost all respect for him then, and all affection. How could I keep either? The man was more like a crazy monkey than like a human being. His pranks surpass all description. There are things that I cannot tell you of, for very shame. I did hope, when I brought you here, that, for your sake and out of fear of our family, he would control himself. But he is irreclaimable. He is contemptible. He is horrible."

"Nellie, you have a way of speaking that makes my blood run cold," said Kate. "If you stay here, will you not be over-tempted some day, and do something wrong?"

"I shall never commit a crime," replied Mrs. Armitage. "I am a lady. I would not disgrace myself and my family by even considering such a thing as poisoning. Is that what you fear? You may be tranquil."

"How dreadful it is even to think of such things! I never thought before that anything in life could be so dreadful."

"Well, we will say no more about it today," sighed Nellie. "I will try never to speak of this subject to you again. Hereafter I can bear my troubles better. Some one knows, some one sympathizes."

There was an embrace, and a mingling of tears between the two sisters, followed by a long and sad silence.

"Some one has come," was Nellie's next remark. "I heard a carriage drive up to the door. It is probably Bent Armitage. Scarcely any one else stops here."

"I am so glad," said Kate. "Won't he help us? Won't he have some influence?"

"He has influence when none is wanted. At such times as this no one has any influence, at least none for any good end. But Bentley will try to make things easy for us. He is good-hearted, and he never becomes a madman in my presence, although he is taking the same road with his brother. It is in the blood to go that way."

"I wish nothing unpleasant had passed between him and myself," said Kate, coloring slightly.

"Don't care for that," returned Nellie, proudly. "You were right in avoiding him, and he knows it. He knows that no Armitage has any claim on any Beaumont. My only wonder is, that he dared court you when he knew what his brother had done to me. If he begins again, tell me of it. I won't have it, certainly not here. I am mistress in this house, so far as he is concerned. Remember now; we ask no manner of favors of him; he is just a guest and nothing more."

There was a little glancing into mirrors, a little arranging of curls and shaking out of dresses; there was the sacrifice to becomingness which woman rarely neglects to pay, however unhappy she may be and indifferent to the eyes that are to pass judgment upon her; then they went down to receive their visitor. Bent Armitage was walking the parlor, staring abstractly at the old faded engravings which he had seen a thousand times, his "clapper," as he called his partially paralyzed foot, slapping the floor in its usual style, and his queer smile curling up into his dark cheek as a confession of embarrassment. Remembering Nellie's interference between him and her sister, he feared that he should be received as an intruder, and he was ill at ease. He was even humble to an extent which was pathetic; he had laid aside all his self-respect in coming here. "Let me look at her a moment," his face seemed to plead; "then turn me away forever, if you must; at least I shall have seen her."

"I hope I am not indiscreet," he said meekly, as he kissed the cheek of his sister-in-law and shook hands with Kate. "I am just up in these diggings from a grand tour as far as Charleston," he went on, talking slang to gain courage. "I heard at Brownville that you were both here, and I thought I might venture to rein up for a minute."

"We are glad to see you," replied Kate; and Nellie added, "You must stay a few days."

Bentley brightened a little; loving hopes rose out of their graves.

"We may need your assistance," Nellie explained quietly.

His countenance fell at once. He understood that his brother was making trouble; that was the reason why he was wanted, or endured. But, although the revelation was a painful one to him, he did not turn sullen under it. Impelled by a fine movement of soul, he resolved to serve these women, who demanded service without offering reward or scarcely thanks. In spite of his slang, his willingness to shed blood on occasion, and his hereditary tendency to strong drink, there was much good and warm feeling in Bentley. He was not such a detestable egotist as his brother; he was capable of a love other and stronger than the love of self.

"I will stay as long as I can be of use," he said. "Shall I hitch up in the old spot?"

"I would rather you should take the room next to Randolph's," replied Nellie.

"Just as handy," assented Bentley, at the same time thinking, "So I am to be his keeper."

"How are things at Hartland, Miss Beaumont?" he now inquired. "Everybody chirk there?"

"All well, thank you," Kate said. "At least so my last letters told me."

"The fight with the Philistines keeps up, I suppose."

"With the — the McAlisters? I suppose so," answered the girl, coloring perceptibly.

She was almost angry with him for speaking so carelessly of the feud and so irreverently of the McAlisters. Bentley perceived that he had made a blunder, and for a moment looked absolutely frightened as well as embarrassed, so anxious was he to stand well with this girl. As to being sorry for the renewal of the quarrel between the Beaumonts and their neighbors, he could not of course reach that state of grace; in fact, he could not but rejoice in the event, inasmuch as it had relieved him of one whom he knew to be a preferred rival, and made the winning of Kate seem possible. It was this new hope, to a certain extent, which had brought him to Saxonburg.

"Well, I'll go to my nest and arrange my feathers," he remarked, presently, shuffling and slapping his way up stairs.

Before attending to his toilet, he stepped into his brother's room. No one was there but Quash, lazily setting things to rights.

"Hi, Mars Bent," chuckled the darky. "I'se mighty glad for to see you, Mars Bent. You's jess come in good time. Wah, wah, wah. You's wanted, Mars Bent."

"If you's so mighty glad to see me, brush my boots," returned Bentley, seating himself.

"Yes, Mars Bent," said Quash, getting out his brushes cheerfully, quite sure of a dime, or perhaps a quarter.

"Whar's Mars Ranney?" continued Bentley, imitating the negro dialect and pronunciation, as he loved to do.

"He jess done gone down sta'rs; dunno whar."

"Is he on a bender?"

"Yes, marsr."

"Big one?"

"Well, nuffin pertickler; nuffin great, so fur."

"From fair to middlin', eh?"

"Yes, marsr."

"Couldn't you hide his whiskey?"

"Wouldn't dast do it, Mars Bent," replied Quash, looking up earnestly. "Lordy, Mars Bent, you knows how he kerries on. He'd jess bust my head."

"I s'pose so," growled Bentley. "Well, what of it? You ought to have your head bust, Quash. You are a rascal."

Quash merely sniggered and continued to polish away, sure of his dime. The boots were just done when a loud crash of furniture was heard down stairs, followed by a wrathful shouting.

"Thar he goes," observed Quash. "Smashin' things like he allays does."

"Here's your quarter," said Bentley, rising hastily. "If you'll break his whiskey-jug, I'll give you two dollars."

Hastening down to the parlor, he discovered Randolph dancing on the fragments of a delicate work-table, a present to Nellie from her brother Vincent.

"Halloo!" shouted the drunkard. "Is nobody coming? What am I left alone for?"

Just then Kate Beaumont entered the room; she was very pale, and her soft eyes were dilated with amazement and horror; but she advanced calmly to the maniac and said, "Randolph, what do you want?"

At first he simply glared at her; he seemed to be ready to strike her. Bentley Armitage picked up a leg of the table and came close to his brother, perfectly resolved to knock him down if he raised a hand upon Kate.

"Go away," said Randolph, hoarsely. "I didn't call for you. I wanted Nell."

Bentley made a sign of the head to the young lady, and in obedience to it she retired without a word further.

"Oho," exclaimed Randolph, discovering his brother and turning short upon him. "So you are here. What the —— do you want?"

"I've come to bear a hand generally," returned Bentley, endeavoring to smile, but anticipating a difficulty, and showing it in his face.

"You bear a hand somewhere else," screamed Randolph, all at once beside himself with an insane rage, approaching to *delirium tremens*. "You bear a hand out of this house. You leave. It's my house. You've had your share. We divided, didn't we? You took the Pickens land, didn't you? You've no claim here. You travel. Take your traps and travel. By the Lord, I am master here. I won't be overcrowed by anybody. Lay down that club. Leave it, and leave here."

"Come, come, Randolph," expostulated Bentley. "There's no sense in this, and I don't deserve it. I've come to make myself agreeable and bear a hand at anything you like."

"I've no use for you; I tell you I've no use for you," Randolph went on screaming, utterly out of his senses. "You just hump yourself and get to your own district. You travel, or I'll —"

Here he caught up a glass lamp and hurled it at his brother's head, the missile narrowly missing its mark and smashing against the wall. Then he made a charge. The younger man struck, but unwillingly and faintly: his blow only exasperated the assailant. Bentley, far less muscular than Randolph, and lame besides, was thrown and badly beaten. This horrible scene was ended by the entrance of Mrs. Armitage and several of the house-servants, who with great difficulty dragged the drunken maniac off his victim and pushed him out of the room.

"You must go," said Nellie to Bentley, when they two were alone.

"Ah, if he wasn't my brother!" exclaimed the youth, furious from his conflict, "I would finish him."

"But he is your brother, and you can do no good here, at least not now. You will have to go."

"What, and leave you with that madman! Leave *her* with him!"

"We can manage him better than you. Seeing another man here only makes him want to fight. We shall be better off without you."

"I never was called on to do so mean a thing before," said Bentley.

"I don't wish to charge you with being capable of meanness. Besides, it won't be mean to do this when I insist upon it."

"Well," assented the young man, unwillingly and sullenly. "But I won't go farther than Rullet's tavern, on the road to Brownville, you know, five miles from here. If you need me, you can send a nigger, and I'll put over."

"Very good," said Nellie. "You will have to take your Brownville carriage back. You can slip through the garden and meet it below the house. Quash will look to your baggage."

"I never saw him so bad before," muttered Bentley, meaning his brother.

"He gets worse every time. His constitution is breaking down. His nerves are not what they used to be."

"Be sure you send for me slap off, if there is any serious trouble," were the farewell words of Bentley.

Randolph Armitage, totally forgetting his brother's visit, spent the rest of the afternoon in his room, drinking, singing, breaking such furniture as he could break, and at last going to sleep among the ruins. The women remained together, talking rarely and sadly, the younger sometimes crying, the elder never.

"I wonder at you," said Kate once. "I never imagined that a woman could have such fortitude."

"Fortitude!" returned Nellie. "I am intelligent enough to know that it is not the fortitude that you mean. It is mere hardened callousness and want of feeling. I ceased some time ago to be a woman. I am a species of brute."

"If ever I am tried as you have been, perhaps I shall become as noble as you are," was the answer of Kate, faithfully admiring her sister.

When bedtime came the younger woman said, "I shall stay with you to-night."

"You can't," replied Mrs. Armitage. "My husband has a right to come to my room at any time."

"Ah!" murmured Kate, recoiling at once before the authority of marriage.

"You are not afraid for yourself, are you?" asked Nellie.

"I had not thought of that," answered the girl. "Besides, my door bolts and locks."

"Good night," said Nellie, with a kiss. "You are a great comfort to me. I am glad that you know everything; I am glad that I told you everything, though I did it in a fit of madness, and it was wrong. I bear things the better because you know them. I was growing savage and wicked with lack of sympathy. Thank you for your sympathy, darling. Good night."

Kate went to her room, fastened her door with lock and bolt, then deliberately unfastened it and left it ajar, fearing a little for herself, but far more for her sister. She was worn out; it seemed to her that the day had been years long; that she had stepped from youth to middle age since morning. Could it be that the degrading and miserable tragedy which she had looked upon was marriage? What might be her own future, even should the feud once more be allayed, and life promise as fairly as it had done weeks before? Even should she, by some incredible chance, become the wife of the man whom she preferred and trusted above all other men, what then? Would the end of her once fair hopes be like the end of the once fair hopes of Nellie? Her mind ran all towards evil foreboding; the future seemed a wilderness, complex, pathless, and sombre; merely to think of it was a weariness and sorrow. Yet she was so exhausted with the unrest of the previous night and the emotions of the day, that, even while saying to herself that she should never sleep, she lost her consciousness.

After a time some noise partially roused her; it was painful to lose her hold on slumber, and she strove not to awake; but the noise persisted, and so alarmingly that of a sudden she started up in her full senses. It was clear to her now that she heard the voice of Randolph in loud altercation with his wife; and, hastily slipping on a dressing-gown, she glided down a dark passage to the door of Nellie's room. The door was ajar, and there was a faint light within as of a candle, but she was so placed that she could not see the speakers. The conversation, however, was but too audible.

"Will you tell me —?" demanded the husband, in a hoarse, thick utterance.

"No, I will not, Randolph," answered Nellie, in that monotone of hers which meant unshakable persistence.

"Then, by heavens —! Look here, you obstinate fool; don't you know what I'll do to you? Don't you know?"

"I know, Randolph," said Nellie. "I don't care for your threats."

The answer to this speech was a sound as of a struggle. Kate hesitated no longer; she stepped swiftly into the room. By the flicker of a candle dying in its socket she saw Randolph holding his wife down on the pillow with one hand, while with the other he brandished a long knife.

CHAPTER 25

 The cry and rush with which Kate entered the room startled the tremulous madman, who was attempting murder, or counterfeiting it.

"Whooh!" he exclaimed; it was a beastly sound, like the short, explosive growl of a surprised dog; but as he uttered it he let go of his wife and faced about.

"Oh, it's you, is it?" he stammered, staring at the girl with watery, uncertain eyes, and with a grin that was half embarrassed, half defiant. "I forgot there was another woman in the house. What the Devil do you want?"

"Randolph!" exclaimed Kate with an imposing air of reproach; then, dropping to a tone of entreaty, she implored, "Won't you go away?"

"I want my whiskey," he replied, exposing without shame the degrading motive of his brutality. "She's hidden it."

Kate turned on Nellie an appealing glance which said, "Can't you let him have it?"

"It is not here," answered Mrs. Armitage, speaking to her sister. "When I say that it isn't here, you may know that it isn't."

"Do you know where it is?" demanded the husband, evidently believing her, unable to disbelieve her.

"I do not," she said, still not looking at him. "I know nothing about it. If I knew, I would not tell."

"Then I'll leave," he growled, after a moment's hesitation, meanwhile staring at his knife as if still uncertain whether he would not use it. "That's all I came here for. Do you suppose I wanted *you?*"

With this parting insult to his wife, he seized his candle, reeled by Kate, and went out. A few seconds later a howl of joyous oaths announced that he had found his treasure; the bungling and lazy, and also, no doubt, timorous Quash having concealed it instead of destroying it.

"What shall we do?" asked Kate, who had meanwhile locked the door, and now stood by it listening.

"Let him drink," said Nellie, with the sad common-sense born of long trouble. "It is the easiest way to get rid of him."

"Isn't it horrible!" Kate could not help groaning, still hearkening at the keyhole for Randolph's return.

The unhappy wife, invisible in the darkness, made no reply. Presently Kate became alarmed at the silence; she whispered, "Nellie," and then called aloud; still no answer. The terrible thought crossed the girl that Randolph might actually have stabbed his wife, and that she might now be dying, or dead. Groping her way to the bedside, she threw her arms around her sister, dropped kisses and tears upon the cool, damp face which touched hers, and sobbed repeatedly, "Nellie! Nellie!" But wild as she was with alarm, she perceived soon that the heart was still beating, and she guessed that this was not death. By the time she had found matches and lighted a lamp, Nellie began to draw the long sighs which mark restoration from a swoon, and presently opened her eyes.

"I have been faint," she whispered, with a bitter smile. "I didn't know there was so much of the woman left in me. I ought to have got over this sort of thing long ago. I am ashamed of myself."

"Nellie, what can I do for you?" asked Kate.

"Nothing. I will get up in a moment, and go to packing."

"Are you going to leave him? Ah, — well."

"At all events I shall take you away. You have seen enough of this, and too much. I ought not to have brought you here at all. It is quite sufficient for one man that he should make one woman wretched. It is as much success as is due to a drunkard. My dear, you won't marry a high-strung gentleman, I hope. Marry a Quaker first, or a Yankee pedler, — anything that doesn't get drunk and fight, anything that isn't high-strung. I hate the word. It's a mean, slang word, and it stands for a curse."

"Will Randolph let you go?" Kate asked.

"His whiskey-jug will attend to that," replied Nellie. "He has a noble master, hasn't he? He prides himself on not being ruled by his wife. It is so much more manly, more chivalrous, more high-strung to be ruled by a jug! Come, go and do your packing. I will do mine and the children's."

An hour or so later the trunks were ready, the little ones dressed, and the carriage at the door.

"I will go and bid good by to my husband," said Nellie.

Kate followed her, fearful lest Randolph might awake and a collision ensue. There was no trouble; the man lay on the floor, stone-blind drunk; an earthquake could not have shaken that stupor.

"Handsome Armitage!" murmured Nellie, looking at the sodden countenance with a strange mixture of scorn and grief in her own pale face. Then turning to Quash, who rose drowsily from his usual sleeping-place in the passage, she said: "Take care of him. But tell him nothing about our going away. Let him find it out for himself."

"Yes, missus," yawned Quash, and proceeded to lie down again covering his shoulders and head with his blanket-coat.

The bays were started off at their speediest trot, for ten miles of rough, hilly road lay between the Armitage place and the Brownville station, and the down train, the only train of the day, left at six in the morning. At the half-way house, known as Rullet's Tavern, or more commonly as Old John Rullet's, Nellie looked at her watch, and said calmly: "It is useless. We sha'n't get there till after six. We may as well stop and see Bentley."

The younger Armitage, a bad sleeper in these days, and consequently an early riser, came out to the carriage.

"Travelling?" he said, with a wretched attempt at a smile, thinking meanwhile that this might be his last interview with Kate. "I rather judge it's the healthiest thing you can do."

"We can't catch the train," replied Nellie. "We shall have to wait in Brownville till to-morrow morning."

After glancing at his watch, shaking his head, pondering a minute, he remarked: "I suppose I had better go and amuse Randolph."

"Bentley, it is a hard thing to owe you so much," said Nellie.

"Oh, it's all in the family," he smiled. "And it doesn't square the family account either."

"Be careful," said Kate, honestly anxious for him.

He looked greatly pleased; he seemed to think it very kind of her merely to care a little for his life; the humility of his gratitude made it absolutely pathetic.

"No particular danger, I reckon," he replied, shaking her hand cordially. "You won't mind it, I hope, if you hear of our drinking a little. A prosperous journey to you. Good by."

"Good by, Bentley," said Nellie, bending down and kissing him. "I wish I could do more for you."

It seemed to Bentley also, that he deserved more than a kiss of a sister-in-law; but none the less he set about his ill-requited work promptly and courageously. As he turned his back on Kate Beaumont, and prepared for his horrible *tête-à-tête* with his brother, he said to himself, "Noblesse oblige."

When he reached the Armitage place, Randolph was just coming out of his drunken slumber. Then followed a tragi-comedy which, considering that the two leading actors in it were brothers, was a little less than infernal. Bentley's purpose was to keep Randolph so far under the influence of liquor that he should not notice the absence of his family, or should be indifferent to it if he discovered it. To this end he drank, jested, gambled, quarrelled, exchanged blows even, went through reconciliations, drank again, squabbled again, and so on for twenty-four hours. It must be observed that, although he had not sought the spree for its own sake, he did in a certain measure enjoy it. But for anxiety as to the result, and also for the somewhat burdensome reflection that he was tippling under compulsion, he would have had a truly delightful carouse. Perhaps we ought to consider in his favor that he was a disappointed lover, and that liquor helped to drown his sorrow. In short, Bentley had a downright honest bender, although he never quite forgot his object in commencing it.

The day passed in freaks beyond the imagination of monkeys. Whenever Randolph demanded his family, Bentley invented some new madness. For instance, late in the afternoon he proposed that they should mob Nancy Gile, on the plea that Randolph had been insulted and attacked by her low-down following. So, mounting their horses, they galloped four or five miles to surprise the "lone woman," turned her furniture topsy-turvy, drank her last gill of whiskey, and then, giving her a couple of dollars to pay the damages, departed hooting. The next thing was a wild-goose chase through swamps and oldfields, on the supposed trail of Sam Hicks, both the brothers being now in strenuous earnest and intent upon killing their man if they should find him, which they did not. Giving up their fruitless hunt when night came on, they made a circuit to reach the cabin of Redhead Saxon, and held another festival in his society.

And now came the climax of the saturnalia. Randolph, who in his cups would have quarrelled with angels or devils, became irritated at Saxon for some cause never afterwards heard of, and laid that faithful henchman prostrate with a fisticuff.

"Square, that's low-flung business," roared Saxon, so drunk that he forgot his fealty. "You've no call to hit a chap when he ain't a lookin'," he continued, rising with difficulty and by instalments, first on all fours, and so on. "You wouldn't 'a' dared fetch me that lick, ef your brother hadn't been here."

"You needn't count in Bentley," replied Randolph. "He sha'n't take a hand. I'll play it alone."

He tried to get off his coat, but in the effort went down and struggled some time on the floor with the garment over his head. When he regained his feet he accused Redhead of pushing him, and proceeded to draw his revolver. At this point Mrs. Saxon, a powerful young amazon of at least six feet in height, rushed upon the scene from the one other room of the dwelling, shouting, "Quit that. No fightin' yere. Ef you want to fight, go out do'."

This pacifying admonition not being heeded, she sprang at her husband, scratched him smartly, and bundled him out of the cabin. Then, holding the door against him, she turned upon the Armitages, and broke out: "Now say. What d' you two want? You've got the man out of his own house. S'posin' you try your hand on the woman. Ain't you a high-tone gentleman, Square Armitage? Then go whar you b'long, an' fight with yer own sort. Oughter be shamed of yerself, pickin' musses with crackers. Wish I was yer wife, and had the breakin' of ye. I'd learn ye to go in harness. Don't ye p'int yer shootin'-iron at me. I'll take it away from ye, an' lam yer face with it. You cl'ar. You jest cl'ar, or I'll light on ye."

"We'll go," answered Bentley, grinning at the scene like an amused monkey and surveying the pugnacious housewife with bland approbation. "Randolph, we're getting the hot end of the poker. Come, old lady, let us out."

"No sir-ee," declared the contradictory Madam Saxon. "You want to mount my old man outside. — Jimmy," she screamed, through a crack of the door, "you travel."

"I won't," vociferated Redhead, who all the while was trying to re-enter.

"Dog gone these men!" objurgated the lady. "Why can't they be peaceful like women-folks? It takes a woman to every man to make him behave."

"Let me in!" roared the husband. "Ef you don't, I'll fire through the do'."

"Hold up a minute, Redhead," called Bentley. Then addressing Mrs. Saxon in a caressing whisper, meanwhile patting her stalwart shoulder, he added, "Look here, old girl. The best way is to powder it out. Let's have a sham fight. You load your husband's pistol and I'll load Ranney's. Blank cartridges, you understand. What do you say!"

"All right," grinned the amazon, her wide mouth stretching from ear to ear to embrace the joke. "Git hold of the Square's shooting-iron. I'll fix Jimmy's."

When the duel was proposed to Randolph, he assented at once with a drunken solemnity which finely satirized the behavior usual with principals in real affairs of honor, and delivered his revolver to Bentley to be discharged and reloaded.

"Hand over yer five-shooter, old man," demanded Mrs. Saxon, rushing out upon her husband and disarming him. "We're gwine to hev a duel."

"Who's a gwine to?" asked Redhead, falling into the cabin.

"You be; you an' the Square."

"You go to —!" retorted the man of the house, who, intoxicated as he was, discovered an absurdity in the proposition.

"Redhead, you are a gentleman, I suppose," began Bentley.

"No, I ain't," interrupted Saxon, his reason perfectly sound on that point.

"Wal, you're a man, ain't ye?" put in his wife, flying at him and giving him a shake. "You stan' up in that corner till things is ready.

Mr. Bent, you set the Square up in t'other corner. Thar's a bar'l thar for him to hold on to."

The two principals being placed, the seconds went out of doors to prepare the weapons. The ball cartridges in the barrels were discharged, and other cartridges substituted with the bullets broken off.

"It'll be mighty slim huntin', won't it?" said Mrs. Saxon, bursting into loud laughter. "Wouldn't my old man be mad, ef he sensed the thing. He ain't used to goin' a shootin' with nothin' but powder."

This idea amused her excessively, and she returned to it several times. "To think of Jim firin' away at a feller with nothin' but powder!"

"Well, old lady, are you loaded?" asked Bentley.

"Reckon I be," grinned Molly Saxon, revolving the chamber of her pistol with experienced dexterity. "No bullets in *them*. Let's see yourn. All right, my blessed stranger. Now what'll we do next?"

"Just hand your old man his cold iron, and caution him to wait for the word. I'll give the instructions."

They re-entered the cabin. There were Saxon and Randolph Armitage, each propped up in his corner and holding fast, their faces very solemn and stolid. Molly's broad physiognomy twitched all over with suppressed laughter as she presented the pistol to her husband.

"Now, Jim, ha'n't you got any last words for yer woman?" she asked by way of joke.

"Git off the course, ole gal," replied Redhead, thickly. "An' take care yerself."

At this moment Randolph, trying to stand independent of his barrel, fell over it and rolled on the floor.

"Set'm up agen," muttered Redhead calmly, and without showing the slightest amusement.

By the aid of Bentley the prostrate man rose and braced himself once more in his corner, smiling the monotonous smile of intoxication.

"Catch hold," said Bentley, delivering the revolver. "And don't fire till I give the word. Gentlemen, listen to the instructions. I shall pronounce the words, 'one, two, three, — fire.' At the word 'fire,' you are at liberty to commence, and you will go on until you have exhausted your barrels."

"That's so," sniggered Molly, cramming a yard or so of her calico apron into her mouth to keep from laughing outright. "Jim, do you understand?"

"You shut up," snapped Redhead in a tone of impatience which re-doubled his wife's amusement.

"Now, then," called Bentley. "One, two, three, — fire."

A deliberate firing ensued; it was curious how cool the two drunk-ards were; though they could scarcely stand, they meant business.

"That's all," mumbled Randolph when he had exhausted his barrels.

"No 't ain't," called Saxon. "I've got a charge left."

"Well, blaze away, old Redhead," returned Randolph, still smiling his alcoholized smile.

Old Redhead took steady aim, resting his revolver across his left arm, and blazed away to the best of his ability. Randolph fell across his barrel once more, but it was whiskey which upset him, and not a bullet.

"Square, are you bad hurt?" called Saxon, advancing slowly and un-steadily. "Square, I'm sorry for it; dog goned if I ain't."

Then seeing his antagonist rise, with the assistance of Bentley, he added, "Did I miss you, Square? Wall, I'll be dog-rotted!! However, never mind. Glad you come out of it safe. Bully for you, Square. Stood it like a sojer. Let's shake han's."

There was shaking hands accordingly, as in more elegant and sober affairs of honor, the two late enemies complimenting each other as high-toned gentlemen, etc., etc., while Molly Saxon fairly capered and stamped with delight.

"An' now you two cl'ar," she presently whispered to Bentley. "I want room to larf. Ef I don't hev it, I shall bust."

Bentley hurried his brother away the more willingly because Saxon, a blazing pine-knot in hand, was searching for the marks of his bullets, and not finding them, might be led to suspect and denounce the trick which had been played, to the manifest risk of further altercation.

"You needn't look for 'em, Jim," Molly was heard to giggle. "You're too drunk to aim at anythin'. You fired out o' winder an' up chimney an' everywhar but at him."

"I'll be dog-rotted ef I ever see any such doin's befo'," returned the confounded Jim. "When a man can't hit a house, standin' inside on't, he'd better quit shootin'."

And now, as it was getting towards midnight, the Armitages went home. Bentley was still afraid that Randolph might discover the absence of his wife and set out in pursuit of her. He resolved to floor him completely, if the thing could be done; he commenced a fresh drinking-bout and kept it up for hours. It was the very saturnalia of doing evil that good might come. It was ludicrous and it was horrible.

CHAPTER 26

 Affairs of state, a shouting of stump-orators, and a buzzing of swarming fellow-citizens recall us to Hartland.

The canvassing for the election of representatives to Congress was at the boiling-point. There was speechifying, discussion around groceries and at street corners, generous betting and chivalrous squabbling every day. The principals in the contest, as well as their partisans, had gone into the struggle in the highest-toned fashion, prepared to exterminate their adversaries if the latter persistently refused to hearken to reason. When Peyton Beaumont went forth on his stumping progresses, his sons guarded him with revolvers under their shooting-jackets; while Judge McAlister was escorted in a similar manner by his warlike progeny, even Frank admitting that he must defend his father. As for the Colts and derringers, and bowies and toothpicks, which were carried by the rank and file, they were beyond enumeration. Excepting that the weapons were concealed, these election scenes resembled the political assemblages of the ancient Gauls, who discussed questions of war and peace with spear in hand and buckler on shoulder. All these gaunt and long-legged men, whether clad in "store-clothes" of black broadcloth, or in short-backed, long-tailed frock-coats of gray or butternut homespun, were as bellicose as so many Scotch

Highlanders of three hundred years ago.

It must not be supposed, however, that fighting was continuous or even very frequent. As every man took it for granted that every other man was armed, discussions were usually conducted with great civility of speech, unless the disputants had become inflamed with whiskey. Even if angry words were exchanged and weapons drawn, there were generally friends at hand to do the proper amount of coat-tail pulling, and bloodshed was generally averted. As for such harmless blusterers as Crazy Naylor and Drunken John Stokes, they were allowed to roll each other in the dust at their pleasure, it being understood that they would merely furnish innocent amusement to their fellow-electors. The fun which their conflicts afforded was increased by the fact that the defeated athlete usually turned upon some boy or nigger who had laughed at his overthrow, and kicked him with much swearing around the nearest corner. Let us state, by the way, that John Stokes and Crazy Naylor were not landless crackers or penniless village loafers. Although they dressed in homespun and held such high-caste people as the Beaumonts and McAlisters in deep reverence, they were well-to-do farmers, owning their five hundred acres and their twenty or thirty head of niggers. John Stokes, in spite of his frequent benders, was "captain of patrol" in his "beat," or magisterial precinct. Crazy Naylor never went howling about the streets and making a spectacle of himself, except when he was in liquor.

Notwithstanding the serious sensitiveness of Southerners, and the danger of jesting with punctilious men who carry revolvers, much sly, coarse ridicule was current in the Hartland political debates. For instance, John Stokes, a violent adherent of the Beaumonts, set afloat laughable tales about the McAlister chieftain, representing him as a man of little less than idiotic simplicity, which was true in so far as this, that the Judge had not the remotest idea of a joke.

"He go to Congress!" sneered John Stokes. "Them Yankees would come games on him an' poke fun at him from Sunday morning to Saturday night. I'll tell you what sort of a man he is. The Judge started out to canvass the district. How did he do it? Got up his coach. Sure as you're bawn he got up his coach an' four horses to go an' ask poo' men for their votes. Well, he druv round an' kissed the young uns an' talked Sabba' school to the women folks, an' subscribed to meetin'- houses an' all that sort of nonsense. An' you bet he made mistakes.

You bet on it an' win every time. Durned ef he didn't take short-haired Dolly Hicks, — she a settin' by the fire wrapped up in blankets because of the chills, — durned ef he didn't take her for the old man an' ask her to vote for him. Now you don't believe that, you fellers of the Mc-Alister crowd. But it's true; you bet your best bale on it; old Hicks he told me. Now that's a lively man to go to Congress from Hartland District *and* South Carolina. Why, he wouldn't know a he Yankee from a she one. Them fellers up thar in them foreign States would stock the keerds agin him an' clean him out every time. Now look at the Honable Peyton Beaumont in a poor man's cabin. *He* don't come in no coach; he comes a horseback. He walks in square an' strong, like he was to home. He straddles out before the fire, an' parts his coat-tails behind him, an' hollers for his tod of plain whiskey, an' chaws an' spits like one of the family. *He* don't make no mistakes betwixt the old man an' the old woman. He knows other folks as sure 's he knows himself. He knows the name of every voter in this part of South Carolina an' the name of that voter's dog. He's that kind of a man that rouses your entuzzymuzzy. He's a man that South-Carolinians will take a heap of trouble for. We never had an election yet but what loads of fellers would pile over the line from every district round here, walkin' or ridin' ten or fifteen miles perhaps to give him a lift, an' that too after going as fur for their own men whar they belong. An' they're right; they're right in takin' all that extra trouble for him; he deserves it. I tell you, ef thar's a gentleman in this district who's fit to stand for the people of this district *and* South Carolina, it's old squar'-shouldered, open eyed, true-handed, big-hearted, high-toned Peyt Beaumont."

Of course we are not to put absolute faith in the partisan declamations of John Stokes. There is no doubt that he exaggerated both the innocence of Judge McAlister and the slightly demagogic courtesy with which Beaumont did occasionally temper his patrician haughtiness.

But we must leave the political background of our story and return to the personages who occupy its foreground. Very sad in these days was Frank McAlister, miserable over the past, and despondent over the future. He did not even believe in the success of his party in the election, for he had almost of necessity taken the measure of his prim, solemn, unbending father, and had guessed that he could not carry Hartland electors against hearty, full-blooded, off-handed Peyton Beaumont. The Beaumonts would triumph at the ballot-box; they would add contempt for his family to hatred for it; there was not a chance for him to win their daughter and sister. He was in these days so gloomy, so haggard, so unable to sleep, so unable to eat that his mother became terrified about him.

Of course she had guessed the cause of his trouble; a woman and a mother could not fail to guess it. But what could she do to raise the spirits of her stricken giant, and renovate his health, and save his life? It was impossible to quiet the family feud, and consequently impossible to get Kate Beaumont for him. That sovereign remedy being out of the question, was there no other? Time? Alas, time is very slow in his work, and affection abhors waiting. Mrs. McAlister knew of a cure which was quicker than that and every way more consonant with her own feelings; it occurred to her that it would be the best thing in the world to get another young lady in the place of the one who had been lost.

The proposition may shock a sentimental man, but I suspect that it was both motherly and womanly. A woman believes in love; if one love affair fails, she requires that another should commence as soon as may be. The single adventure, though very great to her, is not so great as the passion. Moreover, her sister-women are cheaper in her eyes than they are in ours, and she sees no sufficient cause why the loss of one of them should stop a man from using his heart, especially in view of the fact that his heart is, in her opinion, his noblest organ.

It was in consequence of these reasons (which Mrs. McAlister did not of course take the trouble to reason upon, not even with herself) that she invited Jenny Devine to make a visit under her roof. Stating the case plainly, she meant to have Frank fall in love with Jenny, and so forget the girl whom he could not get. True, Wallace was enamored of Miss Devine: the all-seeing mother was not ignorant of that. But Wallace, it was pretty certain, could not have her; and, moreover, Wallace did not stand in pressing need of matrimony, not being broken in spirits and shattered in health; and finally Frank, her youngest and handsomest, was her favorite child. Small, plain, bald-headed Wallace must be sacrificed just a little to save his magnificent, his suffering brother. The plan savored of cruelty, but it was the cruelty of intense affection, perhaps also of wise judgment.

Thus it was that pretty, flirting, jolly, good-hearted Jenny Devine became an inmate of the McAlister mansion. She did not come at all unsuspiciously; she guessed that coquettish passages awaited her; she was somewhat like a cat entering a buttery. In the first place, she was accustomed to be begged for from house to house to entertain young gentlemen visiting in Hartland, and to enliven hops and teas with her music, her dancing, her small talk, and her bright eyes. In the second place, she knew that Frank McAlister had been fascinated by Kate Beaumont, and so must have found it a sad business to be divided from her.

That Jenny was at least willing to run a risk in the matter is shown by the fact that she accepted the invitation. She liked Frank, and she thought no less of him for having liked Kate; for she was not one of those sensitive girls who recoil from a man because he has loved some one else; she had had too many courting affairs of her own to be fastidious on that point. As for cutting out her absent friend, there could be no question of it. Kate had been cut out already by the revival of of the old hate between the two families. Moreover, Kate was not in love with Frank; so much Jenny believed that she had discovered. Accordingly, with conscience clear of unworthy intent, and with heart prepared for either great or little emotions, she repaired with her select armor of finery to the enchanted palace of the McAlisters, to take the chances of such adventures as might befall her there.

She was received with a gladness, which, considering the grave character of the family, was equivalent to festivity. Mrs. McAlister fairly leaned towards the girl; she enjoyed her in anticipation as a daughter-in-law, the chosen one of her favorite son; she secretly loved her and blessed her in a spirit of prophecy. It was the yearning of a bereaved mother, who trusts that she is yet to obtain a child in place of of the one that has been taken away. Not but that Mrs. McAlister would still have preferred Kate as a daughter; she had no spite against the Beaumont men even, and she loved their loved one dearly. But Kate being lost beyond recovery, she must positively have some one in her place, and in her longing she grasped at Jenny.

One result of this craving — a result which looks like the effect of witchery — was that she at once lost sight of the girl's defects, though plainly discernible by her heretofore. Jenny was a flirt; so Mrs. McAlister had thus far always admitted; she had even been angry at her for trifling with Wallace's affections; very angry because of the quarrel which had been set up between him and Vincent. She had said to herself that Jenny Devine, notwithstanding her good temper and mainly good intentions, would make no fit wife for a man of high character and sensitive feelings. Now she forgave all these shortcomings and peccadilloes so completely that she forgot them. Jenny was no flirt; it was not supposable that she could jilt Frank; she would accept him and be an excellent wife and a charming daughter. Mrs. McAlister reasoned about the girl as a lover reasons about the mistress of his heart. Desire and hope did the whole of the argument, and of course reached the most agreeable conclusions.

To all these feelings and wishes Mary McAlister assented with the instantaneous facility and energy of her loving soul. The tall, thin, gray-haired mother and the tall, slender, chestnut-ringleted daughter, both shooting rays of love out of large mild eyes, embraced Jenny Devine with the same tenderness.

"I am so delighted that we have not lost you as a friend," said Mrs. McAlister. "It seems as if there were no friends of late. Everybody is a partisan."

"The Beaumonts will not be angry at you for coming to us?" asked Mary. "We did hope not when we begged for you. But you must tell us."

"I am not their kin," replied Jenny. "And I am not a man either. I claim a woman's right to be sweet to everybody. Don't worry about my good standing with the Beaumonts. If the Honorable Peyton looks glum at me, I shall take his arm and smile in his face, and the next I know he will be patting my head. These old gentlemen are all fools with girls. If you had a speck of courage and impudence, Molly, you could go and tame him in fifteen minutes. I do believe that, if I were in your place, I could make him call on the Judge, and ask the whole family to dinner."

"Jenny, I wish we could work such miracles," sighed Mrs. McAlister. "I would go on my knees to do it."

"Oh, you wouldn't answer at all," laughed the frank and saucy Jenny. "It would take somebody as young as Molly. By the way, there is an idea; why, wouldn't that be nice? Molly, you could be Mrs. Peyton Beaumont the third, merely for winking; only, poor thing, you don't know how to wink."

"What nonsense!" protested Mary, in blushing amazement. "Who could imagine such a thing? Nobody but you."

"I could make Dr. McAuley imagine it," whispered the teasing Jenny. "Wouldn't he rage?"

Mary blushed still deeper, and glanced with maidenly alarm at her mother, who, of course, pretended not to hear, and looked all benignity.

Jenny's frolicsomeness was one cause why the McAlisters continually forgave her misdeeds and liked her. They were a grave generation while not meaning it, and finding persistent gravity a burden; and, like all such, they extracted much comfort from jolly people and craved them as thirsty souls do water.

Thus it may be conceived that Frank McAlister, weighted always with seriousness of spirit, and just now crushed under disappointment, should incline kindly to the company of this prattling and gleesome young lady. Because she made him smile in spite of himself, he liked to listen to her. Because she turned whist into mere fun, he took a hand as her partner. Presently he came to walk with her, and then to ride with her. The intimacy, ripened by his sorrowful tenderness of feeling, burgeoned rapidly into confidences. Before long the subject of Kate Beaumont was broached between the two, and after that there was no end to their talking together.

What an enticing, abundant, limitless subject it was! It was like a Missouri prairie to a herd of buffalo; there was room there to browse forever. Little by little Frank told Jenny all that was in his heart, — how he had loved, how he had hoped to win, and how he had lost. The girl, in spite of her levity, was like almost all other women in the matter of quick sympathy, and especially could not help being touched by a tale of wounded affections. She forgot herself; she opened her heart wide to his procession of sorrows; and of course it followed that he found her charming. In a certain sense she was Jenny Devine and Kate Beaumont in one. To talk to her about Kate was the next best thing to talking to Kate about herself.

Who has not smiled at the ease with which many a grief-stricken widower has been won by a woman who sincerely pitied him for the loss of his wife? Shall we have cause to smile thus at our hitherto unchangeable lover, Frank McAlister?

"How tedious I must be to you!" he said one day, ashamed of his egotism.

"You are not tedious at all," declared Jenny, her cheeks coloring with the enthusiasm of honest and earnest feeling.

"Is it possible that you can like to hear me tell how I love another woman?" he asked, amazed.

"I do like it," said Jenny. "She so splendidly deserves it."

"Miss Devine, you are admirable," he replied with profound reverence. "I am astonished at women, the more I know of them. They have so much unselfishness and sympathy. I think a great heart is nobler than a great brain."

"Ah, don't give me too much credit," sighed Jenny, dropping her eyes. It occurred to her just then that perhaps she was playing falsely by her friend, and running risk of winning that friend's lover. In the next breath she said to herself: "But Kate does not care for him; she told me so."

In fact Jenny was becoming interested and even fascinated. At the time this dialogue took place she had been over a week in the McAlister house. During that crowded week she had seen much of Frank, and had grown to be his intimate and his confidante. She had looked further into his heart than she had ever before looked into the heart of man; and all that she discovered there had led her to admire him exceedingly; to judge that his love was worth any woman's having. It was not for her now; it was for her friend Kate; but would it always be? She had not distinctly asked herself this momentous question, nor any other that concerned her future relations with Frank. Rather she had gone on blindly, first sympathizing, then sympathizing more, then admiring, then liking, then — No, not loving; not at all that; at least, not yet. But there was danger of it, and at times she saw the danger.

During the evening following this conversation she announced her intention of returning home on the morrow. But Mrs. McAlister, in whose opinion things were going on passing well, would not hear of it; and Mary McAlister, guessing at once her mother's ideas and consenting to them, also would not hear of it. So strenuous was their opposition, that Jenny gave up her wise project and meekly stayed on, not knowing what might happen to her heart, and beginning not to care. "I shall be disappointed in love," she sometimes thought; "but it does not matter a bit; I shall deserve it."

Meantime Wallace McAlister was wretched with jealousy. His mother saw it and grieved over it, but did not change her plan for all her grief. To save Frank, it seemed that Wallace must be sacrificed; it was very sad that it should be so, but she could not help it. After all,

Wally must not be a dog in the manger. Unable to get Jenny himself, he must not prevent her from saving his brother; that would be the extreme of selfishness. The unlucky young man himself thought something like these thoughts in his more rational moments. But none the less he suffered; felt his heart shrivel when Jenny strolled out with Frank; clapped his beaver on his poor bald head, and went off to be miserable alone.

Another person who was troubled and alarmed by this sudden intimacy between Frank and Jenny was Major John Lawson. He did not learn it from the McAlisters, of whom he saw very little in these days, he being still a guest of Kershaw's, and consequently more or less tied to the Beaumonts. It was Mrs. Chester who told him of this new peril which threatened his romance of Romeo and Juliet in South Carolina. Mrs. Chester had met Mrs. Devine; and Mrs. Devine had been over to see Jenny in the McAlister hunting-grounds; and the result was certain motherly smiles and hints of a prophetic and exultant nature. Thereupon Mrs. Chester, who had turned to speaking evil of her lost Titan as strenuously as she had once followed after him, spread the report that he was about to marry the greatest flirt in Hartland District, namely, Miss Jenny Devine.

"You don't tell me so, Mrs. Chester!" grinned the disquieted Major, when she had exploded this bit of news under his nose like a firecracker. "My dear Mrs. Chester, you don't seriously believe it! Why, it would be a most delightful arrangement," he continued, recovering his self-possession and wishing to stick some sly pins in Mrs. Chester. "Really delightful! Jenny is an admirable girl. A little of a flirt, no doubt, as you say. But so are all women until they are married. All the same, she is admirable. Deserves him. Deserves anybody. I had had hopes, by the way, that she would have caught Vincent. I am a little disappointed. Do you suppose, Mrs. Chester, that our excellent friend Mrs. Devine winks with authority? Mothers are so apt to deceive themselves, you know. They are sharp-sighted, wonderfully sharp-sighted; I admit it. But nevertheless they do sometimes hang up a scalp for their daughters which has not yet been taken. Do you suppose, Mrs. Chester, do you really suppose —"

"I know nothing about it," replied the imbittered lady. "Mrs. Devine throws out her hints and I repeat them. Miss Jenny Devine is nothing to me, and Mr. McAlister is of course less than nothing. I merely mention the thing as a matter of common uninteresting gossip."

"Ah," bowed the Major, smiling unspeakable compliments at Mrs. Chester, while in the same breath he investigated her with twinkling, analytic eyes. "Of course. Certainly. Not worthy of your attention. Certainly not."

"I never was more mistaken in any man than I was in that Mr. Frank McAlister," the lady went on vixenishly. "I thought well of him for a short time; I thought him good-hearted and a gentleman. He is a selfish, stupid, low fellow. I never saw another man so vulgarly and stupidly ungrateful for civilities. It is well for our family that we got shut of him and his breed. I hope Jenny Devine will catch him. The little cross jilt is just fit for him, and he is just fit for her. They will punish each other nicely."

"Ah — you think so?" nodded the Major, hardly able to keep from grinning in her face. "Really, how dull we male creatures are! Here I had been thinking well of the girl; wishing my young friend Vincent could catch her; envying him the chance. God bless my soul, — God bless my soul! Mrs. Chester, I am positively not fit to go about the world alone. I need your guidance at every moment; absolutely need it, must have it," he fluted in his finest trills and quavers, cocking his head on one side like a curious parrot, and puckering his face into a thousand wrinkles, all expressive of adoration and servitude. But the moment he got out of her presence he muttered, "Spiteful, disappointed old beldame!"

"What does the woman lie for in that style?" he went on, commencing a long soliloquy about this worrying bit of gossip. "I don't believe a word she says. Frank McAlister in love with Jenny Devine! Frank McAlister forgotten Kate Beaumont! Romeo false to Juliet! Impossible. I can't have been so mistaken in the young man. I know him; I have studied him; I have looked him in the eyes; I have sounded his character. Sounded it, — sound-ed it," he insisted, smirking and twinkling as if he were talking to some one else than himself and trying to carry conviction to his auditor. "I must see Romeo," he continued vehemently. "I must say to him, 'This won't do; this spoils our drama; this will make the plot a nullity; this will draw a storm of hisses.' I *will see* him. It will be awkward; it may lead to difficulties; the Beaumonts may scowl at me. But no; the Beaumonts prize me; they are under obligations to me; they know that I fought Tom well; yes, fought him well, begad," affirmed the Major aloud, chuckling over the recollection of his only duel — as a second. "And if the heathen do rage I must defy them. In the name of the poetic unities, I must defy them. I can't have my romance, the darling romance of my life, broken up because of an election, a mere tempest in a teapot, a squabble sure to end in six weeks. God bless my soul, I can't have it. It would make me miserable. I should leave this part of the country. And I have already written to Charleston about my little drama. Prophesied about it, — bragged over it. I couldn't go back to Charleston. Where the deuce could I go?"

And, mounting his horse, the Major rode off boldly toward the McAlister place, not caring in his desperation what the Beaumonts might think of his confabulating with their enemies. He neared the house; he got a view of the garden from the high road; and there, among the roses he saw — what? Frank McAlister walking with Jenny Devine, bending over her in a manner which indicated close amity, and holding her — yes, her hand.

In his indignation and despair, the Major at once wheeled his horse and galloped back to Kershaw's.

CHAPTER 27

 Nellie and Kate passed their twenty-four hours of detention in Brownville without disturbance from Randolph Armitage.

That high-flung gentleman had been stranded by his debauch on the outer reefs of that horrible country which is haunted by the afreets and rocs and serpents and apes of *delirium tremens*, remaining for several days so bruised and shaken with his shipwreck that he was content to lie in bed and submit to the nursing of Quash and Bentley. But the women, not knowing his wretched state, had no anxiety for him and much for themselves, expecting to see his inflamed visage from minute to minute. Consequently they sought a refuge from him, hiding for the day in the house of a venerable friend of the Beaumont race, and returning in the evening by back streets to the hotel.

"You shall not come with us," said Mrs. Armitage to her host, fearing yet lest her irrational husband might find her and not willing to lead her old friend into an unpleasantness. "We shall do much the best without you. Only let us have your Cæsar."

As Cæsar marched behind at a decorous distance, the two women had a chance to commune together, and, being women, did commune. Nor is it any wonder either that their talk, after fluttering unsatisfied from subject to subject, should alight upon Frank McAlister. Kate did not mean to speak of him; indeed, she had made a resolve that she would never utter his name again; but there seemed to be a magical power about the man, and he would get himself mentioned. On the present occasion he made his entrance upon the scene by dint of that sorcery which is commonly called "an impression."

"I have such a strange feeling," said the girl, when her sister charged her with absent-mindedness and inattention. "It seems to me that we are about to meet — one of the McAlisters."

"Which one?" demanded Mrs. Armitage, crisply.

Kate hesitated; she did not like to expose her weakness; moreover, she found "Frank" a great word to utter.

"I know which one," added Nellie. "Ah, Kate, do you think a woman doesn't understand such things? I have had just such impressions. Oh dear, how well I remember them yet! You make me sad; you make me think how happy I was once; it is dreadful to look back upon lost happiness. Oh yes, I can't help understanding you."

"I don't wish you to impute too much to me," said the girl, gently.

"Kate, let us be frank," returned Nellie. "If we are women, we are Beaumonts. Let us speak the whole truth as our race does."

"I try to do that," murmured Kate, remembering with a flush of shame how she had once glided by the direct fact in prattling with Jenny Devine about Frank McAlister. "But is there any need of talking about this?"

"Perhaps there is," said Nellie, pensively. "It is hard to decide whether silence or talk is best. Don't you want to talk about it?"

Kate made no answer.

"I know that you like him," Nellie went on. "I know that it must pain you to find yourself separated from him for life. I don't blame you."

Still Kate spoke not. Denial and confession were both beyond her power; she walked on silently, with tears in her eyes.

"Ah well, Kate!" sighed Mrs. Armitage, fully comprehending this dumb suffering. "There is nothing left now but to bear bravely what is and must be. But if ever you want a heart to lean upon, here is mine for you, the whole of it."

Kate caught her sister's arm, bowed her head upon her shoulder, and walked thus for a few steps, still without speaking.

"Oh my poor darling!" exclaimed Mrs. Armitage, stopping and embracing the girl passionately. "It's lucky that life isn't very long. That is the best thing about it."

After some further walking she resumed: "He is better than most men, in spite of his treatment of Tom. But it is useless to talk of him. There is the feud. I suppose you must marry some one else when the time comes."

"I won't be married at all," whispered Kate, her mind suddenly reverting to that horror of a husband, Randolph Armitage. She was in a state of feeling to believe that all men were like him, except the one man from whom she was divided forever.

On reaching the hotel they hurried to their rooms to prepare for the early start of the morrow. But presently Kate missed her travelling-bag, and guessing that she might have left it in the parlor, went down in search of it. The room was deserted and darkling, for sojourners in that season were few, and the kerosene lamp had not been lighted. The girl found her bag, but there was something in the spacious gloom and lonesomeness which suited her feelings, and she lingered. There were two sets of windows; the front ones looked upon the street, and the rear ones upon a veranda and garden; outside, everything was illuminated and idealized by the abundant moonlight. Kate walked slowly to and fro, glancing first at one of the little landscapes and then at the other, and perhaps wondering that the world could seem so much more like an abode of happiness than she found it. She remained thus for ten or fifteen minutes, unconscious that she was watched.

In the rear veranda a man lurked, trembling with agitation. The night was cool, but he did not notice it; if it had been freezing, he would not have noticed it. When Kate approached him he slipped shamefacedly away, and when she receded he placed himself once more at one or other of the windows, there to gaze after her with an air of anxiety which was like the greediness of hunger. Occasionally he started, as if under some violent impulse, and moved towards a door which opened into the parlor; then as suddenly he checked himself, fell into a meditation and shook his head sadly; then hastened back to his spying-place. It was evident that he wished to speak to the girl, and that for some weighty reason he did not dare.

This man was Frank McAlister. We must explain how he came here. South Carolina had at last summoned him to prove his science; he had been commissioned to report upon an iron-mine in Saxonburg. Ailing and in low spirits, his first impulse had been to decline the job and continue to coddle his sorrows at home under the pitying eyes of his mother and within prompt reach of the sympathy of Jenny Devine. But he made out to remember that he was a metallurgist and that it was high time to magnify his calling. He bade a grateful good by to Jenny (under the eyes of Major Lawson, as one happens to recollect), and left her without suspecting that he had won her fervent admiration, not to say somewhat, be it more or less, of her affection. Then he journeyed to his mine and collected specimens of the ore for analysis; and now here he was, waiting like the two ladies for the morning train eastward. The presence of Kate in the hotel parlor he had discovered while taking a stroll in the moonlit veranda.

The one great question which at once occupied his mind was, should he speak to her? Of course he answered it as a gentleman and a man of sense, saying over and over that it would be useless, that it could only do harm, that he ought not and would not. But on the other hand an impulse which cared not for reason or reproof insisted that he must. Only one word, pleaded this passionate impulse; what that word should be it did not suggest; simply that he must find and utter it. Rationality and sense of propriety fought their battle in vain against emotion. After advancing repeatedly to the door, and retreating from it as often, he opened it and was before her.

It will be remembered that she had had an impression that he was at hand. That impression, absurd as she believed it to be, had so prepared her for the meeting, that she was not surprised by his appearance, and recognized him at once in the obscurity. She did not, however, speak, further than to murmur, "Mr. McAlister."

"I beg your pardon," he said humbly. "I could not help entering."

It seemed for a moment as if these words must end the conversation, and he would have to retire ignominiously without uttering a syllable to any purpose. Kate could not answer him, and there was a moment of terrible silence, equally terrible to both.

"I wish to ask your forgiveness, — yes, and that of your whole family," recommenced Frank, luckily remembering his difficulty with Tom, and so finding something to say. "I was a brute to tie your brother and a madman to go out with him. There must be some natural want of delicacy in me. I did not see it then, but I see it now. I see it just in time to repent of it uselessly."

"Mr. McAlister, I do not want to talk of this," replied Kate, pained at his so humbling himself.

"No. Of course not. I had no right to speak of it to *you*."

He would go on bowing in the dust; would prostrate himself unnecessarily.

"Don't!" she imposed with the simplicity and brevity of earnest feeling. "I am not angry at you. If I was angry, it is over."

"Is it possible?" he asked, so grateful for what he esteemed unmerited pardon, that he wanted to fall on his knees, as if to a forgiving deity. "This is more than I ever hoped to hear from you. I have hated myself for my folly, and believed that you hated me for it. I thought also that you must share the natural feelings of your family towards me. I have been in despair over it."

"Mr. McAlister, you don't know how you pain me," Kate could not help saying in reply to this supposition that she could hate him.

"Oh yes, I have done you injustice," he went on. "I suppose my thoughts have sprung from my fears. Well, I am greatly relieved; I am just a little satisfied. You at least forgive me."

"If I blamed you, it was for the duel."

"But I did not challenge, and I did not fire at him," he insisted, still bent on excusing himself. "I wanted to be shot."

"Oh, how could you!" whispered Kate.

"I was in despair. You did not answer my letters."

"Perhaps I was wrong. I did not know what to do. There was this miserable quarrel, and all intercourse forbidden. I did not like to write, not even to say good by, unless my father knew it."

"I ought to have had more patience," confessed Frank, perpetually ready to condemn himself.

"It does seem to me that you ought, Mr. McAlister. I expected a great deal of patience and calmness from you."

"And it is you who have shown all the patience and all the good sense," declared the young man, in a passion of humility. "And I have played the part of a madman and an idiot. I am so much your inferior."

"Oh no!" Kate could not help saying it, and could not help advancing a little towards him, she so wanted to console him under his burden of self-reproach.

Before she knew what he was about he had taken her hand.

Meantime Mrs. Armitage, wishing to give some direction concerning the start in the morning, had gone to her sister's room in search of her, and thence descended to the parlor.

"Mr. McAlister, is this proper conduct?" she demanded, flaming at once into anger. "Is this keeping your promise to me?"

Frank's soul was in a confused whirl; but he tried to look down the maelstrom and discover the truth at the bottom of it; and he thought he saw that he had not broken his word in regard to paying court to Miss Beaumont without her sister's consent.

"I was asking her pardon," he said. "I asked her pardon for ill-treating her brother and for going out with him. She granted it, and I thanked her."

He spoke with such a manly self-respect and such a sincerity of tone, that Mrs. Armitage could not help believing him. Moreover, his shaking voice moved her; it was eloquent with uprightness of character and fervor of emotion; it made a music which she had heard and been well pleased with heretofore. Her confidence in him and her liking for him returned upon her with such force that she could not at once go on with her scolding.

"I ask your pardon also, Mrs. Armitage," he added presently.

"Oh, let it pass," she replied impatiently, vexed with herself for losing her anger at him. "That has all been cancelled in the proper way, I suppose. But what right have you here? Why did you come here?"

He told her how he happened to be in Brownville, and added that he had discovered her sister by accident.

"Then you go down in the train with us to-morrow?" she inquired.

"If you object, I will wait over."

"I don't see that I have any right to object," mused Mrs. Armitage. "As things stand between our families, I have not the least authority over you."

"I concede the right and the authority," bowed the young man.

"I don't object to your going. It would be asking a favor of you, — placing ourselves under an obligation."

"I assure you that I would not so consider it."

"I tell you that I do not object," repeated Nellie, a little annoyed by this bandying of courtesies with a man to whom she ought not to speak at all, as she believed. "But —" she added, and then checked herself.

Frank waited respectfully.

"I may as well say it," she went on, her vexation rising as she found the interview more and more embarrassing. "You should not have spoken to my sister. I am not blaming *her*; she could not well help listening; I am blaming *you* for speaking. You should not have done it."

"I know it," the repelled lover burst forth. "But, Mrs. Armitage, are you no woman at all?" he continued in a whisper, which Kate overheard as a sob. "Can't you concede any latitude to misery? Just look at me," he added, turning his thin face to the moonlight. "Am I the same man that I was? You at least ought to guess what this change in me means. I have borne wretchedness enough in the last month to make me lose my reason. Indeed, I have lost it; I have behaved like a madman; I have behaved so, I suppose, this evening. I never meant to speak to your sister until I saw her; and then I could not help it. I was driven to ask her forgiveness, and driven to humble myself before her all the more because she forgave me. Why, don't you know, can't you understand, what has happened to me? Separated from her! separated for life! Can't you imagine what that means to me? It means a broken heart, if there can be such a thing."

"Oh, stop!" begged Mrs. Armitage, as Kate fled to the other end of the room, threw herself on a sofa and covered her face. "Oh, these men! there is no doing anything with them. Don't you see what mischief you are making? You shouldn't have come here. Do go away."

"No, I shouldn't have come here," said Frank, recovering a little of his self-possession. It has only made bad worse."

"Yes," sighed Nellie. "And here I am pitying you. How could you charge me with not being a woman?"

"Oh, if I said that, I did you great wrong. I did not know that I said it. I beg your pardon."

"It doesn't matter. I am not angry with you. No, I am not angry with you about anything, though I suppose I ought to be. When you are so wretched, how can I be angry with you? But come; all this talk is useless, worse than useless. As long as the quarrel between our families lasts you cannot be near to Kate, nor even to me. If it should ever end, then — perhaps —"

"So you will still be friendly to me, or at least not hostile?" he asked, his face so lighting up that it fascinated her.

"I must not say too much," she answered; but she could not help giving him her hand. He pressed it in both his, and barely stopped short of kissing it. Then turning a last long look upon the silent girl on the sofa, he left the parlor and went straight to his room a lighter-hearted man than he had been for a month.

"Ah, Kate!" said Mrs. Armitage, taking her sister's arm and leading her away. "What with a crazy man and an idiotic woman, you have had a wretched time. Oh, these lovers! I may as well say the word. He has told you all about it, — with my help. There is no stopping them. No woman really and heartily wants to stop them. I was fool enough to let him go on, and provoke him to go on. I ought to suffer for it, and I do. For it was so useless! oh, it was so useless! Come, let us go to our room and go to sleep. I wish I could sleep all the while. I wish you could, my poor darling. The insensible hours are the happiest hours of one's life. Even nightmares are not so bad as realities. Here is one of the unhappiest women in the world talking nonsense to the next unhappiest. That is what waking life is. Let us get to sleep as quickly as possible. If we could sleep half the time, we should just balance accounts between wretchedness and pleasure. It is a poor consolation."

They were by this time at the door of Kate's room. Mrs. Armitage kissed her sister, lingered a moment on the threshold, and then entered.

"I can't leave you yet," she said. "It is only ten o'clock, although it seems late enough to be morning, to be the next world. You will sleep the quicker if we talk awhile. What a comfort talk is to women. How did our poor ancestresses get along before they learned how to do it, if there ever was such a time?"

"How are we to treat him to-morrow?" asked Kate, not even hearing her sister's prattle, though meant to divert her.

"Ah!" returned Mrs. Armitage. "That is true. Circumstances have changed since I allowed him to go in the train. Perhaps, when he told his story, I ought to have forbidden his coming."

"Are you going to forbid it?" inquired Kate so anxiously that Nellie could not reply, Yes.

"It does not seem to matter much," she said, after a moment of hesitation. "It surely cannot matter so very, very much. I shall leave him at liberty in the question. I shall trust to his judgment."

Did it not occur to her that trusting to the judgment of a man in love, especially after what had happened during the evening, was leaning on a reed? The truth is that Nellie remembered her own time of loving; she guessed that these two must long beyond expression to look at each other, only to look; and in her sympathetic woman's heart she could not find the hardness to forbid it.

But half an hour later, as she went to her own room, she said to herself earnestly, "I do hope he will stay behind. Will he?"

CHAPTER 28

 Warm hearts, as you already know, had the Beaumonts; hearts quick to spring and demanding incessant activity; not, however, in the manner of lambs, kids, and other playful creatures; rather like blood horses, puissant for either good or evil.

Mrs. Armitage was like the rest of her kind; when she was not hating she was loving. By nature she was a woman of the marrying sort, disposed to rush into matrimony herself and to help others do the like. Even now, despite her sad experience in wedded life, she believed in making love and taking the consequences. It was impossible for her to conceive how a person of her own sex could have a heart and not use it. That a girl, under any circumstances, should become an old maid as a matter of preference, was a thing outside of her credence. Not to love and not to marry was in her eyes to be either a wilful monstrosity or a victim of horribly adverse circumstance. She was born to think thus, and could not for twenty-four hours together think otherwise, not even under the pressure of her hardest wifely troubles, not even when flying from her husband. It was no wonder that a woman of such an affectionate and sympathetic character should remember

Kate's declaration that she would never marry, and should revolt against it.

"See here," she began upon the girl early in the morning. "I don't like your saying that you will never take anybody at all. You mustn't get into that state of mind. It is unnatural in a woman. It can't lead to happiness. I don't believe there is any such thing as single-blessedness, — at least not for our sex. The phrase is ironical; it really means single misery. There are no contented and cheerful old maids; you never saw one, and you never will. An old maid is a complete failure. She is like a man who does not succeed in man's careers. Rather than be one, you had better marry a scoundrel, even if you get a divorce from him. You would at least have some short use of your affections; and you would, besides, occupy your mind and your time. Now that is the deliberate, serious opinion of a wife who has failed almost as completely as a wife can. I want you to lay it to heart."

"Oh, tell me about it some other time," sighed Kate, wearied of the subject of marriage, or fancying that she was so.

They reached the station without seeing Frank McAlister or learning whether he would be with them on the train. When the cars started he had not yet appeared, and they supposed that he had remained behind. Kate was disappointed; she had hoped to have him near her, though she might not even look at him; she had expected to draw just a little consolation from that unsocial propinquity. And strange to say, Mrs. Armitage was also disappointed, in spite of her feeling that his absence was a relief, and that it was for the best.

"I did not expect such discretion," she said to herself; "he is not so mannish a man as I took him to be; he is almost too gentlemanly a gentleman."

Turning presently to throw a shawl over her seat, she saw him standing on the rear platform of the car, and glancing sidelong through the window. She was so amused, and, in spite of her uneasiness, so gratified, that she could scarce forbear laughing outright. "I might have known it," she thought; "he has got there to look at Kate undisturbed; just to look at the back of her bonnet."

She absolutely longed to beckon him in and offer him her own place. A few minutes later she discovered that he had slyly entered and was sitting on the rearmost seat, with his face settled straight to the front. "Oh dear!" she reflected, "how is this going to end? I am afraid I shall be wickedly weak about it. I haven't half hard-heartedness enough for a duenna."

She was so interested in this love imbroglio, that during most of the journey she forgot her own troubles. She was so bewildered by it that she could not remember her prejudices as a Beaumont, her sage deliberations as a woman who had seen life, and her anxieties as an elder sister. The near presence of strong love intoxicated a nature given to affection and full of sympathy for it. That man behind her, sending all his soul through his eyes at Kate's hat-ribbons, she could not help thinking of him continually, could not help wishing him success. "If it only could be!" she repeatedly said to herself; and presently she began to inquire, "Why should it not be?"

Her former fancy for the youngster came back upon her in full force; and from liking him the next step was to consider him unexceptionable as a match. After an hour or so of sympathizing with the longings of this faithful and fascinating lover, it seemed clear to her that Kate could not find another man who would make her so good a husband. As for the intervening family feud, could it not be got rid of by defying it? It had blocked the engagement; but if the engagement should be brought about by main force, that might block the feud; the initiative, the aggressive, counted for so much in these matters. She remembered two scolding negresses whom she had once seen, one of whom was pouring forth a stream of abuse, while the other listened with an air of patient menace, merely muttering, "Ef you coughs, you's gone up." She smiled at the recollection and said to herself, "If the quarrel coughs, it is done." In spite of her conscientiousness, her manly sense of honor, and her strong family feeling, Nellie was soon dallying with the idea of a runaway match. Her principles were as high and solid as mountains, but her sympathies were as strong as the volcanic fires which devour mountains. Vigorous in every point of her character, she was all the more a changeable creature, a woman of the women.

At last — Oh, how impatiently Nellie had waited for it! — the younger sister rose, arranged her travelling-rug, looked about her and discovered Frank McAlister. He ventured to remove his hat as he caught her glance, and she just drooped her long lashes in acknowledgment of the salute. When she sat down again her cheeks were rose-beds of blushes, and her hazel eyes were full of flashes which blinded her.

"Ah, you saw," whispered Nellie, trembling with an excitement which was almost glee. "I knew an hour ago that he was there."

"Oh Nellie, what shall I do?" asked Kate, reeling between terror and an irresistible gladness.

"Jump out of the window," advised Nelly, fairly giggling. We must surely pardon her slightly hysterical frame, when we remember how little she had slept of late.

"Nellie, you are laughing at me," said Kate piteously. "It is shabby and cruel of you."

"So it is. But I can't help laughing. He is actually browsing on your bonnet trimmings."

"Be still, Nellie," begged the girl, raising both hands to her cheeks, as if to push back the crowding blushes. "You shall not make me so ridiculous. Oh, I wish he had stayed away! Why didn't he?"

"It is too absurd," declared Mrs. Armitage, with a nervous start. "I can't have him there making an image of himself and making everybody wonder what we are. I must bring him up here where he will have to behave himself."

"Oh, no!" pleaded Kate. "It will lead to misunderstanding and trouble of all sorts."

But, impelled by her nerves, Mrs. Armitage sprang to her feet, faced toward the young man, and beckoned him to approach. He obeyed her in great anxiety, expecting to be requested to leave the car, and fully prepared to make the rest of the journey with the baggage-master, or even to jump off the train if so ordered. This last feat, by the way, would not have been an eminently dangerous one, inasmuch as the railroad velocity of that region rarely surpassed ten miles an hour. It must be understood also that the train had only one passenger-car, and that one by no means full. Negroes travelled not at all, except as nurses, etc.; the low-down population travelled very little; high-toned people were scarce.

"I suppose that you have no provisions," said Mrs. Armitage to the youngster. "Since you are here, you must share in our basket. Would you mind turning over the seat in front and riding backward?"

"I am very grateful to you," replied Frank, who would have ridden on a rail to be near Miss Beaumont.

Then followed a conversation of several hours, — a conversation managed with good taste and discretion; not a word as to the family quarrel or the love affair; all about travelling, Europe, and other unimpassioned subjects. Sensible, full of information, and for the time in good spirits, the young man was fairly luminous, and more than ever dazzled Mrs. Armitage. By the time the party separated she had arrived at a solid resolve to break up the family feud if possible, and to bring about a match between these two, whether it were possible or not. Of course the male Beaumonts would not fancy her projects, and perhaps would oppose them domineeringly and angrily. But she determined to fight them; her long contest with the brutalities of her husband had made her somewhat of a rebel against men; and besides, the law of the "survival of the fittest" had blessed her, as it had blessed all her breed, with abundant pugnacity.

"I am his sworn ally," she said to her sister as they drove homeward from the Hartland station. "If he proposes, do you accept him. Then I will go to papa with the whole story, and if he is naughty, I will appeal to your grandpapa."

"I will neither do nor permit anything of the sort," replied the almost over-tempted Kate, with tears in her eyes.

"We will see," prophesied Nellie. "Oh, you good little cry-baby! Kiss me."

As there had been no time for advisatory letters, the two ladies were their own heralds at the plantation. But while the father and brothers were surprised by their advent, they were all the more delighted. The family sympathy was so strong in this race, that in the matter of welcoming kinspeople the Beaumont men were more like women than like the generality of their own sex. Moreover, in the dull routine of plantation life, every visit is a gratification.

"Why, my babies!" trumpeted Peyton. "This is the blessedest sight I have had in a month. So, Kate, you couldn't stay away any longer from your old father? God bless you, my darling. And Nellie, — why, I hadn't a hope of this, — this is too good. So you escorted her down, did you? Nellie, you were always a wonderful girl; always doing some nice thing unexpectedly. And the little fellows too! Heavens, what boys they are! what boys!"

When the brothers came in there was an incomprehensible clatter of talk. The eight Beaumonts, old and young, babbled in a way which would have done honor to their French ancestors. Despite the sad secrets lurking in some of these hearts, it was a scene of unmixed enjoyment and *abandon*.

Not till the next morning, not till Peyton Beaumont had had time to settle upon the fact that his daughters were paler and thinner than when they went away, were any unpleasant subjects broached. Drawing Nellie into his favorite solitude and sanctum, the garden (the old duellist loved flowers), he demanded, "What the — what is the matter with you two? Here I sent Kate up country to get rosy and hearty, and she has come back as pale as a lilly. And you, too; why, I never saw you so broken down; why, I thought you had a constitution: what *is* the matter?"

"See here, papa," began Mrs. Armitage, and then for a breath was silent. "Well, it has come time to act, and of course it is time to talk," she resumed. "I have had to leave my husband, and I am excusable for telling why."

"Had to leave your husband!" echoed the father, his bushy eyebrows bristling and his saffron eyes turning bloodshot. "The infamous scoundrel ! !"

He was so much of a Beaumont that he never doubted for a moment that his own flesh and blood was in the right. The fact that his daughter had felt herself compelled to leave her husband was all that he needed to enable him to judge the case at once and forever.

Then came the wretched story; at least a part of it; enough of it.

"The infamous scoundrel!" repeated Beaumont, breathing hard, like a tiger scenting prey. "Be tranquil. Be perfectly easy. He won't live the month out."

"Have a care what you do," replied Nellie. "I don't want the whole world to know what I have suffered."

"Who is going to know it?" interrupted the old fire-eater. "By heavens, I'll shoot the man who dares to know it. If any man dares to look as though he knew it, I'll shoot him."

"You can't shoot the women," said Nellie.

"We can call out their men," was the reply of a gentleman who knew the customs of good society.

"And every stone thrown into the puddle will rile it the more," sighed Nellie. "Besides, I don't want blood spilt."

"But, good heavens, you don't mean that I shall bear this abuse of you in patience, — bear it as though I were a Yankee pedler or a Dunker preacher! It can't be borne."

"Father, here is what I want of you," declared Nellie, as emphatic as her parent. "Bear it as I do. You are surely the least sufferer of the two. All I want is to be allowed to live apart from my husband. Help me in that; protect me in that. I not only do not ask anything more, but I forbid anything more. In this matter I have a right to command. I want you to promise me that there shall be no challenging on my account. If you won't promise that, I will go back to him."

After a long argument, and after a good deal of bloodthirsty glaring and snuffing the air, Beaumont grumbled an ungracious and partial assent.

"Let him keep away, then," he said, shaking his iron-gray mane. "If he wants to go on breathing, let him keep out of my sight."

"You won't tell the boys anything of this?" begged Nellie, remembering that her influence over her brothers was slighter than that over her father.

"Why not?" demanded Beaumont, who had half meant to tell the boys, knowing well their pugnacity.

"Father, you comprehend why, of course. Do grant me this favor; do promise me. I want this whole matter in my own hands. Leave it to my judgment. Promise me not to tell them."

And so, unable to resist a child, and above all a daughter, Beaumont sulkily promised.

"But of course you will go on staying here," he insisted.

"I don't know where else to stay," groaned Nellie, suddenly wounded by a sense of dependence.

"My God, my girl!" he exclaimed, throwing an arm around her waist and drawing her close to his side. "Where else should you stay?"

"And my children, too," added the mother, hardly able to keep from sobbing.

"I would like to see anybody get them away from here," returned Beaumont, squaring his broad chest as if to face a combatant, and thrusting his hands into his pockets with an air of drawing derringers.

Left to himself, he muttered a great deal about Armitage, shaking a clenched fist as if he had the brute before him, elevating his bushy eyebrows as a wild boar raises his bristles, halting abruptly to stare fiercely at vacancy, etc.

"After all, I fancy that her way of managing the scoundrel is the best," he finally decided. "What a woman she is, that daughter of mine! What fortitude and sense! In her place I should have made fifty scandals long ago. By heavens, these women amaze me, they do indeed. In their own business — that is to say, in matters that belong to — well in short, their own business, they are wonderful."

When he thus praised women he of course meant such as were born ladies, and more particularly such as were born Beaumonts, though he could hardly have been thinking of Mrs. Chester.

Nellie's next notable conversation with her father began with a reference to the controversy with the McAlisters.

"When does the election take place?" she asked.

"In about three weeks," calmly responded the veteran politician.

"And the misunderstanding with the Judge still continues."

"Humph," grunted papa. It occurred to him that in discussing his affairs of state she was getting beyond woman's business.

"It would be well to devise some plan to make him give up his opposition," continued Nellie.

"Humph," repeated Beaumont. He was determined not to talk with her on this subject; he preferred to be left to his own will and judgment in masculine matters.

"Couldn't he be got to withdraw his candidature?" persisted the daughter.

"I don't want him to withdraw," snorted Beaumont, starting like an angered horse, and forgetting his purpose of reticence. "I prefer to have him run. I want to beat him."

"Oh," said Nellie, somewhat disappointed, "I had an idea that beating him was not so certain. Poinsett tells me that it is likely to be a very close contest."

"Did Poinsett say that?" asked the father, clearly a little alarmed. "Well, I must admit that the Judge is working very hard. There is a great deal of money being spent, — I don't know where it comes from, — but it does come. By heavens, if I get a hold on them!"

"It would be a capital thing, then, to induce him to withdraw," inferred Nellie.

"But how the deuce is it to be done?" answered Beaumont, in a pet. "Do you know what you are talking about? I don't think you do."

"Perhaps not," assented Nellie, sagaciously; she was leading the way to a change of subject; she was devising a new approach.

"Then let us drop the matter," said the bothered candidate.

"I have something to say to you about Kate," resumed Nellie, opening her second parallel. "Did you ever know that Bent Armitage is very fond of her?"

"Bent Armitage!" exclaimed the father in great wrath. "I'll have no more Armitages in my family. I won't have one in my house. It's a bad race. They run to drunkenness and brutality. One of them is enough and a thousand times too much. Bent Armitage may go to the Old Harry. He can't have my daughter. He sha'n't speak to her. He sha'n't come here."

"I thought you liked Bent pretty well."

"So I did, in a fashion. I liked his gabble and his stories well enough. I've no objection to hearing him talk now and then. But when it comes to his paying attention to Kate, that is quite another thing. Besides, I didn't fully know until now what a beast an Armitage can be. I didn't thoroughly understand the nature of the breed. Now that I do know all that, I don't want to see him at all. I don't want any of the crop on my place."

"Bent is better than some men," softly said Nellie, remembering his kindness to herself.

"I tell you I don't want to hear about him," insisted Beaumont. "The moment you talk of the possibility of his courting Kate, I hate him. No more Armitages."

"McAlisters would be better," suggested Nellie.

"Yes, even McAlisters," assented the father. Although his words were ungracious, his manner did not show much bitterness, for at the moment he thought of Frank, and how he had once felt kindly towards him.

"A good deal better," added Nellie.

Beaumont glared and bristled. "What are you talking about now? I can't always keep track of you."

"Frank McAlister is altogether the best of the family," said Nellie, picking a flower or two with a deceptive air of absent-mindness.

The father stared in a puzzled way; but at last he gave a humph of assent.

"That's no great matter," he presently growled. "It doesn't take much of a man to be the best of the McAlisters."

"I don't see how the Judge could have such a noble fellow for a son," observed Nellie.

"Nor I either," declared Beaumont, thrown off his guard. "By heavens, he *is* a fine fellow, considering his surroundings. He is a perfect contrast to that sly old fox, his father. It's just as though a Roman should be the son of a Carthaginian. He has the making of a gentleman in him. To be sure, he did treat Tom — But never mind about that; he did his best to make amends for it: he did very well. I must say, Nellie, that I was grieved to break with that young fellow. I had begun to like him."

"Ah, you liked him because he liked Kate," replied Nellie, insinuating the love affair into the conversation with admirable dexterity.

"Nonsense!" denied Beaumont. "Well, of course I did," he immediately confessed, for he abhorred lying, even to white lies. "Naturally I like to have my children appreciated, and think well of people who do appreciate them. I admit, too, that I admire a man for exhibiting a proper perception of character, and especially of such a noble character as Kate undoubtedly has. But if you mean to say that I meant —"

"No, I don't mean to say that you meant anything," interrupted Nellie. "I will just say what I mean myself. I wish that match had come off."

"No, no," protested Beaumont. "I should have lost my daughter. We never can have a year's peace with that family. I can't have Kate married among people who would drag her away from me and set her up to fight me. I did think of it; I admit it. I was taken with that fellow, Frank, and I did think of letting him try his chance. But what has happened since then puts an end to the idea forever. No marriage with McAlisters. I can't allow it; I can't consider it. And if you mean to suggest that I ought to favor the match for the sake of getting rid of my political rival and assuring my seat in Congress, you are not the child that I have taken you for. Before I would sell one of my daughters in that way, I would let myself be shelved forever and I would step into my grave."

"Don't do me injustice," said Nellie. "If I hinted at that idea, I laid very little stress upon it, even in my own mind. But there is one thing that I want you to consider seriously. It is Kate's happiness. You must understand fully that she likes this young man, and, as I believe, likes him very much. You must understand, too, that he is one of the best men that she can ever hope to have. She may never receive so good an offer again. He hasn't a vice, not even of temper. You don't want her to marry an Armitage." (A growl from Beaumont.) "Well, there are plenty of Armitages who don't bear the name. To be sure, there are other young fellows as good perhaps as this one; there is Poindexter and Dr. Mattieson and our clergyman and so on; all nice fellows. But Kate does not care for them. And for *him* she does care."

"Oh Nellie!" groaned Beaumont. "Stop. I can't talk about this now. Some other time, when we get out of this fight, if ever we do. But I can't discuss it now. Do let me alone. Do you want to break my heart?"

"No, nor Kate's either," said Nellie.

CHAPTER 29

 There is a propensity in the human being when overtaken by trouble to want to know the worst.

If it were not for the mystery and the decisiveness of the act of death, the man who is sweeping down rapids towards a cataract would undoubtedly long to reach the plunge. It may even be that to those who have gone over Niagara the moment of catastrophe has been a moment of relief.

Like most worried people, Peyton Beaumont proceeded to seek out the culmination of his worries; he stumbled on from his trying talk with Nellie about Kate to a still more trying talk with Kate about herself; he did it against his intention and desire, but he could not help doing it. It so tormented him to suspect that his pet daughter was sorrowing, that he could not rest until he had laid his finger on the pulse of her sorrow and made certain of its feverish throbbing.

First he watched her; he noted the unwonted paleness and the sad though sweet seriousness of her face; he observed that, no matter how cheeringly he might prattle to her, he could not make her gay. The smiles that came on her lips, and the sparkles that rose from the lucid depths of her eyes, were transitory. Her demeanor was similar to an overshadowed day, during which the sun steals forth again and again, but only by moments.

"My child, I can't bear this," he at last broke out; "you are unwell or unhappy, and you don't say why. You make me anxious and — and miserable."

Kate glanced at him with a surprised and frightened expression. Her feelings were of such a delicate nature, that to have them handled by a man, even by a father whom she loved and who worshipped her, was terrible. The Creator has seldom fashioned a being more sensitive, more maidenly modest, than was this girl. Excepting with those eyes of a scared fawn, she made no reply.

"What is it, my darling?" insisted Beaumont, taking her hands and drawing her against his shoulder. "Is it something unbearable?"

His manner was as tender as if he were a mother instead a father. In view of the seeming paradox contained in the fact, we cannot too strenuously repeat that this war-like old chieftain, scarred with duels and stained with the heart's blood of more than one of his fellow-men, was a singularly affectionate parent. His children were a part of himself; indeed, he held them as the finest and most precious part; he would have risked fortune and life to right the wrong of any one of them. His parental feeling was all the stronger because of the spirit of family which possessed him, as it possessed all his race. His progeny were Beaumonts; he was the sheik, the patriarch of the Beaumont tribe; he was responsible for the welfare of every member of it.

"Is it more than a Beaumont can endure?" he repeated gently, though with an appeal to the family pride.

"No, it is not more," answered Kate, quivering with her struggle to bear, as an overladen man quivers under his load.

The father was not satisfied, for he did not want his daughter to suffer at all, and she had tacitly confessed to suffering. His strongest impulse, however, was to justify himself.

"I did not seek this new quarrel," he said. "I can declare truly, that Judge McAlister forced it upon me. I could live with the man decently, if he would let me."

"Oh father, I have nothing to say about those matters. Why do you explain them to *me*?"

"Because I don't want you to blame me. I can't bear it. I say I could live with these people. As for the young man, — I mean Mr.

Frank McAlister, — I respect him and like him."

Kate, in spite of her virginal modesty, gave him a glance of gratitude which stung him. He started, and then resigned himself; the girl did love that man; well, he must bear it.

"The deuce knows how it has all come about," he mumbled. "One thing has happened after another. We are all in a muddle of quarrelling. I wish we were out of it."

She made no answer, but he knew by the way she leaned against him that she echoed his wish with many times his earnestness.

"I must speak out," he declared. "It is my duty as a father. I know that this young man likes you and wishes to marry you. If your happiness is concerned, I must know that. Then I will see what I can do."

Kate could endure no longer; she was fairly driven into a burst of tears and sobbing; she clutched her father and buried her face in his neck, all the while kissing him. It was the same as to say, "I am very miserable, but do not be unhappy about it and do not be vexed with me."

"Oh my poor child!" he repeated several times, patting her shoulder in a helpless way, the most discomforted of comforters.

At last she recovered her self-possession a little, gradually lifting her head until her lips touched his ear.

"Papa, I will tell you everything," she whispered. "I did love him, and Oh, I do! If you had let him propose to me, I should have taken him. But now it is different. Since I have seen how it must always be between our families, I have decided that I never will marry him, not even if you consent. I will not risk being put in hostility to my own family. And now let me go, quick. Let me run."

The instant he loosened his embrace she rustled out of the room and away to her own chamber, shutting the door upon herself with a noise of hurry which he could plainly hear.

Peyton Beaumont remained alone in a state of profound depression. After a while he exploded in a torrent of profane invective against Judge McAlister, making him alone responsible for breaking the peace between the two houses by his attempt to sneak into Congress, — the sly, perfidious, rascally old fox, the humbugging possum, the greedy raccoon! Fnally, making a strong effort at self-control, an effort to crush his proudest aspirations, he exclaimed, "Hang the House of Representatives! I won't run for a seat. Let him have it. For once."

But the Honorable Beaumont had other business in the world besides that of being a vehicle for domestic and sentimental emotions. When he came to suggest to his sons and to his political confederates that he thought of throwing up his candidature, he found that they did not look upon him merely in the light of his duty as a father, but expected of him knightly service as a champion of State Rights and Southern principles.

"Going to drop us, Beaumont!" exclaimed seedy old General Johnson, his eloquent jaw falling so that he looked like the mummy of an idiot. "Why, good God. Beaumont, if our Alexander is to turn his back in the very moment of crossing the Granicus, what is to become of us?"

"General, I object to that expression, 'turning the back,'" responded the Honorable, his eyebrows ruffling until they made one think of two "fretful porcupines." "I must be allowed to say that I do not consider it a phrase which can be properly applied to any act of mine. General, I dislike the phrase."

"Metaphor, my dear Beaumont," bowed the General, restraining himself (pugnacious old tiger) for political reasons. "No offence intended, I do assure you. Mere poetical metaphor. Moreover, I withdraw it. Let us say prosaically and plainly, resigning your candidature. And now, the matter being thus posed, will you allow me to argue upon it?"

"Certainly, General, I shall be most happy to consider every suggestion you may have to offer."

"By God, I believe I'd fight him, if he didn't," thought Johnson. Then, speaking with unusual sententiousness by reason of the pressure of the crisis, he proceeded as follows: "Changing leaders in the moment of the shock of battle is equivalent to defeat. If we attempt to run any other candidate than yourself, particularly at this vital moment, we shall be beaten. A traitor to South Carolina will misrepresent South Carolina in the Federal Congress from this heretofore most truly and nobly represented district. The Southern phalanx will be broken in its very centre; and into the gap will rush the centralizing legions of the North. The sublime flag which our great Calhoun unfolded will be borne to the ground. It will be defeat all along the line. States Rights will be trampled under foot. Southern principles will be scattered forever. Beaumont, my dear and revered Beaumont, you are standing on a tripod of the most fearful responsibility. Upon you rests the prediction of our future. Your action will be its prophecy and its creation."

In his "flight of eloquence" the minute old General trembled like a humming-bird.

"Pardon the emotion of a veteran who sees his flag in danger," he resumed, mastering his alcoholized nerves. "Excuse the earnestness of a legionary who has grown gray in the service of his State, and who now sees the fair fame and even the sovereign existence of that State imperilled. Hear me in patience and with solemn consideration, while I implore you not to leave our noble cause to its own unassisted strength in this hour of supreme trial. By those who conquered at Fort Moultrie, and by those who fell at Eutaw Springs and — ahem — at various other places, and by those who dropped from bloody saddles beside Marion and Sumter, I conjure you to hold fast the banner of South Carolina and lead her as heretofore onward to victory. Duncan McAlister to represent this district at Washington? What a downfall for us all! Duncan McAlister to stand in your place? What a downfall for you! Ah, my dear Beaumont, consider, before it is quite too late; con—sid—er!"

We must observe that Beaumont's speechifying was very unlike the Johnsonian; it was mere talk, plain and straightforward talk, somewhat disconnected and jerky, but earnest and often forcible; it consisted in saying outright what he thought and especially what he felt. But although he thus differed from the General in style, and although he knew in his secret mind that the eloquence of the latter was mainly flummery, he on the present occasion could not help being moved by it. Those magic names, Hartland District, South Carolina, Fort Moultrie, Eutaw Springs, etc., always stirred him, no matter by whom pronounced or in what connection. He was a true son of the sacred soil of his State, and his veins thrilled at an allusion to his world-famous parentage. When "the old man eloquent" left the house, Beaumont shook hands with him cordially and thanked him for his friendly remonstrances.

"General, I will consider the matter further," he said. "If private affairs to which I cannot allude will permit, I will go on with my candidature. I will decide within two days, and let you know my decision at once. Meantime, not a word, I beg of you."

"Beaumont, I am the grave," solemnly responded the General, rising on the toes of his shabby boots; "I am a sarcophagus sealed in the centre of a pyramid. This secret is cemented in my breast; all I ask is, may it rot there; may it rot unexhumed and unsuspected. By those who fell at Fort Moultrie and Eutaw Springs," he was indistinctly heard to perorate as he descended the steps.

When Beaumont discussed his proposed demission with his sons, he encountered further earnest, though respectful opposition.

"It seems to me sir, that our family honor is concerned in this matte," observed Vincent, more of a Beaumont even than a South-Carolinian.

"Our family honor!" repeated the father, reddening at the suggestion that he could be indifferent to that lofty consideration.

"I beg your pardon, sir, if I am offensive. It is out of respect for you and regard for your reputation that I speak so plainly. Here is the way in which I look at the affair. You have said, Follow me; all our friends have rallied to your call; now you propose to turn back."

"Vincent, this is monstrous severe," said Beaumont, half scowling and half cringing.

"I beg your pardon, sir, but I can't see it differently. If Poindexter, for instance, had offered himself as candidate, and had gone on at it until within ten days or so of the election, and then withdrawn without assigning cause, what should we have said of him? I won't suggest the answer."

Beaumont quailed before his son; but the next instant he thought of his suffering daughter; so he turned for help to the fat, lazy, indifferent Poinsett.

"Why not assign cause?" suggested this young gentleman.

"It is unassignable," and Beaumont shook his head.

Poinsett knew or guessed somewhat of the affair between Kate and Frank, and was not entirely devoid of sympathy with it, being slothfully good-hearted, like many fat people.

"Could you not say that you prefer peace with a neighbor above a seat in Congress?" he asked. "Men have done that sort of thing, and still been widely respected on earth, and found favor at last with St. Peter."

"I beg pardon; it is too late," broke in Vincent. "It should have been thought of before, or never. We can't afford to buy the friendship of the McAlisters at such a price as must be paid now. Why, this very motive for resigning the candidature is condemnatory. Are we afraid of those people? Do we want to get a favor out of them? Suppose, after all, we should not get it! What would be said of our purpose? What would be said of our disappointment?"

It was evident that Vincent guessed at the gentle motive which influenced his father, and that he did not sympathize with it. There was a hard and pitiless substratum to the young man's character: a substratum which frequently came to view in the form of irony or a sneering smile; not unlike volcanic trap or granite breaking through the softer materials of earth's surface.

Meantime Tom Beaumont, not very quick-witted, and understanding the discussion only in part, prowled about the group of talkers with a sort of showing of the teeth, like a bull-dog who awaits a signal to fight.

"On reflection, I take courage to bow to Vincent's opinion," said Poinsett, waving away the smoke of his cigar as if it were so much demoralizing sentiment. "On reflection, I beg leave to concede that a withdrawal just now would be an error. I beg leave to add that it would be more than an error of conduct; it would be, if I may use the expression, an error of character; it would mark a man's reputation and future."

Beaumont was driven to the wall, and knew not how to defend himself. He could not say to his sons, your sister loves Frank McAlister. The declaration was too tender and too awful for Kate's father to utter even to Kate's brothers.

"Poinsett, you are harder than Vincent," he muttered, more in sorrow than in anger.

"I beg pardon, I was philosophizing," said Poinsett. " I have a habit of considering a thing from a general point of view. It is a result, I perhaps mistakenly suppose, of my Germanic education. It leads, I believe, to truth. I meant no offence, my very dear father. If I have annoyed you, please lay it to a system of thought, and not to my intention."

"All the same, none of you agree with me," grumbled Beaumont, feeling himself quite alone among men, and consequently much depressed. Notwithstanding his passionate nature, and, indeed, precisely because of it, he lived and moved by the breath of human beings, and especially by that of his own kin.

A weak man, the cold-blooded may say; but they would not be more than half right. Just because he was sympathetic, he easily got people to rally round him, and made a pretty good local leader for a party, and had the name of being a man of action, and was one. Moreover, it was only among those who had a strong hold upon his affections that he showed himself gentle and pliable. The generality of men chiefly knew him as headstrong and pugnacious; the Yankee Congressmen at Washington considered him one of the frightfullest of Southern bugbears; and against him the "Tribune" felt bound to hurl some of its weightiest Free-Soil thunder. Really, it is amazing how little a great man may be in his own house. One dares to wonder sometimes whether George Washington was august in the eyes of Mrs. George Washington.

Well, within twenty-four hours, revolving in the same time with the earth, Peyton Beaumont swung completely round on his axis. As he had decided for the sake of Kate to give up his candidature, so he decided for the sake of his sons, his honor, his party, and his State, to stick to it. He had let go, as it were, to get a better hold. He resolved now that he would fight his very best; that he would beat and smash the chief of the McAlisters utterly; that he would bring down his confidence and pride forever. When General Johnson called again on his political flag-bearer, he found him breathing forth brandy and battle.

"I was all wrong, my old friend," confessed Beaumont. "I had a strange moment of weakness, and I came near committing an error. An error of character," he repeated, quoting from Poinsett, whose subtle distinction he had much admired. "I came near forfeiting my own respect, and I fear yours and all men's. Bless my soul and body, what a muddle it would have been. Well, henceforth, the motto is, Forward."

"Forward to victory, my dear young friend," cackled the General, who, being fifteen years the senior of the two, and yet not feeling himself to be very old, naturally looked upon Beaumont as a man in the springtime of life.

Such was the issue at the Beaumont place of the struggle between the masculine and feminine views of existence.

Meantime the same contest was being carried on in the abode of the rival family. Mrs. McAlister and Mary had discovered that Jenny Devine could not fill the aching void in Frank's heart, and had sorrowfully permitted that young lady to return to her own home. Then they had hoped that his job in mining analysis would divert him, that he would plunge into those mysteries of metallurgy and chemistry which they could not see the sense of, and pasture his hungry soul on a knowledge which to them was but dry husks. But this hope was a poor consolation to them; for what woman can approve of a life without love?

Furthermore, Frank returned from Saxonburg in a moody state; working assiduously, indeed, over his blow-pipe, crucibles, and other infernal machines; but abstracted, and, as his two adorers thought, more gloomy than ever. This last supposition, by the way, was a mistaken one, for the youngster had been much cheered by his meeting with Kate. But as jolly, sympathizing Jenny Devine was no longer at hand to make him laugh over whist and keep him prattling about the subject nearest his heart, he did appear unusually sombre.

Thus the McAlister ladies concluded that nothing would fill his needs but Kate Beaumont, and that without her he must perish from off the face of the earth, or lead only a blighted existence. Of course they were frantic to get hold of the damsel and thrust her into his bosom. But how to do it? Such getting hold was impossible as long as the family quarrel lasted; and the quarrel would endure while the Judge tried to oust Beaumont from Congress. To bring about their sweet purpose, they must controvert the awful will of their lord and master, and trip up his revered political heels. But this sacrilege was horrible to think of, and, what was worse, hard to execute.

"Oppose your father!" said Mrs. McAlister with a spiritual shudder.

"Not precisely that," replied Mary, courageous with the courage of an only daughter. "But you might represent the whole case to him. Perhaps he does not really understand about Frank. After all, Frank is his son."

"Oh, if it was only a family matter, I should deem it my duty not to quail," observed the wife. "But there are the Judge's political plans to be considered," she added with profound respect. "There is this great contest, — the interests of the country."

"It seems to me that the country might get along without us. The country is always in a crisis. It is ridiculous. I almost hate it."

"Mary, you mustn't say such things. Your father would be shocked at you."

"But perhaps he has only looked at the political side of this matter. Why wouldn't it be well to show him both sides? Why isn't it your *duty?*" added Mary, using a word which was very potent with her mother.

And so at last Mrs. McAlister saw her duty, and, seeing it, went with a trembling heart and did it.

To her exposition of Frank's awful state, and of the only device which could pluck him out of it, the Judge listened with his usual bland patience, looking down upon her with the sagacious, benevolent air of an elephant.

"My dear, I am glad you have spoken to me of this matter," he said, precisely as if he had known nothing about it. "Frank's happiness and Frank's prospects," he added, thinking of the Kershaw estate, "certainly deserve my earnest consideration."

Then he meditated quite at his leisure, while his wife quivered with anxiety. He had already satisfied himself that he could not carry the election; he had carefully counted noses on both sides, and come to that disagreeable conclusion. Such being the case, he had coolly and intelligently said to himself, "Can I not sell out my supposed chances to advantage? Beaumont would pay handsomely to have me quit the course; suppose I strike a bargain with him and get something for nothing. I can trust him; he is a straightforward honest brute; much as I dislike him, I can trust him."

Finally, that very morning in fact, he had decided that he would be contented, at least for the present, with a certain vacant judgeship of the United States District Court, looking forward, of course, to quitting it whenever there should be a good chance to jump for something higher. This honor he believed the other party would puissantly recommend him for, on conditioning of his relinquishing his congressional candidature. As for his bargain with that Northern wirepuller, Mr. — Mr. — the Judge really could not remember his name at the moment, — and as for the money of the Democratic National Committee, which he had received and spent, he did not care for such trifles a whiffet. The five thousand dollars had strengthened him in the district; it was seed sown for a future harvest; very good.

The only thing which troubled him was the difficulty of proposing his dicker to Beaumont, without sacrificing his personal dignity. Here, now, was an opportunity; here were the women and the young people ready to aid him; here were the domestic lares and the god of love at his service. He smiled very kindly upon his wife as he pronounced his decision.

"My dear, I will surprise you," he said. "In consideration of what you tell me, I am willing to give up my candidature and take the risk of its doing the good you hope."

Mrs. McAlister advanced to her husband, placed her thin arms about his ponderous shoulders, and gave him an embrace of honester gratitude than he deserved.

"Thank you, my dear," observed the Judge, always a model gentleman, always sensible to a politeness. "We understand one another," he added, as if in irony, but really quite serious. "And now please send Frank to me. Or Bruce. No, let it be Frank. I presume he is most likely to have influence with Beaumont. I will despatch him over there with my message."

An hour later Frank was on his way to the Beaumont house, bearing a letter which Peyton Beaumont was to read, reseal, and return by his hand, the said letter containing of course the Judge's offer, couched in the language of pure patriotism.

A little later still, after Frank had got beyond recall, Mrs. McAlister reappeared before her husband with an anxious face, asking, "My dear, do you think it is safe for him? He is going among our bitter enemies. How could I let him!"

CHAPTER 30

 Matters worked like a seesaw: one end of the feud went down, only to see the other go up; McAlister wanted peace just when Beaumont had taken in fresh fuel for fight.

But with all his sense of the honorableness of wrath, and of the duty of running at his highest speed for Congress, Beaumont could not forget that his wrath and his running might trample on his youngest daughter's chances of happiness. He strove to escape from the piteous remembrance; but he was like a man who scrambles on the slippery footing of adverse dreams; he leaped and leaped, and made no progress. Oh these women, these children; how puissantly we are bound to them; how inextricably the varieties of humanity are entangled; how well for the race that it is so!

This deep-chested, heavy-shouldered, bushy-browed, lion-eyed, pugnacious gentleman not only could not help thinking of his daughter's troubled heart, but could not help talking about it. One day, looking at her as she walked with drooping head in the garden, he turned with an excited start to Mrs. Armitage, and demanded, "What am I to do with that girl? She mopes about here as if her own home were a place of confinement, a prison, or a lunatic asylum, or something of that sort.

ll have to send her over to her grandfather's; that is, till the election is over, and all these confounded uproars."

"Then I shall go too," responded Nellie, promptly and rather spunkily. She had lately had more than one argument with her father in favor of the McAlister match, and she was somewhat irritated because of his persistent opposition to the measure which her heart had desired.

"You will!" exclaimed Beaumont with a stare. He was no longer the hub of the family then; his tribe was to gather around Kate, instead of himself; the new generation was decidedly mounting upon the throne of the old. His face wore an expression of annoyance, but even more of depression.

"Let us talk like men about it, papa," continued Nellie, in her heroic way. "Let us call things by their true names, without any fear of the subject or of each other. Here, because Kate is not happy, you want to send her away from her home, and away from her father and brothers and sister."

"For her own good," broke in Beaumont, eagerly. "Things are going disagreeably here, and she can't want to see them. Besides, Kershaw is her grandfather, and you know how they pet each other. He can cheer her. He is such a kind, good old man! Oh, he is so confoundingly good!" he added with a groan of self-depreciation. "I wish I was half as good. I wish I could respect myself as I do Kershaw."

"Bring him over here," advised Nellie.

"What?"

"Bring him over here, for a few days. And when Major Lawson returns from his visit to Charleston, bring him too. Then Kate will have all her best friends around her, — all but one."

Beaumont did not notice the allusion to Frank McAlister; he was taken up with considering Nellie's plan, and with dreading it. Kershaw, that great pacificator of quarrels, he did not quite want him in the house just now. From such a presence there might emanate an influence which would once more beguile him into the weakness of resigning his candidature and washing off his war-paint generally. But after due argument and solicitation, after it had been borne in upon him that the old Colonel, in the temporary absence of Lawson, must be leading a dreary life in his own house, he withdrew an opposition for which he could not allege his reasons and of which he was secretly ashamed. Riding over to Kershaw's place, he invited his father-in-law to visit him for a fortnight, pressing the point with his characteristic cordiality and hospitality, and securing an acceptance. So the next morning the Colonel alighted from his carriage on the gravel-walk before the Beaumont door.

"Isn't he beautiful, papa?" whispered Kate, as she and her father hastened to greet their venerable visitor.

"He is the white rose of South Carolinian chivalry," murmured Beaumont. "Not a leaf fallen by reason of age, and not a stain by reason of sin."

The sympathetic and passionate nature of this rough fighter enabled him to appreciate and worship a character which was beyond him.

In truth, the Colonel was beautiful, as healthy and good old men can be beautiful. He had fully recovered from his late severe illness; to look at him, it seemed as if he might live twenty years longer. His white hair, waving over his heavy, old-fashioned coat-collar, was as yet abundant and almost luxuriant. His massive aquiline face, rendered only the more expressive by deep wrinkles and large folds, was full of dignity, intelligence, and sympathy. Eighty or nearly eighty years of the life of this world, so generally commonplace, so often full of temptation, so often sorrowful or exasperating, had not dimmed the sunshine of that benignity which must have been the core of his character. He looked as George Washington might have looked, had he reached the same age. He made one think of what an angel might be, could an angel become white-haired and wrinkled. Very tall, and as yet of goodly fulness, he seemed a colossal statue erected to physical beauty and moral worth, grown venerable.

Kate soon took possession of her pet, and led him to his room. She wanted to have him all to herself, and she wanted the luxury of serving him with her own hands. After prattling for some minutes, after seeing anew that he was furnished with everything which he could need, she left him to wash off the dust of his drive and went below to wait for him, her eyes sparkling with impatience. Presently she ran and called up the stairway, "Grandpapa, are you never going to come down?" As he did not answer, probably not hearing her, she hurried to his door, drummed on it with eager fingers, and said in a tone of loving reproach, "Why, how long you are!"

That was always the way with her when Kershaw came over. She was as impatient to get at him and as greedy of his company as a hungry child is impatient and greedy for its dinner. Moreover, she had absurd, charming little terrors, if he were long at a time out of her sight, lest he had hurt himself, or perhaps died. When she was a child and visited him for short terms at his plantation, she used to say, night after night, "Promise me, grandpapa, that you won't die before morning," The benignant and affectionate old man, so like her lost mother, and indeed so like herself, exercised a sort of bewitchment over her, which was all the more potent because it had begun before the dawn of reason, because it had begun as an instinct. It was in vain that her other relatives sometimes jealously chafed because of this fascination, and sometimes good-humoredly laughed at her for it. On this point she remained sweetly childish, and could not be otherwise, nor wish it.

The bewitchment was mutual, as such affectionate magic often is. Despite his rational, grave, and one might say rather slow nature, the old man worshipped the girl as the girl worshipped him. At this moment, when he heard the well-known and expected drumming on his door, his solemn blue eyes and massive folds of his face lighted up with a deep, serene pleasure.

"Come in, my little girl," his hollow and tremulous voice called. "I am only brushing my hair."

"Let me brush it," begged Kate; and would do it, making him sit for the purpose.

"It needs cutting, doesn't it?" asked the Colonel, who was in the habit of seeking her guidance, at least in little matters.

"Not yet," said Kate. "It is too handsome to cut."

"Handsome?" asked Kershaw, thinking of her chestnut curls.

"It is every bit as white as snow," continued the girl. "It makes me think of Mont Blanc. What color was it once?"

"A little darker than yours, child, if I remember right," said the old man, after pausing a moment to send his memory backward many years. "There, you have taken trouble enough with it. Now sit down where I can look at you."

"Wait a little," begged Kate. She was intent upon making the silver cataract fall behind his ears and roll evenly over his coat-collar. The work done, she drew a childlike sigh of satisfaction, and seating herself in front of him, smiled in his face. Her smile, could he have understood its under-sadness, would have told him that she loved him all the more because the out-reachings of affection towards another had been rudely put aside.

"You don't look in good flesh," said the Colonel. His phrase was old-fashioned, but it suited his venerable mien, and it was made sweet by a tone of tender anxiety.

"I am a little thinner than usual," replied Kate. A spasm passed across her mouth, but she quelled it by an heroic effort, and presently the smile reappeared.

"If you are ill, you must tell me," urged Kershaw. "We must have advice."

He knew nothing of her love-affair, and suspected nothing; even the garrulous, sympathetic Lawson had refrained from hinting it to him.

"Grandpapa, you are always thinking about other people," observed the girl, willing to change the subject of conversation.

"Of course," he replied, simply. "My own affairs are of so little interest."

At this moment Kate's face turned as pale as death. Glancing out of a window near her, she had seen Frank McAlister dismounting at the gate, and the idea at once crossed her mind that his life was in peril.

"What is the matter?" inquired Kershaw, who noted her start and dimly perceived her change of color.

"Oh, do go down there," she begged, springing to her feet and seizing his arm. "Do go, before there is trouble."

"What is it?" he repeated, slowly rising.

"I don't know," stammered Kate. "What can he be here for? It is Mr. Frank McAlister."

"McAlister!" exclaimed Kershaw, in a tone which showed that he realized the full gravity of the situation. "The young man, — the tall young man? I remember. The one who saved your life. Of course I remember him. But he shouldn't be here. I will go down."

"Oh, do, do," implored the girl, almost hurrying him, almost pushing him. "Don't let any trouble happen."

"No, no," said Kershaw, as he stalked out of the room, leaning forward in the manner of old men when they are in haste. "But what can he be here for? It is highly imprudent."

We shall best see the end of this adventure by joining Frank McAlister. Dismounting at the high post gate which whitely glared in front of the house, he left his horse in charge of one of half a dozen pickaninnies who were kicking up the dust of the road with their bare black feet, and walked straight towards the veranda, where stood Peyton Beaumont grimly staring at him, a statue of mistrust and amazement. When he had got within a few yards of his father's rival and enemy he halted, lifted his hat entirely from his head, and bowed without speaking. At the same moment Tom Beaumont came out of the door behind his father, and, seeing this most unexpected and somewhat alarming visitor, slipped a practised hand under the skirt of his shooting-jacket, obviously feeling for the handle of a pistol. Frank noted the threatening gesture; but he did not change countenance, nor move a muscle; he remained with his eyes fixed on the face of Peyton. The latter, after hesitating for a moment, slightly waved his hand in salutation.

"Mr. Beaumont, I beg leave to deliver you a friendly letter from my father," said Frank.

"From your father, sir!" exclaimed Peyton. He reflected for an instant, thought of his political confederates, thought of the feud, too, and added, "I do not feel at liberty to receive it, sir."

Tom Beaumont drew his derringer, supposing that Frank would draw also, and determined to be beforehand with him. But just then Colonel Kershaw stepped slowly into the veranda and laid his hand gently on the elbow of the aristocratic young desperado. Tom glanced sidewise, recognized the old man, and slowly returned the weapon to his pocket, still however keeping his hand on it, while he watched Frank steadily.

"Am I intruding, Beaumont?" asked Kershaw.

"Ah!" started Beaumont. "Why no, certainly not. In my house you are in your own. And by the way, Kershaw, by the way — Mr. McAlister, have the kindness to wait one instant. — Kershaw, I want your advice. A letter from the Judge," he whispered, blowing out his cheeks with an air of demanding amazement. "Shall I open it? *Would* you? Would you, *indeed?* Well, perhaps so; decidedly so. Just to see what the scoundrel wants. Exactly."

Turning to Frank, he said with ceremonious civility: "Mr. McAlister, by the advice of Colonel Kershaw, I will now, with your permission, receive the letter. If I was discourteous to you personally in my first refusal, I ask excuse."

He read the Judge's communication with mingled feelings. First came the expression of that gentleman's desire to resign his candidature to Congress for the sake of the peace of Hartland and the unity of South Carolina. Beaumont approved. He approved promptly, fully, and energetically; for once he was harmonious with Duncan McAlister. But next came the hint that, in return for this concession, a seat in the United States District Court would be acceptable. Beaumont hesitated; there were good men of his own party to be thought of; his brow darkened with an ominous look of dissent. Then he went through his rival's elegantly written, dignified, and almost pathetic peroration. It moved him; the expression of noble sentiments always moved him; he was just to that degree simple and sympathetic. Well, what should he do? Obviously it was his personal interest to close with the bargain, and so get rid of his rival in the coming election. But he was not an ordinary politician; he was honest, high-minded, and unselfish, at least so far as he knew how to be; if he was ever moved by interest, it was unawares. Thus he had no difficulty in putting aside this egotistic consideration immediately.

On the other hand, here was a favor; the Judge was going to give up his candidature in any event; and surely he deserved a favor in return. The fact that he could say to Beaumont, "You ought to have the seat in Congress," made Beaumont want to say, "You ought to have the vacant judgeship." The heart of this impulsive, unreflecting, headlong knight-errant began to warm towards his rival and enemy. He had scarcely read his letter through before he desired to serve him. He became, as it were, his partisan. To be sure, old bellicose feelings boiled and bubbled somewhat in his heart; but they were kept down in a measure by thoughts of Kate and of Kershaw. On this score the impulses of peace and war remained in even balance.

"This is very important," he observed, turning to the old Colonel. "Kershaw, I must have your advice. Mr. McAlister, will you do me the kindness to walk into my parlor. Tom, oblige me by seeing that we are not interrupted."

In the parlor he seated his guests, closed the doors, and then approached Frank.

"Mr. McAlister," he said, "Colonel Kershaw's character —"

"It is sufficient," bowed Frank. "I am confident that my father would be willing to intrust any secret to Colonel Kershaw."

Then the letter was read aloud. A blush inundated Frank's face when he heard Beaumont clarion forth his father's demand for a *quid pro quo*, offering to dicker his chance for Congress against a seat in the temple of justice. For a minute or two he could not look Kershaw or Kate's father in the face. His shame was only in part removed by Beaumont's calm consideration of the bargain and charitable comment upon it. Beaumont, it must be understood, was by this time quite impulsively in favor of the Judge, looking upon himself as the patron of his rival, and desiring to do him a good turn.

"Wishes to withdraw from politics, you see," he remarked blandly. "Well, it is about time I should do the same. After this campaign, Kershaw, — after this campaign, you may rely on me. No more candidatures, no more stumpings."

If he meant to make a bridge of gold for a retreating enemy, he certainly did his engineering rather neatly. The truth is, that, being now anxious to accept his rival's offer, he was anxious to have Kershaw advise him to accept it.

The good old man responded to the wish from good motives of his own. He saw a chance before him to turn the swords and spears of the feud into the ploughshares and pruning-hooks of amity.

"I approve of the proposition," he said slowly and after deliberate consideration. "Judge McAlister is better fitted for the position in question than any other man in the upper country. He is our ablest lawyer and our most judicial mind."

"I have always admitted it," Beaumont declared, and with entire truth. "He deserves the place."

"In appointments to the judiciary there should be no question of partisan politics," affirmed Kershaw.

"Certainly not," assented Beaumont. "By heavens! the President who should consider politics, in making appointments to the judiciary, ought to be impeached and deposed."

There was no questioning his honesty in saying this. He looked like truth incarnate, and none the less for his bellicose expression.

"What a gentleman he is at bottom," thought Frank, only too glad to judge kindly of Kate's father.

"Why didn't we come to this before?" continued Beaumont, delighted that he had secured Kershaw's adherence, and quite resolved now to back McAlister. "I shall rejoice in recommending the Judge to a position which he will fill so nobly. And so will my friends I am confident. By heavens! if they don't I won't run for them; I'll throw up my candidature immediately; I will, by heavens! Kershaw, I want you to bear witness to that, and stand by me in it," he added, remembering that giving up candidatures did not come easy to him.

"I think our friends will make no objections," said the Colonel, knowing that Beaumont's will and his own would be law to the party in the district.

"I should say not," answered Peyton, swelling and ruffling at the idea of opposition. By heavens! I should like to see the man who would be fool enough and brute enough to object to such an appointment," he went on, forgetting that he would himself have opposed it but for circumstances. "Well, it is understood. Mr. McAlister, please do me the favor to say to your father that I assent most cordially to his chivalrous proposition. I make this declaration in the presence of Colonel Kershaw. If I made it alone, I would be equally bound by it. And now, Mr. McAlister, a glass of wine together."

He fairly beamed upon the young man. The moment that he could be friends with him at all, he was as much his friend as he ever had been. He inclined towards him with all the vivacious promptness of his mercurial, yet energetic nature. He let himself remember distinctly that this was the man who had saved his daughter's life, and with whom his daughter's chance of happiness was perhaps intertwined. There was no mistaking the kindliness which glowed in his martial black eyes and his dark red visage. Frank was instantaneously as happy as a king is vulgarly supposed to be.

"I am more gratified than I can possibly express," he said, in a tone which told infinitely more than the words.

After the sherry had been tasted, the young man rose to take his leave, remarking, "I must carry this good news to my father."

"Add that I cannot sufficiently thank him for sending you on this mission," said Peyton, shaking hands.

"I entirely concur with Beaumont in sentiment," added Kershaw in his brief, weighty way, few words always, but every one doubly meant.

"I trust that this begins a lasting peace," ventured Frank.

Beaumont could not decide at once what to answer; but the Colonel, pressing the youngster's hand warmly, said, "I trust so."

Frank glanced gratefully at his benign face and glorious crown of white hair, admiring him as noble young men do admire noble old ones, and thinking him too good for this world.

In the entry hall they encountered Nellie, who, seeing these demonstrations of amity, saluted Frank with a smile and a few words of commonplace civility.

During this brief moment Peyton Beaumont had one of those revulsions of feeling or opinion to which he was subject. A doubt, a scruple, troubled his sense of honor. He had been accustomed to call Judge McAlister an old fox, a carthaginian, a perfidious rascal. Would a man whom he had thus stigmatized, and as he believed properly stigmatized, be the right man for the district court bench? Would he render just judgment, and honor the Beaumont recommendation? "What do you think, Kershaw?"

The Colonel had none of Peyton's hereditary prejudice against the McAlisters. He replied gently and gravely, "Have no fears, Beaumont. Whatever McAlister may be as a politician, in his official character he is a gentleman. There is not a stain upon his professional honor. You have done well."

"Kershaw, you relieve me inexpressibly," nodded Peyton with a sigh of deep satisfaction. Then, advancing quickly to Frank, he took his hand and said, "I trust, with you, that this begins a lasting peace."

As the young man heard this phrase, which filled him with inexpressible joy, he heard also a rapid step in the veranda. He did not turn, but the others did, and saw Randolph Armitage advancing, his hand under his coat as if seeking a pistol, and his drunken, fierce eyes fixed on Frank McAlister.

CHAPTER 31

 It must be remembered that Randolph Armitage had passed several days on the verge of *delirium tremens,* either caring nothing for the exodus of his wife and children, or unaware of it.

But on recovering his wits he wanted his Israel back, as is apt to be the case with abandoned Pharaohs of our household Egypts, however vicious and unloving they may be. It is such a disgrace to be deserted, and involves such a diminution of sweet authority, besides loss of domestic comforts! — Conceited, confident in himself, passionately wilful and headlong, he soon determined to go in pursuit of Nellie, believing that at the sight of him she would fall under the old fascination and return to her wifely allegiance.

Sober when he left home, Randolph was quiet in demeanor and even somewhat anxious in spirit. He feared lest his wife or her sister might have told tales on him; and, if such were the case, he would probably have to listen to a remonstrance from "old man Beaumont"; and he knew that when that gentleman did remonstrate, it was in the style of a tornado. But with the fatuity of a shallow soul, incapable of appreciating its own scoundrelism, or of putting itself fairly in the place of another, he trusted that he could easily turn wrath into favor by a week of sobriety and of the superfine deportment which he prided himself on being able to assume.

At Brownville he heard for the first time that Frank had met Nellie there and gone on with her to Hartland. The news was angering; the man, being a McAlister, had no right to travel with *his* family; moreover, it looked as if he had helped the woman to run away. Randolph took a dram and then several drams. By the time the train started (it was early in the morning, observe) he was in a state to go on drinking. He treated himself at every station, and he accepted treats from fellow-passengers who carried bottles in their wayfarings, as is the genial habit of certain Southerners. Long before he reached Hartland he was fit to shoot an enemy on sight, and to see an enemy in the first man who stared at him. He forgot that the object of his journey was to wheedle back his wife to her married wretchedness. His inflamed brain settled down upon the idea that it was his duty as a gentleman to chastise Frank McAlister for abetting Nellie's elopement, and for daring to associate himself to Beaumonts. Clenching his fists and muttering, he carried on imaginary conversations with that criminal, reproving him for his impertinence and threatening punishment.

"You've no call to speak to a Beaumont," he babbled, identifying himself with the famous family feud, for which when sober he did not care a picayune. "My wife is a Beaumont, sir. She's above you, sir. My people have nothing to do with your people. I'm a Beaumont — by kinsmanship. You sha'n't travel with my wife, sir. You sha'n't go in the same car with her. You sha'n't lead her away from her home and her husband. We'll settle this matter, sir. We'll settle it now, sir." And so on.

At the Hartland station his first inquiry was for Mr. Frank McAlister. "Never saw him in my life," he explained. "Don't know him from Adam. But he's a tall fellow. He's a blackguard. I'm after him, I'm on his trail. Seen anything of him?"

Frank's person was more exactly described to him by a little, red-eyed, seedy old gentleman, who seemed to be doing "the dignified standing round" in the grocery attached to the station, and in whom we may no doubt recognize General Johnson. The General, smelling an affair of honor, and always willing to give chivalry a lift, made prompt inquiries as to the whereabouts of young McAlister, and presently brought word that he had lately been seen riding in the direction of the Beaumont territories.

"Gone to attack my relatives!" muttered the drunkard, honestly believing at the moment that he loved the Beaumonts. "I'll help them. I'm on his trail. I'll be there."

He was mad as Don Quixote. He was in a state to succor people who did not want to be succored, and to right wrongs which had never been given, and to see a caitiff in every chance comer. He was one of those knight-errants who are created by the accolade of a bottle.

Reaching the castle which he meant to save, just as Frank, Beaumont, and Kershaw came out of it, he had no difficulty in recognizing his proposed victim. The obvious amicableness of the interview did not in the least enlighten this lunatic. In the smiling and happy young man, who was shaking hands with the master of the house, he could only see a villain who had deeply injured himself, and who was now assaulting or insulting his connections. Clapping his hand on the butt of his revolver, he strode, or rather staggered, towards Frank, scarcely observing Beaumont and Kershaw.

It was a singular scene. Frank McAlister, who did not know Armitage by sight, and did not at all suspect danger to himself, towered calmly like a colossal statue, his grave blue eyes just glancing at this menacing apparition, and then turning a look of inquiry upon Beaumont. The white-haired Kershaw, nearly as tall as Frank, was gazing blandly into the face of the young man, unconscious that anything strange was happening, his whole air full of benignity and satisfaction. Beaumont, the only one of the three who both saw and recognized the intruder, had turned squarely to face him, eyes flaming, eyebrows bristling, and hands clenched. It must be remembered that he hated Armitage as a man who had filled Nellie's life with wretchedness. At the first glimpse of his insolent approach and air of menace he had been filled with such rage, that if he had had a pistol he would perhaps have shot him instantly. In a certain sense he would have been pardonable for such action, for he supposed that the drunkard's charge was directed against himself. There he stood, undismayed and savage; all the more defiant, because the odds were against him; all the grimmer because he was unarmed, gouty, and in no case for battle; as heroic an old Tartar as ever scowled in the face of death. When the reeling desperado was within six feet of him he thundered out, "You scoundrel!"

Armitage made no answer to Beaumont, and merely stared at him with an indescribably stupid leer, not unlike the stolid, savage grin of an angry baboon. Then, lurching a little to one side, he passed him and pushed straight towards Frank, at the same time drawing his revolver. Halting with difficulty, he looked up in the astonished face of the young giant, and demanded in a sort of yell, "What y' here for?"

"I don't understand you, sir," replied Frank. "I don't know you."

"What does this mean?" exclaimed Beaumont, suddenly realizing that his guest's life was threatened, and trying to step between him and Armitage.

"Let me alone," screamed the drunkard. "He's run away with my wife."

The coarse suspicion thus flung upon Nellie inflamed her father to fury. Without a word he seized his son-in-law, pushed him toward the low steps which led down from the veranda, and sent him rolling upon the gravelled walk at their base.

Frank had no weapons. He had come unarmed into the house of the hereditary enemies of his house. He had resolved to put it beyond his power to do battle, even in self-defence, under the roof of Kate's father. But he now stepped forward hastily, calling out, "This is my affair, Mr. Beaumont."

Kershaw stopped him, placing both hands on his arms, and saying, "You are our guest. I do not understand this quarrel. But we are responsible for your safety."

At the same moment Beaumont hastened to the door and shouted, "Tom! Vincent! Nellie! Here, somebody! Bring me my pistols!"

Then he turned to look, for a shot had been fired. The overthrown maniac, even while struggling to rise, had discharged one barrel of his revolver, aiming, however, as a drunken man would naturally aim, and missing his mark. Kershaw let go of Frank, stepped a little aside and sat down in a rustic chair, as if overcome by the excitement of the scene, or by the weakness of age. Thus freed for action, the youngster plunged towards his unknown and incomprehensible enemy, with the intention of disarming him. Two more shots missed him, and then there was a struggle. Of course it was brief; the inebriate went down almost instantly; his pistol was wrenched out of his hand and flung away;

next a heavy knee was on his breast and a hard fist in his neckcloth.

At this moment the younger Beaumonts, aroused by the firing and by the call of their father, swarmed out upon the veranda, every one with his cocked pistol. Seeing their brother-in-law (of whose domestic misconduct they knew nothing) under the hostile hands of a McAlister, they naturally inferred that here was a fresh outbreak of the feud, and rushed forward to rescue their relative.

"Stop, gentlemen," called Kershaw, but he was not heard.

"Boys! boys!" shouted Beaumont, limping after them down the steps. "You don't understand it, boys."

All might have been explained, and further trouble avoided, but at this moment there arrived a rescue for Frank, a rescue which comprehended nothing, and so did harm. It seems that Bruce and Wallace McAlister, learning from their mother what mission their brother had gone upon, and having little confidence in the sense or temper or good faith of their ancient foes, had decided to mount and follow up the adventure. When Armitage's first pistol-shot resounded, they were in ambush behind a grove not three hundred yards distant. A few seconds more saw them dashing up to the gate which fronted the veranda, and blazing away with their revolvers at the Beaumonts, who were hurrying towards Frank. A sharp exclamation from Tom told that one bullet had taken effect.

"Come here, brother!" shouted Wallace. "Run for your horse."

Frank sprang to his feet and stared about him in bewilderment. He saw Tom handling his wounded arm; he saw Vincent and Poinsett aiming towards the road; turning his head, he saw Bruce and Wallace, also aiming. It was the feud once more; the two families were slaughtering each other; all hope of peace was perishing in blood. At the top of his speed he ran towards his brothers, calling, "You are mistaken. Stop, stop!"

Vincent fired after him. Poinsett, pacific as he was, discharged several barrels, but rather at the men on horseback than at Frank. Tom picked up his pistol with his sound arm and joined in the skirmish. The two McAlisters in the highway, sitting calmly on their plunging horses, returned bullet for bullet. At least thirty shots were exchanged in as many seconds. That amateur of ferocities, chivalrous old General Johnson, ought to have been there to cure his sore eyes with the spectacle. Never before had there been such a general battle between the rival families as was this hasty, unforeseen, unpremeditated combat, the result of a misunderstanding growing naturally out of lifelong hostility. Peyton Beaumont alone, knowing that the *mêlée* was one huge blunder, took no part in it, and indeed tried hard to stop it, calling, "Gentlemen, gentlemen! Hear me one instant."

When Frank reached his brothers there was a streak of blood down his cheek from a pistol-shot scratch across his temple. Moreover, he was in peril of further harm, for Randolph Armitage had regained his feet, and followed him, and was now reeling through the gate with a drawn bowie-knife.

"For God's sake, stop!" implored Frank, unaware both of his wound and his danger. "It was not the Beaumonts who attacked me. It was some drunken brute!"

Wallace made no reply except to spur past his brother upon the pursuing Armitage and knock him senseless with a pistol butt blow over the head.

"Mount your horse," shouted Bruce. "They are reloading. Mount your horse."

"I must go and explain," cried Frank, turning back. "I forbid you to fire," he added in a terrible voice. "Don't you see *her?*"

His dilated eyes were fixed upon Kate Beaumont, who, with the aid of a negro, was leading Kershaw into the house. When she had disappeared and he believed that she was in safety, he lifted his clasped hands toward heaven, and reeled as if he would have fallen.

"Come, Frank," begged Wallace, throwing his broken pistol at him in his desperation. "Do you want us all shot here? Mount your horse."

In his confusion and anguish of soul, just understanding that his brothers would not leave him, and that he must ride with them to save their lives, the young man sprang into his saddle and galloped away.

"I ought to go back," he said, after he had traversed a few rods. "I must know if anything has happened to them."

"This is the second time that you have barely escaped being assassinated by those savages," replied Bruce, sternly. "If you are not a maniac, you will come with us."

"Oh, it was a horrible mistake," groaned Frank. "You meant well, but you were mistaken. The Beaumonts did not attack me. It was that madman."

"That was Randolph Armitage," said Wallace. "Do you mean the fellow that I knocked down? That was Peyt Beaumont's son-in-law. He is another of the murdering tribe. They are all of a piece."

Perplexed as well as wretched, Frank made no reply, and dashed on after his brothers. The retreat was a rapid one, although two of the horses were wounded, and Bruce had received a shot in the thigh which made riding painful. As there was now only one pistol among the McAlisters, and as their enemies were well armed and had fast steeds within easy call, it was well to distance pursuit.

But the Beaumonts did not think of giving chase; they were paralyzed by the shock of an immense calamity.

At the firing of the first shot Kate was sitting by a window of her own bedroom, looking out upon the yard through a loop in the curtain. We may guess that her object was to get an unobserved glance at Frank McAlister when he should remount his horse and ride away. She had so much confidence in her grandfather's influence, that she did not expect trouble.

The first pistol shot surprised her into a violent fright. To her imagination the feud was always at hand; it was a prophet of evil uttering incessant menaces; it was an assassin ever ready for slaughter. Her instantaneous thought was that the old quarrel had broken out in a deadly combat between her pugnacious brothers and the man of whom she knew full well at the moment that she loved him. She could not see the veranda from her window, and she hurried down stairs into the front-entry hall. There she heard her father's voice calling for pistols, and beheld her sister running one way and her brothers another. In her palpitating anxiety to learn what this turmoil meant she stepped into the veranda, and there discovered Frank McAlister holding down Randolph Armitage. Next she heard a faint voice, — a voice familiar to her and yet somehow strange, — saying earnestly, "My dear, go in; you will be hurt."

Turning her head, she beheld her grandfather in the rustic chair, motioning her back. Had she looked at him closely, she would have perceived that he was very pale, and that he had the air of a man grievously ill or injured. But she was in no condition to see clearly; the hurry and fright of the occasion made everything vague to her; she recognized outlines and little more. Accustomed to obey her venerable relative's slightest wish, she sprang into the house and shielded herself behind a doorpost. Then came the sally of her brothers; then the trampling of horses arriving at full speed, and the calling of strange voices from the road; then a cracking of pistol-shots, a hissing of bullets, and a shouting of combatants. She was in an agony of terror, or rather of anxiety, believing that all those men out there were being killed, and screaming convulsively in response to the discharges. Without knowing it, she was struggling to get into the veranda; and without knowing it, she was being held back by her sister.

Next followed a lull. Nellie leaped through the doorway, and Kate at once leaped after her. There were her father and her brothers; they were staring after Frank McAlister and his brothers; these last were already turning away. She did not see Tom's bleeding arm, nor the prostrate Randolph Armitage. Her impression was that every one had escaped harm, and she uttered a shriek of hysterical joy.

But when she turned to look for her grandfather, she was paralyzed with horror. His face was of dusky or ashy pallor, and he seemed to be sinking from his seat. For a moment she could not go to him; she stood staring at him with outstretched arms; her whole life seemed to be centered in her dilated eyes. Then seeing black Cato step out of a window and approach the old man with an air of alarm, she also ran forward and threw herself on her knees before him, with the simple cry of "Oh grandpapa!"

He was so faint with the shock of his wound and the loss of blood, that he could not answer her and probably could not see her. He sat there inert and apparently unconscious, his grand old head drooping upon his chest, and his long silver hair falling around his face.

Of a sudden Kate, who had been on the point of fainting, was endowed with immense strength. Aided only by the negro boy, who trembled and whimpered, "Oh Mars Kershaw! Mars Kershaw!" she lifted the ponderous frame of her grandfather, and led him reeling into the house.

CHAPTER 32

 By the time that Kate and the negro had laid the Colonel on a settee in the broad entry, he was in a dead faint.

The girl, believing that life was extinct, fell on her knees by his side, clasping one of his drooping hands in both hers, and staring at his ashy face with dilated eyes, the whites showing clear around the iris. Feeling, presently, a little flutter at his wrist, she regained some hope, but only so much hope, only such a terrible hope, as to gasp, "He is dying."

Just then the Beaumont men, getting news in some way of the catastrophe, hurried into the hall one after the other and gathered around the senseless octogenarian. Peyton was for a moment so overcome by the calamity that he actually lost his head and called like a frightened child, "Kershaw! Kershaw!" Then, catching sight of Vincent, he turned sharply upon him and demanded, "Why don't you see to him?"

"He is living," replied the young man, who, it will be remembered, had been bred a physician. "Cato, bring some wine and cold water. He has swooned away entirely. He must have been hit early."

"In my house!" groaned Peyton. "My best friend shot in my own house!"

"Why didn't he call for help?" wondered Tom. "An old gentleman like that —"

"Ah, Tom, you don't know him," muttered the father. "He isn't the man to call for help when his friends are under fire."

"Are none of you going to do anything?" sobbed Kate, turning a piteous and reproachful stare from face to face.

"My dear sister, he has simply fainted," replied Vincent. "The wound is in the thigh, and probably a mere flesh wound. Let go of him now, and let us get him to bed."

By this time the hall was crowded with the house-servants, most of them uttering suppressed whimpers of grief, for Kershaw was worshipped by these poor people. Under the direction of Vincent, four of the strongest men took up the settee with its heavy load and bore it to a bedroom, followed by the trembling and crying Kate.

"I say, Vincent," whispered Tom. "When you get through with him, take a look at me. I want to know if any bones are smashed."

"You hit?" stared the elder brother. He took hold of the wounded arm, moved it up and down, and added, "It's all right, Tom. Nothing broken."

Meantime Beaumont senior was glowering about him and asking, "Where the deuce is Nellie?"

"She's jess done gone out to look after Mars Ranney, what's out thar in the ditch," explained Cato.

"Ah!" grunted Peyton; "that's what I wanted to tell her. Drunken beast! I hope he's dead."

A little later his heart smote him for thus leaving his eldest daughter to face her perplexities and troubles alone. He sought her out and found that she had already caused her husband to be carried to her room and laid on her bed.

"Nellie," he whispered, just glancing with aversion at the soiled, bloody, and still insensible drunkard. "I don't want to be hard. He can stay here till he is able to go. But no longer, Nellie; at least I prefer not. He is the cause of all this. But for him there would have been no difficulty. Besides, he has been such a brute to you, — such a cruel, insulting brute! I don't feel that I can have him here long."

There were tears in Nellie's eyes. It is not easy for a woman to look at blood and suffering without pity. As she gazed at Randolph's disfigured face and thought that possibly he might be dying, she could not help remembering that he had once been Handsome Armitage, and that it was not many years since it had been her greatest joy to worship him. Much reason as she had for despising and abhorring him, there had come into her heart now some sympathy and tenderness, and she had almost thought that she might again endure, might even again love him. Nevertheless, she was rational; she admitted that her father was right; the man must not stay long in this house.

"I ask nothing more," she said, shaking her head hysterically. "Only that you will please send for a physician. I don't want him to die like a dog."

"He shall not," replied Beaumont, seizing and pressing her arm. "Send yourself for everything you want."

Hurrying now to Kershaw's room, he found that the old man had recovered his consciousness, and was able to speak.

"Ah, my dear friend, you are quite yourself again," exclaimed Beaumont, his grim face brightening with a joy which made it beautiful.

"We will hope for the best," murmured Kershaw. In reality he had little confidence; there were pains in his body which led him to believe that the ball had glanced upwards and made a mortal wound; but Kate's eyes were fixed on him with a piteous anxiety which would not allow him to utter forebodings.

"Oh my dear!" she sighed, partly divining the affectionate heroism of this sublime utterance, and thanking him for it by pressing his wrinkled hand against her wet face.

"Do not be troubled, my little girl," he continued, noticing her tears. "Even if the worst comes, it is well. I have lived a long while with you. I have seen you grow up. It is a great deal. I was an old man when you were born."

"You were already wounded when you told me to go in," said Kate. "Oh, why didn't I see it then?"

"It would have made little difference," he replied. "I could wait."

It was evident that he spoke with difficulty, and that his faintness was returning.

"Here, take this, Kershaw," interposed Beaumont, pouring out a glass of wine. "My dear child, you must not make him talk, and I think you had better go. She can't help talking to you, Kershaw; she never could."

"Oh, don't take me away!" implored the girl, rendered childish in mind and speech by her grief. "I won't say a word."

"She will do me no harm," whispered the invalid. "She helps me."

Presently, recovering his strength a little, he added in a clear voice, "Don't trouble yourself, my dear Beaumont. You will suffer with this standing. Sit down."

Quite overcome by this thoughtfulness for himself at such a moment, Peyton turned away with the spasmodic grimace of a man who struggles not to weep. When he had somewhat regained his calmness, he dropped wearily into an arm-chair, and gazed at Kershaw with humid eyes.

The spectacle was worthy of his or of any man's wonder and worship. In that dusky face, seeming already stained with death, — in that noble face, sublimely sweet with native goodness and with the good thoughts and deeds of a long life, — there was not a look, not even a passing paroxysm of selfishness. Neither pain, nor the loss of vital power, nor the belief that he was drawing near his end, could make Kershaw utter a complaint or a claim for pity. If he had words that were pathetic, it was because they were touching with self-forgetfulness, eloquent with sympathy for others.

After a while Dr. Mattieson, who had been sent for in all haste, was shown in by Vincent. Beaumont and Kate had to leave the chamber in order to allow of a thorough examination of the wound. "Will they hurt him?" asked the daughter in the crying tone of a grieving child; and then, without waiting for an answer, she fled to her room and locked the door. Meantime the father walked softly up and down the hall, expecting evil tidings, but striving to hope. At last Vincent came out with a grave face.

"What is it?" demanded Beaumont, dragging the young man aside. "Not bad, I hope."

"Very bad," said Vincent. "The ball has glanced upward and probably penetrated the abdomen. There is only too much danger of peritonitis, and of death."

"Death!" whispered Beaumont, his ruddy face turning to a brownish pallor. "Oh my God, no, Vincent!" he absolutely begged, smiting his nails into his palms. "We can't have it so. Kershaw to die! Kershaw murdered in my house! Oh no, Vincent!"

His first thought was grief; his next was vengeance. His eyes were reddened with tears, but they were also bloodshot with rage.

"Oh, what an account those brutes have opened for themselves!" he went on hoarsely. "They have murdered the noblest man I ever knew. Murdered my best friend. What an account — in the next world — and in this! God will remember them. But I can't leave it to him," he burst out, after a pause. "I and my boys must take them in hand. Lest God should forget," he added, wiping away with his short, thick, hairy hand the sweat of grief and wrath which stood on his dark forehead.

Vincent made no demonstrations and muttered few words. He was a calmer and more taciturn man than his father, and valued himself on doing more than he looked or said. He scarcely scowled and his voice was almost soft as he replied, "No one will blame us, whatever happens."

"You are right," returned Beaumont. "Public opinion will be with us. Hartland can't support desperadoes who shoot such men as Kershaw."

Presently a new thought and a very painful one startled him for a moment out of these ideas of vengeance.

"Who will tell this to Kate?" he asked. Almost immediately he added with vehemence, "I can't."

Vincent, though not a sensitive or very affectionate being, was perplexed and made no answer.

"She worships her grandfather," groaned Beaumont. "I can't tell her he is going to die."

Still Vincent offered no suggestion. "I *won't* tell her," decided the father. "Time will let her know all."

"It is the best way," assented Vincent. "Distribute a great emotion over as many pulsations as possible. It is generally the best way."

During the afternoon Kershaw rallied a little, and even the physicians began to have faint hopes of him, impossible as it seemed that so old a man could survive such a wound. But early in the evening the horrible agony of peritonitis, or inflammation of the abdominal case, declared itself. Wonderful as was the self-control of the invalid, he could not help moaning and writhing under his torture. No sleep; opiates could not render nature insensible to that pain; all night he was conscious and on the rack.

When in the morning Kate succeeded in fighting her way with tears and pleadings to his bedside, he was a pitiable spectacle. His face had fallen; his forehead, nose, and chin were prominent; his eyes were of a leaden blue, and surrounded by dark circles; his complexion, notwithstanding the fever, was ashy and deathlike. His natural expression of benignity had been so changed by long straining against intolerable anguish, that, had the girl seen him thus otherwise, she would not at once have recognized him.

Now and then there was a moan; it was a feeble one, it is true, because he tried still to hold himself under restraint; but, breaking as it did through a life-long habit of self-command, it was significant of immense agony. It was like the last ripple, the feeble remnant of a mighty wave, which dies almost without noise among the reeds of a sloping shore. Little in itself, it told of a tempest.

"My dear," he whispered to Kate as she sat down paralyzed by his side. "I wish to see our clergyman."

"Oh, you are not going to die," she burst out, wringing her hands.

"My dear, have they not told you?" he answered. "Doubtless they meant it in kindness. Neither did they tell me. But it is so."

Kate was crushed. She could neither weep nor speak. She seemed to herself to be of stone.

"Will you send for him?" he asked, after waiting for some time in patient silence, striving meanwhile to suppress all utterance of pain.

Starting from her chair, Kate reeled out of the room on her awful errand, moving by jerks, as if she were a piece of imperfect mechanism. During the half-hour which elapsed before the arrival of the clergyman, she walked the house without speaking, except to whisper now and then, "It isn't true, it isn't true." Her reason, tried for months past by trouble after trouble, nearly sank under this new catastrophe. She retained intelligence enough, however, to know that her agitation would harm the invalid if he should witness it, and to keep away from the sick-room until she should be able to re-enter it calmly. Her father and sister, fearing for her sanity, sought to condole with her, and to hold her quiet with caressing arms.

"Let her walk," whispered Vincent. "If she could be got to gallop twenty miles, it would be still better. I never saw such infatuation," he muttered to himself. "However, he is like her, and we are not like her. It is a case of natural sympathy, exaggerated by circumstances."

When Kate saw the minister arrive and go in to Kershaw, she suddenly became calm, and went to her own room, there, no doubt, to pray for strength and resignation.

The Rev. Arthur Gilyard was a man of twenty-eight or thirty, tall and slender, slightly bald, his skin fair and very pale, with calm, serious blue eyes, and an expression of natural firmness alternating with an acquired gentleness. Firm as he was, however, and disciplined as he had been by the trials and duties of his profession, he faltered when he saw the death-marked face of his venerable parishioner, one of the chief supporters of his little church, and his own model of deportment and life.

"My dear friend and brother," he began, and stopped there, overcome by grief. His next words were forced from him by deep humility of soul, arising from a sense of his own unworthiness to stand forward as a preceptor to this elder disciple, this man to whom from his childhood he had looked up as his superior. "I have come to you," he said, "to learn how to die."

"My dear pastor, I cannot teach you," sighed Kershaw. "Pray that we may both be taught."

But we will not ascend farther into the solemnities of this more than earthly interview.

When it was over, the doomed man sent word to his son-in-law that he wished to see him alone.

"Well, Kershaw, what can I do for you?" asked Beaumont with assumed cheerfulness as he seated himself by the bedside and took the hand of his revered friend.

"Beaumont, you are a kind-hearted man," murmured the Colonel. "You have warm and generous sympathies."

"Ah, Kershaw, I am a poor, rough, old fellow," returned Peyton, shaking his head.

"Beaumont, you love your children," continued the invalid. "I wish you could love your fellow-men as you do your children."

"I do love some of them. I have loved you, Kershaw —"

Here he stopped a moment, his hard face twitching with emotion, and his grim eyes filling with tears.

"If they were all like you, it would be easy," he went on. "But some of them are such — such rascals! Those McAlisters, for instance. How can a man love those savages?"

"I was thinking of them," resumed Kershaw. "You know, Beaumont, that I have wanted you all my life — my latter life, at least — to be at peace with them. I want it now."

"But they have just shot you, Kershaw," blurted out Peyton. "I could have forgiven them before. Now I can't."

"I can," said the dying man, fixing his eyes solemnly on his friend. Beaumont bowed his face under that gaze.

"'Vengeance is mine, saith the Lord,'" continued Kershaw, his voice falling to a whisper under a paroxysm of pain.

Beaumont shook his iron-gray head, as if the text proffered aid to his vengeance, and he could not accept it.

"It was a misunderstanding," went on Kershaw. "Those young men thought we were attacking their brother."

"But they knew *you*," persisted Peyton. "They knew that *you* never did harm to a human being. Why should they fire so as to hit *you*? The miserable, barbarous wretches! Kershaw, I never can forgive them, never!"

After a short silence, during which he wrestled with his agony, the old man said deliberately, "We South-Carolinians are not a law-abiding people."

"Not a law-abiding people!" exclaimed Peyton, in such surprise that he forgot where he was and spoke quite loudly.

"No. We take punishment into our own hands. We cannot wait for the law. We do not trust the law. We make of ourselves judge, jury, and executioner. The consequence is that the State is full of homicide. It is wrong, Beaumont. It is a violation of the faith of man in man. It strikes at the base of society. It tends to barbarism."

"Kershaw, you astonish me," said Peyton, who thought his friend's reason was beginning to fail. "But are you not tiring yourself? Hadn't you better rest a little?"

"I cannot rest, Beaumont. I must not rest until I have an answer from you. I ask you not to avenge me upon the McAlisters. Can't you promise it to me? Beaumont, can't you?"

"Ah, Kershaw, you push me to the wall," groaned Peyton. "Well — yes, I must promise. I do."

"And will you beg of your sons not to avenge me?"

"Yes, I will do even that," assented Peyton. He did not want to agree to so much, but he was fairly driven to it by a sudden spasm in Kershaw's face, which he thought was the invasion of death.

A glass of wine partially restored the invalid, and he continued his plea for humanity.

"I know that I can trust you," he whispered. "You always keep your word. And now, if I could obtain one other promise from you, I should die contented. Can you not forgive these men altogether, Beaumont? Can you not make peace with them? Has not this feud shed blood enough? Remember that I am one of its victims. I have a right to bear witness against it. Can you not, for my sake as well as for the sake of humanity, for the sake of those whom it still threatens, and for the sake of their Creator and yours, can you not promise to do your utmost to end it?"

It may seem strange that Peyton Beaumont should not have told some gentle falsehood with regard to making peace, for the purpose of soothing his dying friend. But this rough man was profoundly honest; he would not have uttered a white lie, if he had thought of it; and he did not even think of it. No, it was not in his nature to promise to end the feud, unless he meant to end it. So, with Kershaw looking at him, as it were, from the other side of the grave, he remained silent until he could come to a decision. When it was reached, such as it was, he uttered it.

"Yes, Kershaw," he said. "I will — yes, I will do — the best I can. You know how old this thing is. You know how it is tangled up with our lives and our very natures. Don't make me promise more than I can perform. But I will remember what you ask, Kershaw. I will do what I can."

"It is enough," said the invalid. "I trust you and thank you."

Here he fainted quite away and was thought for a time to be dead; but the charge of vitality was not yet exhausted, and he came back to consciousness. It was during this insensibility that Lawson arrived and was shown into the room. The dying man received him with a smile which triumphed over a spasm of agony.

"Lawson, I am glad to see you," he said. "I bear this the better for seeing you once more. But I can only say a few words. I must bid you good by quickly. You are a good man Lawson; you have a gentle, loving heart. I think you never wished a human being harm. I have seen the sweetness of your soul and loved you for it. You are one of the children of peace. God reward you, Lawson. God bless you.

It was visible at this moment that the Major was not that shallow and merely babbling being which many people judged him to be. Completely overwhelmed by this parting from the man whom he loved and reverenced above all other men, he could not utter a word beyond a convulsive, "Kershaw!" Then he knelt down suddenly, hid his face in the bedclothes, and sobbed audibly.

The invalid next bade a calm farewell to Nellie Armitage, to her three brothers, and to Mrs. Chester.

"My dear young friends, I have left something for each of you," was one thing which he said to them. "And in my will I have ventured to beg that you — you young men, I mean — will strive to be at peace with your fellow-men. I trust that you will not be vexed with me for that exhortation, and that you will bear it in mind. God guide and bless you all, my dear friends."

After this he was left alone, at his own gently hinted request, with Peyton Beaumont and Kate.

"Hold fast to my hand," he whispered to the girl. "I go straight from you to your mother."

At these words the tears burst loose from Beaumont's eyelids and rolled down his grim, unshaven face.

"Kershaw, give her my love," he said with impulsive faith, alluding to his dead wife. "But I never was worthy of her. God forgive me."

Kate, with the hand that was free, reached out and took her father's hand. She was not crying; her grief was too hard to give forth tears; but with all her suffering, she could pity.

"I *will* be good to her child, — to my child," added Beaumont, with a sob.

"God help you so," replied Kershaw in a voice so solemn that it seemed to come from the other world. "God be with you both."

These were the last rational words that he spoke. For some time, unobservedly to those about him and unconsciously to himself, he had been struggling, not only with weakness and anguish, but also with the commencement of that delirium which invariably results from the intense inflammation of peritonitis. He had, as it were, fought with devils for his reason in order that he might bid farewell to those whom he loved, and exhort them to a better life. This duty accomplished, he fell on his field of victory. Incoherence came upon him, like reeling upon a wounded hero; and then followed hours on hours of wandering without one gleam of sanity. The final stage was come; there were hours more of sleep, or rather of stupor; he saw nothing, heard nothing, and, happy at least in this, felt nothing. Then, before any one perceived it, he was dead.

"He is gone," said Beaumont, taking one of his daughter's hands, and passing an arm around her waist, as if he would prevent her from flying also to the other world.

For a minute she made no reply, her whole soul being absorbed in gazing into the face of the dead and searching there for some signs of life. At last she said with strange deliberation, "My last hope of happiness is gone."

Having thus summed up the catastrophe that had overtaken her, she fell back on her father's shoulder, pallid and apparently senseless.

CHAPTER 33

 Before Kate fairly recovered from her fainting fit, her brother Vincent placed a powerful opiate at her lips and she drank it, so that the first hours of her bereavement passed away in sleep, or rather in disturbed and spasmodic dozing.

Leaving her in the hands of this merciful insensibility, let us see how others were affected by the death of Kershaw. Even previous to that event Peyton Beaumont had made it his duty to exorcise Randolph Armitage from his house. When that high-flung gentleman made his appearance, on the morning after he had been put to bed drunk and with a broken scalp, his father-in-law's first words to him were, "Are you able to travel, sir?"

"I suppose I am," sullenly replied Randolph, with a scowl of mingled pain and anger.

"Then travel, sir," growled Peyton, the brown veins in his forehead and the red veins in his cheeks swelling with wrath.

Randolph started, placed one hand to his bandaged head as if to repress its beatings, made an evident effort to recover his self-possession, and seemed about to remonstrate.

"Don't you speak, sir," thundered Beaumont. "You can't have your wife and children. As a husband and as a father, as well as in every other way, you have been a brute. Get out of my house. Get out of this district. If I find you in the neighborhood to-morrow, I'll have you hunted like a wolf. Not one word, sir. Be off!"

With the air of a cowed but savage cur, Armitage walked silently out of the house, and that very day quitted Hartland for parts unknown.

Sadly and heavily, Beaumont now went to find Nellie, and said to her, "My poor child, I have sent him away."

Nellie placed her hands on her father's shoulders, as if for support, and laid her head against his cheek so as to hide her face. She remembered that it was her own husband, once very dear to her, who had thus been driven out, and she remembered also that she could not reasonably say a word against his ingnominious expulsion. In that bitter moment she was fully conscious of her loneliness, her degradation as a wife, her failure as a woman. She expressed her wretchedness and her resignation in one brief sentence, "I have ceased to be a wife."

"My dear, it was time," murmured Beaumont, in hoarse, tremulous bass. "My dear child, no one can blame you," he presently added in a louder tone. "I should like to look the man in the face who would dare blame you."

The next notable event in the household, an event already related, was Kershaw's death. In the village, in the district, and even in all the midland part of the State, it produced a prodigious excitement. The profound popular respect which had for many years surrounded this "last of the barons" (as some men called him) blazed up in a flame of wrath against his murderers. All the fighting men of the region, as well as all the non-fighting men and the women, were for once virtuously indignant at an assassination. Even the intimate friends of the McAlisters found it hard to excuse them, and their numerous enemies were in a state of mind to lynch them gladly, had lynching highborn planters been ethically permissible.

The Judge, honestly horrified by the tragedy, had moral sense enough to foresee the storm which it would arouse, and to shrink from encountering it. He promptly published a card in the "Hartland Journal." In this card he expressed his sincere grief for the death of Colonel Kershaw; he eulogized the old man's character in a style which strong feeling made eloquent; he flatly denied that his sons were responsible for the homicide, and asked the public to suspend its judgment until further information. Bruce and Wallace also put forth a joint statement, in which they asserted that neither of them had aimed at the deceased, and that their action in the *mêlée* was a justifiable defence of their brother.

But their plea was useless. Nearly all Hartland believed that they had killed Kershaw, and that in so doing they had committed an abominable crime. Even their assertion that they had not aimed at the old man was turned against them by this community of marksmen. John Stokes, a fervent adherent of the Beaumonts, be it charitably remembered, expressed very pithily the prevailing opinion.

"Popped the Colonel by accident, did they?" said Mr. Stokes, taking a fresh quid and chewing it vigorously, while he meditated upon the infamy of the confession. "Sech men no business carryin' shootin'-irons," he resumed, in his leisurely way. "Why, I consider it one of the highest crimes an' misdemeanors to pop a man by accident. I'll leave it out to all Hartland, if it ain't. Why, look hyer. Ef I save a man beknownst an' a purpose, I may hev good reason for it. Anyway, I know what I'm after. I do what I set out to do, an' nothin' else. You know how to count on me. You know what I'll do next time I put my hand under my jacket. Take the Beaumonts, now," instanced Mr. Stokes, after another prolonged grinding. "*They* don't go round shootin' the best men in the country by accident. When they pop you, they mean it. They've shot as many as any other crowd in the State, an' never had no damn foolish accident yet, but allays bored the feller they drew bead on, an' no other. Now thar's men you can tie to; thar's men you can hev a confidence in; thar's men you can feel safe with. I tell you, I love an' respect them Beaumonts, for what they do, an' for what they don't do, for what they hit an' for what they miss. A man that's allays doin' jest what you reckoned he was gwine to do is the man that John Stokes swings his old broadbrim for. That's *so*."

After another stern assault upon his quid, he concluded his virile profession of faith, worthy surely of the heroic age.

"But as much as I love business, I hate foolin' round an' firin' wild. A feller that goes about killin' by accident, you can't tell what he'll do nor whar he'll stop. He may clean out the whole poppylation by one accident after another. Children an' niggers an' stock an' property at large ain't safe when sech a feller is loose. He can't be trusted. A decent community has no use for sech a man. In a general way he oughter be strung up with the nighest grapevine. I don't want to raise a crowd agin the McAlisters," added Mr. Stokes, remembering that they were high-toned gentlemen and owned hundreds of negroes. "I've allays considered 'em hitherto as straight-shootin' men an' tollable reliable men every way, except in politics. I'm willin', as the Judge requests in his keerd, to suspend my judgment. But I must say that so fur, accident or no accident, things is agin 'em. Yes, *sir*, sure as cotton is white an' niggers is black, things is powerfully agin 'em."

Things were so much "agin 'em," and the Judge was so clearly aware of it, that he persisted in withdrawing his congressional candidature, though dismally uncertain whether Beaumont would now recommend him for the United States Court. In explanation of this step he put forth a second card, which was dictated, like many other political effusions, by a mixture of subtlety and right feeling, but which expressed such admirable sentiments, and expressed them so well, that it regained for him a certain measure of popular consideration.

"In consequence of the universal horror and grief at the death of the late lamented Colonel John Kershaw," he wrote, "and in view of the as yet mysterious circumstances which seem to throw the responsibility of the tragedy upon members of my family, I withdraw my name as candidate for the House of Representatives, merely begging my esteemed fellow-citizens, and especially my faithful political friends, to believe that it is not an evil conscience which impels me to this step, but solely respect for, and sympathy with, a community mourning its noblest citizen."

"At least," thought the Judge, "I have a good excuse to send to Mr. Choke and his committee. And, moreover, I think the card must bring people around a little."

It did bring them around somewhat, but not enough and not soon enough to influence the election, even had the Judge's adherents still persisted in considering him a candidate. The voting took place the day after Kershaw's death, and resulted in an overwhelming triumph for Peyton Beaumont, two thirds of the electors supporting him and the other third staying at home. The Judge received the news of his rival's gigantic success with the calmness of a strong man accustomed to misfortunes.

"It is what I looked for," he said to his excellent wife, with whom he consorted much in his times of trouble. "It was inevitable, — once *my* name withdrawn. Well, the clouds must clear up some day. Heaven," he added, feeling somehow that, because he was chastened, therefore he was good, — "Heaven will some day see that justice is done me."

He did not even show petulance to Bruce and Wallace because of the calamity which they had brought upon him.

"In general I disapprove of rencontres," he said to them. "If gentlemen must fight, they should fight under the code, in most cases. But this was an exceptional case. It was defence against assassination. You were unquestionably right, you were right in the sight of God and man, in trying to rescue your brother. The Beaumonts themselves, unreasonable and savage as they are, must see it. I have no doubt that you saved Frank's life. I approve of your action. Approve? God bless me, I thank you for it! As for the death of poor Kershaw, time will show that your statement is correct, and that you are not responsible for it. All-discovering time and Heaven's own justice," perorated the Judge, trembling eloquently with his faith and piety.

The Judge's affairs took on brightness quicker that the reader probably sees reason to hope. The public prejudice against his family was destined to receive a prompt and potent shock. There was a grand-jury inquest into the death of Kershaw, and necessarily a post-mortem examination. Then was satisfied a craving curiosity which had kept all Hartland awake of nights. To understand this inquisitiveness, it must be stated that the fighting men of the region frequently marked their bullets, partly perhaps out of a chivalrous feeling that every one ought to take the responsibility of his own shots, and partly that each might be able to vindicate his marksmanship by identifying his proper game. It was a custom which had been introduced by those leaders in chivalry, or, as some few people said, in savagery, the Beaumonts. Of course it was expected by all the enemies of the McAlisters that the fatal bullet would disclose the letter *M*. What then was their astonishment when the letter was found to be *A*!

"*A*!" whispered Vincent, as he handed the tragical bit of lead to his father.

"*A*!" gasped Peyton Beaumont, after a long stare of amazement and a quick glance at Vincent.

"It was an ugly hieroglyphic — for us," observed Poinsett, sombrely.

"What! — was it Armitage?" demanded Tom, blurting out what the rest had shrunk from uttering.

"He was the man," responded Beaumont with drooping head. "The calamity is ten times more dreadful than we knew."

All four were silent for a little, weighed down by the same terrible reflection, that upon their house rested the responsibility of the death of Kershaw.

"It must have been a pure accident," said Poinsett at last. "Armitage had nothing against our old relative."

"It was a stupid drunken accident of a miserable drunkard and idiot," muttered Beaumont, dashing tears of grief and rage from his eyes.

"One thing puzzles me," resumed Poinsett, whose legal mind was already cross-questioning the circumstances of the tragedy. "Armitage did all his firing before Bruce and Wallace came up. Consequently the Colonel must have known that it was not they who hit him. Now, why did he not state it?"

"Wanted to save the honor of our family," thought Tom.

"No," sighed Beaumont, shaking his head. "Kershaw was our friend, but not to the point of injustice. He was too truthful a man to let the responsibility lie at the wrong door deliberately. It was more likely that he thought the secret would perish with him, and so no one would be punished for his death. That was like Kershaw. He had no spite in him. He was the gentlest-hearted man that ever drew breath."

But Vincent had a surgeon's explanation, and it was noticeable that it at once secured the assent of his auditors, so chirurgical in mind had they become through fightings and hearings of fightings.

"Sometimes a man is not at once aware that he is hit," he said. "I have seen a fellow who had lost first blood insist upon going on with his affair, quite unaware that he was wounded, and smartly wounded at that. I have known a fellow, shot through the shoulder, who complained that the ball had gone down into his thigh, and finally discovered that the pain in the thigh was caused by a second ball which had struck him there, without causing at first any noticeable sensation. It is wonderful what hits a man may take in a moment of excitement, without immediately remarking them. I suspect that Kershaw never really knew when he was wounded. Had he known it I think he would have told us, he was naturally so straightforward and frank."

"You must be right, Vincent," answered Beaumont. "I remember something of the sort happening to myself."

The reminiscence was uttered quietly, and no one looked surprised at it, nor were any questions asked. The Beaumonts never bragged about their combats, and rarely mentioned them, except incidentally or when business demanded it.

"What are you going to do with *that?*" asked Tom, as Vincent walked away with the proof of Armitage's homicide.

"I am going to put it in Mattieson's hands to exhibit it to the jury," was the response.

Beaumont gave Tom a grave glance which seemed to ask, "Would you think of concealing it?"

The young fellow dropped his head and made no further remark.

When the story of the ownership of the fatal bullet spread through Hartland, there came a mighty change in public sentiment. The Mc-Alisters were cleared of Kershaw's blood as if by a hurrah. People wanted Randolph Armitage brought to justice, and were not far from ready to lynch him, gentleman as he was. Peyton Beaumont was freely criticised (behind his back) for having allowed his son-in-law to disappear, and was even charged with having urged him to escape before his guilt should become known. Nor were there wanting low-minded gossips incapable of appreciating the pugnacious old planter's unselfishness and strenuous sense of honor, who hinted that he had long been waiting for the Kershaw estate, and had become impatient. Furthermore, the Beaumonts were held accountable for Armitage's breach of hospitality in attacking Frank under their roof. Bruce and Wallace were justified for defending a brother in danger of assassination. In short, popular feeling and opinion had never before run so strongly in favor of the McAlisters, and against their rivals; and had the election been held after the inquest, instead of before it, the Judge might have gone into Congress by a respectable majority. Of this fact, by the way, he was the first to take notice; and he groaned over it in a spirit that was pardonable, if not praise-worthy.

At last, however, all the circumstances of the *mêlée* became public, and then Hartland settled down to blaming Randolph Armitage alone, considering that the other combatants had done what was right according to their knowledge, and so merited, not reprobation, but eulogy.

Nevertheless, the Beaumonts remained in a state of grief, wrath, and humiliation. Considering themselves responsible in a measure for their relative, Armitage, they were ashamed of his attack upon their father's guest, and furious at his homicide of their noble Kershaw. The death of the good old man was an awful loss to them in more ways than one. He had been not only their adviser in doing what was right, but their ægis against criticism when they had done what was wrong. On the rare occasions when society dared to condemn them for their battlings and other peccadilloes, they had been able to respond, "But we keep the friendship of Kershaw, and therefore cannot be very culpable." Without him, they felt less strong than hitherto, and they mourned him on that account, as well as because they had loved him.

It would seem now as if Beaumont ought to have fulfilled his promise to Kershaw to do his best at burying the hatchet. But, instead of sending pacific messages to the McAlisters, he turned his back on them and on Hartland, and went off to Washington. He remained absent some weeks, during which nothing was known of his purposes or his doings, except that he was much seen in political circles. From him, therefore, we turn to his sorrowing daughter, Kate.

This affectionate, sensitive girl had been bruised to the core by the great calamity which had fallen upon it. Her best and wisest friend, the sweet old man of whom she had made a pet from her infancy, the being toward whose purity her own pure spirit had instinctively inclined, had been torn from her by a hideous accident, a brutal mistake. At first she had received the blow with an amazement which had the effect of incredulity. This often happens to the afflicted, and it is well that it is so. Sorrow, to use the intelligent phrase of Vincent Beaumont, is thereby distributed over a greater number of heartbeats, and thus permits the heart to beat on.

But day after day passed and Kershaw did not return. Little by little Kate fully realized her bereavement, and little by little it appeared that she could not well endure it. To those who loved her, and therefore watched her comprehendingly, it was a terrible thing to see the storms of grief which sometimes came upon her, even when she was striving to maintain a sunny countenance. In the midst of a conversation she would be stricken dumb; her head would fall slowly back, and her eyes turn upward as if seeking to pierce other worlds; then, with a quiver of the throat, she would utter a loud, shuddering sigh. It was only a momentary spasm, for almost immediately she would regain her usual air, and perhaps finish a sentence. But short as the tremor had been, her heart had given forth a portion of its vitality, and less remained for the purposes of living. There are eruptions which at once show the power of the volcano and eat away its case.

Of course her trial was a complicated one, and her grief a legion. In losing her best and dearest friend, she had lost her chances of domestic peace, and her hope of being able to live for love. Who, now that Kershaw was gone, would keep quiet those wild broods of Beaumont and McAlister men, always ready to fly at each other's throats? What probability was there that she would ever be able to place her hand in the outreaching hand of him who had won her heart? Her father and brothers, kind as they meant to be to her, were so many causes of anxiety and terror, such was their readiness to expose life and to take it. From her sister, more unfortunate than a widow, a wife whose husband was an outlaw, she had no right to demand consolation. If she looked to the past, it was a series of troubles, billow raging after billow. Its successive shocks had already weakened her, so that she was the less able to withstand the present.

The human being, bodily and spiritually, is a unity. The mind cannot chafe long without causing the strength of the body to fail. Sorrowful brooding by day, and nights of broken, unrefreshing sleep, soon made the girl an invalid, and gave her the air of one. Her rich color faded, her limpid hazel eyes became dull and despondent, and her fine figure lost somewhat of its rounded outlines.

But sadly as the physical languished, the spiritual suffered even more. Before long Kate fell into a melancholy which took an unwholesome theological cast, akin to superstition. In her diseased imagination God became a Moloch, demanding the death of the innocents of her heart. She was possessed by an impression that some great sacrifice was demanded of her. What could it be, except the man whom she now loved, as she was compelled to admit, above all other living beings?

Heavy laden with this terrible idea and striving in vain to shake it off by efforts of reason, the girl wandered in deserts of gloom. Restless with an emotion which claimed to be remorse, she went from room to room with such a haggard face and abstracted gaze as to draw wondering stares from her relatives. One whole day she passed alone in her chamber, praying that the intolerable cup might pass from her. But the heavens were of brass; it seemed to her as if the sun refused to shine upon her; as if all nature reproved her for selfish rebellion.

At last, overcome by the reproaches of her mock conscience, she bowed her will to this supposed duty. Kneeling before her Bible, sobbing forth supplications for resignation, she promised to expel Frank McAlister from her heart, and to think no more of marrying him, no more of loving him.

She had expected that this vow, could she ever utter it, would give her peace. But it did not; something else was now demanded of her; the cruel Moloch of broken health and shattered nerves was insatiable; she must still sacrifice, choosing whatever was pleasantest and dearest. She must give up her home, go forth from her own flesh and blood, and labor somehow, suffer somehow, alone.

This new requisition of the mocking spirits of invalidism drove her almost frantic. Unfortunately there was no one in the family to whom she would naturally turn for counsel in such difficulties. Her aunt and brothers were not in any sense spiritually-minded; even her sister, notwithstanding her puissance of sympathy, could not comprehend her. Once, when Kate ventured to hint some of her dolorous impressions to Nellie, that healthy woman broke out in sound-minded indignation, telling the girl that her scruples were whimsical, and calling her a silly.

Under such circumstances it is no wonder that Kate began to receive with pleasure the consolatory visits of the Rev. Arthur Gilyard.

CHAPTER 34

 As the Rev. Arthur Gilyard will be of some importance in our story, we must say a word or two concerning his character.

He was a model gentleman, and, making allowance for the narrowness of his moral education, a model Christian. In all those duties of his profession which he clearly saw to be duties, he was faithful in the extreme.

If he had neither public nor private reproof for some of the characteristics of Southern society which other societies denounced as sins, it was because he had not yet been able to decide that they were unmixed evils.

He doubted, for instance, whether duelling were not an instrument for the development of civilization by elevating the sense of honor and polishing manners. As for slavery, if the Bible did not assail it, why should he? If in these views he was illogical, antiquated, and provincial, he was at least perfectly honest.

These things apart, he was admirable. By nature proud, ambitious, and combative, he had made himself humble, unselfish, and gentle by assiduous self-culture. The best of sons, a fervent friend, a tireless pastor, an earnest preacher, he was loved in private and respected in public.

Notwithstanding his peaceful profession, even bellicose Peyton Beaumont admired him heartily, and said of him, "He is a gentleman," sometimes adding, "Well, of course he is. Good blood, sir; Huguenot blood. Even a clergyman, sir, can't be a gentleman without descent."

Such was the man who now came often to console Kate Beaumont, and who very soon became infatuated with his mission. In spite of her thinness and pallor, the girl was still beautiful; and in spite of her despondency and her fits of silence, she was fascinating.

There are women who charm men because they take the pains to do it, and who take pains because they are themselves interested. They are of the nature of magnets; they attract potently for the reason that they are attracted; they are creatures of strong sympathies and therefore of indefatigable activity. They win triumphs, but they pay for them. For every pulsation that they cause, they have given a pulsation. They are admirable for what they do, and for the power which enables them to do it, and for the health of moral and physical constitution which supplies this waste of power.

The life of such a woman is as stormy and as full of exhausting labor, one may almost say, as that of a Napoleon. She can hardly be encountered without subjection, and she cannot be intelligently considered without wonder. Let no one who is not born to do it, who is not furnished by nature with the force to do it, hope to rival her. This power of fascinating, of being fascinated, and still living, is not acquired, but given. It is unconscious. She who possesses it is not aware of the possession. She acts by it, and does not know why she so acts, and does not even see that she so acts. And it is surely one of the mightiest of the gifts that are conferred upon mortals.

But there is another enchanter, very different from this one, yet equally wonderful. She is not gifted for effort, and she puts forth none. She waits, like a deity, for the worship which is due her, not even perceiving that it is due. She is as calm in appearance as Greek art, and as sure of admiration. She may be called the Washington of women, as the other is the Napoleon. Her purity and nobility of soul, obvious to every worthy beholder, are what draw adorers. The more unconscious she is of worship and the more indifferent to it, the more she commands it.

In sorrow, in the sublime forgetfulness of self which grief brings, she is especially irresistible. Whoever sees her grieving wishes to comfort her, and brings offerings of pity and then of love. She inspires the respectful, the solemnly reverential affection which a true Catholic feels in gazing upon a *Mater Dolorosa.* A maiden, perhaps, yet already a mother of sorrows, she is at once fascinating and imposing. Men long to sound her sombre mystery, and are willing to use their lives to dispel it.

Such at this time was Kate Beaumont. Her face, of that sweet and dignified aquiline, which we call Oriental, was both tender and grand with trouble. Her profound, imploring hazel eyes demanded the pity which she never or rarely asked for in words. No man of refined feeling could look on her without querying, What is the matter with her, and what can I do for her?

How could a clergyman, whose profession it is to utter the mercy of Heaven, fail to be urgent in proffering consolation? Arthur Gilyard performed his duty with emotion, and he suffered the penalty of so performing it. We have not space to show how sympathy grew in his heart from one form into another; we must compress the whole of this passionate evolution into one phrase, — he fell in love.

Now imagine Kate Beaumont in daily intercourse with this pitying, worshipping young man, and receiving from him the only ideas that could give her any semblance of peace or joy. What wonder if an impression should come upon her, like a message delivered by some invisible archangel, commanding her to revere her comforter, to imitate his beautiful life, to renounce like him a dying world, and like him devote herself to the good of others? She had thoughts of entering a hospital as a nurse, or of going abroad as a teacher of the heathen. But, woman-like, with all her self-abnegation, she felt that she needed in these labors a fellow-apostle, who should be her support and guide. So also felt and thought the Rev. Arthur Gilyard, remembering meanwhile that his people had been urgent with him to take a wife, and trusting that Heaven had shown him one who was worthy to share his mission.

But this strange courtship, this courtship which strove to be unconscious of its own real nature and purpose, must have the go-by for the present. We are called upon to turn to an unpleasant figure in our drama. Mrs. Chester is about to make trouble, and must be watched.

Notwithstanding a certain constant jealousy of Kate, notwithstanding that it always annoyed her to see another woman admired, Aunt Marian's first feeling with regard to the Gilyard courtship was mainly gratification. The harebrained, spiteful old flirt had not yet forgiven Frank McAlister for preferring a niece to an aunt; frivolous as she seemed, she had sincerity and earnestness enough to hate him heartily and to want him to be miserable. "If Kate takes this stick of a minister," she said to her unamiable self, "it will plague that tall brute properly."

But we must be more serious than usual with Mrs. Chester. A singular change, capable of germinating ugly consequences, had come over this always sufficiently singular woman. Whether it was that the late startling events in the family life had shaken her nervous system, or whether it was that some constitutional transition or some occult decay of health had suddenly diminished her power of self-control, at all events she was in an uncommonly excitable state. She was as restless, dissatisfied, and fretful as a teething baby. Always troubled with plans and wants, she had them now by scores. Every day some new project for being happy was proposed, advocated with pettish eagerness, and dropped for another. She was as agitated in body as in spirit. She could not sit still; into a room, and out of it; changing from sofa to settee: always in movement. At last people began to notice how she buzzed about, how incessantly and eagerly she talked, how oddly her black eyes sparkled.

"What the doose is the matter with Aunt Marian?" grumbled Tom, annoyed by her humming-bird activity. "I'd as lieve have a basket of hornbugs in the house. If she should bang against the ceiling and come down kicking on the floor, I shouldn't be astonished."

"She is only a good deal more like herself than usual," observed the philosophic Poinsett. "We are all of us annoying when we are excessively in character."

"She is behaving queerly, even for her," judged Vincent, the semiphysician.

Well, among her numerous projects, Mrs. Chester conceived that of going to Washington with Representative Beaumont, keeping house for him during session time, giving grand receptions, having members of the Cabinet to dinner, coquetting with mustached secretaries of legation, and becoming nationally famous as a queen of society. A judicious portion of this enchanting prospect, that is to say, such part of it as included having one's own nice bed and excellent cookery in a capital not famous for such things, she had set before the mind's eye of her brother just previous to his leaving Hartland.

"I would take a house there, if I could have my daughters with me," replied Beaumont, always a father.

Mrs. Chester frowned: she did not want the daughters along; they would be her rivals with the secretaries.

"Do you think I couldn't take care of you, Peyton?" she asked, reproachfully; "an old housekeeper like me!"

"That isn't it," answered Peyton, who nevertheless had his doubts. "I don't want the expense of a Washington house, and Washington hospitalities, of course, unless my children, my girls at least, can share the pleasure with me. You are very kind, Marian," he added, with judgment. "But, you see, I am an old fool of a father."

"I know you are," retorted Mrs. Chester, snappishly. But in another instant this versatile gadfly changed her direction and decided to accept her nieces.

"Let the girls come, if they wish it," she said. "We shall be all the gayer."

"Gayer!" almost growled Beaumont. "How can they be gay? How can they go into society at all? You know what a row Armitage has made, and that he has disappeared."

"Oh certainly, Nellie can't go," admitted Mrs. Chester, thinking, so much the better.

"Nor will Kate, I am sure," added Beaumont.

"Why not? Kershaw was only her grandfather."

Peyton gave his sister rather a black look, and replied, "That is a good deal, especially when he was the man he was. My God, we let the dead slip out of mind soon enough. Would you have us hurry up our forgetting?"

"You are always snapping at me," said the lady, with a violent gesture which showed how slight was her self-command. "You are very hard-hearted."

Beaumont stared in amazement and indignation. Then, for the first time perhaps, he noticed the unusual brilliancy and unsteadiness of his sister's eye, and wondered whether she were as well as usual. Deciding that she was not fit for controversy, and that he as a man ought to show forbearance, he made no answer to her attack. She will discover on reflection, he said to himself, who it is that has been hard-hearted.

He ought to have known his sister better; she was not a person to see herself as others saw her; she was as incapable of introspection as a cat. It is worthy of note, by the way, as an instance of her unhealthy versatility, that she had promptly withdrawn her favor from the Gilyard courtship, on discovering that it might interfere with her Washington whimwham.

"I think you don't sufficiently consider Kate's interests," she resumed. "Her health, poor child, is suffering. She ought to be taken away from a place where she has met with such affliction. She needs amusement. You ought to have her with you, whether she wants to go or not. She needn't be very gay, you know," explained Mrs. Chester, thinking that she herself would receive the mustached secretaries while Kate should sit up stairs and read her Bible. "I could take the heaviest part of the entertaining off her hands. She could just drive about and see the sights and recover her cheerfulness."

Beaumont grinned, almost audibly. His sister had already set up a carriage at his expense in Washington. He said to himself, How like her!

"You are right about Kate," he observed, aloud. "She does need change of scene and air. Well, when session opens, if she feels disposed to go with me, I will take a house."

The next morning he departed for the capital on the mysterious business of which we have already spoken.

Mrs. Chester now turned her mind to bringing Kate into the Washington project. Seizing a moment when the girl seemed more cheerful than usual, she went at her with the smile of an angel, that is, of a fallen one.

"Your father is very anxious to keep house, this coming session," she began. "He is sick of those wretched hotels, and wants his own bed and his own table. His plan is to take you and me with him, and have a comfortable home, you know, and give a few dinners and receptions, and be somebody in society there. It will be so much for his interest, and so much for his comfort too! I am so glad he has settled upon it."

Now this was stating the matter pretty strongly, was it not? Did Mrs. Chester mean to lie or to exaggerate? Well, not exactly; she did not see that she was lying or exaggerating much; perhaps she did not see that she was doing so at all. She was one of those persons who desire so impulsively and passionately, that they easily impute their desires to other people. She stretched the truth, and annexed what was not the truth almost unconsciously. No doubt, also, her present abnormal nervousness may account for somewhat of her audacity of invention.

"Reception in Washington!" murmured Kate. The sorrowing soul shrank from gayeties as an invalid might shrink from a voyage among the chilly glitter of icebergs.

"Oh, I will see to them mainly," offered Mrs. Chester. "You could be in or out, as you wished."

"I don't see how I could well avoid them, if I were in the house."

"Well, why should you avoid them?" demanded Mrs. Chester, with shocking cheerfulness.

"But, dear aunt, I cannot go into society," replied the girl, piteously. "How can I think of it?"

"Oh, don't be so weak-minded," exhorted the dear aunt. "Do try to think of somebody besides yourself," she added, finding one of the most sympathetic beings in the world guilty of egotism. "You ought to get at your sewing at once," she continued, remembering perhaps what a fascinating business dressmaking is to women, and how quickly it can give them a fresh zest for life.

"If my father really wishes me to go to Washington, I must go," said Kate, sadly.

But during the day she wrote to her father; and before long she received a reply, leaving the matter entirely to her choice; and, armed with this letter, she once more faced her aunt.

"There, you have spoiled all," snapped Mrs. Chester. "You went and cried to him, and melted him as usual. You are the most selfish, the slyest, the —"

"Aunt Marian, you do me injustice," interrupted Kate, her eyes opening wide with the astonishment of maligned innocence.

"Oh, do I? I should think I did. Ha, ha! Well, I suppose so," replied Aunt Marian with incoherent irony. "Perhaps I do the young man injustice, too," she added, more intelligibly.

Kate, however, did not understand. A blush slightly tinted her cheek, but it did not refer to the Reverend Gilyard. She simply saw that she was attacked, and she flushed under the outrage.

"But *I* understand, miss," proceeded Mrs. Chester, in a truly irrational passion. "A young minister, a sweet-voiced young minister, with solemn, saintly blue eyes, is a great consolation. Oh, I have seen many young girls comforted that way before now! I am not a fool, miss. I know my own sex."

The coarse insult pierced even through Kate's incredulity that an insult could be meant. Without a word she put her hands to her ears and escaped from her denaturalized tormentor.

"She will tell her father of me," thought Mrs. Chester, with a transitory terror. But after a minute of reflection, or rather of certain emotions which served her in place of it, she burst out violently, "I'll stop this courting."

Her next notable dialogue on this subject was with Mrs. Devine, the mother of our little coquette, Jenny. Mrs. Devine was one of those mild, soft-spoken women who have no mind nor will of their own, but who, in carrying out the desires of some adored being, can show the unexpected persistence and pluck of a setting hen. Unlike Mrs. Chester in character, and much disapproving her worldly ways, she nevertheless consorted with her a good deal, because of old fellowship in the langsyne of boarding-school, and because of the intimacy between Jenny and Kate.

Now Mrs. Devine's heart was bent on getting her darling minister married, and she had settled upon Kate Beaumont as the best match attainable for him. Such a dear, good, lovely girl was surely a very proper prize for such a dear, good, lovely man. There was money there, too, and Mr. Gilyard undoubtedly ought to have money, he was so indifferent to it, and knew so little how to keep it. There had been a time when Mrs. Devine had pinched and saved on his account, thinking that perchance he might become the steward of Jenny's moderate fortune. But he had not been so guided; and the mother had finally had the grace to see that her daughter was unfit to be a minister's wife, — had acknowledged with humility that she was much too thoughtless and gay. And surely Providence was in it; for, if her idol had married Jenny, he could not have married Kate; and Kate was just the girl to be able to appreciate the idol and make him comfortable on his altar.

Well, Mrs. Devine had prayed for this match, had intrigued for it, had prophesied it. Accordingly Mrs. Chester, who did not desire the match lest it should prevent her from going to Washington, had a bone to pick with Mrs. Devine.

"I hear that you want your minister to marry my niece," was the opening attack of this energetic, though desultory woman.

The setting hen struck out promptly and gallantly in defence of the eggs which she was hatching.

"I am sure she could not find a better husband," she replied. "I am sure it is better to marry a man like Mr. Gilyard than to plunge into the dissipations of Washington."

Mrs. Chester was very excitable in these days, remember; and this attack upon her favorite project touched her where she was most sensitive.

"It seems to me, Mrs. Devine, that you trouble yourself too much about other people's girls," she replied with flashing eyes. "I should say that you had quite enough to do with keeping your own duckling out of puddles."

"What have you got now to say against Jenny?" demanded Mrs. Devine, forgetting even her minister in defending her daughter.

Mrs. Chester had nothing special to say against Jenny; so she changed her front once more.

"And what have you got to say against Kate's going to Washington?" she asked.

"I have much to say against it," replied Mrs. Devine, with the bland but annoying firmness of people who know that they are doing their duty. "I think it would be very wrong to take her into the gay world just when her heart has been softened by the death of dear, good old Colonel Kershaw. I think that I am bound, as her friend, and as one who wishes her highest good, to bear my testimony against any such step."

Mrs. Chester would hear no more. She was quite unable to restrain the nervous irritability which of late perpetually gnawed her, and set her flying not only at her fellow "humans," but also at cats and dogs, and even at things inanimate. She broke out in such a fit of passion as one seldom sees in a lady outside of a lunatic asylum.

"I know what you mean by your pious talk, Sally Devine," she chattered. "You want to keep Kate here so that your stick of a minister can court her. You are stark crazy about that pale-faced, white-eyed, white-livered creature. You know that Kate Beaumont is the best match in the district, and you want her money and niggers to support him. Oh, you needn't make eyes at me as if I were breaking all the

Ten Commandments at once. I don't care if he is a clergyman. I don't like him. I don't like his looks. He has a white liver. He's just that kind of man that the niggers call a white-livered man. And he's a poor stick of a minister. When he looks at the daughter of Peyton Beaumont, he looks altogether too high for him. Kate Beaumont is for his betters. She is fit for any planter or any politician in the State. When you put up your little man to jumping for her, you put him up to making himself ridiculous."

Mrs. Devine was dumbfounded with horror and amazement. Mrs. Chester was talking with a violence which even in her was extraordinary. Not only was her language violent, but her manner also. Her gestures, her flashing eyes, and her loudness of tone all showed an unwomanly and abnormal excitement. Mrs. Devine even thought, just for one moment, "Is she crazy?"

"I want you to let our Beaumont affairs entirely alone," resumed Mrs. Chester, who had merely paused to catch her breath. "We are able to take care of our own young lady. Do you take care of yours." At this point, remembering how much Jenny had made of Frank McAlister some time previous, her anger received a fresh accession, and she added, "She needs it enough, — the little flirt!"

Even sense of duty and of martyrdom in a just cause could not enable Mrs. Devine to hear more. Insulted through her daughter, and with a sense of degradation in being made the butt of such glarings and such language, she rose and hurried out of the room, crying with vexation.

We beg that the reader will not be equally shocked, and shut his eyes upon the very name of Mrs. Chester hereafter. Sooner or later he will learn the true cause of her unwomanly outbreak, and will probably in a measure pardon her for it.

It so happened that while hastening across the yard, Mrs. Devine met Kate Beaumont. In the weakness of abused femininity suffering from instant outrage, and remembering also how Mrs. Chester had formerly abused Jenny to her face, the injured woman did not wisely conceal the cause of her weeping.

"I have been insulted by your aunt," she sobbed. "Insulted because I thought it my duty to protest against your being dragged into the vanities and follies of Washington. I have done my duty in this house for the last time. I am sorry, but I can't help it."

With these words she tore away, rushed into her carriage, and was driven off. It will be observed that she kept silence as to the Rev. Mr. Gilyard, either because she thought it was right so to do, or because she thought it was wise. Even conscientious people, when of the illogical turn of Mrs. Devine, are apt to indulge in such concealments, regarded by stronger heads as prevarications.

Kate, although a hater of duelling, rencontres, and the like, had what may be called gentlemanly ideas of hospitality and of honor. The fact that a Beaumont had insulted a guest under the Beaumont roof-tree, roused in her such indignation that she forgot her sorrows, forgot her melancholies, and lost somewhat of her habitual gentleness. As she entered the house and advanced upon Mrs. Chester, with a marble face and the step of a Juno, she looked much more like her spirited sister than like herself. For the first time in this whole story she was angry. We regret to use the word in connection with her, it has such ugly associations; and yet her anger was just, honorable, and becoming.

"Aunt Marian," she said, "I hear that you have been attacking Mrs. Devine, and because of my affairs."

"I did not," asserted Aunt Marian.

"I do not know what to make of this," replied Kate, steadily gazing into Mrs. Chester's wandering eyes. "Mrs. Devine tells me that you had words with her about my going to Washington."

Mrs. Chester had at first been strangely afraid of her niece. But as the girl stood there calling her to account, she became suddenly very angry with her, so angry as to lose all her self-control and to forget her cunning.

"Yes, I did have words with her," she broke out. "I let her know her place here. She wants to prevent our going to Washington, and to marry you to that white-livered minister. I let her know that she was an interfering gossip. I did, and I will again."

"Aunt Marian, this cannot be," said Kate, speaking with the steadiness of a Fate. "This is my father's house, and guests cannot be insulted in it. If you do not write an apology to Mrs. Devine, I shall lay the whole matter before him."

"Will you go to Washington?" was Mrs. Chester's only answer.

"I am not going to Washington," decreed Kate.

"Then I won't stay here another day," declared Mrs. Chester in loud anger. "I won't stay here to be ground down and insulted. I'll go and keep house for Bent Armitage."

Kate did not believe her. She was mainly occupied in wondering at the woman's unusual excitement. She decided that time would be the best medicine for it, and that for the present she would say nothing more to irritate her. When Mrs. Chester should come to herself, and should get over her disappointment about the collapse of the Washington project, she would probably have a mild turn and send an apology to Mrs. Devine. So trusting, Kate left her.

But the next morning Mrs. Chester slyly set off for Saxonburg with bag and baggage, alighting upon the hospitality of the astonished Bentley Armitage, who was keeping bachelor's hall in his brother's house. And there, inspired perhaps by a bee in her bonnet, she commenced making fresh trouble for Beaumonts and McAlisters.

CHAPTER 35

 "What is up now?" were Bent Armitage's first words to Mrs. Chester when she rustled suddenly into his lonely lodgings.

Puzzled by her unexpected advent, he supposed that she could only have come to bring him some startling news of Randolph, still a fugitive from such justice as homicidal high-flung gentlemen had in those days to fear in South Carolina.

"I am driven from my brother's house by my brother's children," answered Mrs. Chester in an excited tragical way which struck him as both singular and ludicrous. "Have you a place where I can hide my head?"

"Lots of places to hide heads in," answered the reassured Bentley, his queer smile, a smile indescribably and perhaps unintentionally quizzical, curling up into one cheek. "This old rookery is just the spot for hiding heads, or bodies either, for that matter. Any number of handy closets for skeletons."

Mrs. Chester dropped various bundles on the floor, and then dropped herself with equal helplessness into an arm-chair, gasping as if she had run all the way from Hartland.

"So the boys have been turning up rusty?" inquired Bent.

"It's the girls," said Mrs. Chester. "I can get along with men."

Bentley smiled again; she was partly right there.

"I had hoped, or rather I was afraid, that you brought news of Randolph," he added, turning grave.

Starting off suddenly, like a turbine-wheel when the water is let on, Mrs. Chester told the whole story of the killing of Colonel Kershaw. Her distinctness of memory was wonderful; she related every incident of the tragedy with amazing minuteness, picturesqueness, and fluency; she was extremely interesting and even amusing. Another noteworthy circumstance was that she talked with such rapidity as to throw off a slight spattering of foam from her lips.

"I knew all that," said Bentley, when he found a chance to speak. "But where is Ran now? That's the point."

"I don't know," replied Mrs. Chester with curious dryness and indifference. "Give me some writing-materials. I want to write a letter."

Pen and paper being furnished, she commenced writing with singular slowness and hesitation, using first her right hand and then her left.

"I am disguising my hand," she presently explained. "It is an anonymous letter."

Before Bentley could fairly say, "The dickens it is!" she added, her eyes flashing spitefully, "It is to Frank McAlister."

Bentley was astonished, but amused. He had heard somewhat of the woman's fancy for the young giant. Was she going, at her respectable age, to send him a valentine?

"I want to make him miserable," she continued.

"I've no objection," observed Bent, lighting a cigar, and watching her through the smoke. "Sock it to him."

"I am going to tell him," went on Mrs. Chester, with a sullen, absent-minded air, — "I am going to tell him that Kate is engaged to Arthur Gilyard."

Bentley turned pale and dropped his cigar.

"He'll believe it, and he'll be miserable, — he'll believe, and he'll be miserable," repeated Mrs. Chester, with an air of savage pleasure in the iteration.

"But it isn't true?" asked, or rather implored, Bentley.

"It is," answered Mrs. Chester. "And oh, ain't I glad of it? I hate those McAlisters!"

The unhappy youngster reeled to his feet and left the room. When he returned, a few minutes later, he had the look of a man who has risen from an illness. Mrs. Chester, who had by this time finished and directed her letter, went on talking about the McAlisters precisely as if she had been talking about them all the while, unconscious of his absence.

"The feud has lasted seventy years now," she said. "There have been three generations in it. There have been fourteen Beaumonts shot in it and thirteen McAlisters. We still owe them one. Just think of it: Peyton is the only one left of seven brothers; all the rest died in their boots, as the saying is. Until three years ago, our family has never been out of mourning since I can remember. And now Kate is in mourning for her grandfather."

Bentley softly whistled a plaintive Methodist tune which recalled a chorus commencing, "Oh, there will be mourning, — mourning, mourning, mourning."

"Yes, there has been mourning," said Mrs. Chester, recognizing the air; "and there will be more. It can't stop here. We owe them one, and we must pay the debt. I don't know who will do it, but somebody will. Your brother missed his mark. He fired at a McAlister, and hit Colonel Kershaw. Perhaps you'll be the next one to take up the old quarrel. Ain't you Beaumont enough?"

"Scarcely," was Bent's dry answer.

"Oh well. You are not married into the family; but you may be. I thought at one time you were going to take Kate. Why didn't you?"

"Didn't hear any loud call to do so," said Bent. His words were jocose, but his face was tragic.

"Oh, I know," went on Mrs. Chester. "That Frank McAlister got in your way. He stopped it."

"Did he?" asked Bentley.

"You could have got her, if it hadn't been for him."

False as this undoubtedly was, Bentley had himself supposed it to be true, unwilling to believe that his love had been declined simply on account of his own demerits.

"Of course he slandered you," said Mrs. Chester.

"Oh no," protested Bentley, who, notwithstanding the credulity of sorrow and eagerness, found this hard to credit.

"He began it with his eyes," continued Mrs. Chester. "He used to look at you and then look at her in a way that was the same thing as a warning. She understood him. I could see that she did. After one of those looks, she used to avoid you. Oh, you don't know how quick women are at taking hints! I know them. A hint goes further with them than a long argument. They think it over by themselves and make ever so much out of it. It is the best way to lead them, to give them little hints and winks. I have found out a thousand things that way. But Frank McAlister didn't stop there. After a while he went on to talk to her about you. He said you were a drunkard and would make her miserable."

Mrs. Chester's disordered imagination invented so rapidly, that her tongue could hardly keep up with it. She talked so volubly and by moments so indistinctly, that Bentley found some difficulty in following her. It may seem singular that he should have credited her babble; but it must be remembered that she had him upon a subject where his wits were at a disadvantage; that in talking to him of Kate Beaumont she used a spell which paralyzed his judgment.

"Look here, this is too much," he exclaimed at last, starting up and striding about, his partially disabled foot slapping the floor more paralytically than usual.

"Of course it is too much," replied Mrs. Chester, eagerly. "I don't see how you can endure it."

"I can't," said Bentley, rushing out of the room.

It was evening when this conversation took place. Before bedtime Bent was under the influence of the hereditary devil of his family. In trouble as well as in joy, in seasons of wrath as well as in seasons of conviviality, in all times of excitement and too often in times of dulness, it was the custom of the Armitages to betake themselves to whiskey. As certain peoples in a state of revolution elevate a tyrant to power, so this breed, when distracted by emotions, enthroned alcohol.

In the morning, rising from the irritation of evil slumbers, Bentley resumed his drinking before breakfast, keeping it up all day and for days following. There were some strange scenes of carousal in the lonely mansion. Mrs. Chester, we remember, was an ardent admirer of men, and especially of young men; and even in her present excitement she did not forget her old predilection. She took to flattering and petting Bent Armitage, as she had once flattered and petted Frank McAlister. She was so thankful for what little attention she got from him, that she did not mind his semi-intoxication, and indeed ministered unto it. She mixed his liquor and set it before him in a coquettish, hoydenish, juvenile way, sincerely gratified to serve him. She was a cracked old Cleopatra waiting on a totally indifferent young Antony. It was a spectacle which would have been farcical had it not been woful.

The more Bent drank, and the more irrational and savage he became with his long debauch, the more completely he credited Mrs. Chester's tales concerning Frank McAlister's slanders of himself. For the feud he cared nothing; even in his present wild state, he knew that he had nothing to do with it; his native clearness of head asserted itself thus far. But he did believe that Frank had injured him, and he did want to shoot the fellow. He used to go to sleep muttering, "Hang Frank Mc-Alister! Hang all the McAlisters! Hang Frank McAlister particularly! Hang him particularly!" Only, in place of the word "hang," he used a stronger objurgation.

Alcohol is a magician. It tears down a man's natural character in an hour, and builds him a new one. It accomplishes miracles which re-mind one of the doctrine of the transmigration of souls. Under its enchantment your body is forsaken by the spirit which belongs to it, and entered upon by a spirit which you knew not of, any more than if it came from another world. Bentley Armitage, a good fellow by nature, and well furnished with common sense, was presently on his way to Hartland to fight Frank McAlister, following precisely in the steps of his addle-pated brother, under the same frenzying influence. It was the stupid iteration of that stupidest of possessing demons, "rum-madness."

But, though playing Randolph's part after him, he did it with another port and mask. Even in his inebriety he kept his tranquil air and quiz-zical smile, rather exaggerating them than otherwise. Moreover, in-stead of improvidently depending for drink on station bar-rooms and on the bottles of wayfarers, he carried with him a full demijohn. In his slangy way he called this his "wine-press," and when he treated his fellow-travellers, which he did often and liberally, he said with tire-some repetition, "Won't you have some of the wine of astonishment?" It must be understood that he was not helplessly and idiotically tipsy; that he did not reel and stammer and hiccough and talk incoherences. He was simply in an exasperated nervous state because of a long drinking bout.

Arrived in Hartland, he had sense enough not to go to the Beaumont house, knowing to a certain extent what his condition was, and not wishing to present himself thus before Kate. He took the one hack of the little town and drove to the one hotel with his valise and demijohn. After tea he thought himself sober enough to face his relatives, the Devines, and repaired to their house with the hope of learning that the Gilyard engagement was a fiction. The moment that Jenny laid eyes on him, she detected his status; for being a student of men, she knew him thoroughly, habits, expression, and all.

"What are you here for, Bent?" she asked at once, with not a little tartness.

"Oh, I am around," he replied, trying to smile naturally. "I am going to and fro in the earth, like Satan, you know."

"Exactly," said Jenny. "What are you going on in this way for? You'll be doing something to worry us. Where is your baggage? Why didn't you come here at once? You had better trot up stairs and take a nap."

"Come, don't jump on a man the minute you see him," protested Bentley, with a momentary sense of humiliation at being so quickly guessed out and so sharply lectured. "I am a two-legged creature without feathers, I believe. I don't need a coop."

"I wish you would come here and let us take care of you," insisted Jenny. "You are not fit to be about alone. Shame on you, you great baby! There, you sha'n't go," she added, running to the door, shutting it upon him and placing her plump shoulders against it. "Now I want to know what you are in Hartland for."

"How you do jockey me!" he said, with the magnanimous smile of a man who feels that he could resist if he would. "See here, Jenny," he added, after a scowl of trouble. "Is — is Kate Beaumont — is she engaged? Mrs. Chester tells me that she is engaged to the mininster, Gilyard. Is it true?"

Jenny hesitated; a flash passed through her hazel eyes; it was a gleam of mingled reflection and decision.

"He has been very attentive to her," she replied. "And if Mrs. Chester told you so, why, of course, Mrs. Chester knows."

Bentley, his face sobered and ennobled at once by intense grief, advanced to the door and seized the knob firmly.

"Where are you going?" demanded Jenny, without giving way.

"I am going back to Saxonburg," he whispered.

"Right," she said, letting him out. "I am sorry for you, Bentley; I am indeed. But you had better go."

Unfortunately there was no train up country till the next day. During the evening a number of Bentley's boon companions found him at the hotel, and beguiled him into a carouse which lasted till near morning. When he awoke from a brief and feverish sleep, he had lost the gentle sentiments which Jenny's feminine magnetism had instilled into him, and was ready in his semi-delirium to fight the first creature which approached him, whether it were a man, or a royal Bengal tiger, or a turtle-dove. He resolved to stay in Hartland and do battle with Frank McAlister. Part of the day he passed in wandering about the streets, heavy laden with bowie-knife, pistols, and ammunition, including whiskey, waiting for the appearance of his slanderer. But after dinner, meeting with that martial young lawyer, Jobson, he communicated his griefs to him, and under his dictation drew up a challenge in the approved style of old General Johnson, the document being as rhetorical and almost as voluminous as Cicero's Orations against Verres. This "flight of eloquence" was despatched to its destination by the hands of that most bloodthirsty paradox, invented by the code of honor, and ironically denominated "a friend."

We must see now how the cartel was received at the McAlister residence.

Perhaps, however, we ought first to note what was the general state of mind of the challenged party, and what had been his moral history, since we left him retiring from the *mêlée* in which Colonel Kershaw had fallen.

His moral history referred solely to Kate Beaumont; he thought of nothing else, and as it were knew nothing else. But while he thus lived solely for her, he believed that she could never live for him. It was not her heirship to a large estate which put her beyond his reach. He was not ashamed to sue for her because she had become rich; he respected himself too much to entertain that kind of coyness; or he loved her too much to suffer it to trammel him. Besides, he would one day be rich himself, at least sufficiently so to live like a gentleman. In his magnanimous and manly opinion, the match would be an equal one, only for this, that Kate was individually far his superior, as she was far the superior of any man.

But the perpetual conflicts and tragedies, — that last degrading *mêlée* and that last horrible tragedy, — how could he bridge them over so as to reach her? It seemed impossible; a sea of blood blown upon by winds of hate lay between them, — a sea which grew wider and stormier at every attempt to span it. Fate had been so long and violently against him, that it had almost wearied him out and stripped him of hope. But not of desire: he still longed passionately for her; all the more passionately because of disappointments and barriers.

While he was thus fighting weakly with despair (as a man fights who only receives blows and cannot return them) he received Mrs. Chester's anonymous gossip as to the Gilyard engagement. At first he declared to himself with angry contempt that he would not believe it; and then, comparing it with what he knew of the young clergyman's visits to the Beaumont place, he did believe it. It may be supposed that life had very little value in his eyes when, a few days later, he opened Bent Armitage's challenge.

He read the challenge with amazement, and it was surely an amazing paper. It was as full of specifications as an old-time indictment; it charged him with calumniating Bentley and Randolph Armitage at divers times and in sundry places; in short, it contained the whole substance of Mrs. Chester's malicious or crazy inventions.

"I wonder he didn't add, and for kicking up a blamed fuss generally," remarked Wallace, to whom Frank handed the three or four sheets of foolscap. "But I say, old fellow, for a man who pretends to be peaceable, you get into an awful number of squabbles."

"I know nothing about these things," declared Frank. "He must be insane."

"I'll fight him myself," offered Wallace, who had lately been rejected by Jenny Devine, and did not feel that life was worth keeping.

"It is not your business," replied Frank, remembering the story concerning Gilyard, and feeling far more acutely than Wallace that existence was a burden.

"Well, what do you mean to do, with your notions about duelling?" asked Wallace.

"I shall deny these ridiculous charges. Then, if he persists in picking a quarrel with me, — and I suppose that is his object, — I shall defend myself."

"You mean a rencontre?"

"I hate the word," said Frank. "But poor as life is, I have a right to defend it, and I shall do so."

"Of course, you might put him under bonds to keep the peace," suggested Wallace, doubtfully.

"Oh, is it worth while?" groaned Frank, almost wishing for a bullet in his brains.

"No," said Wallace. "We gentlemen don't do it. We gentlemen are like necessity; we know no law. Law is for our inferiors."

"Or for our betters," said Frank.

CHAPTER 36

Within two days after Bent Armitage left the lonely old house in Saxonburg, Mrs. Chester quitted it also, turning it over without the least compunction to the care of the negroes and the rats, and flying back, of all places in the world, to the Beaumont homestead, against which she had so lately shaken off the dust of her feet.

It was singular conduct certainly, but there was one thing which was even more singular than the conduct itself, and that was that it seemed to her perfectly natural. It also seemed to her quite natural to throw herself into Kate's arms, kiss her with sobbings and gaspings of affection, hug and kiss Nellie in the same ecstatic manner, and weep with joy at getting home. A few minutes later, her now very peculiar form of rationality led her to relate with astonishing volubility how Bent Armitage had come down to avenge the Beaumonts on their hereditary enemies, and how it was her intention to attend the funeral of Frank McAlister in the family carriage, and therefrom give the survivors of his race a piece of her mind.

Peyton Beaumont was not at home to care for his sister in this sad moment. But Vincent, a cool and clear-headed young man, his apprehension quickened by his medical knowledge, did all that was necessary. He soon had his unfortunate aunt in her room and in bed, under the guardianship of two muscular negro mammas. When he came out from her he said to his brother Poinsett, "I think you had better ride yourself after Mattieson. Tell him it is a clear case of delirium."

Kate was present, and heard these words. A flush started into her pale cheeks, and clasping her hands she exclaimed, "Oh Vincent!" It seemed as if this girl's affections followed the line of her natural duty, without the slightest regard as to whether those allied to her were lovable or not. Gentle and pacific as she was, abhorring bloodshed and all wild ways, we have seen how loyal and tender she has been to her free-drinking, pugnacious father and to her ungovernable cata- mounts of brothers, although their flighty and violent tempers have slaughtered the dearest hopes of her heart and filled the outlooks of her life with darkness. Mrs. Chester, too, had been a perpetual plague and perplexity; hardly a day had passed but she had vexed Kate's soul with some foolish interference or spiteful assault; and at last she had driven her into that to her most dreadful of extremities, an open con- flict. Yet the moment that misfortune settled upon this pest of a blood- relation, the girl was full of pity and sorrow.

"Am I to blame?" she asked, ready to accuse herself. "She went away from here because of a difficulty with me. Do you suppose that made her ill?"

"Nonsense!" declared Nellie, somewhat hardly. "She is always hav- ing difficulties. If they could hurt her, she would have died thirty years ago."

"Don't worry yourself, my dear," said Vincent, patting Kate's arm. "This is a trouble which has long been hanging over her."

"But she has been very well of late," replied the girl. "I never saw her more vigorous and clever, — in her way."

"She has not seen a thoroughly well day since I have been able to observe her medically," continued Vincent. "She has been for years in a state of abnormal excitement. We Beaumonts are all, always, pretty near a brain-fever. Except Kate here; and Kate is a Kershaw."

"She is not in immediate danger, I suppose," quietly observed Nellie, who did not love her aunt, and would not pretend to, not even now.

"No," judged Vincent. "Even if the affair should terminate fatally, it will be a lingering case."

"Oh Vincent, how calmly you talk of it!" said Kate.

"I am a physician," he answered. "I am professional." Then, patting her arm again, "You are a good, sweet girl; too good for use in this world, Katie."

"She is just a little bit silly," added Nellie, kissing her sister in a pitying way. "Come, child, don't worry so much about Aunt Marian. I dare say she will live to plague us a good many years yet. I have great faith in her."

"I am not thinking entirely of her," replied Kate, musingly. Then, raising her head suddenly, like one who resolves to speak in spite of scruples, she asked, "Vincent, how much truth has Aunt Marian been capable of telling this evening?"

"Who knows? A mixture of truth and error, I suppose."

Kate walked slowly away, and signed to her sister to follow her. When they were alone she said, "Nellie, there is no sense in this difficulty, if there is a difficulty, between Bent and the McAlisters. They cannot possibly have anything to do with each other. It must, in some way, be a pure misunderstanding."

Nellie reflected with the rapidity of lightning. It was evident that Kate wished to save the life of the man who loved her, and whom almost certainly she had once loved, if indeed she did not love him still. Should she be encouraged to talk of the matter, or should she be checked at once? It was impossible for a woman of more than average affection and sentiment to decide otherwise than in favor of Kate's purpose.

"I have no doubt that Bent is in fault," said Nellie. "Bent has probably been drinking, and when he does that he is a savage, like all his race. The Armitages are no more fit to have liquor than so many Seminoles. I sometimes think there must be Indian blood in them. Yes, I suppose Bent is going the way of his family; he has been drinking, and wants to fight some one. But what can we do?"

"I cannot ask *you* to do anything," answered Kate, with tears in her eyes, the pathetic tears of a retired soul which finds itself forced to step out into the hard, glaring world of action. "But I must do something. Both these men have liked me; I owe them kindness for that. I never shall be anything to either of them; but it is my duty to try to save their lives. Moreover, — you can understand it, Nellie, — this quarrel may be about me. Well, I shall try to stop it; woman as I am, I shall try. People will say it is not a lady's affair; but I cannot and shall not mind that. A lady surely cannot be wrong in seeking to save life. I cannot go to Mr. McAlister, but I certainly shall see Bentley. Will you help me?"

It was about as impossible for Nellie Armitage to say to her sister, "I will not help you," as it would have been for her to die outright by a mere effort of will. She reflected just one moment; but in that moment she resolved to do herself what Kate proposed to do, — resolved, furthermore, that she would do it without informing the girl of her purpose. All that she said was, "Yes, I will help you."

"You are my own darling," cried Kate, embracing her. "You are the strong and brave part of myself. Oh, it is a comfort to lean upon you!"

"I am something, in a weak way, like a husband, am I not?" returned Nellie, smiling away the scene.

"Will you send for Bent here?" asked Kate. "Papa has forbidden his family the house. But for such a purpose as this —"

"I will see to everything," promised Nellie. "It is late now. Go and sleep. Leave everything to me."

Kate hardly closed her eyes that night. The anxieties and sorrows of the last few months had got her into a way of lying much awake. Slumber is very largely a matter of habit; the less you do of it, the less you are likely to be able to do; and this troubled soul had acquired an unhappy facility for easy wakings and prolonged vigils. That night she tossed for hours, often turning her pillow to find a cool spot for her fevered head, and repeatedly rising to seek refreshment in the damp air that flowed in from the outer world. Most of the time her mind oscillated between her crazed aunt and the image of Bent Armitage hunting Frank McAlister to his death. She went through scene after scene in insane asylums, and stood witness to a succession of fatal duels.

It was unendurable, and she sought relief in devotion; but she prayed in vain. There is no comfort in the truest piety, as the case of Cowper ·bears witness, when it is presided over by a shattered nervous system. To no wicked soul, to no criminal called upon to expiate unparalleled guilt, could the heavens seem more pitiless than they seem to this scrupulously unselfish, this pathetically conscientious innocent. The Moloch of superstition which arises from deranged health, or overtasked sympathies, or a wearied brain, deigned no reply to her petitions but a demand for sacrifice, sacrifice! I *have* given him up," she replied in her despair. " I *do* give him up. Only, spare his life."

Once an apparition from the real life of the world — an apparition which would have moved and troubled her profoundly, had she understood it — came to give her a moment of distraction and slight relief. She had risen, seated herself by the window, and was drawing deep gasps of the cool night breeze, her aching eyes wandering through the broad moonlight. Suddenly the dogs barked; next there was the trample of a horse's feet advancing slowly and as if with caution; at last the figure or a horseman showed hazily in the road which passed the house. It remained a few minutes motionless, and then went the way it had arrived. Kate did not know that Frank McAlister came four miles every night to look at the windows of her room. Much as she thought about him, this never entered her imagination. She languidly watched the unknown out of sight, wondered a little who he might be, went back to her bed, and at last slept.

Before the younger sister was up in the morning, the elder had set out on her mission. Nellie had no difficulty in finding Bent, for he too had risen early, as was his custom.

This ill-starred youth was very sad, mainly because he was a little sick. The liquor which had been for the week past his chief motive-force, and almost his food, had become a dose. It had temporarily paralyzed his digestion, and it palled upon his taste. He had thrown away in disgust the cocktail which was to prepare him for breakfast; and, deprived of his usual stimulus, shaken moreover by his long drinking-bout, he was in low spirits. He was in that state of mind in which a man sees himself, not merely as others see him, but as he appears to his enemies and despisers. Remembering how for two days, or perhaps three, he could not tell which, he had been blustering publicly about Hartland, threatening death on sight to Frank McAlister in places where Frank McAlister never went, he queried whether he had not seemed a fool to everybody else, and whether he had not, in fact been a fool.

He thought of going back to Saxonburg; then he had a mad impulse to rush over to the Beaumont house and propose to Kate; then, knowing that she would refuse him, and probably even decline to see him, he queried whether he had not best shoot himself. At last it occurred to him that he might feel the better for a gallop; and, taking a horse from the hotel stables, he rode out breakfastless into the country, directing his course towards the long, low eminence on which stood the

Beaumont residence; for he too wanted to look at the home of Kate. By the way, he had his revolver under his coat and a brace of derringers in his pocket; being not yet decided in mind that he would not fire upon Frank McAlister if he should see him.

Nellie Armitage, also in the saddle, and followed by a mounted servant, encountered him half a mile from the village. Both drew rein as they met, the negro remaining at a little distance.

"Good morning, Bent," said Nellie. "I am glad to find you. I came to look for you."

"I hope you mean kindly," replied the young man, with a look which was both sullen and piteous. "I couldn't stand much of a lecture this morning." (He chose to pronounce it "lectur'," according to his slangy habit.) "I feel up to blowing the top of my head off if anybody I like should scold me. It's one of the black days."

The kindly nature of this youth, so much worthier a man than his thoroughly selfish and shameless brother, showed itself in the fact that tears of remorse and humiliation rose to his eyelids, and that his glance cowered under the gaze of a noble woman, a woman whom he respected.

"Yes, it is one of the black days," said Mrs. Armitage, surveying gravely and not without pity his haggard face. She well knew the meaning of that pallor; she had studied it often in her husband; she had seen it before in Bent.

"I will be as gentle as things allow," she went on. "Bentley, is it true that you are here to bring about a meeting with one of the McAlisters?"

He had a mind to say that surely no Beaumont should find fault with him for such a purpose as that; but he was a straightforward man, and he remembered that he was talking to a straightforward woman; he decided that it would be in bad taste to bandy words.

"That is what I waded in here for," he replied, almost involuntarily using his slang to carry off his embarrassment; for he recollected his absurd blustering about the village, and supposed that Nellie knew of it.

"Is this on our account?" continued Nellie. "I heard that you were here to take up the feud."

"That is all nonsense," he burst out. "I have been — wild; but I know perfectly well that I am not a Beaumont; I have not been fool enough to want to meddle in your family affairs. I have my own quarrel with this Frank McAlister."

It is about Kate, thought Nellie. She did not want to say a word further; she hated to be always talking with men about her sister; it seemed to make the girl too public. But she had undertaken this job of sending Bent home, and she must go through with it.

"Does your quarrel refer to one of us?" she asked unflinchingly.

Bent did not speak, and in truth could not speak, but his look said, yes.

"I know it has nothing to do with *me*," she continued. "What right have you to quarrel about *her*?"

After a long pause Bent answered, "He has slandered me to her."

"I don't believe it," abruptly declared Nellie, remembering Frank's manly face and deportment, unmarked by a trace of meanness.

"He told her that I was a drunkard," Bent added with a crimsoning face. "Even if I am one, he had no right to say it. It killed me," he went on, after a brief struggle with his emotion. "You know that I loved your sister. Well, she had a right to avoid me. You had a right to check me. But he, what business had he to say anything? Oh, curse him!"

And here his voice gave way utterly, sinking into a sob or a growl.

"There is one sure way to clear this up," observed Nellie, not looking at him the while, for his grief touched her. "My sister will tell us the absolute truth. You must go with me and see her."

"Hasn't your father forbidden me his house?" asked Armitage.

"If you have scruples about entering it at my invitation, she will come out to meet you," said Nellie, evading a direct reply. "Come."

"I suppose it will be proved to me that I am a fool," muttered Bent, as he rode on by her side.

Presently they halted in the road before the Beaumont mansion. Kate, dressed in black, was sitting in the veranda, anxiously awaiting the return of her sister. At a sign from Nellie she came hastily down to the gate and halted there breathless, looking up at Armitage with an expression which was partly recoil, partly pleading. Thin, haggard, and anxious, her pallor marking more clearly than health could the exquisite outline of her Augustan features, her lucid hazel eyes unnaturally large and bright with eagerness, she was beautiful, but also woful and almost terrible. At the first sight of her thus, so changed from what she had been when he last met her, Bentley was horror-stricken and terror-stricken. He dismounted and took off his hat; he wanted to prostrate himself at her feet.

"Miss Beaumont, are you ill?" He could say nothing else, and he could say nothing more.

"I am not well," she replied. "How can I be?"

There seemed to be a complaint in the words, but there was none in the tone. Her utterance and her whole manner were singularly mild and sweet, even for her. Gentle as she always had been, she had of late searched her conduct with such exaggerated conscientiousness, that she had found herself guilty of impatience and tartness, remembering with special remorse her controversy with Mrs. Chester; and by her efforts to curb a petulance which in reality had no existence she had acquired a bearing which resembled that of one who has passed years under the discipline of a convent; she was an incarnation of self-control, resignation, and humility.

"Let us say what we have to say at once," observed Mrs. Armitage, who had also dismounted. "Bentley, can you ask your own questions?"

"I can't," murmured the young fellow.

Nellie was too purely a woman not to pity a man so thoroughly humbled and wretched as was this man. But after one merciful glance at him, she turned to her sister and went on firmly: "Kate, I have promised Bent that he shall know the truth. Is it true, — he has heard so, — is it true that Frank McAlister has spoken ill of Bent to you?"

Kate's calmness vanished; all her face filled with excited blood; she answered hoarsely and almost sternly, "No!"

"In no way, in nothing?" continued Nellie.

"In no way, in nothing," repeated Kate, still with the same air of agitated protest.

Bentley suddenly flushed crimson with anger. He had been duped into outrageous folly which had pained the being whom he worshipped; and in his indignation he burst forth, "Then there is one Beaumont much to blame. Your aunt told me this."

The two women glanced at each other, and shrank backward as if under a blow.

"It must be uttered," said Nellie, at last. "Our poor aunt is crazy."

"Crazy?" demanded Bentley.

"She is in the house, under confinement."

"Crazy!" he repeated. "So am I. I have been crazy for a week. I always shall be."

There was another silence, an intensely tragic one, — one of those silences which do not come because there is nothing to say, but because all that can be said is too painful for utterance.

"Yes, I am no better than a madman," resumed Bentley, suddenly lifting his eyes and staring eagerly at Kate, with the air of one who bids an everlasting farewell to all that is dear. "I am and always shall be a miserable wretch. But at least, Miss Beaumont, I will never torment you again. This is the last time that you will see me, or, I hope, hear of me."

Without even offering his hand for a good by, he sprang on his horse and spurred away.

When he was out of sight, Nellie turned to her sister and said with a serenity which would be amazing, did we not remember the hardening misery of her married life, "It is a happy riddance."

"He had never done me any harm," replied Kate. "I am very, very sorry for him."

"Think of the harm he would have done you, had you liked him."

"Perhaps he would not have been the same," was the pensive response. "Perhaps I could not employ my life better than in trying to reform some such person."

"As I have employed my life," said Nellie, bitterly.

"There is nothing left me but to live for others," murmured Kate.

Her face was sadly calm, with the calmness of despair. Suddenly a little light of interest and perhaps of pleasure came into it. Nellie followed the direction of her sister's eye and beheld the approaching figure of the Rev. Arthur Gilyard.

"Must that be the end of it?" she thought. "Is Kate to become *his* wife, and wear herself to death on his sense of duty?"

CHAPTER 37

 What was to be the ultimatum of destiny to Kate Beaumont as a young lady?

Quite as much interested in this question as Nellie Armitage was Major John Lawson. From the time that the girl had returned from Europe, a wonder in his eyes of beauty, and grace, and graciousness, he had fairly worshipped her. The grandfather had broken out in him, as it sometimes will break out in old bachelors.

He never saw Kate and never thought of her, but he wanted to pat her hand, to praise her to her face, to minister unto her happiness, to be the good fairy of her future. He had a daguerreotype of her which he kept constantly with him and looked at twenty times a day, if not fifty. He used to say to himself, and sometimes to his confidential friends, "If I were young enough and rich enough and good enough, I would offer myself to her. Not that I should hope to be accepted, — certainly not, in no case. But I should consider it an honor to be refused by her. I should feel it a great privilege to be allowed to lay my heart unnoticed at her feet. I should feel that I had not lived in vain."

In truth, this elderly, simple-hearted, sweet-hearted gentleman had been for months little less than foolish over the child. And of late, now that she was the only representative of his deceased friend, the noble, the venerable, the revered Kershaw, he adored her as if she were more than human. Impulsively and fervently he transferred to her the allegiance which he had for years paid to the sublime old Colonel. How should he not love her when they mourned together? He gave her his sympathy because of her great bereavement, and demanded hers because of his own great sorrow. His head bowed, holding her hand tenderly (but not making eyes, nor grimacing, nor saying fine things), he softly bewailed the death of her grandfather and his friend, so sincerely bewailing it that more than once he wept. Vain and yet unselfish, whimsical and yet earnest, he was on the surface something of a bore, but at bottom a heart of gold. If, considering his tediousness, he was not worth the digging, he was at least worth having when he gave forth his treasures of affection freely.

It must be understood that, at Kate's request, he had taken charge of the Kershaw place until some one who could work it might be put in permanent tenantcy, and that consequently he was able to ride over to the Beaumont house every day to visit his favorite. Of course, he saw that his other pet, Frank, never came there, and that the Rev. Arthur Gilyard came there very often. Was this young minister going to spoil the romance of "Romeo and Juliet in South Carolina"? Was he going to prevent an alliance between the Beaumonts and McAlisters, and thus make himself the instrument of prolonging the feud? Major Lawson, though reverent of clergymen in general, and heretofore an admirer of Gilyard himself, began to have doubts of his piety. When he was not talking with him (in which case he of course grinned and complimented in his usual fashion) he watched him with a suspicious air, and, in fact, rather glared at him, as if he would have liked to send him on missionary work to the Cannibal Islands and get him eaten out of the way. With respect to Kate, much as he loved her, he almost felt that it would be better for her to take poison over Frank's dead body, than to become the happy wife of any other gentleman.

"What is Mrs. Armitage about?" he demanded, talking to himself, as was his frequent custom. "Has she — a woman — a woman too who has suffered — no true womanly sentiment with regard to this matter? Bless me, I had supposed that Woman had, of all the human race, the truest eye for what is beautiful in life! And this — *this* marriage — *this* instead of the other — would be so unbeautiful, so unartistic! I had supposed that women were our superiors in a perception of the gracious fitness of things. They surely are so in the affairs of ordinary existence. They decorate our houses. To them we owe carpets, curtains, tassels, laces, *parterres* of flowers. Without them our dwellings would be bare walls, mere shelters, dens. But for their æsthetic guidance we should spend our money entirely on the useful, the ponderous, the unamiable. We should have aqueducts and no sofas, fortifications and no upholstery. And when it comes to making our lives beautiful with poetry, with the romance of artistically arranged events, with the facts which naturally arise from true sentiment, is woman — *woman* — to fail us?"

The Major was thinking his best; he felt that he ought to take notes of himself; he resolved to put these ideas into his next essay (for private readings); perhaps, if it were possible, into a poem. He grew oratorical; he started backwards and started forwards; he ran from basso up to soprano, and down again; he broke a wineglass and did not know it.

Presently, however, he recollected the urgency of the case, and resolved to have a talk with Mrs. Armitage as to her sister. He was a little afraid of Nellie; there was about her a manly frankness which was rendered more potent by a womanly impulsiveness; and this mingling of weight and rapidity gave her a momentum which he did not love to encounter. Nevertheless, alarmed for his romance, and anxious for the happiness of his two pets, he sought her out and unfolded to her his mind.

"I am quite of your opinion," replied Nellie, when she had discerned, through many smiling and flattering circumlocutions, the fact that the Major did not like the Gilyard courtship.

Lawson was stunned as usual by her directness, but delighted with her assent.

"My dear lady, — gracious lady, as Dante says, — you fill me with joy," he exclaimed, seizing her hand and patting it in his caressing way. "I have not had such a moment of gratification for months."

"But what can be done?" asked Mrs. Armitage. "Kate is her own mistress."

"Go to Mr. Gilyard," replied Lawson, firmly; meaning, however, that Nellie should go, not he himself. "Hint to him, if necessary say to him plainly, that he is standing in the way of much good. Don't you see, my dear Mrs. Armitage? If he marries Kate, she can't marry Frank

McAlister. Then what means have we left for ending this horrible feud? Pardon me, — I really beg your pardon, Mrs. Armitage, — I am speaking severely of your family *fasti*, of your hereditary palladium. But I remember my old, noble, revered friend Kershaw, and I venture to utter my mind boldly. I know that it was his earnest desire for many years that this quarrel should terminate. Have I offended you?"

"Never mind, Major," replied Nellie, quietly waving her hand as if to brush away his apologies. "I am altogether of your opinion in this whole matter. We have had enough of quarrels. I have seen enough of them."

"You delight me beyond expression, — beyond the power of a Cicero to express," chanted Lawson, his eyes twinkling with an unusual twinkle, as if there were tears of joy in them. "And now, gracious lady —"

"I will make one more effort for peace," interrupted Nellie. "I will — But never mind what; you shall know in a day or two."

Quite tremulous with his gladness, the Major thanked her copiously, squeezed her hand again and again, and at last fairly kissed it by force, subsequently waving affectionate and cheering farewells to her while he got out of the house, mounted his steed, and ambled out of sight.

The characteristic step which Nellie Armitage decided upon was to go straight to Arthur Gilyard with her story and her demands.

"I want a great thing of you," said this sympathetic woman, knowing full well the pain that she gave, and watching it with the emotion of an angel overseeing the necessary chastening of a saint; "I want you to make peace between us and the McAlisters, so that my unhappy sister may meet the man who loves her, and whom I believe she loves. I ask this of you for her sake, and for the sake of the father and brothers whom I want to keep in life, and in the name of all my relatives who have fallen in this long quarrel."

Kate's lover, thus summoned to give her up to a preferred lover, half started to rise from the chair in which he was sitting, and then dropped his head upon his bosom as if he had been shot. His habitually pale cheeks turned quite white; he was so dizzy that he could not see the woman who was torturing him; the words that he heard during the next minute were merely as a drumming in his ears.

But, fortunately for his honor as a man, he was of the same heroic mould with the person who demanded of him this tremendous sacrifice, and who had had the greatness to believe that he could be great enough for it. As he came back to his full consciousness, he passed rapidly in review the procession of horrors which had marked the history of the feud, and resolved that he would do what lay in him to close such a source of bloodshed, no matter what suffering the labor might bring him.

"Is it too much to ask?" murmured Nellie, her heart almost failing her at the sight of his quivering face.

"No duty is too much to ask," were his first words, — words spoken on the rack. After a moment more of struggling for breath and purpose, he added, as if by way of exhortation to himself, "A Christian must not hesitate before duty."

She remained silent; she was revering him. But surely it was also a grand thing in her that she could be noble enough, in that eager and anxious moment, to perceive his nobility.

"How can I best serve your purpose?" he presently inquired.

"May I beg you to join with me in urging a reconciliation upon my father?" she answered.

"I will do so, with all my heart," said this man whose heart was bleeding.

"He will return this evening," added Nellie. "Will you see him with me to-morrow?"

"I can talk with him best alone," he replied. "Will you allow it?"

Then, perceiving assent in her eyes, he hastily rose, bowed, and got himself away, conscious that he was tottering.

"It was worse than I looked for," said Nellie, as she gazed after him with admiration and pity. "He is to lose her in showing himself worthy of her."

In the little space which we can allot to Arthur Gilyard, we must strive to do him justice. It was characteristic of him that from the moment when he resolved to tear out his heart for the good of others, he never faltered in his purpose. What struggle remained to this clear-headed and heroic sufferer was simply a struggle for resignation. He would do his duty; oh yes, that would be done; that of course. The hardness of the thing was to do it in a spirit which should be held acceptable in that unseen world which he tried to think of as the only real world. Oh, how unreal it seemed to him as he rode homeward! Earth, this earth of emotions, this passionate, mortal life, they were very near and terribly puissant. He was like Christian, resolute upon going through the valley of shadows, but seeing Apollyon "straddled quite across the way," dreadful to behold and threatening woful wounds.

It was not until he had locked himself into his accustomed place of devotion that he could get one glimpse of that sphere which Kate Beaumont did not yet inhabit, and where her influence must not reign. But here, on the threshold of a sanctuary, we stop.

When, during the next day, he presented himself before Peyton Beaumont, he was so pinched and pale that his host asked him if he had been sick.

"I have been favored with my usual health," he replied calmly. "Perhaps the consciousness of a great and difficult duty has weighed upon me more than it would have weighed upon a stronger and better man."

Beaumont could hardly fail to understand that this word "duty" referred to himself; that towards him was coming some plea, some remonstrance, or perhaps some reproof. High as was his temper, and savage in certain points as had been his life, he had an imaginative reverence for religion, and a well-bred respect for clergymen. His wide-open black eyes stared into the firm blue ones of Gilyard with mere grave surprise and expectation, not showing a sparkle of annoyance.

"I beg beforehand that you will hear me patiently until I have discharged my conscience," continued the minister.

"Mr. Gilyard, speak boldly," said Peyton. "I give you my thanks already, if what you have to say concerns my conduct."

"It does in part," went on Gilyard. "I have come solely to beg you to stop the account of blood between your family and the McAlisters. Heretofore more than once, if I remember, I have ventured to speak to you of this matter; but not plainly enough, and not urgently enough. I did not do my full duty. I was weakly and wickedly vague. I did not clearly set before you your responsibility, and — I must say the word — your guilt."

"Guilt!" exclaimed Beaumont, his astonishment very great, and his eyes showing it.

"In the presence of God I repeat the word," insisted Gilyard. "It condemns me as well as you. I should have uttered it years ago."

After a moment's reflection, after drawing a long breath of surprise, Beaumont said, "We are not the only guilty ones."

"It is too true. The McAlisters also come under condemnation."

"They do," declared Peyton, in an excitement of self-justification. "I made peace with them once. And they broke it: *they* broke it."

"Offer it again," exhorted the minister. "Urge it."

"See here," said Beaumont, after further thought. "I can tell you something — a secret, please to observe — which will give you pleasure. I have been engaged lately in preparing a way to peace. Kershaw asked it of me. I pledged him my word on his death-bed, and I have not forgotten it. In a day or two — in a few days at least — I hope to hear from Judge McAlister, hope to receive a friendly message from him. In that case I will give him my hand for life, if he will take it and do what he should to keep it. I will, so help me — It is not easy work, this. But it shall be done; it shall, I promise you. Will that content you?"

"I am merely a messenger from One who is infinitely greater than I, Mr. Beaumont," returned Gilyard. "I can only say that personally I thank you for this assurance."

"And thank you, sir, for coming to me," said Peyton. "I do in all sincerity. But bless me! you are very pale. Won't you have a glass of wine?"

Mr. Gilyard had understood that peace between the Beaumonts and McAlisters meant the cession by him of Kate Beaumont to Frank McAlister. On obtaining the promise of this peace, the assurance of this cession, he had turned dizzy.

It was some minutes before he could muster fortitude to seek out Mrs. Armitage and say to her, "We have reason to be grateful. Your father, I believe, and hope, will end the feud, if it is humanly possible."

"It will take us a lifetime to thank you for this," replied Nellie, ready to kneel at the feet of this martyr, who had, as it were, lighted his own pyre of torture.

"I should have done my little long ago," he said.

Then, suddenly remembering that in such a case he might not have loved only to lose, he added in his heart, "My sin has found me out." If he had thought of confessing his hopeless affection, if he had had an impulse to utter a complaint and a cry for sympathy, his mouth was sealed now. Bearing a burden of self-condemnation which only a saintly nature could heap upon itself, suffering as perchance only the perfectly conscientious and the high-minded can suffer, this noble though limited spirit went out speechlessly from the household which he had blessed, bearing his cross alone.

That very day Judge McAlister received his appointment as Judge of the United States District Court of South Carolina. This was Beaumont's doing; it was to bring this about that he had spent weeks in Washington; it was to this that he had alluded when he told Gilyard that he had prepared a way for peace. He had fought hard for it, combating the partisan prejudices which ruled at the national capital, and beating down the pretensions of claimants of his own following. Of course he knew that he was not under any practical obligations to McAlister, inasmuch as his own election would have been a certainty, even had not his rival withdrawn from the canvass. But his word had been passed; and that word it had been the pride of his life to keep sacred; and in this matter it must be kept all the more sacred because given to an enemy.

The favor was received in a spirit not unworthy of that in which it had been conferred. Judge McAlister was not often troubled by magnanimous impulses; but now the best blood in his mainly selfish heart boiled to the surface.

"This is Beaumont's work," he said, handing the commission to Frank, who happened to be with him at the time. "By heavens, he is a gentleman!"

The young man's face flushed crimson; he saw all the possible consequences of this fine deed; he trusted that there was yet for him love and happiness. It was impossible for the moment that he could do more than merely endure his heartbeats. He was either far above or far below the faculty of speech.

"I could not have demanded it," continued the father. "That miserable rencontre had put my claims in chancery. He is certainly a gentleman."

"What will you do, sir?" the son could at last inquire.

"What do you mean?" stared the Judge.

"If you accept the commission, you will owe an expression of —"

"Gratitude," admitted the Judge, with a grand bow. "Unquestionably. I shall owe it, and I will pay it. The gift, to be sure, is not overwhelming," he added, his conceit, or, as he conceived it to be, his dignity, beginning to come uppermost. "I suppose I had claims to the position which no man could gainsay. I may say that I had rights. This thing, at the least, was due me. But I consider the good-will," he went on, with an air of magnanimity. "A bit of good-will from an old enemy is doubly an obligation. Certainly I shall thank Beaumont. I could not do otherwise so long as my name is McAlister."

Heavens, what a pride he had in being himself, and how loftily he bugled the word "McAlister!" He was grandiose over his gratitude; he would so return thanks for the favor received as to overpay it; he would make Beaumont glory in having served him.

"I will go in person," added this Artaxerxes of a country gentleman and local politician.

"I beg pardon," observed Frank. "We must take precautions against another misunderstanding. You are not perhaps aware that there is a second drunken Armitage on hand."

It must be understood that, although Bentley had already left Hartland, Frank had not heard of it.

"Indeed?" demanded the Judge, not minded to get himself shot unnecessarily, at his time of life.

Then the young man told the elder how Bent had challenged him, and was supposed to be lying in wait to take a shot at sight.

The father gave the son a queer look. He was saying to himself, "In my day, when a fellow proposed to ambush us, we used to look him up and root him out." But he could not make this speech to his own child, and especially not under the present circumstances; for the Armitages were kin to the Beaumonts, and with these last it was not well to open a fresh account of blood, at least not immediately.

"That is bad," he observed, arching his eyebrows thoughtfully. "I hope you are — taking precautions."

"I am not ashamed to say that I am keeping out of the lunatic's way. Of course, if he attacks me, I shall defend myself."

"Unquestionably you would be justified in so doing," declared the man of law. "Indeed, it would be your duty, to yourself and society. But I am sorry to hear this. It complicates matters; it is dreadfully inconvenient."

After a moment of worried meditation he added, "I am greatly tempted to put this rascal under bonds to keep the peace."

"It would excite discussion, sir," observed Frank, who knew that certain families were too lofty and honorable to appeal to the law for protection against their foes.

"It would," admitted the Judge of the United States District Court, remembering that he was a high-toned gentleman first, and an expounder of the statutes afterwards. "I must confess that I hardly know what to do in the premises. On the whole, I must, I think write to Beaumont, asking his permission to call upon him with one or two of my family."

"With our revolvers in our pockets, sir?" smiled Frank.

"I see no impropriety in that, under the circumstances," answered the Judge. "Of course we shall have the gentility and the sense to keep them out of sight, except in the last extremity."

"On the whole I can suggest nothing better," assented the young man, knowing that his father would do nothing better, though it should be suggested by an angel.

Anything for a chance to bring the two families together in peace; anything to obtain one more look at Kate Beaumont; anything for love!

CHAPTER 38

 Judge McAlister did not call upon his ancient enemy and present benefactor attended by an armed retinue.

Having made inquiry in the village after Bentley Armitage, and having learned positively that that unhappy young man had gone to parts unknown, he went alone to the Beaumont place with his calumets and his wampums.

There had been an appointment, but, watches disagreeing, Peyton had miscalculated his visitor's arrival, and was at his stables, with all his sons and not far from half his negroes, inspecting a newly purchased racer.

It was Kate Beaumont who received and welcomed Frank McAlister's father. She had learned that he was coming, and learned or guessed that it was in peace. In spite of her conscientious struggles to be calm, in spite of the spiritual melancholy which had settled upon her, she was in a state of feverish excitement. Would there be a renewal of amity? Would the dry bones of feelings and expectations which she believed to be dead clothe themselves again with life and stand upon their feet, a mighty army? How the questions, the doubts, the hopes, the scruples, the self-reproaches, the longings, the fears, and still the hopes again, thronged through her spirit! Impossible to give more than a feeble and vague idea of the contest which agitated her soul and caused her very flesh to tremble. One word she kept repeating, "I have given him up, given him up." Nevertheless she went forth to greet his father.

When the Judge met her in the veranda, he saw a girl who had not slept the night before, and who was even then striving to lay her heart upon the altar of a Moloch, but whose face was so colored, and whose eyes so brightened by fever that she looked the picture of health.

"My dear young lady!" he said, the exclamation being actually forced from him by his amazement at a beauty which was even more wonderful now than formerly, because more spiritual. "I consider it a good omen that you should be the first to meet me," he added in the flush of his enthusiasm.

"You have my earnest thanks for this visit, sir," she replied, pressing his hand fervently, and then dropping it suddenly, with a strange mixture of impulse and self-repression.

"Heaven bless you, my dear young lady!" said the Judge, still in a sort of daze as he bowed gigantically over her, wondering and admiring. "You show your native goodness in divining me," he continued, regaining his intellectual self-possession. "I have come for peace."

She led him into the parlor with the air of a dethroned and sorrowing but resigned queen, receiving a king who brings sympathy. Her fine figure rendered only the more willowy and elegant by emaciation and by her closely clinging black dress, she was an incarnation of grace.

"I have but one regret," she sighed, her eyes turning upward sadly as if seeking her grandfather.

"Miss Beaumont, I share it," he answered, understanding her with a quickness which did him honor. "I wish John Kershaw could have seen this day."

"I wish so," whispered Kate, almost inaudibly.

The Judge rose to his feet and took both her hands tenderly, while a dimness came into his eyes as of half-born tears.

"My dear child, you have my very heart's sympathies," he said. "What a man he was! What a loss!"

Kate bowed; she could not answer; she could not look at him. She bowed very low, let fall a few bright drops upon the carpet and left the room. When she had gone, the ponderous Judge took a large white handkerchief out of a capacious pocket, slowly wiped away something which obscured his sight, and murmured, "Poor — beautiful — creature!"

As soon as Beaumont learned that McAlister had arrived, he hurried to meet him with such speed that he entered the parlor quite out of breath. To honor the occasion and the visitor, he had dressed himself with scrupulous care. He had on a blue dress-coat with gilt buttons, a buff vest also with gilt buttons, and buff kerseymere trousers tightly strapped under the instep, as was the fashion of the time. The strong colors, so suggestive of military uniform, perfectly became his bold, trooper-like, officer-like expression and the dark ruddiness, almost as deep as mahogany, of his complexion. His costume contrasted with the solemn black of the Judge, much as his impetuous character contrasted with the other's deliberate subtlety.

"I beg your pardon, Judge, for making you wait a single instant," were Peyton's first words, at the same time cordially giving his hand.

"I have not waited," said McAlister, with a certain grave emotion. "I have been gratified, honored by an interview with your youngest daughter."

"I am glad that she was here to receive you," returned Beaumont, bowing thanks for the compliment to his child.

"She is a wonderful woman," declared the Judge, momentarily forgetting the object of his visit. "I thought I knew her already; but she always astonishes me. I have never seen in any other person such expression of feeling and character. She spoke of her grandfather in a way —"

The Judge stopped. Beaumont bent his head as if beside a grave.

"Lamentable tragedy!" resumed McAlister. "Mr. Beaumont, I hope it will be the last in the history of our families."

The Judge, profoundly in earnest, was talking above himself. It was the contagion of Kate Beaumont's tender nobility of soul, quite as much as a consciousness of the weighty importance of the occasion, which thus evaluated him. His host looked at him with surprise and respect, and answered fervently, "I sincerely hope and trust so."

He too, as well as McAlister, was at his moral zenith. He was quite aware that this was one of the most impressive and important moments of his life. Its gravity exalted and purified him; he showed it in his deportment and utterance. Throughout the whole interview he exhibited not one violent impulse, not one start of his characteristic eccentricity of feeling, not one amusing trait of unconscious humor. Never before, at least not since his days of youthful diffidence, had he been such a calm, contained gentleman as he was during this scene.

"Mr. Beaumont, I am your debtor," resumed McAlister, remembering that he had come to return thanks.

"I have fulfilled my promise. Let us say no more about it."

"I must say this, that I owe you my earnest gratitude, and give it."

"Judge, your merit has at last been acknowledged, at least in part. That is all."

Considering the life-history of these two men, it was surely a grand, as well as perhaps a grandiose, dialogue.

"You are very kind to express yourself thus," bowed the Judge. Then he fell silent. He wanted to ask for peace. He remembered Frank, and wanted to give him a chance. But the feud was a very old denizen of his heart and habits. It made the word "peace" a hard one to mouth.

Beaumont broke the silence. He felt that McAlister had said as much as could be demanded of him. It was his own turn now. His rival must be met half-way. Moreover, his promise to Kershaw must be kept. The two families must, if the thing were possible, be brought into some kind of compact, so that bloodshedding at least should cease.

"Judge, let me be frank," he began, speaking slowly, like one who weighs his words, and who speaks because he must. "There has been a feud between your house and mine. I propose that it shall end; that you and I shall do our utmost to end it; that we shall pledge our faith and character to that work. Sir, will you give me your hand to it?"

His face was crimson with his struggle to say this. Judge McAlister's oaken countenance also turned to a deep red. Both men felt that it was a weighty agreement to offer and to accept.

"Here is my hand," replied the head of the McAlisters. "Our honor is plighted."

After this great deed had been done they sat down, both at once, two tired and breathless men. This making of peace had been to them a more wearying effort than would have been a wrestling-match.

"We shall keep this treaty," said the Judge, after a moment. "We never fully and freely and in set terms made it before."

"That was our mistake," answered Beaumont.

He seemed absent-minded; he was thinking of Kershaw.

"It is the spirit of my old friend who has done this," he presently exclaimed, rising and walking the room. "He is stronger in death than he was in life. God forgive me for not having let him see this day and hear these words."

His martial and grim face worked with emotion, and there was a prayerful, piteous stare in his black eyes. The Judge rose also, seized and wrung Peyton's hand anew, and even patted him comfortingly on the shoulder. He had not for years been in such a state of tender emotion over a man. He absolutely thought well of Beaumont, absolutely admired him.

Soon the conversation became calmer, turning easily to subjects of an unpathetic nature, as is natural with masculine talk. For a while it was mutually satisfactory; but at last McAlister made a remark which showed his thick-skinned nature, his born incapacity for distinguishing what might offend the feelings of a man of acute sensibility.

"I trust that you will be reassured before long as to the fate of your son-in-law," he said. "Excuse me," he added, perceiving a change in his host's countenance. "I wish to say that he could hardly be held culpable as to the fate of your lamented friend. So obvious an accident, you know!"

Beaumont's brow had darkened unpleasantly; he did not want to hear about a son-in-law whom he had despised and hated; above all, he did not want to discuss his character and chances with a McAlister. For an instant it seemed as if he would reply offensively; but after a struggle, he smoothed his forehead and spoke softly. What he said, however, was startling.

"He is dead, sir. I am quite reassured as to his fate. Shot dead, sir, by some mountaineer or other, in the Dark Corner. Don't trouble yourself to condole with us, sir."

The Judge had blundered, and of course he saw it. He bowed meekly, mumbled some unnoticed words of apology, and passed to other matters. But it seemed well now not to prolong the interview; and, having begged Beaumont to do him the honor of a visit, he took his leave.

"Ah!" burst out Peyton, when his visitor had got out of hearing. "How can I get on with such a man? Even when he means to be civil he tramples on one's soul."

After a little, however, he recovered his good-nature, and added, with a smile of grim resignation, "But he will die some day, and, for that matter, so shall I; and perhaps our children will find each other more endurable. I must use the rest of my life in trying to give them a chance to live."

Considering the man's sensitive nature and pugnacious habits, the resolution was surely self-sacrificing, and showed not a little paternal affection.

But Peyton Beaumont became more distinctly and agreeably reconciled to the idea of peace with the McAlisters, when Frank called on him. The habitually stormy depths of his eyes grew calm, and a hospitable smile flew like a dove to sit upon his wide, strong mouth, as he beheld the almost sublime stature and the handsome, gracious, dignified countenance of this gentle giant. Painful and humiliating as the task was to him, he apologized for the untoward incidents of Frank's last visit.

"It was a shameful, horrible breach of hospitality, sir," he said. "But you will surely not hold us accountable, especially as we were the greatest sufferers. That — that scoundrel is dead, sir," he added. "He will make no more mischief."

"God have mercy upon him!" Frank murmured. Beaumont made no reply; his nostrils were distended and his eyebrows working; he was thinking of the dead Kershaw and the sorrows of his daughters, not praying for Armitage.

After some amicable dialogue, the young man asked leave to pay his respects to the ladies of the family.

"They will be happy to see you, sir," answered Beaumont, graciously. "You will find my youngest daughter very much changed. She has received a terrible blow."

So Frank perceived for himself when he encountered Kate. It is true that the first sight of him brought a flush to her face and a tremulous brightness to her eyes; but in a moment came the thought that she had given him up, turning her to the whiteness and coldness of marble; and presently the tumult subsided into the calm pallor of physical languor and of grief. Thin as she was and faded as she was, Frank found her more beautiful than ever. His pity for her increased his affection magically, and he thought that he had never before seen her so enchanting.

Of course, in this first meeting after great calamities, awed by the melancholy of those eyes whose pathos made the room holy, and still believing somewhat in the tale of the Gilyard engagement, Frank could not breathe a word nor throw out a look of courtship. The interview passed in talk on commonplace subjects, and he retired from it so unsatisfied that he thought himself unhappy. It had been a great joy to look upon her once more; but he believed that he was doomed never to win her as a wife.

Several weeks passed without visible change in the relations of the two young people. But meantime Kate's health rapidly returned to her, and brought with it a fresh outburst of her girlish beauty. She grew well at Hartland; she made a little trip to Charleston, and came back still better; in two months she had recovered her plumpness, her tints of damask rose, and the brightness of her eyes. The moment that life had ceased to be merely a sorrow, it had ceased to be a disease.

As if to pile miracle on miracle, health of body restored health of mind. The clouds of superstitious gloom and ascetic purpose, which had lately wrapped her in wretchedness, rose, grew thin, dispersed, vanished, she knew not why, she knew not when, but utterly and forever. It was as if a terrible enchantment had been lifted by a spell, restoring her from cavernous dungeons to light, from a false world of horrors to a real world of happiness. Suddenly and to her amazement she found herself free; she could do what she would with her pure heart and will and life. "No voice nor hideous hum" of her Moloch any longer deceived her; and she knew that her late vows of self-sacrifice were senseless and nugatory. Indeed, she was so perfectly healthy in spirit that she at times asked herself, "Have I been crazed?" No, she had not been crazed; but she had been near it.

It must be understood, by the way, that Arthur Gilyard had facilitated her recovery by keeping altogether away from her, so that she the more easily got rid of her impression that it was her duty to become his wife. It was the final act of self-abnegation in this noble spirit to seek a prompt dismissal from his parish, and take up his labor for souls in a distant part of the State. It was well, no doubt, for his own peace, but it was well also for the peace of Kate.

Meantime, the two families remained on friendly, and, so far as the women-folk were concerned, on cordial terms. Mrs. McAlister and Mary once more twined the tendrils of their hearts around Kate, claiming her as one whom they had a right to love and must love. It was they who first learned, and who quickly reported to their son and brother, that the Rev. Arthur Gilyard never came to the Beaumont house, and so could not be troth-plighted to its fairest inmate. They threw out hints of encouragement to the young man which sent the blood through all his six feet and four inches of stature. These affectionate urgencies were the more open because the Judge was impatient for a proposal of marriage, and actually pushed the women to push the boy up to it.

"Why doesn't he take advantage of the present favorable circumstances?" said this unsensitive old gentleman. "A woman who is in affliction, and who of course needs consolation, is all the more likely to accept an offer. Depend upon it, madam, that I know something of human nature. He ought to speak at once, before any one else comes in."

In a modified form, made delicate and pure by a mother's lips, these suggestions reached Frank's ears.

"I should be so overjoyed to take such a daughter to my heart," said Mrs. McAlister in a cooing, happy tone. "I think, considering what she already knows of your feelings, that she would not be shocked if you should speak to her. You need not press her for an answer; it would be best not, I think and feel. But you certainly may tell her that you have not changed. It would be only fair and kind to tell her that."

So Frank McAlister resolved to tell Kate Beaumont that he had not changed.

CHAPTER 39

 Before going to the daughter, Frank went to the father, whose consent it will be remembered that he had once asked but not received; matters between the Beaumonts and McAlisters being then in a highly explosive state, smoking with a promise of lofty flame and red-hot lava. He found the Honorable Peyton in his veranda, walking up and down with the short, careful steps of a gouty man, and smoking a cigar with an air of grinding it.

"Good evening," said the lord of the manor in the strong and rather too trumpet-like tone which was habitual with him, but at the same time amicably producing a spare cigar. "Will you join me?"

"I wish to join you for life, Mr. Beaumont," replied Frank, not even seeing the proffered Havana.

It was evident that Kate's father comprehended, and that he was not entirely gratified. Over his hard and highly colored but expressive face there came a cloud, which, if not downright displeasure, was anxiety. Nevertheless, he looked into his visitor's eyes with an air of attentive and respectful meditation.

"Once more, Mr. Beaumont," continued Frank, unfalteringly, "I come to ask you to let me tell your daughter that I love her with all my heart."

The simple earnestness of the phrase, and the tremulous sincerity of the tone in which it was uttered, shook all the father in Peyton.

"Look here," he said, throwing away his cigar, and seizing both of Frank's hands. "I have but a single objection. To yourself I have none. I believe in you, Mr. McAlister; I believe in your head and your heart. But, I sometimes ask myself, how long will peace last between our families, much as we now prize it? How do I know that you will not some day separate me from my child?"

"From my wife, sir, you shall never be separated," answered Frank, returning the other's spasmodic grasp. The two men were locked together by their emotions; it seemed to Beaumont as if he could not escape, as if a fate held him fast.

"I know that this marriage will be a bond of union for us all," continued Frank, speaking for the moment with the sublimity of a prophet.

"Ah, well, — so let it be," returned Beaumont, unable to resist this enthusiasm. "Go and find her."

Frank raised the hand of Beaumont, and suddenly pressed it to his heart. It was a hand which had shed McAlister blood, but he forgot that; it was also the hand of his loved one's father, and that alone he remembered.

Next, descending into the garden, where he had already seen Kate through the twilight, he sought her amid a perfumed tangle of shrubbery and flowers. The faint golden radiance which lingered in the west revealed her; she appeared to him to be standing in a delicate, unearthly halo of luminousness; she reminded him of Murillo's Immaculate Virgin showing through hazes of aureoles. Although the comparison sprang from the hot imagination of strong affection, it was not altogether extravagant. The greatest fact possible to young womanhood, the consciousness of loving and of being loved, had given Kate the sweet serenity of a seraph. Moreover, unmarried though she was, there was about her something of the Madonna. Her face had that various richness of expression which we see in the faces of wives and mothers so much oftener than in the faces of maidens. Under suffering her mind and heart had both expanded, and this development of thought and feeling had given every feature a new light, rising at times to a fulness of meaning which seemed to comprehend all womanhood.

There was just one blemish to the picture, if so tender a thing may be called a blemish. There was a tear; it hung upon her eyelash as he softly approached her; and when she turned at the sound of his footsteps, it fell upon a white rose which she held to her lips. She had been kissing the rose because it was her grandfather's favorite flower.

"Will you let me spend the future in trying to console you for the past?" he said, gently taking her hand.

Yes, such had been her history and such was his nature, that his first words of love to her must be words of comfort.

It was just what she craved; she could hardly, under any circumstances, have answered nay to such a plea; and loving him, trusting him as she did, she only answered by leaning on his breast and weeping there. It was one of those sublime moments in the life of the soul when it is mightier than the body; when its emotions are so overpowering that the voice fails at their mere advent and can give them no utterance.

"I will console you for all," he whispered, his arm supporting her. "Every breath that I draw shall be drawn for your happiness."

What further was said between them we will not repeat. The few syllables which they exchanged had to their souls a fulness and richness of meaning which would not appear to those who should read them. Their lips, touched by fire from heaven, ennobled language far beyond its wont, and made it like the speech of some better world. Words became emotions, pouring heart into heart, and mingling them forever.

As they returned to the house, Nellie Armitage met them, gave one glance at her sister's face, read with a woman's sympathetic insight all that was in it, passed a tremulous arm quickly around her neck, and kissed her. Then pressing Frank's hand vehemently, she went and wandered alone in the darkling garden, calling to mind how this same cup of happiness had once been put to her lips, and obstinately struggling to forget how it had been dashed from them.

Major Lawson, lounging on the gravel-walk before the house, also saw the young couple, comprehended what had happened to them, and halting with a start, stared after them in ecstasy, muttering, "Bless my body! It is done at last. The Montagues and Capulets reconciled! Romeo and Juliet to be married! Bless my body! I could caper like a nigger. Bless my body!"

"I have won her," was Frank's simple address, when, wearing Kate proudly on his arm, he reached Beaumont.

"Take her," replied the father. "Only remember that I have put my happiness as well as hers in your hand."

He kissed his child repeatedly, and then resumed his solitary walk and cigar, feeling deserted and sorrowful.

Well, a year more saw many events: the marriage of Frank McAlister to Kate Beaumont; the young man's installation over the Kershaw estate, he giving up science as a thing not yet required by Carolinians; the marriage of Vincent Beaumont to Mary McAlister, who became lady of the house in the mansion of her ancestors' enemies; the marriage of Jenny Devine to Dr. Mattieson, — "Just to console him for losing you, my dear," she said to Kate; finally, the death of poor worn-out Mrs. Chester by softening of the brain.

It will be understood, of course, that there was no renewal of the famous feud which had so long kept Hartland in cheerful tragical gossip, and made it feel itself to be the most illustrious village of South Carolina.

It must be stated also that Peyton Beaumont always remained satisfied with the son-in-law who had come to him through so many difficulties and whom he had accepted with so much hesitation.

"By heavens, sir, he is Kershaw over again," he used to say. "I don't wonder Kate picked him out of twenty. It's astonishing what a perception of character that girl has. He is Kershaw over again."